RED BLOODED MURDER

LAURA CALDWELL

MIRA®

Recycling programs
for this product may
not exist in your area.

ISBN-13: 978-0-7783-2658-8

RED BLOODED MURDER

www.MIRABooks.com

Printed in U.S.A.

Dear Reader,

The Izzy McNeil series is fiction. But it's personal, too. Much of Izzy's world is my world. She's proud to be a lawyer (although she can't always find her exact footing in the legal world), and she's even more proud to be a Chicagoan. The Windy City has never been more alive for me than it was during the writing of these books—*Red Hot Lies, Red Blooded Murder* and *Red, White & Dead.* Nearly all the places I've written about are as true-blue-Chicago as Lake Michigan on a crisp October day. Occasionally I've taken license with a few locales, but I hope you'll enjoy visiting them. If you're not a Chicagoan, I hope you'll visit the city, too, particularly if you haven't recently. Chicago is humming right now—it's a city whose surging vibrancy is at once surprising and yet, to those of us who've lived here a while, inevitable.

The Izzy McNeil books can be read in any order, although Izzy does age throughout, just like the rest of us. Please e-mail me at info@lauracaldwell.com to let me know what you think about the books, especially what you think Izzy and her crew should be doing next. And thank you, *thank you,* for reading.

Laura Caldwell

ACKNOWLEDGMENTS

Thank you, thank you, thank you to
Margaret O'Neill Marbury, Amy Moore-Benson
and Maureen Walters. Thanks also to everyone at
MIRA Books, including Valerie Gray, Donna Hayes,
Dianne Moggy, Loriana Sacilotto, Craig Swinwood,
Pete McMahon, Stacy Widdrington, Andrew Wright,
Pamela Laycock, Katherine Orr, Marleah Stout,
Alex Osuszek, Margie Miller, Adam Wilson,
Don Lucey, Gordy Goihl, Dave Carley, Ken Foy,
Erica Mohr, Darren Lizotte, Andi Richman,
Reka Rubin, Margie Mullin, Sam Smith, Kathy Lodge,
Carolyn Flear, Maureen Stead, Emily Ohanjanians,
Michelle Renaud, Linda McFall, Stephen Miles,
Jennifer Watters, Amy Jones, Malle Vallik,
Tracey Langmuir and Anne Fontanesi.

Thanks to all the TV and broadcast people
who offered their insights, especially Jeff Flock
and everyone at Fox Business News, as well as
Steve Cochran, Anna Devlantes, Amy Jacobson,
Elizabeth Flock, Jim Lichtenstein, Pamela Jones
and Bond Lee.

Much gratitude to my experts—Detective
Peter Koconis and Chicago Police Officer
Jeremy Schultz; Janet Girtsen, Deputy Laboratory
Director of the Forensic Science Center at Chicago;
criminal defense lawyers Catharine O'Daniel and
Sarah Toney; private investigators Paul Ciolino and
Sam Andreano; and physicians Dr. Richard Feely,
Dr. Roman Voytsekhovskiy and Dr. Doug Lyle.

Thanks also to everyone who read the book or offered advice or suggestions, especially Dustin O'Regan, Jason Billups, Liza Jaine, Rob Kovell, Beth Kaveny, Pam Carroll, Katie Caldwell Kuhn, Margaret Caldwell, Christi Smith, William Caldwell and Les Klinger.

The hands that grabbed her were greedy. They shoved her, pushed her, not caring when she cried out. And although she wanted more—more now, more later—she felt the need, even in this faraway moment, to say the truth. "We shouldn't be doing this again. At least I shouldn't. This is the last time, just so you know."

"Shut up," *came the reply.*

"I'm not kidding. I want you to know that this is it. It's over after today."

"Shut up."

Those hands moved lower, clawing and probing as though they'd been waiting for this, lying in wait until she was vulnerable, when they could strip her bare and plunge her into oblivion.

She threw her head back and clutched at the bed sheets, holding herself down until the moment when she would step into the void that she so craved.

A breeze trickled in the window, enticing after the biting winds that had battered Chicago for months. Yet nothing could touch the heat that boiled inside, carried her in small but growing crests, reaching her in places she always forgot until moments like this.

The hands stopped suddenly, startling her.

"Why?" *she said, desperate.*

*A mouth crushed against hers, bit her. "I said shut up."
And she did.*

Later, when she was alone, she slipped into her clothes
for the evening—white, ironically. Tonight, she would smile,
and she would be engaging. After all these years, she knew
how to do that—how to shine her eyes at someone, how to
direct her energy so they felt seen and heard and touched.
No one at this event would know what she'd just done. She
would carry the last two hours in her head, like little
packages whose pretty wrappings hid the shame and the
pleasure. Those thoughts would please her when she mentally unwrapped them; they would send pangs of delight
throughout her body. But they would remove her from
everyone, too. Secrets were always like that. They put a film
between you and the rest of the world, so that you could see
everyone else, but no one could see the whole of you.

Searching for her bag, she walked through her place and
found it by the door. She remembered now that she'd
dropped it there in the heat of that first moment, when she
had let herself be devoured by her wants.

She sighed and picked up the bag. She took it into her
bedroom, where she transferred a few essential items into
a smaller bag more appropriate for the evening. She
brushed her hair.

For a second, she studied herself in the mirror. She didn't
look any different than she had that afternoon. There wasn't
a blush to her cheeks or a shine to her eyes. She'd gotten so
good at hiding the evidence.

Her gaze dropped. It was hard to look at herself these
days. She walked to the front door, trying to clear her mind
of the last few hours, of everything.

She stretched out her arm for the doorknob, but suddenly
it turned on its own, surprising her, making her gasp.

The door opened.

"You scared the hell out of me," she said, when she saw who was there.

She stopped short, looking into those eyes—eyes that saw her, knew what she was really like. She opened her mouth to say something sexy, but when she looked again, she saw those eyes shift into an expression of cold anger. She turned away for a moment while she collected words in her head and shaped them so that they would be earnest, pacifying.

But before she could form the sentences, she felt something strike her on the back of the head. She heard herself cry out—a cry so different from those she'd made earlier, a cry of shock and of pain. Instinctively, she began to raise her hands to her head, but then she felt another blow. Her mind splintered into shards of light, the pain searing into pink streaks. She felt her knees buckle, her body hit the floor.

Something tightened around her neck, squeezing her larynx with more and more force, stealing the breath from her. The light in her brain exploded then, filling it with tiny spots. Strangely, it seemed as if each of those spots encased the different moments of her life. She could see all of them at once, feel all of them. It was a beautiful trick of the mind, a state of enlightenment the likes of which she hadn't known possible. She felt more alive than she ever had before.

1

Three days earlier

The bar, on the seventh floor of the Park Hyatt hotel, had its doors propped wide, as if boasting about the suddenly dazzling April weather.

We stepped onto the bar's patio—an urban garden illuminated by the surrounding city lights.

"Spring is officially here," I said. "And God, am I ready for it."

The thing about spring in Chicago is that it's fast and fickle. A balmy, sixty-eight-degree Friday like tonight could easily turn into a brittle, thirty-five-degree Saturday. Which is why Chicagoans always clutch at those spring nights. Which is why a night like that can make you do crazy things.

The maître d', a European type in a slim black suit, spotted the woman I was with, Jane Augustine, and came hustling over. "Ms. Augustine," he said, "welcome." He looked at me. "And Miss…"

"Miss Izzy McNeil," Jane said, beaming her perfect newscaster smile. "The best entertainment lawyer in the city."

The maître d' laughed, gave me a quick once-over. A little smile played at the corner of his mouth. "A lawyer. So you're smart, too?"

"If so, I'm a smart person who's out of a job." I'd been looking for six months.

"Maybe not for long," Jane said.

"Meaning?"

Jane shrugged coquettishly as the maître d' led us over the slate floor to a table at the edge of the patio.

"Our best spot," he said, "for the best." He put two leather-bound menus on the table and left.

We sat. "Do you always get this kind of treatment?" I asked.

Jane swung her shiny black hair over her shoulder and looked at me with her famous mauve-blue eyes. "The treatment was all about Izzy McNeil. He's hot for you."

I turned and glanced. The maître d' was watching us. Okay, I admit, he did seem to be watching *me*. "I think I'm giving off some sort of scent now that I'm single again."

Jane scoffed. "I can't stop giving off that scent, and I'm married."

I studied Jane as the waiter took our drink orders. With her long, perfect body tucked into her perfect red suit, she looked every inch the tough journalist she was, but the more I got to know her, the more I listened to her, the more I was intrigued by the many facets of Jane. When I was lead counsel for Pickett Enterprises, the Midwest media conglomerate that owned the station where Jane worked, I'd negotiated her contract. And while she was definitely the wisecracking, tough-talking, shoot-straight journalist I'd heard about, I had also seen some surprising cracks in the veneer of her confidence. And on top of that was the sexiness. The more I knew her, the more I noticed she simply steeped in it.

"Seriously," Jane said. "I know you're bummed that you and Sam had that little problem—"

"Yeah, that *little* problem," I interrupted her. "We're seeing each other occasionally, but it's just not the same."

Six months ago, my fiancé, Sam, disappeared with thirty million dollars' worth of property owned by my client, Forester Pickett, the CEO of Pickett Enterprises, and it happened on precisely the same night Forester suddenly died. After nearly two agonizing weeks that seemed like two years—weeks in which my world had not only been turned upside down, but also shaken and twisted and battered and bruised; weeks during which I learned so many secrets about the people in my life I thought I'd been dropped into someone else's life—the matter had been resolved and Sam was back in town. But I'd lost all my legal work in the process and essentially had been ushered out the back door of my law firm. As for Sam and me, the wedding was off, and we weren't exactly back together.

"Whatever," Jane said. "You should enjoy being single. You're dating other people, right?"

"A little." I rubbed the spot on my left hand where my engagement ring used to rest. It felt as if the skin were slightly dented, holding a spot in case I decided to put it on again. "There's a guy named Grady, who I'm friends with, and we go out occasionally, but he wants to get serious, and I really don't. So mostly, I've been licking my wounds."

"Enough of that! Let someone do the licking for you. With that red hair and that ass, you could get anyone you want."

I laughed. "A guy at the coffee shop asked me out the other day."

"How old was he?"

"About forty."

"That'll work. As long as he's eighteen, he's doable."

The waiter stepped up to our table with two glasses of wine.

"Would you go out with her?" Jane asked him.

"Uh…" he said, clearly embarrassed.

"Jane, stop." But the truth was I was thrilled with the randomly warm night, with the hint that the world was somehow turning faster than usual.

"No, honestly." Jane looked him up and down like a breeder sizing up a horse for stud. "Are you single?"

The waiter was a Hispanic guy with big, black eyes. "Yeah."

"And would you go out with her?" Jane pointed at me.

He grinned. "Oh, yeah."

"Perfect!" Jane patted him on the hip. "She'll get your number before we leave."

I dropped my head in my hands as the waiter walked away, chuckling.

"What?" she said. "Now you've got three dates when you want them—the waiter, the coffee shop dude and that Grady guy. We're working on the maître d' next. I want you to have a whole stable of men."

A few women walked by. One of them gasped. "Jane Augustine!" She rushed over. "I'm so sorry to bother you, but I have to tell you that I love you. We watch you every night."

"Thank you!" Jane extended her hand. "What's your name?"

The woman introduced her friends, and then the compliments poured from her mouth in an unending stream. "Wow, Jane, you're attractive on TV but you're even more gorgeous in person…. You're beautiful…. You're so smart…. You're amazing."

"Oh, gosh, thank you," Jane said to each compliment, giving an earnest bob of the head. "You've made my day." She asked what the woman did for a living, then graciously accepted more compliments when the woman turned the conversation back to Jane.

"How do you do that?" I asked when they left.

"Do what?"

"Act like you're so flattered? I know you've heard that stuff before."

Jane studied me. "How old are you, Izzy?"

"Thirty this summer." I shook my head. "I can't believe I'm going to be thirty."

"Well, I'm two years away from forty, and let me tell you something—when someone tells you you're beautiful, you act like it's the first time you've heard that." She looked at me pointedly. "Because you never know when it'll be the last."

I sipped my wine. It was French, kind of floral and lemony. "How's your new agent?"

"Fantastic. He got me a great contract with Trial TV."

"I've seen the billboards."

Trial TV was a new legal network based in Chicago that was tapping into the old Court TV audience. The billboards, with Jane's smiling face, had been plastered up and down the Kennedy for months.

"It's amazing to be on the ground floor," Jane said. "They've got a reality show on prosecutors that's wild. It's gotten great advance reviews. And we're juicing up trial coverage and making it more exciting. You know, more background on the lawyers and judges, more aggressive commentary on their moves."

"And you'll be anchoring the flagship broadcast each morning." I raised my glass. "It's perfect for you."

Jane had always had a penchant for the legal stories. When she was a reporter, she was known for courting judges and attorneys, so that she was the one they came to whenever there was news. She got her spot as an anchor after she broke a big story about a U.S. Senator from Illinois who was funneling millions of dollars of work to one particular law firm in Chicago. It was Jane who figured out that the head partner at the firm was the senator's mistress.

Jane clinked my glass. "Thanks, Iz." She looked heavenward for a second, her eyes big and excited. "It's like a dream come true, because if I was going to keep climbing the nightly news ladder, I'd have to try and go to New York and land the national news. But Zac and I want to stay here. I love this city so much."

Jane looked around, as if taking in the whole town with her gaze. This particular part of Chicago—the Gold Coast and the Mag Mile—had grown like a weed lately as a plethora of luxury hotel-condo buildings sprang into the skyline.

"Plus, aside from getting up early, it's going to be great hours," Jane continued. "I don't have to work nights anymore, and trials stop for the weekends. They even stop for holidays."

"Is C.J. going with you?" Jane's current producer was a talented, no-nonsense woman who had worked closely with Jane for years.

She shook her head. "She's staying at Chicagoland TV. That station has been so good to me I didn't want to steal all their top people. Plus, I wanted to step out on my own, start writing more of my own stuff." She gave a chagrined shake of her head. "You know how I got all this?"

"Your new agent?"

"Nope. He only negotiated the contract. It was Forester."

Just like that, my heart sagged. I missed him. Forester had not only been a client, he'd been a mentor, the person who'd given me my start in entertainment law, the person who'd trusted me to represent his beloved company. Eventually, Forester became like a father to me, and his death was still on my mind.

"I miss him, too," Jane said, seeing the look on my face. "Remember how generous he was? He actually introduced me to Ari Adler."

"Wow, and so Ari brought you in." Ari Adler was a media mogul, like Forester, but instead of owning TV and radio stations, newspapers and publishing companies all over the Midwest, as Forester did, Ari Adler was global. His company was the one behind Trial TV.

"Forester knew I loved the law," she said, "so he brought me to dinner with the two of them when Ari was in town."

"Even though he knew it meant he might lose you."

"Exactly." Jane put her glass down and leaned forward on her elbows. "And now I'm bringing you to dinner because I want you."

I blinked. "Excuse me?"

"The launch is Monday. We've been in rehearsals for the last few weeks." She paused, leaned forward some more. "And I want you to start on Monday, too."

"What do you mean?"

"I want you to be a legal analyst."

"Like a reporter?"

"Yeah."

"Are you kidding? I've never worked in the news business. Just on the periphery." And yet as logical as my words sounded, I got a spark of excitement for something new, something totally different.

"We had someone quit today," Jane said. "A female reporter who used to be a lawyer."

"And?"

"Well, let me backtrack. Trial TV has tried to put together a staff that has legal backgrounds in some way, including many of the reporters and producers. We have reporters in each major city to keep their eye on the local trial scenes. You know, interview the lawyers and witnesses, prepare short stories to run on the broadcasts. But one of our Chicago reporters hit the road today."

"Why?"

Jane waved her perfectly manicured hand. "Oh, she's a prima donna who wants everything PC. She couldn't handle our dinosaur deputy news director." Her eyes zeroed in on mine. "But you could. After working with Forester and his crew, you know how to hang with the old-boys network."

"Are you talking an on-air position?"

"Not right away. We'll give you a contributor's contract, and you'll do a little of everything. You'll assist in writing the stories and help with questions when we have guests. But eventually, yeah, I see you on-air."

"Jane, I don't have any media experience."

"You used to give statements on behalf of Pickett Enterprises, and you were good. Either way, the trend in the news is real people with real experience in the areas they're reporting on. Think Nancy Grace—she was a prosecutor before she started at CNN. Or Greta Van Susteren. She practiced law, too."

The spark of excitement I'd felt earlier now flamed into something bigger, brighter. If you'd asked me six months ago what the spring held for me, I would have told you I'd be finishing my thank-you notes after my holiday wedding, and I'd be settling into contented downtime with my husband, Sam. But now Sam wasn't my husband, and things with him—things with *my future*—were decidedly unclear.

"What would it pay?"

She told me.

"A month?" I blurted.

She laughed. "No, sweetheart, that's a year. TV pays crap. You should know that. You've negotiated the contracts."

"But I'm a lawyer," I said.

"You'd be an analyst and a reporter now."

Just out of principle, I considered saying no. I *was* a lawyer; I was worth more than that. But the fact was, unless I could find entertainment law work, I was worth almost nothing. I knew nothing else, understood no other legal specialties. I'd been job hunting for months, and trying to make the best of the downtime—visiting the Art Institute, the Museum of Contemporary Art, the Museum of Science and Industry and just about every other museum or landmark Chicago had to offer. But, depressingly, there was no entertainment work up for grabs in the city. Though most Chicago actors and artists started with local lawyers, when they hit it big, they often took their legal work to the coasts. The lawyers who'd had it for years wisely hoarded the business that remained. And, months ago, after the dust had settled after the scandal with Sam, Forester's company had decided to use attorneys from another firm, saying they needed a fresh start and a chance to work with someone new.

I couldn't blame them, but it had left me in the cold. My bank statement had an ever-decreasing balance, teetering toward nothing. I hadn't minded the lack of funds so badly when I couldn't buy new spring clothes, but soon I wouldn't be able to pay my mortgage, and that would be something else altogether.

For the first time in my adult life I was flying without a net. Fear nibbled at my insides, crept its way into my brain. I was buzzing with apprehension. But the job offer from Jane was a ray of calm, clean sunshine breaking through the murky depths of my nerves.

I knew, as the negotiator I used to be, that I should ask Jane a lot of other questions— What would the hours be? What was the insurance like? But in addition to needing the money, I needed—*desperately* needed—something new in my life.

So I leaned forward, meeting Jane's gaze and those mauve-blue eyes, and said, "I'll do it."

2

When we left the Park Hyatt, Jane told the waiter where to meet us, and three hours later, when he walked in the club, Jane and I were surrounded by five other guys.

I was talking to one in particular, a tattooed twenty-one-year-old with shiny, light brown hair that fell halfway to his shoulders. He knew Jane—they'd met at a party a year ago—and he strolled up to us within moments of arriving. But it was me he was talking to, and although he was way too young for me, he was so pretty in such a big, strong kind of way, I couldn't tell him to beat it.

"Theo Jameson," he said, when we first met. He reached for my hand, shook it, squeezed it, then held it…and held it. He smiled at me as if he had been waiting to see me for a long, long time. "Great hair." His chin—strong and tanned—jutted toward the top of my head. But his eyes didn't move from mine.

"Thanks." I pulled my hand away, patted my head idiotically. My hair had a life of its own. When the gods smiled, which was infrequent, it corkscrewed into perfect spirals. Most of the time, like now, it twisted prettily in some places and frizzed about in others, and the result was a long tangle of orange-red curls.

The club was on Damen—lounge-ish and made to look like a French salon. Apparently Jane went there frequently and knew the manager, and even though we'd had too many celebratory glasses of wine earlier, she'd convinced me to stop in with her and "say hello." She needed to cut loose, she said. She'd been working for a month straight, and she'd be in rehearsals all weekend. In days of yore, I would have declined, and then I would have skidded over to Sam's place and crawled in bed with him. I would have woken him up with a few select kisses up his thighs—I loved those thighs, dusted with gold-blond hair. Back when I was with Sam, I would never have known such lounge-ish salons existed. But now was a different time, and there was something about Jane that made it very, very hard to say no.

Theo and I started talking. When he told me his favorite meal was champagne and mussels, I was mildly interested. When he told me he ran a company that made Web design software, and that his clients included a bunch of Fortune 500 companies, I was intrigued, but not sure I bought it.

Two of his friends were standing nearby at the time. From the very few words they spoke, they seemed younger than Theo. One wore a T-shirt that read *Objects Are SMALLER Than They Appear.* I stared at that shirt. Being a decade older than him, was I somehow missing the joke? Or was the slogan what I thought it was—an odd, thinly veiled reference to the kid's small penis?

"Come sit," Jane said, herding Theo and me to a large, round powder-blue booth. Two guys were already sitting there. Jane gestured at them. "Writers," she said. "They write books." She mentioned their names, but with the jazzy, club music pumping loud, I couldn't make them out.

We all shook hands. One of the writers was an attractive guy with thick, prematurely gray hair that contrasted with his youthful, tanned face.

"How are you?" he asked me, after all the hand shaking. He had the kind of eyes that looked right into yours, not necessarily in a romantic way, just a way that was truly interested, that was keen to other people.

"I'm great. Jane just offered me a job at Trial TV."

"Really?" His eyebrows rose. "Congrats."

"Yeah, congrats," the other writer said. He had blond hair and a shy smile.

Theo slid into the booth and began talking to the writers, but Jane held me back. "Theo is the real deal," she said. "Started this software company while he was in high school. Went to Stanford on a full-ride scholarship but he dropped out after a year. Making millions upon millions now."

I looked over my shoulder at him. "He's so young."

"Who cares?"

I changed the topic. "How do you know the writers?"

Jane shrugged. "I've met the one with the tan once before. Something about him intrigues me." She playfully shoved me into the booth. "Someone needs to buy me a drink," she said loudly to the group.

Ten minutes after we sat down, Theo's buddies joined us, and ten minutes after that, the waiter walked in, looking unsure in his black jeans, his hair newly wet and combed back. He saw Jane and me packed into that leather banquette with five men and shook his head as if to say, *Nooooooo.*

"Jane!" I called toward the end of the banquette, gesturing at the waiter as he began to walk away, but she was engrossed in a conversation with the two writers.

I tried to move around Theo, but he glanced from me to the waiter and then put his arms on the table, blocking me. "If you think I'm letting you get up to talk to some other guy, you're wrong." He leaned closer, his sleek hair brushing my cheek. "Sorry. I don't want to be pushy, but I'm into you." His last few words hushed themselves into my ear. And just like that, I forgot about the waiter.

Vodka bottles came and left the table, wine bottles disappeared even faster. I went to check my watch at one point. I thought I caught a glimpse of well past midnight, but Theo covered the watch with his hand. "It's Friday, remember? There's all sorts of time on Friday night."

"You're right. I have lots of time," I said, quite tipsy by

then and thinking I might be philosophical. "And I used to have no time. I mean, I used to be *inundated*. Work and billable hours and an assistant and clients and a wedding and—" I thought of Sam "—and people. But now, I have all sorts of time. My time is empty, my time is…" I died away, trying to come up with something profound and falling short. I closed my mouth. If there was one thing I'd learned as a lawyer it was when to shut up.

But then I remembered my time wasn't empty anymore. Monday morning, I'd start as an analyst for Jane. Even sooner, tomorrow afternoon, I'd meet with John Mayburn to consider working another case with him.

Mayburn was a private investigator who had helped me out when Sam disappeared. In return for the huge fee I couldn't pay, I'd worked for him on a case where he needed a North Side Chicago female type to blend in and conduct surveillance. He'd practically gotten me killed, and I vowed never to take another job with him, but I needed the cash in a fierce way. With luck, he could get me something that could minimally bridge the cavernous salary gap between my profitable days of yesteryear and my intriguing, but nonetheless impoverished, future in TV.

I tried to catch Jane's eye to thank her for that opportunity. Despite the miserable salary she'd told me I'd be making, I was thrilled in a way I hadn't been in a long time. There was nothing like a wedge of opportunity to make the whole sky open up.

But Jane was leaning in close to the writer. His gray hair looked whiter than it really was because of the smooth tan of his skin. His brown eyes were decorated with lashes longer than normally seen on a man. He had one of those overly handsome indents in the center of his chin, but that, combined with the gray hair, somehow gave him the look of an intellectual. The other guy had disappeared. Neither Jane nor the writer seemed to care. They were completely intent on their conversation. And clearly flirting.

Right then, Jane unbuttoned her suit coat and slipped it off. It seemed that all the men in the bar paused to look at her at that moment. The black blouse she wore underneath was held by only a thin velvet band around her neck. The fabric was gauzy and fell in soft folds around her breasts. Jane seemed too entranced by her conversation with the writer to notice the attention, but then she glanced up and swept the room with her eyes, drinking in all those gazes. She looked at me, and she winked.

I laughed, tossing my head back. It was as if I could feel the laughter burbling up inside me, and by releasing it I was letting go of all the tension of the last six months—all the deep, troubled talks with Sam about why he hadn't trusted me to tell me what he'd done, why he'd taken off from the city, leaving me blinking like a newborn, unattached and unsure.

When I looked back at Jane, she and the writer were talking low, staring at each other's mouths.

As I watched them, Theo bent toward me and kissed my neck. Just like that.

Instead of pulling back and saying, *Hey, excuse me, what are you doing?* I tilted my head to let him do it again. His tongue flicked gently against my skin. I let my head fall back farther. It didn't occur to me to care that a strange man (a child, really) was kissing me in public. Nothing mattered but that moment. I turned my head to him and met his mouth with mine. I expected rough; I expected insistent; I expected demanding. But Theo was nothing like that. He kissed patiently, like someone with lots of time to get where he wants, and very sure he's going to get there.

My cell phone vibrated in my purse, but I ignored it. I shifted my body in the booth, touched Theo's silky hair. It fell on my cheeks as he leaned over me.

A minute later, the phone vibrated again. Our bodies were so close by that time, the sensation traveled from me to him.

"Want to get that?" he said into my mouth.

"No."

His tongue flicked against my lips and he put his arms around me, scooping me, as if I were a small and tiny creature, even closer into him.

Once again, that phone.

"Hold on," I mumbled. I extricated myself and opened my bag. *Sam, cell,* the display read. I clicked Ignore, then looked at the caller ID list. He'd called three times.

Despite the fact that Sam and I were just dating now and it was legal for me to be kissing a total stranger, a little guilt sparked inside me. Then paranoia hit. *Was Sam here? Had he seen me somehow? Was that why he was calling?*

I swiveled my head around.

"What's up?" Theo asked.

The place was packed now—lots of guys with gelled hair, lots of women in dresses and stiltlike sandals. No Sam. "Nothing," I said.

"You sure?"

"I'm sure." I stuck the phone in my purse, annoyed that everything in my world had been focused on Sam lately. I wanted tonight to be about fun, about celebrating a new job (and maybe another one tomorrow when I met with Mayburn). I looked at Theo's mouth—deeply curved at the top, sloped low at the bottom, wide and yet masculine. I licked my lips, glanced up into his eyes. They were on my mouth. I leaned forward and bit his bottom lip. He pulled me back into him, and soon we were making out once more.

The phone buzzed again. And again. And again.

I groaned, pulled away and yanked the phone from my purse. *Sam, cell.* I felt a pang of panic. What if it was an emergency? "Hello?"

"Hey, Red Hot." Sam said, his nickname for me. The sound of it softened me, made everything disappear—the bar, Theo, the bottles, the people. They all vanished as if pulled into a hole, deep and black.

"Hey," I said.

"Where are you?"

It all filled back in then—the booth, the crowd. Suddenly the music's bass seemed to pump louder, harder. "Some place on Damen."

"Who are you with?"

"Jane. You know, Jane Augustine?"

I looked over to the end of the booth, but Jane was gone. Probably in the bathroom.

From behind, I felt my hair being lifted up, then replaced with a mouth, wet and questioning on my nape. I almost moaned.

"Come over," Sam said.

"I can't."

"Why?"

"It's late."

"Exactly, so come over." A pause. "I miss you."

Theo was suckling the skin on the back of my neck now. I thought to warn him that I was a redhead, and redheads acquired hickeys very, very easily, but I couldn't exactly say anything while I was on the phone with Sam, and the fact was I didn't want Theo to stop. Not even a little bit.

For a moment, I was suspended there, hearing Sam say sweet things—how he missed me, how he loved me. And at the same time, I was feeling those persistent lips on my neck, sucking something of me into the room, some part of me that had been veiled until now—a part that enjoyed a dark lounge in the wee hours of a Saturday morning, a part whose whole body responded to the boy with long hair and tattoos, a part that reveled in the off-kilter and the fresh and the surreal.

"Iz?" Sam said. He'd stopped talking, I realized, and I hadn't said anything.

"Yeah, sorry, I'm here."

"Come over."

I was torn in two then. One part leaned toward my old life, toward Sam, the other pushed back into Theo, thrilled with the new. The truth was, the new was a stronger pull, if only because I'd been living in the past for so long and I was tiring of it. Sam and I spent hours and hours trying to piece together what had happened between us. Once a week, we talked to a therapist about our "communication patterns." Now I wanted, just for a moment, levity and life, fun and frolic.

"Sam, I told you earlier that we couldn't get together. I told you I had plans."

Theo's arms slid around my waist. He whispered in my free ear, "Get off the phone."

"Sam, I'll call you tomorrow."

"Don't bother."

"Excuse me?"

"I'm sorry, but I'm sick of this, Iz."

"So am I!" Exasperation crept in, messing with my levity.

"I know I caused you a lot of pain. But it's in the past, and at this point, it's your hang-up."

"What are you talking about?"

"I've been talking, and I've been explaining, and I've been telling you how much I adore you, but you just won't let it go."

"Are you kidding? It's kind of a big thing to just *let go*—"

"Have fun, Izzy." And he hung up.

I stared at the phone in dismay. Sam had never hung up on me. At first, I was scared—scared I'd lose him, scared I'd already lost him, scared that if I didn't patch things up, and right now, he'd be gone forever. Then anger swept in. How dare he blame this on me?

And then at last, calm entered my mind. It said, *Leave it alone. Just for now. You want frolic? Then frolic.*

Theo was kissing my ear. I stared at my phone. One finger itched to call Sam back, but that voice spoke again. *Leave it alone. For now.*

In that instant, I wanted so badly to forget everything, to forget even myself.

I put the phone back in my purse, turned around and placed my arms around Theo.

3

Jane Augustine opened her eyes and let her gaze sweep over the strange bedroom. A small skylight, drawing in the morning sun, illuminated the otherwise dark room. She could make out an antique shelf packed with books in a meticulous way—the taller books at the beginning of each shelf. Next to it was a dresser, which also looked antique. Above that hung an oil painting, which showed a single green apple on a table. The brush stroke was heavy, the painting textured contemporarily. The place looked as if it had some cash behind it.

And then there was the address—Goethe Street, right off State. Impressive, Jane thought. Writers usually made so little money. Not that she cared. It wasn't as if she was looking for a husband; it was simply that she'd woken up in more than one strange bedroom, and they weren't all this nice.

She turned her head, trying not to shift the bed, and glanced at the writer in question. Last night, he had seemed worldly, but now, as she listened to his light snore, he looked like a little boy despite his gray hair.

But he was a little boy who knew how to fuck. She could tell that even before she went home with him. She could tell that with any man. She had gotten exactly what she wanted from the writer—Mick was his name. She'd needed her fix last night, and he had been her black tar heroin.

That was how she thought of what she did—like an addiction—but in all honesty, it was inaccurate to say that she was addicted to sex. She'd once visited a sex addict Web site, and what she found there wasn't her. She didn't search the net for porn. She hadn't been arrested for voyeurism, exhibitionism, prostitution, sex with minors or indecent phone calls.

What she was addicted to, though, was the rush of someone new, the smell of a body so unlike her husband's, the feeling of instant intimacy with a stranger. She was addicted to the way an evening with someone like the writer would walk her right into a world so dissimilar from hers. She had always been able to see, even as a child, that there were so many different lives to be had. Sex with someone other than her husband gave her a key to those other lives, let her crawl right into them and look around with awed eyes.

She and Zac loved each other with a ferocious loyalty and an ever-present tenderness, but she and Zac were different when it came to sex. She liked it more than he did, required it more than he did. And so her dalliances—she liked calling them that, thought there was something Virginia Woolf-ish about that word—had been a constant in their life. She knew it sounded like a cop-out, but she was happier with Zac because of what she had outside of him. She was better to him, more devoted to their life together. He always understood that.

But like any addiction, the morning after was never pretty. As she stared around the new bedroom, guilt crept in like smoke. It inhabited the room. It filled her lungs until she found it hard to breathe. Always this guilt, this judgment of herself. She was a bad person, she knew. Anyone who cheated on their spouse was bad, wasn't that right? But she didn't believe in her bones that she was a terrible person.

She stood from the bed and stretched her long limbs. The writer groaned, rolled over. With that groan, flashes of last night flooded in. She could still feel his mouth, his teeth on her breasts. She looked at her body, searching for bruises, any marks that would give her away when Zac got home. But even without a telltale sign, Zac would know. He always did.

There was something wonderful about that knowing. Zac saw everything about her—all her flaws—and he still loved her. It was amazing to have a love like that. And so these dalliances, in their own way, brought her that deep part of their relationship, too.

She went into the bathroom and closed the door, then flipped on the light and sat on the toilet. The bathroom was rather large, with a small, round table across from the toilet. On top was an oval, silver dish. She lifted it and poked her finger at the contents—matches from Cog Hill, a local country club, a small pair of silver scissors, a few Euro coins depicting Mozart.

She finished using the toilet and opened the cabinet under the sink. Typical male collection of crap—shaving cream, gel, a box of condoms.

When she came out of the bathroom, he was still asleep. She cleared her throat to see if he would roll over again. Nothing. She padded softly on the Oriental rug and left the bedroom, closing the door behind her.

The hallway was dark. She stood still a moment, letting her eyes fine-tune to the dimness. When she stayed with someone, this was her favorite part, this nosing around, because she got to walk around in a life that wasn't her own.

The first room on the right was bigger than Mick's bedroom. It was, she realized, the master, but he used it as his office.

A large teak desk dominated the room, nearly covering the window that was set into the wall behind it. The blinds were half-closed, and through them, a gray, early-morning light striped the room. She went to the desk, looked at the four stacks of paper there. Two were made of typed sheets of paper; another was made up of tiny, handwritten notes. The last was a stack of cut-out magazine pages. She flinched. On top of that pile was a photo of a woman in a black suit with tan piping and gold buttons. Her suit. It was a picture of her.

She blinked a few times, confusion clouding her brain. She leaned close, her hands behind her back. The photo had run with an article which had appeared just last week in *Chicago Magazine,* discussing the soon-to-be launch of Trial TV and her position as anchor. In the photo, she also wore her signature red scarf. It had become a thing, that scarf, something that signaled to loyal viewers that there was a big story or that it was a momentous news day.

On the picture, a black arrow had been drawn toward the scarf with a marker. A note in the margin read, *How did scarf get started? Intentional PR schlock or the real deal?*

She recoiled. What was going on here?

Her eyes shot to the other stacks. She tried to read the notes, but they were mostly illegible. One of the other piles had typewritten pages about a CNN news reporter who'd recently been caught sleeping with a Southern governor whom the newscaster had been covering for years.

The final stack… She leaned closer. She froze.

Jane Augustine, was typed on the top of the sheet. Below that was a list:

Gym—East Bank

Grocery store—Whole Foods on Huron or Fox & Obel.

Hair salon—Roberto Puig on Rush

Sports—Bulls occasionally, but only courtside. Bears but only club level.

Her breath caught in her lungs. She literally felt unable to breathe. What the hell was all this? Was he covering her for a story? If so, why wouldn't her publicist or the station know about it? They told her of every tiny story they landed about her. And if he was covering her, why the notes about what gym she went to, where she got her hair cut? She looked closer at the list, scanning it. She cringed when she saw one of the last items there.

Gynecologist—Dr. C. Wiseman on Wabash

She raised the paper and read the item under it.

Guys, it said. Two names were listed below—*Nathan Vatalli, Ben Houston.* Both men she'd slept with.

Right then, she got a whoosh of air into her lungs. She turned and stormed from the room into his bedroom. She pushed open the door. It banged against the wall.

He started, raising himself up on his elbows. "Mornin', gorgeous," he said when he saw her standing there, naked.

She walked to the bed. She put her hand on his chest and shoved him.

He smiled. "Yeah. Get back in here." He threw off the covers.

She glared. She pulled the blanket back over his body. "Just so you can get your information straight, that scarf was given to me by Barbara Brewer, the famous journalist and my first mentor. It was not some 'PR schlock—'" She made air quotes with her hands "—and if you don't stop following me, I'll have you arrested."

She turned and began searching for her clothes, suddenly teary and fluttery instead of angry. The threat was a lame one. If she called the cops and accused this guy of stalking her, he might tell them about her affairs, her dalliances, which he clearly had learned about. And she knew the Chicago cops well enough to know that such information would hit the streets—accidentally of course, but fast. She couldn't risk that kind of bad press, certainly not with Trial TV about to launch.

She retrieved an earring from the floor. Her hands trembled as she tried to get the post through her lobe. She found her skirt, then her jacket, and put them on, trying to steady the shake that was not only in her hands but quivering through her organs, crawling on her skin. She glanced back, expecting to see him with a guilty expression, maybe a scared one now that she'd busted him, but he was just stroking that cleft in his chin that she'd found so sexy last night. And it was he who was studying her.

"What exactly is that?" She gestured toward the hall.

"What are you talking about?"

"Those notes on your desk. The article. The lists."

"So you're a snooper, huh? Wouldn't have pegged you for a snooper."

She finished dressing and put a hand on her hip, willing herself not to show her nerves. She wanted to say something smart in return, she wanted to ask him so many questions, but his cold, assessing stare frightened her, draining away the shock and the anger, leaving only a hyperawareness that screamed that she was alone with this man. *Anything* could happen. Why had she thought for so long that she was immune to danger? That she could screw around with strangers without consequence? She had to get out of there.

She grabbed her purse from a brown velvet chair in the corner and tucked it under her arm. She wished he would say something normal, something that would explain all this—maybe even something that would make her laugh, because she wanted very much to cry.

But all he said was, "You were even better than I thought."

4

When I woke up, I reached for Sam, feeling for that blond fuzz on his thighs. Instead, the legs I touched were smooth, longer than Sam's, so muscled they felt like bone.

I opened my eyes, and there was that child. His brown hair spun out from his head like a Chinese fan. His face was white, his lips a pillowy pink. He was sleeping soundly. He looked like one of those people who could sleep anywhere— a plane, a crowded bus, the bed of a strange woman he'd only met the night before.

My first one-night stand. I'd never thought I'd have one. I was supposed to be a married woman by now.

A twisted sheet had fallen to the floor. I picked it up and wrapped it around me. Then I sat against the headboard and drew my knees up, staring at him. The tattoos on his arms— a gold-and-black serpent on one, twisting ribbons of red on the other—fascinated me. The people I knew with tattoos had tiny ones. My best friend, Maggie, had a shamrock on her ankle, for example. But Theo's covered his entire forearms, his round biceps. High on his left pectoral was an Asian-looking symbol.

A buzzing sound split the silence. Startled, I dashed out of bed and grabbed my cell phone from the dresser. *Sam, cell.*

I hit the off button for the ringer and glanced over my shoulder. Theo moaned, happily it seemed, and curled into a ball.

I took the phone in the hall and shut the bedroom door.

Sam, cell, the phone kept flashing. I felt an irrational guilt about the boy in my bed. I reminded myself that there was nothing to feel guilty about. I was an adult, Theo was an adult—legally anyway—and Sam was decidedly an adult. It was Sam who'd made our lives so crazy months ago; it was Sam who had hung up on me.

But still he was hard to resist. I answered. "Hello?"

"Sorry about last night, Red Hot."

I leaned my back against the wall. I twisted a strand of my hair around my fingers. "How are you?"

"Feeling like a jerk. I'm sorry. This whole thing just gets me crazy, this being apart. I really miss you."

"I miss you, too."

"So what are we doing? Let's just get back together."

"I don't know, Sam. It's not that easy." I grabbed a larger strand of hair, my hand twirling, twirling as I twisted it tighter onto my finger. If Sam were here, he'd gently take my hand; he would untwist my hair and kiss me on the head, just the way he'd always done.

"Yes, it is that easy," he said. "You're the one making it hard."

"*I'm* the one?"

"Well, yeah, now you are. We've gone over and over everything. I had to do what I'd promised to do."

"You promised you'd marry me."

"And I still want to do that!" His voice was raised, and the tenderness was gone.

We were back to where we'd been many times since Sam had returned to town.

Suddenly, a tall band of light moved into the hallway, and there was Theo.

His nude body took up nearly the whole doorway. He crossed his arms, the red ribbons stretching tighter across his biceps, and gave me a lazy grin that was so sexy I felt my mouth hanging open. What was this kid doing in my hallway? How did I get him back to my bed?

"You got any eggs?" Theo asked.

I put my finger to my lips and pointed toward the kitchen.

He walked toward me, slow and steady until he towered over me. Last night I was wearing heels and he hadn't seemed so big. Now, he was a large, strange man. Seeing him like this, naked and in daylight, made everything surreal, as if my world had been shaken like a snow globe.

"What's going on over there?" Sam said.

"Nothing." *Just that there's a molten-hot boy in my condo.*

Theo leaned over me, that silky hair brushing my cheeks again. "I'm gonna make you breakfast," he whispered in my ear. Mundane words, but the way he'd said them made my stomach flip.

"Iz?" It was Sam.

"Can we talk later?"

A pause. "Let's get it out now." But his voice was flat. We were both weary of talking.

I watched Theo's ass as he walked toward my kitchen. I'd never seen such a perfect ass—two smooth orbs at the top of those long legs.

The other line rang. The display showed a number I didn't recognize. Maybe Mayburn? "Sam, hold on a sec."

I switched to the other line and heard an unfamiliar man's voice say my name.

"Yes?" I said.

"It's Zac Ellis."

"Who?"

"Jane Augustine's husband."

"Oh, hi, Zac." Jane had told me that her husband, a photographer, was in New York for an exhibit.

"I got your number from Jane's book. Can I talk to you for a second?"

"Yeah, sure. Hold on please." I clicked to the other line. "I have to call you back, Sam. I'm sorry, okay?"

A beat, then, "All right." I could hear the patience Sam was trying very hard to foster. "Love you."

"Love you, too." That was one thing that was still certain in our lives.

I switched over to Zac. "Hi, I'm back."

"Thanks. Look, Izzy, I have to ask you something—did you go out with Jane last night?"

"Yes."

A pause. "Oh. I guess I thought…" His words fell away. Then, "Were there any guys there last night?"

Theo stepped into the hallway and held up a box of green tea in a silent question. How had he known that green tea was what I drank every morning, what I needed right at this very moment?

I smiled and nodded at him.

"What do you mean?" I said to Zac.

"I mean, was it just you and Jane or did you talk to any guys?"

"Uh…um…" It was a loaded question if I'd ever heard one. I had no idea what the right answer was. "We talked to a few people." *And one of those people is naked in my kitchen.*

He said nothing.

"Is something wrong, Zac?"

"I got an early flight home last night. I waited up for Jane."

"That's nice," I said, still unsure how he wanted me to respond.

"Yeah. It was. Except she never came home."

5

I was still on the phone with Zac a few minutes later, spinning out possible hypotheses for where Jane had spent the night. I didn't really believe any of them.

What I was really doing was taking up time, trying to let myself piece together the end of the evening. After Sam had hung up on me last night, I'd continued making out with Theo, partly out of spite and partly out of booze and partly out of the fact that he was *so unbelievably hot.* Before I knew it, he and I were in a cab on our way to my house. *Before I knew it...* Those were the words of someone who had done something wrong. Someone who should feel ashamed. That wasn't me, I reminded myself.

As for Jane, the more I thought about it, the more it seemed quite possible that she'd gone home with the writer. She believed her husband was out of town, and she and Mick had been flirting madly. I hadn't given it much thought last night. I'd assumed that flirting was all it was, but maybe it had gone further than that.

Shortly before I left, Jane had been there, slipping off her jacket, drinking in the visual praise of the men in the room, and then later when I looked up from my conversation with Sam, she was gone. I left ten minutes after Sam hung up on me, so I assumed Jane was just in the bathroom or at the back of the crowded lounge, somewhere I couldn't see her. I'd searched around, and when I couldn't find her, I'd texted her saying I was leaving and I'd talk to her tomorrow. And then, *before I knew it,* I was in the cab.

To Zac, I dished out more lame-sounding excuses—maybe she'd gone to a friend's house, maybe she'd gotten a lead on a story and she was following that—while I tried to figure out what to do. Should I tell my friend's husband that she'd been flirting with someone else?

"Was Jane talking to any guy in particular?" Zac asked.

"Uh…"

"Look, Izzy," he said. "I shouldn't have called you." Silence. Then, "It's not the first time this has happened, okay?"

"What do you mean?" I was in a robe by then. I went into my living room and sat on my favorite piece of furniture—a wingback chair Sam and I found at an antique store on Lincoln and reupholstered in a whimsical yellow-and-white fabric. The chair was unbelievably comfortable, and sitting there usually made me feel better. It wasn't working today. Behind me in the kitchen, Theo was oblivious, whistling while he cooked.

"How close are you and Jane?" Zac asked.

"We're friends from work. I used to be the lawyer for the company that owns Jane's old station."

"Yeah, I know, and she wants you to work for Trial TV."

"Right. I accepted. But what did you mean that this has happened before?"

He exhaled, said nothing.

"Do you think you should call the cops?" This was all way too familiar. I could remember with crystal clarity the night Sam disappeared and that next morning when he still wasn't around. "Or have you called the TV station?"

"I checked."

"Have you talked to her family?"

"They live in Michigan. Plus, I think I know exactly what happened."

"What?"

"I asked you before if you talked to any guys last night. Tell me the truth."

I wrapped my robe tighter around me. "I did tell you. We spoke to a few people."

"Who were they?" Zac asked.

"Um…let's see." I glanced over my shoulder, stalling for time. Over the breakfast bar, I could see Theo as he shook a small frying pan and flipped a perfect yellow omelet into the air, catching it again.

"You don't remember who you spoke to?" Zac said. Something cold had crept into his voice.

"No, I do. I just…"

"What time did you leave?"

"One o'clock, I guess. Maybe two."

"Who were you talking to?"

"Well, this one guy." A guy who was in my kitchen right now.

"What's his name?"

"Um…" I knew it was Theo, but I had to think about his last name, which mortified me. Jameson! That was it.

Before I could answer, Zac jumped in. "Did Jane leave with him?"

"No." I did.

"Look, Izzy, seriously. Don't try to cover up for her."

"I'm not. I *know* she didn't go home with the person I was talking to."

"Then who? Who was *she* talking to?"

I tried to think of the writer's name. "I'm not sure." I was relieved to be telling the truth. If I had thought it awkward to wake up with my first one-night stand, it was even worse to have a morning-after conversation with a friend's husband.

Then he laughed. A caustic, short laugh. "Look, don't worry about it. She just walked in."

Zac hung up on me, the second man in twenty-four hours to do so.

Theo walked into the room, still naked, still so sizzling hot. He was holding out a white plate, on which was a yellow omelet with two red pepper slices crisscrossed on top. "Hungry?" he said.

I nodded. But I wasn't exactly looking at the omelet. I took the plate. My thoughts crisscrossed too, calling out different directions. *Call Sam back and make nice. Call Jane and find out where she was last night. Save the omelet for later and take Theo back to bed.*

I opted for the last one.

6

Minutes after Theo said goodbye—a goodbye that involved a fair amount of groping—Jane called.

"I'm sorry Zac phoned you," she said.

"Don't be. Are you all right?"

"Can you meet me for coffee in an hour? I want to prep you on some Trial TV stuff, and I want to talk to you about something else."

"Sure." I had to meet Mayburn an hour after that, but I could fit it in.

Jane gave me the address of a coffee shop near her house in River North.

Before I got in the shower, I called my old assistant, Q, short for Quentin.

"How was girls' night?" he said, answering.

"I slept with someone."

Q and I used to be the busiest lawyer-assistant duo at the law firm of Baltimore & Brown, and we never had time for the usual *Hi, Hello, How are you this morning?* kind of stuff. Even though we had both been out of work for six months now—me because the firm had all but ousted me, and Q because he never really wanted to be a legal assistant anyway—we still continued to eschew common pleasantries when we talked and got right to the point.

"Thank, God. Who was it? Sam?"

"No."

"Grady."

"No."

"Someone new?"

"Yes."

"How many dates have you had with this person?"

I paused. "None."

"A one-night stand?" His voice rose a few decibels.

"Yep."

"Your *first* one-night stand?"

"Yep."

"I'll be right over."

Although Q had been in a relationship with a man named Max for most of the years I'd known him, at the end of our tenure at Baltimore & Brown, he'd gotten involved in an illicit affair. I call it illicit because not only was Q living with Max at the time, but he'd fallen for someone who wasn't even out of the closet. But now he was official with the new boyfriend and living up the street from me at North and Dearborn.

True to his word, Q was banging on my door in less than ten minutes, which gave me just enough time to shower and toss on a dress that had been itching to get out of the closet since last fall.

Q sat on my bed, the overhead lights gleaming on his bald, black head, while I dashed around my bedroom putting on makeup and jewelry. When we worked at the law firm, Q's uniform was crisp khakis and a stylish blazer. Now that he wasn't working, he'd kept the blazer, but switched to jeans.

"Cute," I said, pointing to the jacket, which was black.

"It's too tight." He tugged at the sleeves. "Everything is too tight. I thought being in love would give me the motivation to lose ten pounds, but it's been the opposite." Q worked out religiously and attempted every diet he heard about, but so far the flawless gay-man physique evaded him.

"You look great." This was true. Happiness, even if it hadn't translated into weight loss, made Q's gray eyes sparkle and his skin gleam.

"Thanks. Is this new?" He fingered my waffle-cotton duvet cover.

"It's old, actually." I had been using a beautiful ivory spread that Sam and I had registered for and gotten as an early wedding gift. But once everything with Sam blew up, I tucked it in the closet for the time being.

"Is this where the magic happened?" Q patted the bed.

"Here and in the kitchen."

"Tell me."

"His name is Theo."

"Nice. What's he do?"

"Owns a Web design software company."

"Like a real company? Or is he one of those guys who *says* he has a company, but it's really him in his pajamas in his studio apartment?"

"From what I hear, it's a real company, with some big profits."

"Where did you hear that?"

"Jane."

"How is she?"

I almost said, *In deep shit with her husband.* But I held my tongue, since I'd been on a stop-swearing campaign for a while now. The other reason I didn't say it was because I didn't believe in telling one friend another's business. "She's great. She's the new anchor at Trial TV, that start-up legal network that launches Monday."

"It's perfect for her."

"I know. And she's taking me with her."

"What?"

"She asked me to be a legal analyst, kind of a reporter. What do you think? Ridiculous?"

He sat back and crossed his arms. "I think it's *brilliant*. You're TV pretty. You've got that great red hair and that crazy big smile. And you could talk your way out of a Turkish prison."

"But I'm a lawyer, not a journalist."

Q held up a palm in protest. "Are you kidding? Hardly anyone is a journalist anymore. Trust me, the business news stations are always on at our house, and they've got these sweet little children broadcasting from the trading floors. Don't tell me any of those kidlets are journalists. Besides, you're a lawyer, which means you know how to talk and to think on your feet. That's what they want."

"I guess." Now that I was away from the drinks Jane was buying and the enthusiasm she projected, I was a little unsure. "God knows I need the money. Unlike you."

Q smiled. "Yes, I am a kept man, and I love it."

"So everything is sunshine and roses with you two?"

"I have to wear sunscreen all the time, and there are no thorns."

"Wow. It sounds different than it was with Max."

"It *is* different."

"But you were in love with Max."

"I was. At one point. In the only way I knew how to be at that time. And then somewhere it turned into me loving Max like a family member. I still love him, even though he won't return my phone calls. But what I have now is that I'm intensely, absolutely *in love,* Iz. It's like… It's like…"

He trailed off, and I glanced over at him. He was staring into the distance, at the back wall of my bedroom, but it was as if he was watching a sunset fall over the Aegean Sea; he looked that ecstatically happy.

I felt a shiver of envy run through me. Because that's how I used to look when I thought about Sam.

"Anyway," Q said, coming out of his dreamy fog, "enough shoptalk, enough about me. Tell me about this Theo guy. How old? With a name like Theodore and his own company, I'd say forties, but since it's software, I'm going with thirty-six."

I purposely didn't meet Q's eyes in the mirror as I fastened my silver hoop earrings. "Bit younger than that."

"Thirty?"

"Little younger."

"Twenty-five?" Q said, surprised.

"Not exactly."

"Twenty-three?" His voice was incredulous now.

"Um…Twenty-one?"

He whistled and clapped. "Damn, girl. That's illegal in some states."

I turned and leaned against my dresser, facing Q now. "You would not believe how sexy this kid is."

"Oh, this is going to be trouble."

"No, it's not. It's not going to be anything. It was just a…a thing."

Q laughed, his gray eyes glinting. "Believe me, I think it's about time you unleashed your inner slut. I applaud you for it. But this *thing* is going to be a train wreck."

"No, it's not. I might not even see him again."

He laughed harder, throwing his head back. "Who are you kidding? You're hooked."

"No, I'm not." I crossed my arms over my chest. "And why would it be a train wreck?"

"The young ones always are."

"But he's older than his years. He's been working since he was in high school. He went to college for a year. Stanford, I think. He has his own *company*."

"Train wreck. In the best way. Believe me, I think you need this kid. He's going to get you all hot and bothered and loosen you up. It's exactly what you require after all this seriousness with Sam."

We grinned at each other, and I had to admit, I kind of agreed with him. And despite the wisecracks, it was nice to have Q back the way we used to be.

"And I want to thank you," Q continued. "I have been so bored lately, and now I've got a front-row seat for this show."

"Why have you been bored?"

He sighed. "You know how it is. I was miserable when I was working, but…"

"Excuse me?" I put my hands on my hips. "You were miserable when you were working with me?"

"No, no. You know I loved working with you. I just didn't love the *work* I was doing. I wasn't meant to be a legal secretary."

"But you've been taking acting classes again since we left the firm."

"I quit. I'm too old for it now."

"You're in your early thirties!"

"And you should see everyone in these acting classes—they're in their early twenties. Like your boyfriend."

"Shut up."

"I am so going to love this show."

I moved away from the dresser. "There's no show, and there's no train wreck."

Q swung his feet over the side of the bed and stood. "Yes, there is, and, honey, I'm going to be here until the last curtain call and the last crash."

7

I looked at Jane across the table. "Jane, I'm…Well, I'm kind of shocked."

She blew on her half-full mug of coffee, clearly annoyed, then pushed it away.

We were at a coffee shop on Chicago Avenue. And after Jane gave me a bunch of details about Trial TV—the mission of the network, what I'd be doing there, instruction on landing news stories and writing them—she just announced that yes, she'd gone home with that writer last night, and no, as Zac had said, it wasn't the first time something like that had happened.

"Why are you shocked?" she asked.

"I don't know." I stirred a few Splendas into my second green tea. "I guess because I thought you were on top of it."

"What's that supposed to mean?"

"Don't get mad at me. I've seen you get dragged around by your agent on occasion, but generally you seem like someone who's got it together."

"Izzy, nobody has *everything* together." She shook her head and glanced away from me. When she turned back, she looked suddenly exhausted. "Nobody's perfect. Didn't you find that out when Sam disappeared?"

"Yeah, but I know why Sam did what he did."

"And if you're so fine with that, then why aren't you back together?"

A good question. One Sam had been asking me, one I'd been asking myself for months.

A few years ago, when Sam and I discussed getting married, I had journaled about it, I had visualized it and debated the pros and cons. I talked to Sam about it, and I talked to my friends about it. And the conclusion I came to in my heart was...*Yes*. I wanted to be married, and I wanted to be married to Sam. But the big wedding Sam desired and my mother supported entirely had completely overwhelmed me. I was just about to talk to Sam about scaling it back, maybe even cancelling it, when he disappeared. So much had happened since then, and now something felt stuck in our wheel, dragging Sam and me slower and slower.

"I guess we're not back together," I said to Jane, "because it would have to be a hundred percent. I wouldn't be dating anyone else. I wouldn't be sleeping with anyone else."

"Don't judge me because I had sex with that writer last night."

"Actually, I'm not judging you at all. When Sam was gone and I had no idea where he was, I kissed someone else. My friend Grady."

"See? And a lot of times I don't sleep with these people, by the way." She picked up the mug and took a sip. "A lot of times it's just a make-out thing."

"Does it matter, though? I'm really not judging you, I swear. God knows I'm spinning around, trying to figure out my life, so I'm the last person to judge anyone. I just think that cheating is cheating."

"Oh God, are you one of those people who think that even kissing someone else is cheating?"

"Yeah."

"So you cheated on Sam when you kissed that other guy?"

"I'm not proud of it, but yes, it was technically cheating."

Jane's expression was now one of disappointment. "Izzy McNeil, I wouldn't have thought you were such an innocent." The word *innocent* had a bite; it wasn't meant as a compliment.

I was quiet, watching Jane, processing these new bits of information about her. Jane was right—no one was perfect. But she was wrong to say I was an innocent, because I'd learned the hard lesson that no one in my life was exactly who I'd thought they were, a fact that had unsettled me at first. And yet, with distance and time, the altered images I now had of those people delighted me in a strange way. They made me realize that there was no end to the random flotsam of traits, beliefs, habits and secrets that were hidden under the controlled exteriors people wore. Which meant that the world was a mystery and always would be. Although this fact had initially depressed me, had nearly taken me down and left me there, I'd finally decided to see the wonder in it and be amazed.

I knew that Jane prized honesty, so I said, "Here's my thinking on the topic. Maybe it's old-fashioned, but I think if you're fooling around with someone other than the person you're committed to, then cheating is cheating. Whether it's kissing or rolling around or sex."

Jane leaned forward, her eyes lighting again. "Okay, so go with me for a second. Let's say you and Sam are together, let's say you've already gotten married, but you need a break, and you decide to take a vacation with a friend. Who's your best girlfriend?"

"Maggie Bristol. You might know her. She's a criminal defense lawyer."

"Martin Bristol's kid?"

"Grandkid."

"We should get both of them on Trial TV. But anyway, let's say you and Maggie decide to go to South Beach, okay? You head down there with some other girls for a weekend. You're just gonna tear up the town, drink too much, dance your asses off, have bloodies by the pool in the morning."

"Sounds great."

"Exactly. It's just you and the girls. But of course, you're going to talk to guys at the pool. I mean, you can do that, even if you've got a boyfriend or a husband, right? That's not cheating."

"Sure."

"Okay, and when you see the same group of guys out that night, you're going to talk to them again, aren't you?"

"Yes, Jane, I talk to men. What's the point?"

"Stay with me. So there's one guy in particular who thinks you're incredible. You know how you can tell when a guy thinks you're sexy?"

I laughed. "I guess."

"You know. Like Theo last night. There was no question about that, was there?"

I blushed. Nope, there had been no misunderstanding with Theo last night. None this morning, either.

"Okay, so your girlfriend Maggie, is she single?"

"Not really. She recently got back together with a guy named Wyatt."

"Well, imagine this is right before they got back together."

"Sure." Maggie was perennially single, so it wasn't hard to imagine.

"So Maggie is flirting with one of this guy's buddies, and you and this guy who has the hots for you, you're just talking, and he buys you a drink. You'd accept that drink, wouldn't you?"

"Sure, and I'd buy him one, too. I'd probably buy for the whole group."

"Definitely." Jane was talking faster now, her voice excited. "And you think this guy is cool. I mean, he's definitely good-looking, and he's super smart. He's got this great job, doing…I don't know…something that takes brains like running a hedge fund. You're having an amazing conversation. Nothing wrong with that, right?"

"No, there's nothing wrong with talking to someone." I took a couple sips of my tea. I was suddenly exhausted. The night with Theo hadn't allowed more than three hours of sleep. Not that I was complaining.

"You really have a great connection with this guy," Jane continued. "You start to think about how attached you feel to him, just from your conversation, and you realize you haven't felt that connected to Sam, not in the same way, for a while. Not that you don't love Sam, but you don't always feel in sync with him."

I blinked a few times. I knew what she was talking about. "But you can't feel connected to anyone a hundred percent of the time, so of course you're going to feel connected to other people sometimes. Other guys."

"Absolutely. So you're feeling this connection, and it's exhilarating. It's literally making you feel more alive to have this conversation. The drinks are flowing, and your Maggie is gone for the moment, but you don't care, because you feel safe with this guy. He's married, you're married. The bottom line is you just think he's wonderful. You're thinking that maybe you could introduce him to Sam and they could be friends, or maybe you could set him up with one of your other girlfriends. He's that great of a guy."

"Okay, Jane, I got it. What's your point?"

"My point..." She scooted forward in her seat, her long torso stretching toward mine. Her black hair swung over her shoulders and hung in two gleaming sheets along the sides of her face.

"You want to know my point, Izzy?" She leaned closer. She smelled warm, like a cinnamon apple. I could see a few delicate lines that cut through the puff of her bottom lip.

Her voice was hypnotic; I was waiting to find out where she was taking me. "Yeah," I said.

"My point is..." She leaned even closer so that our faces were only an inch apart. "What if..." I could feel her soft breath near my mouth. "What if he moved toward you, just like this? What if you could feel the heat from his body and his mouth when he spoke to you? You know what I mean?"

"Yeah." I didn't move. I felt as if I was holding my breath, waiting for the end of the story.

"No one is around." Jane was now speaking her words in my ear. "It's loud and it's buzzing in that bar, and the more you talk, it just seems like the two of you, no one else. You know what I mean?"

"Yeah." In my peripheral vision, I saw the front window of the coffee shop over Jane's shoulder, but I wasn't truly seeing. I was in South Beach at that bar.

"So what if…what if right at that moment, he stopped talking…" Jane halted for a second, turned her head a fraction of an inch. Her mouth was near mine. "And what if he kissed you?"

We stayed there, Jane's lips close to mine, and for a second I wondered if *she* was going to kiss me, just to prove her point. And though I had never thought of kissing a woman before, it didn't seem a terrible prospect. In fact…

I let myself drift, far away from my mind, which had been so sure of what it wanted and how it would act only minutes before. I closed my eyes. I parted my lips for just a second.

"See?" Jane said. "See? You would have done it!"

My eyes bolted open. "No, I wouldn't."

She sat back and slapped her knee. "Yes, you would. You would have kissed *me*."

"Bullshack," I said, trying out one of my swear word replacements. Then to really make my point, "Bullshit." I picked up my mug and drank a few gulps of tea.

"Fine, then you would have kissed that guy in South Beach."

"No." But the way she'd told the story, she might have been right. In a moment like that, I might have slipped. "If I did," I said, "I would have felt awful. It would have been *cheating* to me."

"No, that's not cheating. Kissing or making out, especially in a situation like that, is not cheating."

"It is."

She sighed. "You know how many of your friends who are in relationships do stuff like that?"

"None that I know of."

"None that tell you."

I laughed. "Maybe you're right." But the truth was I felt like a farm girl led into town for the first time. Was she right? Was this one of those things that everyone believed except for me? Was I some innocent, as Jane said? Someone behind the times?

"You won't tell anyone about me…you know, about me being red-blooded, will you?" She smiled then dropped it.

"No way. I'm a vault."

"Good. You'll be the only one in the news business." She glanced at her watch. "I should get going."

I felt as if I had missed some amorphous opportunity, one that would have allowed me to connect with Jane, and I regretted it. "Hey, Jane. I'm sorry."

She shook her head, silent. She picked her phone off the table, looked at it, then bent down and tossed it in her bag. She straightened up and smiled.

"That's your anchorwoman smile," I said. "I've seen it."

She laughed, her own personal smile returning, one that was natural and made the sides of her eyes crease just a little. She reached across the table and lifted my hand, giving me a little squeeze. Her fingers were smooth but firm. "I'm glad we're going to be working together."

"Me, too. Hey, Jane, don't I need to do something this weekend, like rehearsals?"

She shook her head. "Just the on-air people. But be ready for trial-by-fire on Monday." She took a silver cigarette case out of her purse. Opening it, she pulled out some bills and put them on the table. "I've got to get out of here. Zac has had enough time to cool off. Time for damage control, and then I have to get to the station."

"Will you and Zac be okay?"

She gave a hard, short laugh. "A few months ago, I would have said 'yeah.' Zac knows I'm red-blooded. And he still loves me."

"What's happened over the last few months?"

She gathered her wrap made of taupe-colored cashmere, her eyes downcast. "He's been getting sick of it. I mean, who can blame him? It's just that we had an understanding before, and now he's not… Well, he's not so understanding anymore."

Elegantly, Jane swung the wrap around her shoulders, then released her deep black hair, letting it fall around her like a shiny shawl. She stood. "I forgot to ask you—what happened with Theo last night?"

I said nothing, and in that moment, Jane must have read my face.

She laughed. She leaned over me. "Was it hot?"

In that instant, I saw Theo leaning over me, moving into me, his hair brushing the sides of my face. I blushed with the memory. "Yeah."

"Did it feel like anything you'd ever had before?" When I paused, she said, "C'mon. You've had sex before, Izzy, but *this* was something different, right? Something more electrifying than you've felt."

I could feel his lips biting mine; I could feel his fingers everywhere. I flushed more deeply. "Yeah."

"Was it so good it felt like your whole body filled up with heat? The kind of heat that you didn't know if you could bear, but yet somehow you loved it?"

"Yeah."

"And you felt like your mind was going to explode?"

I saw Theo and me then, slick with sweat, coming together, setting off explosions. "Yeah."

She stood up, taking the heat of the moment, the heat of

the memories with her. "That's how I felt last night, too," she said. "That's how I always feel. That's one of the reasons why I've had such a hard time giving it up."

"What are the other reasons?"

Her eyes went thoughtful. She looked past me for a moment. "There isn't one person who can be everything to me. I think it's unfair to try and make Zac my best friend, my lover, my business partner, the co-owner of our houses, my accountant, the person I cut loose with, the person whose shoulder I cry on." She looked at me.

I said nothing, sensing more.

"Different people inspire me in different ways," she continued. "They fascinate me in different ways. I like to be let into someone else's life, to see what other people are doing with their days." She stopped and shook her head. "I just look at my own life differently after I've gotten a taste of someone else's."

I nodded. I understood a little, I suppose.

"Anyway, I've got lots of other reasons," Jane said. "Those are just some of them."

Before I could respond, she turned, and then Jane Augustine was gone.

8

Jane sat in Zac's studio in their basement. They always did their best talking while he worked. Her husband's back was to her. Years ago, he used to be hunched over the wet tray in the dark room. Now he hunched in front of the computer or over his printer, searching for the blackest of blacks, switching papers from Portfolio to Silver Rag to Maestro.

"You want to tell me who it was?" He didn't turn, his eyes firmly on the screen.

The image there was one of a pink balcony hanging precariously over an orange brick alleyway just off Belden Avenue in Chicago. *Back Alleys* was the title of Zac's photographic exhibit at an art gallery here in town. He'd been successful with these photos of alleys in New York and D.C., and he'd finally felt it was time to feature the town he had called home for almost a decade. The show had been so successful, selling hundreds of photos in the three weeks since the opening, that Zac had been working constantly to fill the orders. He'd been on a roll and had been happy lately. But then he'd returned early from meeting his agent in New York and found Jane missing.

It wasn't that such a thing hadn't happened before. In days past, sometimes, Zac actually wanted to know a few details—what they did to her, what she did to them. Sometimes the details got him excited. Other times, he was only putting up with her and her dalliances because he loved her.

Today was definitely one of the latter.

She could tell this from the way Zac's lat muscles tensed under his stylishly worn T-shirt, originally black but grayed from so much washing. She could tell from the way his movements were fast and sharp, rather than relaxed, almost dreamy, the way he usually worked when he was happy.

"Just some—" she started to say.

"Just some guy?" he interrupted, his voice edged with impatience.

"Something like that." Although that wasn't true. He was some guy who'd been following her. Some creep who'd been making notations about the most minute, private things in her life. Despite her public job, Jane *hated* for her life to be made public. And she'd been lucky because her affairs had always existed in a void for her.

Zac cleared his throat, a habit of his that sprang up when he had something to say which he didn't feel confident about, but something he'd thought about for a long time.

It was so strange how well she knew him. In many ways, she knew him better than she knew herself; she understood the reasons for his behavior so much better than she did her own. For example, she was a wife who cheated, and according to most people she was wanton, immoral and wrong. And although she had her reasons for it, ninety percent of the time she agreed with those people. It was the ten percent she had told Izzy about. The ten percent that got her into trouble.

She'd promised Zac recently that she wouldn't do it anymore, that she would be a proper wife who never strayed. She meant it, too, but it was harder than she thought. And yet, she had expected him to forgive her. But now there was this edge to his back, this fuming energy that poured off him.

"Are you all right?" she said.

He turned to face her.

He rarely looked at her during these types of discussions. Usually he kept working, as if he were more comfortable to let his words rise from a blank canvas rather than let her see his expression.

But now he was definitely looking, and there was nothing resembling forgiveness there. What she saw was anger, along with something she hadn't ever seen before. Something like disgust.

9

John Mayburn walked in ten minutes late. I pointed at my watch as he strolled to the table.

"Sorry," he mouthed, a smile on his face.

It was the smile that threw me.

At his job during the week, when he met with lawyers like me (the lawyer I *used* to be) who wanted him to dig up dirt on a plaintiff, Mayburn wore a boring navy-blue suit or slacks and a jacket, a button-down shirt underneath that was starched so stiff it could stand on its own. When I got to know him better, I learned that on the nights and weekends, he was rather relaxed. So the stylish jeans, Ramones T-shirt and beat-up brown boots he wore now didn't throw me. It was definitely the smile.

"What's with you?" I said, as he slipped into the seat opposite me.

"What do you mean?" He picked up a large, laminated menu. We were at a café on Webster, named John's Place.

"You're chipper."

"I've barely said two words. Why would you think I'm chipper?" He glanced at the menu. "The Cobb sounds good, doesn't it?" He glanced back up at me, then shook his head. "Jesus, that did sound chipper."

"So, what's the deal?"

He shrugged. "Sorry I was late. I had to drop someone off."

"You had to *drop* someone off? Did you have someone spend the night?" *Like I did,* I almost added.

"Shut it." He kept looking at the menu. "I took someone to the hardware store this morning."

It sounded innocuous, but he still had a faint smile on his lips.

The waiter came over then. Mayburn ordered a club sandwich. I asked for an omelet with red peppers, since I hadn't gotten to eat the one Theo made that morning.

"Are you dating someone?" I asked.

He shrugged. "Maybe."

"Who is it?"

"Someone I've known for a while...well, kind of."

"Is it Meredith?" Mayburn had told me that he'd once dated a gallery owner named Meredith Saga, a woman who lived for art and sex and little else.

"No Sagas for me."

"So who?"

"Why are you so nosy?"

"Why won't you tell me?"

Mayburn seemed to be looking at anything but me now. He studied the family at the next table. He frowned at their baby, who was in a stroller as big as an RV and blocking the aisle.

All the while, I stayed silent. It was one of the smartest things I'd learned from being a lawyer—the best way to make someone tell you something is not to badger them with questions but to confront them with silence. And then there were the things Mayburn himself had taught me—when you're surveying someone, listen to everything, look at everything. Especially look at what people do as much as what they say. Look at what they *don't* say, too.

A few seconds ticked by. Then a few more. Finally, Mayburn met my eyes. "You want to know who it is?"

"Yeah."

"Lucy."

One of the other things the law had taught me was to never show shock. But it was impossible at that moment.

"Lucy *DeSanto?*" I blurted so loud that the baby in the stroller began to cry.

"Yeah."

"The same Lucy DeSanto whose husband you and I caught laundering money for the mafia?"

"Yep."

Lucy DeSanto was a tiny, lovely, elegant blonde who lived in Lincoln Park. She was married and had two children. Her husband, Michael DeSanto, was not living at home, however. Rather, he was living at a maximum-security holding cell, awaiting his federal trial for racketeering, fraud and money laundering. Due to the nature of the people DeSanto worked with—mafia people who tended to run for parts unknown if they got even a glimpse of sunlight—bail had been denied.

Mayburn had been hired by the bank where Michael DeSanto worked and he'd pulled me into it when he hit a brick wall with the case. As payback for aiding me in my search for my missing fiancé, Mayburn asked for my help because I could fit in the upscale North Side neighborhood where Lucy lived. He trained me on surveillance techniques and had me pose as a neighborhood mom to get close to Lucy and get inside their house. When Michael DeSanto had come home one day and found me in his office fiddling with his computer, I thought that my time on earth had come to an end. But I managed to get out of it, and the evidence I got out of Michael's computer had sent him away, at least for now. Although Mayburn had never met Lucy during the investigation, he'd spent plenty of hours watching her come and go from the house, and I'd always suspected he had a long-distance crush on her.

"I didn't think you were supposed to meet your subjects," I said.

"You're not. But you know Lucy."

The waitress delivered our food. The omelet didn't look as delicious as the one Theo had created. But then again, if Theo had put a pile of dirt on a plate and handed it to me while naked, it would've looked good.

"I do know Lucy," I said, taking a bite. "She's probably the sweetest person on the planet."

"Isn't she?" Mayburn's voice carried something like awe. "She is such a good person."

I blinked. I'd never, ever heard Mayburn talk this way. He sounded more like one of my girlfriends than the sarcastic, seen-everything P.I. he was.

"How did this get to the point where you know Lucy DeSanto personally, and you're taking her to the hardware store?"

"You know how bad we felt for her after they took Michael away?"

"Yes. I even called her to tell her that."

"Well, I did, too."

"So you admitted that you were the investigator who was hired to watch her husband?"

"Yeah."

"Did you tell her that you'd been spying on her for months, trailing behind her when she took the kids for a walk and following her when she drove to the grocery store?"

"I did."

"That's not the typical pickup line. How did she take it?"

"You know Lucy." He smiled with one side of his mouth and then pushed his plate away, as if the thoughts of Lucy had fed him enough. "She was kind about it. She was actually happy that it all happened. She had no idea Michael was into something dirty. She's filed for divorce."

"And now she's got you, apparently."

That one-sided smile again. "This is it, Izzy."

"*It,* like you're in love?"

"Yeah."

"*It,* like you want to marry this girl?"

"Yeah."

"Wow. I'm jealous. I can't seem to decide if I want Sam or…" Or Theo. Or Grady. Or someone else altogether. Or no one at all. "Anyway, does Lucy feel the same way?"

"Not sure. It's a lot more complicated for her." He pushed his chair back. "All right, enough about me. I need you to eat that omelet fast, because we have to go to the lingerie store." He turned and pointed through the front windows at a store across the street.

"The Fig Leaf? Don't tell me you want me to model lingerie so you can pick out something for your girlfriend."

"Nope. Have you ever worked in retail?"

"No."

"Well, I want you to work there."

"You want me to fold panties?"

"And I want you to sell them and ring them up, and mostly, I want you to watch Josie, the manager. My client, Marie, the owner of the store, doesn't trust her lately, but technically the store is running great, so she doesn't want to fire her."

"This doesn't sound like your usual case." Mayburn worked for big law firms, monster corporations and international banks.

"It's not. Marie is a family friend. Maybe she's being paranoid about her manager. Who knows? But I'm not treating it different from any other investigation."

"Okay, so what's Josie up to? Skimming money off the top?"

He shrugged. "The books seem like they're up-to-date. Inventory seems well-handled. They're just getting a lot more traffic, which obviously is a good thing, but they haven't increased marketing efforts or their PR. Marie can't figure out exactly how it happened. She wants to make sure everything is on the up-and-up, especially since she spends most of her time in Palm Beach now. If there's nothing to find, everyone's happy."

I stared at the Fig Leaf. It was an upscale place I'd been once. The merchandise had been ludicrously expensive, but still I had purchased a white nightie, very short and very sexy, for my wedding night. The nightie still hung at the back of my closet, tags on.

"Since Marie started spending more time out of town, Josie has been telling her they need to hire a clerk," Mayburn said. "This morning, Marie told Josie she'd found someone—her family friend Lexi, who is attending law school during the day."

"Does Lexi have red hair?"

"Yes."

"Lexi," I said, trying the name out. "Lexi what?"

"Lexi Hammond."

"Lexi Hammond," I repeated. "I like it. But wait a minute, what about filling out IRS forms and stuff? Won't I need a social security number?"

"They're paying you cash under the table. And then I'm paying you a freelance investigator fee."

"Shouldn't I be getting an investigator license if I'm going to keep doing this?"

"Nah. It's a pain in the ass to get a license in Illinois. And expensive. Plus, I just need your help to get intel. I don't want you to testify or anything like that."

I thought of something else. I told Mayburn about my job at Trial TV. "But Jane says I won't be going on-air right away."

"Should be fine. I need you to start tomorrow, Sunday, and if we're lucky I won't need you more than a few weeks. So, what do you think, Lexi?"

"Does Lexi get a discount?"

"I knew you were going to ask that. Thirty percent."

I clapped my hands and pushed the omelet away. "Let's go."

10

Zac Ellis opened their weekend house in Long Beach, Indiana, the way he always did. He walked through the place, turning on lights, dialing the thermostat up or down, opening windows just to get some fresh air in the place. Often, he would be followed by Jane when she was done with a broadcast, and the fresh air would twist its way though the house and into their lungs and even into their relationship, and they almost always felt much better within hours of arriving.

But he could tell today would be different. The fresh air, colder today on this side of Lake Michigan, seemed too harsh. And so was the news of Jane's latest bit of messing around. How had he ever thought he could handle it?

He stopped for a moment in their kitchen. It was narrow and crammed with old, kitschy appliances they'd picked up at antique malls and flea markets—so different from their vast, metropolitan kitchen in Chicago. Standing there, he thought about his history with Jane. Before they'd met, he dated deep, brooding women. Artists like his ex Zoey, who were dark and moody, who wore funky clothes and who painted in a studio for days at a time.

Jane was so different from those women—tall and flashy and up-front about everything. He hadn't been mesmerized with the whole TV world, or even really that interested. Which had given him the mistaken impression that he would never fall for Jane. How very, very, *very* wrong he had been.

He left the kitchen and walked down the narrow hallway toward their bedroom. The house was built in 1927, and so, like the kitchen, the room was small, and their antique brass bed had to be pushed into the far corner. He leaned against the wall, shoving his hands into the pockets of his jeans, imagining Jane there. Almost ten years ago, about a year and a half after they'd met, they got married on the beach two blocks from here, and they spent their first night as a married couple in that bed.

It felt good to picture Jane this way, with him. Lately, his mind only held pictures of her with other men.

Yes, Jane was the love of his life. He never doubted that—still didn't—but he was starting to wonder if his love, his passion, his intensity for her could survive these affairs. She'd said she would stop, but she hadn't. And after coming home from New York and discovering her gone again, he saw that fidelity was a lofty goal in Jane's eyes, one she was never going to be able to achieve on a regular basis.

He walked over to the bed and scratched at the brass with his thumbnail. It was starting to blacken, losing its luster. He would have to polish it. He was always the one who had to do these tasks around the beach house—cleaning up the yard, splitting the wood, retouching the crumbling paint. Jane disliked such chores, and it pleased him to take care of them for her, for them.

He kept scratching at the brass. The chalky black wouldn't seem to budge. He wondered if it could be removed at all, or whether it had spread too far. He wondered the same thing about Jane's affairs.

The thing was they weren't even affairs. They were one-night stands mostly. She loved only him, she said, wanted to be married only to him. But damn it, what did it say about *them* that she needed such experiences, that she couldn't give them up?

Suddenly, taken by a rage that exploded in his belly and shot into his hands, he grabbed the rail of the headboard and rattled it violently, as if he might shake away the tarnish. The headboard banged against the wall, which only made him think of Jane, rattling someone else's headboard. He shook it harder, the pounding increasing, the *bam, bam, bam* getting louder and louder. He liked the violence of it, the feeling that energy trapped inside him was coming out, and so he kept shaking the bed, kept hammering it against the wall, until it sounded like the staccato of gunfire.

And then he pictured himself, acting like a teenager, unable to control his emotions.

He stopped. He calmed down. "Enough," he muttered out loud, to no one, his voice forlorn in the empty house.

He turned and kept walking through the rooms, inching open a few windows, wiping the dust from the end tables in the living room, embarrassed at his solitary display of rage.

Zac liked to consider himself a strong person. Jealousy had rarely been a problem before this. When Jane told him about the first guy, a year after they were married, she was so nervous, he almost thought it funny. He had never been possessive, and he had never thought he could possess someone like Jane. And so he told her to be careful and to not make it too much of a habit, but that he understood. Of course, he added, if she was going to do that, then *he* could sleep with the occasional woman if he wanted. But the thing was he never wanted to. Jane was enough for him. He had ventured outside their marriage only once, with Zoey, mostly because he felt it would somehow even the score, but all he could think about was Jane.

And now he was tired of being her fool. Check that. Judging from his tantrum with the bed, he wasn't just tired, he was pissed off. Truth was, he was starting to despise her a little bit. And he hated that. How could he love her so much and hate her at the same time? It was a sadistic circle.

Strangely he had seen the same pattern play out in his parents' relationship. His mother, Martina Ellis, was an artist, a flamboyant woman who hit her stride in the seventies when she changed her fine arts perspective to one of "super realism." His dad, after their marriage, followed her to different places around the world—sometimes Manhattan, sometimes the South of France or London—so she could paint. His father often sat in the background, supporting his wife. When Zac was born, it was no different. He loved his mother, but she intimidated him with her talent and her unapologetic exuberance. That was true even to this day. It was his father he was close to. And so when his dad finally grew weary of taking the backseat, Zac understood perfectly why he had to divorce his mother.

His dad understood Zac well, too. He understood why Zac would be attracted to someone like Jane, and he had been very empathetic lately when Zac called him, asking vague questions about marriage and how his dad handled it. His father answered all such questions with his usual blend of patience and candor. He spoke to Zac of how he "managed" Martina when she needed it, how he propped her up when the critics were ruthless, how he held her arm proudly when they walked through a glittering gallery showcasing her work.

But in a recent conversation, his father paused and spoke a few words that haunted Zac.

"Remember one thing," he said. "It was a battle, and I didn't win it. I had to leave."

Those words blazed through Zac's mind now as he walked through their house one more time, then outside and onto the deck. In the summer, the deck would hold chairs with big padded cushions, a chaise, a hammock, two umbrellas. But now only an iron patio table stood alone, stark and lonely in a cool patch of light.

Usually, he would be relaxing now that the house was open, maybe starting to think about a bottle of wine to uncork for Jane. But Jane would not be coming today. He'd told her to stay the hell away from the beach house, from him. Without her, the house seemed only half-full of its usual vitality, but he couldn't stand the sight of her right now. Her bullshit *dalliances* were causing his mind to swirl, to wonder—Was it him? Or was it them? And how could he get his mind around it? Because he didn't want to lose the love of his life.

And then there was another persistent question—why should he be the one who had to ask these questions, to ponder new versions of right and wrong?—Why was it Jane who got to do whatever she wanted while he had to wade through the muck left behind?

He stormed from the deck back into the house. He would focus on something else, on some work around here. That was what always calmed him.

He hurried down the old, slanted staircase into their basement. On the workbench that was original to the house, amid the house paint and the tools, he found the brass cleaner he had used on the bed when they bought it. He grabbed a few rags from the bin under the bench and took the stairs back up two at a time.

In the bedroom, he chose a spot on Jane's side and furiously scrubbed at it with the polisher. The black started to lift, but the brass remained dull. He grabbed a clean rag and ran it back and forth, hard, over the spot. Still, it wouldn't shine. The brass appeared slightly greenish, as if it had been inhabited by a mold that had simply taken over the bed.

He squirted more tarnish remover on the rag, scrubbed again and again and again. He tried a clean rag. The tarnish couldn't be removed.

"Goddamn it," he said. *"Goddamn it."*

His voice, low as it was, cut through the crisp, spring coolness of the house, and he heard the anguish there. For some reason, it was that sound, that tone, which overwhelmed him.

He sank to his knees and grief washed over him. He couldn't go on like this. *They* couldn't go on like this. He began to sob. He hadn't cried in eight years, not since his grandmother, his dad's mom, passed away.

But the tears were different now. They weren't the soothing sobs to mourn the passing of a life lived well. These were angry sobs, full of despair. And mostly, full of fear.

Because he had no idea how he would handle this grief. He had no idea how to move on from here.

11

"Have you ever cheated?"

Sam shot a sideways glance at me. His green eyes sparkled like olives in a martini. "Not on you."

"On anyone?"

His eyes moved away, looking toward the empty stage. As he did so, the overhead lights glinted in his cropped blond hair, making him look like the California boy he was.

We were no longer engaged or exclusive, but now, as we tried to figure out what to do with our lives and ourselves, Sam and I dated. Which meant that instead of spending our nights making dinner at home or watching the Cubs on TV, we went out for nights like this.

We were at Wise Fools, a bar on Lincoln Avenue, where we often went when we first met. Like a lot of the other bars on Lincoln, it was wood-clad and beer-soaked, the kind of place that brought out the twenty-somethings searching for Bud Light specials. But Wise Fools booked great bands, too, and since Sam was a guitar player and an all-around music lover, we'd been finding ourselves there every few weeks.

The band tonight was Mutha Goose, which I thought was just about the stupidest name I'd ever heard, but Sam's friend R.T. was the lead guitarist. R.T. and Sam often played together, but Sam never had the time to be in a real band. He was always too busy with business school and then work. Sam, who had been Forester Pickett's financial advisor at a wealth management firm, had lost his job, too, after taking off temporarily with Forester's property, but unlike me, he'd landed on his feet. The fact that the whole mess had been in the news hadn't helped me one bit. Lawyers don't like even a whiff of a scandal associated with their law firm. The same was true with Sam's business. None of the wealth management firms would take him on, but a friend gave him a job on the trading side of the business. He didn't seem entirely happy, but I couldn't tell if that was because of the new job or because we had broken up. Or maybe because he didn't have the time to play much music lately, something which made him a little irritable.

R.T. came on stage. By day, R.T. sold computer software, but his passion was his music, and nights like tonight, he looked like a musician—jeans that appeared not to have been washed for weeks, leather flip-flops, brown bangs that fell in his eyes instead of being gelled into submission.

Sam waved hi to his friend, then turned back to me. I could see some kind of struggle in his eyes, but whether it was because he wished he were on that stage or he wished he didn't have to answer my question, I didn't know. I used to be able to read him so well.

"I've cheated." He said it simply, almost resignedly, as if it were something he'd wrestled and come to terms with.

I felt a well of disappointment. Sam was a cheater. At that moment, I wanted to look at anything but him. I picked up my BlackBerry from the table and scrolled through the texts and e-mails. There was a time when my in-boxes would have been choked with cries for help, when someone always needed me or my opinion. Now they were fairly empty, save a text from my brother, Charlie, saying he might stop by the bar to say hello.

I could feel Sam watching me, gauging my reaction to his statement.

I put the phone back on the table and thought of his ex-girlfriend Alyssa, a woman who was beautiful and reed-thin.

She and Sam had dated at the end of high school and into college. She was an angelic blonde who worked in geriatric research, making the world better for the elderly. In short, she made me feel like a shallow devil—the brassy, red-headed entertainment lawyer.

I didn't necessarily like Alyssa, but I felt pain for her now because she must have been the one Sam was talking about.

Finally, I looked at him. "You cheated on Alyssa?"

Sam shook his head. "Carrie."

"Carrie, your first girlfriend ever?"

"Yeah." He lifted his Blue Moon beer from the table and poked at the orange slice with his finger.

"Sam, you were like a freshman in high school."

I thought of the monumentally idiotic things I'd done during high school. Once, when my mother was out of town and trusted me enough to babysit my brother, Charlie, I forced him to be the bartender for the monster bash I threw. He was twelve at the time. Charlie ended up drinking beer as he poured it from the keg and later threw up violently over our balcony and into the alley behind our apartment, one of the most scary and heartbreaking things I'd ever witnessed. Doing stupid things made you smarter, I figured. I'd certainly never treated my brother like that again. If anything, I had cherished and babied him after that. Oddly, he remembered the incident fondly.

"Does that really count?" I asked Sam.

"Hell, yeah. She was my first love." He grimaced, as if what he'd done still tortured him. And that made my heart fill with love, like a balloon given a shot of air from an inflator.

"You were so young," I pointed out. "You didn't know what you were doing."

"Yeah, I did." He looked straight into my eyes. "You want to know why I did it?"

I nodded, almost afraid to say anything. This was one of the things I liked about our breakup—despite the drama and the uncertainty, we were completely honest with each other now. Sure, we were honest before all this, too, but now it was different. Now, it was microscopic, as if we were both laying all our cards on the table and saying, *If we're going to do this, here's the truth. The real, deep-down, not-so-tidy, sometimes-it-will-make-you-flinch truth.*

"You know what my dad is like?" Sam asked.

"A drunken, selfish bastard." I had never met Sam's dad. Neither he nor his sisters had any consistent contact with him, but I'd heard the stories.

R.T. and his band began playing. Their first number was a cover of a song by The Killers called, appropriately enough, "All These Things That I've Done." The lights in the bar dimmed. The stage lights, orange and bold, grew stronger, while the music grew louder until it seemed the stage pulsed like a heart.

Sam pulled his chair closer so I could hear him. "This was a few years before my mom finally got rid of him," he said. "Then I kind of wanted to be like him. I thought the way he acted—tough and swaggering and hard-partying— was how guys were supposed to be. So I acted like that, you know? My mom was mortified, and she tried to stop me, but I didn't care. I just…" His words died away for a second.

"You wanted him to love you." I watched his face for a reaction, hoping he wouldn't close down the conversation because it was too uncomfortable, something that might have happened before our breakup.

Sam blinked slowly a few times, his brown lashes hitting his cheeks, already tan from playing rugby outside. "Yeah. Exactly. I could tell he wasn't going to be around for long, and even though I knew he was a jerk, I was terrified of having to take care of my sisters and my mom, even though no one ever said I had to. So I drank a lot and smoked pot and just kind of pretended I was like him. And then one day…man, I can remember it exactly… I came home from school early because I wasn't feeling good or something.

And he had this girl in the house. I knew her. She was a waitress at one of the pancake houses he owned, and she was the one I'd always had a crush on." Sam shook his head. "They didn't hear me come in. She was on the counter and they were…"

"Going at it," I finished for him, feeling the bewilderment and shock Sam must have experienced.

"Yeah." He laughed, a brittle sound. "Like, right there on my mom's countertop. I just turned around and left. I went down the street to this park and I sat there for four hours. The next night, I went to a party and picked a fight with Carrie, and as soon as she left, I walked up to this girl by the pool. We ended up making out behind the pool house for an hour."

"And you think that's cheating?"

"Yes," he said without hesitation. "Don't you?"

"Yes," I said, relieved to be on the same page with Sam about this, about anything.

Sam moved his chair even closer. He put his arm around my back and nuzzled my neck.

"Red Hot." Sam whispered my nickname in my ear. "I miss you."

I turned my head to nestle into him. But then I remembered Theo. Guilt ripped through me. I hadn't cheated, I reminded myself. I hadn't, I hadn't.

But I felt as if I had. Sam kissed me, and the room seemed to disappear. In the distance, I heard the band play a slow, hard version of "Tempted" by Squeeze. *Tempted by the fruit of another…Alarmed by the seduction…I wish that it would stop.*

Except that I had no interest in stopping Sam now, or whatever would happen with us later that night. Suddenly, I didn't care about the technicalities of dating two men, of whether that made me a bad girl, a temptress or a slut, when before I'd always been the pillar of fidelity, the poster child of monogamy.

"Hey, what am I interrupting?"

Sam and I pulled apart. I blinked at the figure that stood in front of our table, backlit by the stage lights. It took me a moment to make out my brother, Charlie, who wore a bemused expression on his face.

"Hey, man!" Sam jumped up to give Charlie a hug. The two of them loved each other.

Charlie returned the hug, thumping Sam on the back. Charlie had chestnut-brown hair but in the stage lights, you could see a tinge of red. He had spiral curls like mine, which he let grow a little longer than most men's hair. He was one of the sweetest guys I knew. Also one of the laziest. Charlie had been living off a worker's comp settlement for a few years now, and all his friends called him "Sheets" because he spent so much time in bed.

I stood, and Charlie made his way around the table. He hugged me tight, lifting me off the floor. "How are you doing, sister?" He set me down, and we smiled at each other, saying nothing. "Good," he said, reading in my eyes that I was just fine. At least at that moment.

Sam found another chair for Charlie, and as he sat, my phone lit up. A new text message. I picked it up. Somehow I'd gotten three texts in the time Sam and I were kissing. All of them from Jane Augustine.

Are you doing anything tonight? the first said. *Would you be able to come over to my house?*

Hi, Izzy, the next said, *I'm so sorry to bother you but not sure who to call. I'm kind of freaking out here, and I wondered if you were out and could stop by.*

Izzy, the last said. *I need some help.*

I looked at the call log and saw she'd called twice but hadn't left a message.

I went into the front room of the bar, where it was quieter, and called Jane.

"Thank God," she said, answering. "I'm so sorry to interrupt your night, but can you come over?"

"What's going on?"

"Someone has been in my house."

"What? Is Zac there?"

"No, he took off today for our weekend place." She exhaled hard. "I came home, and I found some...well, some stuff in my house." She was talking fast, her voice distressed. "Someone has been in here."

"Have you called the cops?"

"No!" Her voice was alarmed now, anxious. She sounded as if she were bordering on tears. "Izzy, you know how it is. If I call the cops, then this is all over the news. The network is launching Monday. A legal network. *This* is not the kind of PR we need."

"But are you safe?"

"I've been through the whole house. There's no one here now." She sighed. "I didn't know who to call, and you were always the one we went to when there was any problem with work. I don't know... Is there any way you could come over?"

"What's your address?" I asked.

She told me.

"I'll be right there."

12

Jane's place in River North was one of eight town houses, all clearly built at the same time, probably by the same developer, but hers was the nicest—an elegant graystone, nearly white. It was new construction but built to appear old with iron streetlamps with electrical flame that flickered like real fire and a black iron fence with twisted posts. French balconies surrounded the tall upstairs windows.

The house was lit up—all the lights must have been on—but the shades on the first floor, tasseled at the edges, were drawn, hiding whatever was happening there. I hurried up the front steps, trailed by Sam and Charlie.

The brass knocker was shaped like a lion's head. I used it to pound on the door.

Jane answered right away, as if she'd been standing behind the door, waiting for us.

She wore workout clothes—black pants that hugged her long legs and a tight pink T-shirt that proclaimed the name of a local jewelry store and said, *Simply the Best for 20 Years.* Her hair was in a high, swinging ponytail. She seemed younger somehow, almost like a girl barely into her teens who looks like an adult from far away but seems so vulnerable and coltish up close.

Or maybe it was the scared look on Jane's face.

"Izzy!" She launched herself into my arms with a fierce, tight hug. We'd never really embraced before, but I could tell she needed it, and I squeezed her back just as tight. "Thanks so much for coming." She drew back. "You look cute," she said, distractedly.

"Thanks." I was wearing a red, patterned skirt and tall black heels for my date with Sam. "Jane, this is Sam, my..." I still didn't know what to call him. *My ex-fiancé* wasn't right, and *boyfriend* wasn't, either. I decided to just skip it. "And my brother, Charlie."

She shook their hands. "Hi, guys, c'mon in." Jane looked nervously up and down the street before leading us into her house.

Inside was a wide living room with polished wood floors. The walls were a soothing fawn color; the moldings along the high ceilings were painted a creamy ivory. Jane, or her very talented decorator, had filled the place with plump, coconut-brown couches and overstuffed chairs on either side of the five-foot marble fireplace. There were colorful touches everywhere—still-life oil paintings that hung side by side, an Aztec vase which stood on a pedestal, throw pillows with an African print.

"Wow." Charlie looked around in wonder. "Great place." Charlie found everything fascinating. He would have been awed by an eight-by-eight prison cell. But he was right, Jane's place was unique—somehow both chic and welcoming.

"Thanks." Jane glanced around, as if suddenly seeing it through someone else's eyes. "My husband and I have been here for almost ten years."

"You won an Emmy?" Charlie pointed to a built-in bookshelf next to the fireplace. On it was a gold statue of a winged woman holding aloft a globe.

Jane smiled. "Yes. Last year."

"Can I touch it?"

Jane laughed. "Sure. Pick it up."

Charlie walked over to the shelf and lifted the statue. "Wow." He curled it a few times as if it were a barbell. "This thing is heavy."

"Charlie!" I said. "Be careful."

"What? It's cool."

Jane laughed again. "Don't worry about it." She looked at me. "Izzy, can I show you something?"

"Of course."

"We'll be right back," she said to Sam and Charlie.

"Take your time," Sam said. He shot me a smile. If Sam was upset that our date had been interrupted, first by my brother and then by Jane's SOS call, he didn't show it. And that made me love him all the more.

If only, I thought for a second. If only we could base our decisions about who to love (and how to spend our lives) solely on a feeling we have at a given moment. If that was the case, I wouldn't care what Sam had done months before or why he hadn't confided in me about it.

Jane led me from the living room into a massive kitchen with a center granite island marbled in colors of sand and black. On the island sat a tall vase of flowers.

She pointed at them. "When I got home, they were here."

"The flowers?" It was a mixed bouquet, clearly expensive, in orange and red—passionate colors.

"I have no idea who left them. Zac took off this morning for our other house." A pained expression moved into her face. "He left after I got back from coffee with you. He said he couldn't be around me. He went to our house in Long Beach on the other side of the lake. I went to rehearsals and then worked here in my office for a while—there's so much to do to get ready for the launch on Monday—and Zac called me from the lake house when he got there. I finally took a break and went to the gym before it closed. I was gone for an hour and a half, and when I came home, this was here." She crossed her arms and looked at the vase as if it were filled with rotting food.

"Is it possible Zac left it before he went to Long Beach, and you didn't notice?"

"No, I'm telling you, the flowers weren't here before I

went to the gym. And there was no card. Someone came into the house while I was out and left them."

"Any clue who that is?"

She shook her head again.

I stared at the flowers, the kitchen feeling cooler all of a sudden. "Who has keys to your house?"

"Zac and I. Our cleaning lady. Zac's mom, but she's still in London for the winter."

"Was the house locked?"

She nodded. "I always lock it before I go anywhere, even if I'm just walking up the street for the paper. The thing is, we've got a key hidden outside, near the garage, just in case."

"How many people know about that?"

She exhaled. "A fair number. I have this little problem of losing my keys, so all my friends know about it, and some of the…" She raised her eyes to me, asking me to understand.

"Some of the guys." I said this plainly, with no judgment. And the truth was, I really didn't judge Jane for having affairs. It wasn't for me, but I had never believed that the rest of the world needed to conform to my ways. "So you bring people like that here?"

"Occasionally. Very occasionally."

"Did you check to see if the key was still there?"

She turned to the counter behind her and lifted up a magnetic box. "I got it after I found the flowers. It was in the same place. I couldn't tell if the key had been used or not."

"Do you have an alarm?"

"Yeah, but I only turn it on at night or when I'm leaving for more than a day."

"Could Zac have driven back from Long Beach and left the flowers?"

She looked at the vase, thinking, chewing the inside of her mouth. "I don't think so. I mean, I guess it's possible.

Long Beach is an hour and a half away, and that's about how long I was at the gym."

"Are you sure he called you from Long Beach?"

Her eyebrows drew closer together. "He called from his cell phone, and he said he was there. I guess it's possible, technically, that he wasn't. But they don't look like something he'd buy."

"Have you called him since you found the flowers?"

"Yeah, but he didn't answer. I left a message."

I looked at the bouquet. "Maybe it was a friend, someone trying to be nice? Maybe they just forgot the card." I looked at my watch. It was getting late. And Sam had plans with his rugby team tomorrow. If I didn't get to spend time with him tonight, it might be a few days before I saw him again with my new work schedule.

Jane bit the inside of her mouth again. I could tell she was mulling something over. "There's more."

"What do you mean?"

"Can you come upstairs?"

I followed her from the kitchen back through the living room, where Sam and Charlie were sitting on the couch, laughing about something. They looked at us expectantly.

"Just give us a second," I said.

Upstairs, we passed a guest room and a home office, both decorated to the hilt, and like the living room downstairs, accented colorfully with artwork, sculptures and rugs.

"This is our bedroom," Jane said.

I walked in and looked up. The ceiling was at least thirty feet high and vaulted. French doors led to a balcony, where I could see two chaise lounges and a host of plants and trees. A stone fireplace was against one wall with a stack of birch inside. A massive bed with twirled posts stood against the far wall, so high that small steps had been installed on either side. It was made up in a sumptuous way with white linens, plump pillows and a salmon-colored, tufted duvet.

"Great bed," I said.

"Isn't it? This is my favorite room of the house. Or at least it was." Jane pointed to the leather bench at the foot of the bed. On it sat a black box, about the size of a shoe box, but square-shaped. "That was here, too, when I came home."

Even visually, the box seemed to have a weight to it, a presence. "What is it?"

She walked over and lifted the lid of the box, which opened on one side. She held out the box. There was something red inside, something shaped in a circle.

"Is that your scarf?"

Jane had a red scarf that she wore during important broadcasts.

"Yeah," Jane said, her voice brittle. "Look closer."

I stepped toward the box. I felt off-kilter, infused with an irrational fear that she might slam the lid closed on my hand.

I peered into the box. "Jane, is that…?"

"Yeah," she said. "It's a noose."

13

I put my hands behind my back and looked down at the scarf. "Do you always keep it in this box?"

"No, I have it hanging inside my closet door with my other scarves. I mean, it's become my thing, right? And I'm supposed to wear it on Monday when the station launches. But it's not like it's some precious fabric. I just toss it in my closet with the rest of my stuff."

"But you came home and it was here, in this box?"

"Yeah. I was so freaked by the flowers that I came running up here, and this was sitting on the bench. And inside the scarf was tied like that." She dropped the box back on the bench. The scarf flew out and landed softly on the wood floor. "Who would do that?" Her voice was full of pain and panic.

I stared at the scarf. "Do you tie it like that when you hang it up?"

"No! I just hang my scarves over a peg." She was talking faster, her tone more anxious now. "And look at it. I mean, I'm not crazy, right? That's a noose."

There was no mistaking the hangman's knot, tied under a seven-inch loop, just big enough for someone to put their head through. "You're not crazy. But I've got to ask again, could it be Zac? You said he was angry. Maybe he's *really* angry."

With one hand, Jane nervously tugged her ponytail with

her fingers. She reminded me again of a young girl, a scared girl. "I just can't imagine Zac would do this. Why not just tell me to stop it or he'll leave me?"

"Has he ever said that?"

"No. He's said he could never give me up, no matter what I've done."

We both stared at the noose. The scarf was made of a shiny deep red silk. I'd always thought of Jane's scarf as competent, in-charge, bold. Now, it seemed sinister.

Her eyes cut to my own. The mauve-blue of her irises seemed to stand out against the pale of her skin. "I can't believe this." Her look bordered on terror. Fear emanated from her, cutting into the room, filling it, so that everything seemed to hum with intensity. "There's something else."

"What?"

She looked at the scarf again. She gave a little moan. "I don't know how to say this. I mean, I don't talk about this with my friends. And the truth is I think I need a lawyer right now as much as I need a friend. Can you be my lawyer?"

"You want me to tell you I won't tell anyone? That whatever you tell me is private?"

She nodded.

"Jane, that's true whether I'm your lawyer or your friend. But if it makes you feel better, I'll put my lawyer hat on. Say anything."

Jane breathed out hard. "I have this thing I like to do. Sexually. It's…well…have you heard of scarfing?"

I shook my head no.

"Sometimes it's called erotic asphyxiation."

I remembered hearing something on the news. "It's like self-strangulation during masturbation? Something about intensifying the experience?"

She nodded, her eyes on mine, looking for the judgment she seemed sure would come.

I kept a bland expression on my face. "So it's something you *like* to do?"

"Not on my own. I do it with other people. You're basically choking someone. Gently. It could be with a scarf or with your hands, and you don't do it to the point of them passing out, or even close. You just do it a little, and believe me, it makes it incredibly powerful."

"You do it to other people or you have them do it to you?" I felt like a complete sexual neophyte.

"Both." Jane slumped farther against the bed, her arms crossed in front of her chest. "Usually I have them do it to me."

I said nothing.

"You've never done anything like that?" she asked.

I almost laughed. I thought I'd tried just about every position, and I thought that had made me sexually progressive. "I'm not even sure I get it, Jane. Is it dangerous?"

She blew out a puff of air. "If you're stupid about it, yes, or if you're with someone you can't trust, but it's safe when you do it right."

"And what happens?"

"It cuts off some of the blood flow to the brain, and you have these intense…"

"Orgasms." At least I had one word to contribute to the conversation.

"Amazing. Like you've never had before." She exhaled. Her gaze slid to the scarf on the floor, a red ring, like a circle of blood. "But you want to know something? I don't think I figured this out until right now, but the scarf thing? I think it's something I like to do because it's punishing. Don't get me wrong. I do love sex and the asphyxiation thing *does* get me going. But it's also like I'm taking a penalty for cheating."

We stared at each other.

"Boy, I'm messed up," she said.

"You could probably use a little therapy."

We both broke into nervous laughter that seemed to make the room lighter. But then our eyes fell again on that red noose.

"How many people have you done that with?" I vaguely pointed to it.

She shrugged. "More than a few."

A shrill bleat cut through the air, making both Jane and me jump.

"Jesus," she said, a hand on her chest. "It's my cell." She scampered in her bare feet to the nightstand, where she looked at the display on the phone. "Zac." She sounded nervous. She threw a look at me over her shoulder, and I saw that fear again.

She answered. "Hey, hon," she said. "Yeah, I'm all right. What happened? Well, we had a break-in. Sort of. No, nothing was taken. Not a thing. Whoever it was left something." She quickly told him the story, leaving nothing out. She really did tell Zac everything. "Okay," Jane said, "I'll see you soon." She turned around with a sigh. "He's coming home. He'll be here in an hour and a half."

"We'll stay until he gets here."

She smiled, and it made her face light up. "Thanks," she said simply.

I hugged her. I could think of little else to do to make her feel better, to feel safe.

"Please don't tell Sam," she said, her words muffled by my shoulder. "You know, about the scarf thing."

"I told you, I won't say anything to anyone."

We pulled apart and went downstairs. Sam was standing by the unlit fireplace. He and Charlie were talking about rugby, but I could tell by the way Sam looked at me— eyebrows expectantly up, asking a silent, *Are we ready to go?*—that he'd had enough family and friends for the night.

I gave him an apologetic look. "If it's okay, we're going to stay until Jane's husband gets home. They had a break-in."

"Are you serious?" Sam looked alarmed. His arms tensed. He had a bulldog's way of wanting to protect people that I'd always adored.

"It's okay," Jane said. "It wasn't like a robbery. In fact, they didn't even really break in. Someone came in the house using a key, as far as I can tell, and they left some flowers and…well, a gift."

Sam's face registered confusion. He frowned at me. There was more to the story, and he knew it. And I *knew* that he knew it. And yet here I was doing the same thing to him as he'd done to me—promising someone I wouldn't tell anyone about a secret. And keeping that promise. All of a sudden, I felt both closer to Sam, and yet more distant, than ever before.

Jane brought glasses of water for us into the living room. We all sat on her couches for an hour, during which Charlie, who was oblivious to even a hint of social awkwardness, quizzed Jane about her broadcasting career, as if he were meeting her at a local pub.

Jane answered him openly, laughing at stories she must have told a thousand times, but seeming to enjoy them just the same. It reminded me of when I'd seen her with fans at the restaurant—Jane honestly appreciated the attention people gave her.

At 11:30 p.m., we heard a door opening at the back of the house. Jane flinched at the sound. Then said, simply, "Zac."

Aside from the phone call the other day, I'd never met Zac Ellis before. But I'd seen recent spreads on him and his work in the *New York Times* and *Michigan Avenue* magazine.

He came into the living room. He was a short man, definitely shorter than Jane, with wavy, light brown hair. And he was sexy. You could see that from across the room. He wore gray jeans and a leather jacket that probably cost thousands, but was somehow beat-up and tough-looking on him.

"Hi." He threw a glance at us before turning to Jane. "You okay?"

"I am now that you're home." Jane introduced us.

He shook our hands, but in a terse way. He glanced at Jane. "Can I talk to you in the kitchen?" He left.

"Be right back." Jane followed after him.

I looked at Charlie and Sam. "Sorry about this, guys."

Sam picked up my hand and rubbed it. "Don't be. You had to be here for your friend."

We sat in silence for a while, the only sound the ticking of the mantel clock which looked like a miniature grandfather clock.

When ten minutes had gone by, I stood. "I'm going to tell Jane we're leaving."

I walked to the kitchen, but stopped when I reached a pair of pocket doors that were closed most of the way. Through the six-inch crack I saw Jane and Zac standing close together. Her back was to the countertop on the left side of the room. With a wide-legged stance, he stood in front of her. She had her arms crossed, her head bowed. Her face looked splotched, as if she'd been crying, but now it was expressionless, almost devoid of emotion.

I must have made a sound, because both of them looked at me.

"Sorry," I said. "Sorry, I was just coming to tell you—"

Zac stormed to the pocket doors and pushed them open.

Surprised, I backed up. He strode past me, the leather of his coat brushing me, and marched into the living room.

He looked at Charlie and Sam, then over his shoulder at me as I trailed after him. "Thanks for coming," he said. "I appreciate you being here for Jane. But it's time for you to leave."

14

"Chilly," Charlie said when we were on the street. He tilted his head at Jane's house. He meant Zac. But that was about as negative as Charlie could get. "Weird night," he said simply. "See ya, guys."

He kissed me on the cheek, clapped Sam on the back and loped off down the street.

Sam and I stood on a now deserted street next to my silver Vespa.

"What was with the husband?" Sam said. "Just worked up about the break-in?"

"I guess." And probably worked up about his wife's stepping out. The whole thing made me wonder about Zac and why he had put up with her behavior for so long.

I stared at Sam, thinking how incredibly complicated relationships were. Such complications had never been so plain to me until the last six months.

"Why were you asking me earlier about cheating?" Sam said. "Is it because of Jane?"

Surprised, I hesitated. Then, "Why would you say that?"

He shrugged. "Just a feeling I got in there."

I darted my eyes lower. "I don't want to break a confidence."

"You shouldn't. I definitely don't want you to do that."

I met his eyes again. "Thanks." I thought about Jane and Zac for a second. "What do you think about open relationships?"

"You mean where you're together but you can date other people?"

"I guess. Or sleep with other people."

He looked up toward the sky, as if he was thinking hard about this. His green eyes returned to mine again. "I don't think they can work. I mean, monogamy is hard. It's a major sacrifice, but I think that's the only way marriage or a long-term relationship can work."

"But what about all those long-term relationships that fail, even though both people are faithful?"

He said nothing for a second. I knew we were both thinking, *Like our relationship.*

"I think there's a better chance of things working out if you're monogamous," Sam said.

"But there's no guarantee."

I glanced over his shoulder at the outline of the Sears Tower, its top lit with pink lights. It made me think of last spring, only a year ago, an uncomplicated time when we were happy, in love, almost boring in our contentedness. We would sit on my rooftop deck, Blue Moon beers on the table in front of us, and Sam would play guitar, the lights of the skyline behind him.

As much as I missed that, and as much as I was afraid of the lack of guarantees in the world of love, there was something about this new complexity that I liked, that made me feel alive.

Sam kissed my forehead. "Let's go to my place."

I was about to say yes, but then I remembered, after I'd met the Fig Leaf manager, Josie, today, she'd "hired" me immediately, but we both knew she was only giving me the gig because her boss said she had to. I started the next morning. At 7:00 a.m., and I'd been told to wear only black or white.

"I can't." I told Sam about the store job. I'd already told him about the Trial TV gig earlier.

He raised his eyebrows. "Lingerie, huh? I just don't want you to lose your drive for the law. I mean, the Trial TV thing is fun, and at least you're still in the legal field in some way, but c'mon, Iz, you're a lawyer, and you're amazing at it."

"Thanks, but no one is paying me to be an amazing lawyer right now."

I wanted to tell Sam that aside from the money that I needed to make, the other reason I was about to specialize in bras was because Mayburn would also be paying me. I would, essentially, be conducting surveillance on Josie and the Fig Leaf. I'd be studying how she ran the business, how the store was handled while the owner wasn't there— keeping my eye out for, as Mayburn had told me, "anything that smells even a little bad."

But I also remembered his cautions about telling no one, and although I'd told Sam before when I'd worked for Mayburn as a freelancer, Mayburn hadn't been happy about it, and he was insistent I not tell anyone this time. And so there I was, standing in front of Sam, another secret in the tiny space between us.

"Come to my place?" I said.

He shook his head. "I told a guy I'd run sprints with him early. I don't have any of my gear with me."

Sam privately coached some high-school rugby players, often at the crack of ass on Sunday mornings.

"Call you after practice tomorrow?" he said.

"Please."

He kissed me hard. He kissed me in a way that told me how much he loved me. I kissed him back exactly the same way. And then we split apart, that space between us widening even more.

The air felt cool and cleansing on my skin as I drove my Vespa home. I'd driven a scooter since my mother bought me one in high school, too nervous to have me waiting at city bus stops. I had thought that when I started practicing law, I'd get rid of it, but there was something about driving the Vespa that invigorated me, had never allowed me to let it go.

Ten minutes later, I was back at my Old Town condo on Eugenie Street. The building was a converted brick three-flat. Mine was the top unit, which I loved because of the rooftop deck where Sam and I used to spend so much time. The downside of my place was the three flights of stairs.

By the time I reached my condo and let myself in, I was exhausted—from the lack of sleep last night, from Jane's confessions and the creepy break-in, from the weight of having to keep things from Sam.

The small living room had pine floors and a turn-of-the-century marble fireplace with a swirling bronze grate. I slumped into my yellow chair and tried to let the whirlwind of the last few days drain away.

My phone dinged, telling me I had a new text. I picked it up, expecting something from Sam, something about how he was missing me already.

But it was a number I didn't recognize, one with a 773 area code.

It's Theo, the text read. *I've stopped myself 300 times from texting you today. I give.*

I smiled. *I've thought about you a few times today too,* I wrote. It was the truth. I was aware, distantly, of how quickly I had swung from Theo to Sam and back again.

What are you doing? he wrote.

Just got home. Weird night.

Meet me out? There's a great band playing in Bucktown.

I looked at my watch. *It's almost midnight.*

So?

Can't, I wrote. *Have to get up early tomorrow.*

Then let me come over, he wrote.

I laughed, then typed, *Nothing like cutting to the chase.*

You've taken over my head. Let me see you.

I thought of Jane saying, *I get different things from different people… When I'm with them, I get to see myself in a different way than I do every other day.*

Now I knew what she meant. Being with Theo, with someone younger and edgy and tattooed, was, quite simply, different than being with Sam, a blond, rugby-playing financial guy. And it was captivating to get a chance to see myself differently, to see myself through someone else's eyes.

I ignored the memory of Q saying, *This thing is going to be a train wreck.* Instead, I sat forward on my yellow chair now, holding my phone, and I let that captivation sing through my body.

I lifted the phone. I texted, *I'll open the front door.*

15

He walked into my apartment, and the atmosphere shifted. He wore a green Seagram's T-shirt. The gold-and-black serpent on his left arm seemed to slither out of his sleeve. His hair looked newly washed. Oddly, he looked a little nervous, which surprised me. He was a wunderkind from what Jane had told me. And he was hot enough to get anyone he wanted, male or female.

"Can I get you something to drink?" I asked. It sounded so awkward. I didn't know how to date anymore.

He held up a brown paper bag. "I brought refreshments."

He walked into my kitchen. I trailed behind. He reached into my cabinet and took out two highball glasses, as if he'd been there fifty times. "I'm glad I got to see you," he said over his shoulder. "I'm leaving on Monday for Isla Natividad."

"Where's that?"

"Mexico. Little island. You can only get there by boat or plane. My partner and I go once a year for a few days to surf."

"You're a surfer?" For some reason, this made me want to have sex with him.

"Oh, yeah." He crossed the kitchen to my freezer. "And this island is amazing. No cell service, no hotels. Just the sand and the surf."

"Sounds a little remote for me."

He laughed, pulling ice cubes from the freezer and dropping them into the glasses. "It's a little remote for most people." Out of the brown bag, Theo took out three oranges, round and vibrantly stained in a crimson color. He pointed at them. "Blood oranges. No seeds. They make excellent screwdrivers."

I said nothing. I couldn't. He seemed to take over my kitchen with his tall frame—so different from Sam's solid, shorter body. What was I doing asking him to come here after I'd just seen Sam? It was something I wouldn't have considered before. I felt different from any other Izzy McNeil I had been in my life.

Theo selected a knife from the butcher block and quickly sectioned the oranges. With the practiced movement of a bartender, he held a hand over each slice as he squeezed and juiced them into the glasses. He took a bottle of Belvedere Vodka from the bag and poured some into each glass. The kitchen was silent. I stood behind him, staring at his ass, at the red ribbons trailing from his other arm. He must have felt my eyes on him, but he didn't seem to care. Or maybe he liked it. He picked up one of the oranges again, squeezed more juice into the glass.

He turned around, a crimson orange in his hand. His eyes flicked over my body, and I felt as if those eyes were licking me. He walked toward me, took my hand and turned my arm over. He raised the orange and squeezed a few drops of juice on the white flesh of my wrist. Then he lifted my wrist slowly to his mouth and sucked lightly on my skin.

"Good to see you," he said. "Sorry about your weird day."

I opened my mouth. Nothing came out.

He turned and picked up one of the glasses, handing it to me. "Try it." It seemed as though he was talking about more than the drink.

I took a sip. The vodka bit; the blood orange soothed it over. "Delicious." I didn't take my eyes from him. "How was your day?"

"You still want to make small talk?"

My heart tripped around, my body temp went higher. What was this kid doing in my kitchen at midnight sipping blood orange juice and vodka?

"Isn't that what civilized people do?" I asked. "Make small talk?"

He put his glass on the counter. He took my glass from me and placed it next to his. "What I'm going to do to you is not civilized. Not even a little bit."

16

The Fig Leaf was a little jewel of a store. From the front window, you could see silk slips hanging from pink, padded hangers. Delicate panties in dazzling colors overflowed from open wood chests, like piles of jewels. Nightgowns and bustiers were stacked on white cushioned benches. From the ceiling hung billowing ivory fabric, giving the place the look of a sumptuous little harem.

I was about to push open the front door when it opened for me. "You're late," Josie said. She looked down on me at the street level, her body blocking me from entering the store.

Josie was on the tall side. She seemed to tower above me in a white blouse and a long black skirt that hugged her curvy body. Her severe bobbed hair was deep brown with a cherry-cola red tint, and it was sleek, as if it had just been washed and blow-dried professionally.

"I apologize." I decided not to offer any excuses. I had none, except that it had been hard, near impossible, to boot Theo out of my bed.

She jutted one leg out and crossed her arms. Through thin silver glasses that looked like lines of ice around her eyes, she gave me a formidable stare. "Look, Lexi, let's get something really clear, okay?"

I shivered a little and nodded. It was still cold in the mornings in Chicago, but optimistically, I'd shoved my wool coat to the back of my closet. My ivory-colored spring coat with the tulip sleeves was doing little to keep away the chill.

"I know your parents are friends with Marie," Josie continued, mentioning the owner, "and I love Marie for opening this store and for hiring me, but *I* run it, got that?"

"Sure."

"I run this store, and I run it well. In fact, I run it exceptionally." She looked down her nose at me. "Now it's true that I cannot run it alone, and I need assistance, but if I had it my way, *I* would have conducted interviews, and *I* would have decided who my clerk should be. Please don't think that because you know Marie that you'll be treated any differently. I need you to work. *Really* work, do you understand that?"

"Absolutely. Marie said you're the captain of the ship here."

That drew a little smile.

"And I'm very sorry I'm late."

She crossed her arms tighter, but she seemed to have softened. "Let's get going." She turned and made her way quickly through the store, weaving past a round table piled high with sleek pajamas.

For the next two hours, Josie lectured me. First, she taught me the front of the store—the workings of the faux-antique cash register, the location of the two little girly dressing rooms, the placement of the stock. She told me where she wanted me to stand and greet customers. Always, she said, greet each customer individually, and don't say the same thing to each one. She made me stand there and practice. *Hi, welcome to the Fig Leaf… Good morning… Hey, how are you?… Great day out, isn't it?*

As I rehearsed my lines, I pretended I was standing in court, stepping in front of a judge. Suddenly, I missed practicing law. Very, very much.

When Josie was finally satisfied, she declared me ready

for the back of the store. I followed her, taking my first big breath of the day.

But then Josie suddenly stopped and spun around.

"Oh!" I said, practically colliding with her. "Sorry."

"I forgot to tell you something. I have regular customers." Her eyes peered at me through her silver glasses. "I won't have your inexperience causing them to migrate to another store. When my regular customers come in, *I* wait on them. Understand?"

My friend Maggie had worked at a clothing store during our second year in law school, and she told me about the competitiveness that sometimes arose between salespeople over regular clients.

"No problem," I said.

"You do make commissions," Josie said, seeming to feel momentarily chagrined. She lectured for ten minutes on how the commissions were tallied and paid. "But not on my customers. I wait on my regular customers."

"Got it." I gave an affirmative, nonargumentative bob of my head.

She took me in the back, a chaotic and yet somehow organized warren of rooms piled with heaps of panties and mountains of pajamas. She also showed me the big black door where stock was delivered from the side alley. Josie instructed me on how to open boxes when they arrived, how to steam the contents and then how to hang them or fold them gently so they were ready for the "front of the house" when needed.

She watched as I practiced opening and preparing three boxes of merchandise. The bras were the trickiest. Each strap came wrapped in plastic, which had to be removed, and then the strap had to be attached to the bra. Steaming the bras was challenging, too. If you blasted the steam too powerfully it permanently stained the fabric (a loss which Josie told me no less than fifteen times would have to be deducted from my paycheck), but if you didn't steam enough, the cups would retain an unsightly crease.

It was monotonous work. Finally, Josie tapped her watch. "Eleven o'clock!" She smiled for the first time that day. "Open the front door, please, and start greeting customers."

"Sure," I said, grateful for the change in task.

I charged to the front with a burst of energy and unlocked the door. I took a position near the table of pajamas. Josie told me that you had to look busy when customers came in. You didn't want them to feel that you were going to jump down their throats or were desperate for the business.

So I refolded the pajamas, most of which were made of satin in various spring colors. I had refolded the table three times before I decided to move on. When, exactly, did the customers start arriving?

The next table, also sleepwear, held cashmere short-shorts in whites and yellows and matching cotton tank tops. Once again, I refolded the merchandise to perfection, about four times, and still no customers.

As I was moving to the rack of slips on the right side of the store, the front door dinged and two women walked in.

"Hi, guys," I called over my shoulder, before I darted a glance at Josie. She nodded at me to go ahead. Not her regular customers.

One woman was looking for a strapless bra. I remembered the section where Josie kept them. I found three for the woman and showed her to the dressing rooms. When she bought one of the bras ten minutes later, I was proud of myself.

But Josie wasn't. "You should have showed them the spring panties," she said when they left. "And the lounge-wear. We make money in this business not just giving people what they want, but also by showing them what they don't yet know they want. Now, while we've got some time, let me show you how to handle returns."

I came around the desk to stand with her. She rang up a pair of lavender cotton panties with a white branch pattern on them.

"Now…" She held the panties aloft. "First thing, check to make sure the tags are on and ask them if they've been worn." She then started to rattle off a series of complicated steps to return the panties. She gave me more information than I had needed to take the bar exam. I struggled to memorize it all, watching her hands fly across the register, as if she were operating the Space Shuttle.

"*Then,*" she said dramatically, "sniff."

"Excuse me?"

She pointed to the crotch of the panties. "Make sure you sniff."

I had to be misunderstanding something. "Do you mean…" No, she couldn't mean.

"Yes," she said in an irritated voice. "We have to *ensure* that the merchandise wasn't worn before it was returned."

"Would someone do that?"

She gave me a look that made it clear she thought I had reached new levels of stupidity.

"So we have to *smell* the underwear to make sure they didn't do that?" I said, just to make sure I was hearing her right.

"Yes." No hiding her irritation.

"Well, isn't it rude to the customers to smell the panties right in front of them?"

She actually rolled her eyes this time. "You do it surreptitiously, of course. Like this." She turned her body away from the register and grabbed one of the return forms behind the desk. As she did so, she casually and quickly lifted the panties and waved them in front of her face, taking a clandestine inhale.

"Got it?" she said.

"Sure." Despite myself, I giggled a little.

"What's so funny?"

"Nothing." Another small laugh escaped my mouth. God, I wished Q was here. The fact that I was sniffing undies for a living would slay him.

"Lexi..." Josie said in a stern voice, not bothering to complete the sentence.

"I'm sorry. Really." I squelched down a laugh and gave the panties a practice sniff.

From the vantage point of the watcher in the crowd, Jane Augustine looked stunning. She stood in front of the Daley Center, the sunlight glinting off the Picasso sculpture and giving her face a luminescent glow. Her hair and her smile gleamed as she spoke into the camera.

"Welcome to Trial TV," she said, flashing a vivacious grin, "where we bring you gavel-to-gavel coverage of the courtrooms topping the news. From New York to L.A., from Chicago to Miami and from every city in between, we'll bring you up-to-the-minute reporting, but we'll also give you the real stories of what's happening behind the scenes. We've got the best news team in the business. We've got our ears to the ground. If there's breaking legal news, you'll hear it on Trial TV first."

She paused. She flashed that smile again.

"Cut!" her director yelled.

The crowd that had gathered to watch broke into a smattering of applause.

Jane gave a half bow to the onlookers. "Thanks!" she called out.

She began to discuss something with her director, pointing at the courthouse behind her, then at the light. They glanced at their watches. They moved a few inches to the right and seemed to be preparing to try another promo shot.

Some of the crowd drifted away, but there were still enough people to hide behind. It was easy enough to watch her as she checked her makeup in a small compact, as she adjusted her red scarf. She tugged it a little as if she was irritated. A look of distaste crossed her face as she glanced down at the scarf, almost as if she was considering removing it, then the irritation cleared.

She signaled to the cameraman that she was ready again.

"Action," the director yelled.

"Welcome to Trial TV…"

Jane and her crew went on like that, trying different shots from different angles, pausing when she occasionally flubbed a line.

The crowd loved it when that happened, because Jane would joke or make some silly head-rolling gesture. It showed how human she was, despite her exterior of perfection.

But even when the crowd laughed, even when Jane took a mock curtsy in front of them, it was obvious that she wasn't really seeing the individual faces. It seemed to the watcher, the one in the crowd paying the closest attention, that this was typical of Jane. She'd gotten so used to the crowds and the cameras that she never looked behind them. It was as if she perceived a shell around herself that separated her from everyone.

Unfortunately for Jane, she seemed to think that this shell remained firmly around her personal life, as well. She seemed to think that no one could really see inside her, that no one really knew the things she did away from the cameras.

Unfortunately for Jane Augustine, she was wrong.

I spent the rest of the afternoon trying to stay awake, moving between the empty times of no customers and then the abrupt arrival of eight or more who suddenly flooded the store. Most were women who had money to spend and who weren't in the slightest bit embarrassed to discuss whether their nipples would show through a lace bustier. A few, however, were men. They were the funniest, trying to act nonchalant while they cupped their hands in an attempt to describe their girlfriend's bra size.

Only two of the customers were Josie's regulars. Both times, she hopped from behind the register and strode confidently to the front, calling *hello* in a breezy, sparkly-eyed kind of way. Both times, I scurried away and watched as she expertly doted when she needed to and gave people the space when they needed that. And each time, her customers left the store happy, waving goodbye, and with a hell of a lot more merchandise than they had seemed ready to buy when they came in.

At 4:45 p.m., I was starting to fantasize deeply about getting on my scooter and getting out of there. I was supposed to meet Mayburn tonight to tell him about the day, and the thought of a beer and a chat was appealing.

Josie joined me at the front of the store with an armful of what looked like white camisoles. "Bridal wear," she said. "We're getting lots of it." She looked at her watch, then gestured toward one of the sleepwear tables. "Make some room here for these, will you? After we close the door, you can head back and start unpacking the shipments that came in today."

I tried not to let my disappointment show. The back room was exactly where Mayburn wanted me—peering into the operations of the store, keeping my eye out for anything amiss. It was just that I was starting to fade.

"No problem." I took the camisoles from her. They felt silky smooth, almost like water, on my hands.

The door dinged, and a couple walked in, laughing and shoving each other playfully.

"Hello, Nina!" Josie trilled.

The woman was a wisp of a girl dressed in fitted jeans, a long powder-blue T-shirt that matched her eyes and an ivory leather jacket. Her hair was twisted into two braids on either side of her face, a hairstyle few women over the age of fourteen could pull off. But this woman not only pulled it off, she rocked it.

Nina waved at Josie with a slender hand, gold bangle bracelets on her wrists jangling like a wind chime.

The man she was with waved, too, although he could barely take his eyes off his girlfriend.

Josie shot me a glance. I nodded and turned away. Obviously, regular customers.

I moved to the round table to make way for the bridal wear.

"I'm looking for something to wear under a white dress," Nina said.

"And don't forget…" the guy said, laughing.

Nina laughed, too. "He wants me to get one of the pearl thongs."

I looked at them. The guy was raising his eyebrows in a salacious but cute way.

"Oh, sure," Josie said. "I've got them in the back." She turned and headed for the storerooms. She looked at me. "Lexi, can you help Nina find a nude bra?"

"Sure." Josie must have thought I was half-capable if she was letting me at her regulars. I felt a shot of pride that woke me up and propelled me across the store.

Nina shook hands with me as if we were meeting at a dinner party, as if I weren't a store clerk. "This is James."

James, who was rubbing his five-o'clock shadow, smiled and shook hands with me, too.

Josie came out of the back a minute later, holding a flat, black box with a white ribbon. She opened it and presented a piece of lingerie so beautiful, it looked like a piece of art. "We only have the black right now in your size." She raised the lingerie higher—an intricate black lace panty, from which hung two strands of white pearls.

I peered at it. "Do the pearls…?"

Nina laughed, a sweet, burbling laugh. "Yeah, the pearls are the thong part."

"Wow." Dumbfounded, I couldn't say anything else. Though I'd wear just about anything to look sexy, I couldn't imagine having small pebbles running along my ass.

"Lexi is new." Josie gave me a withering look. She took the bras out of my hand, pulled out a few different ones. She told me to go to the storerooms and steam a box of robes.

In the back, I poked around the farthest rooms, which seemed to serve as storage for display equipment, hangers and signs. To me, it all seemed like standard retail stuff. I was flipping through some of the signs when I heard a sound behind me and I jumped.

"Oh, hi, Josie!"

"What are you doing?"

"Looking for the steamer."

"I showed you where the steamer was. You already used it."

This was an excellent point. "I thought maybe there was a smaller one for the bra straps."

She considered this. "That's not a bad idea, but we just have the one steamer." She peered around the room. She looked me up and down. "You can go now."

"Are you sure?"

She nodded.

"You know," I said, wanting to make her like me, wanting to chase away any suspicion. "I think I'd like to buy one of those pearl thongs, so that I'm aware of all the merchandise and how it fits."

She said nothing for a second. She looked me up and down. "You're a medium?"

"Yes."

"They're extremely hard to find, and we're out of the kind that Nina just bought, but I do have another brand in your size."

"Great."

"They're seventy dollars."

"Oh." I definitely didn't have seventy bucks for a pair of undies, even to get me on my boss's good side.

"But you do get your discount, and I could take it out of your first paycheck."

"Great!" I'd chalk it up to research. Maybe I could get Mayburn to pay for it.

"Stay here." She left for a few moments and returned

with a silver-gray box tied with a silver ribbon. She handed it to me. "There you go. I'll see you in a few days." As a part-timer, I'd be working weekends and one or two nights a week.

"You're sure you don't want me to finish the robes?"

She gave me a curt shake of her head, then took my elbow and propelled me to the front room.

My first day on the job was over.

17

I love a good dive bar—the dusty golden lighting, the rickety stools, the scarred wood bar top, the white wine served from a jug (or sometimes a box or tiny airplane bottles), the lingering smell of wood smoke (though there's no fireplace in sight), the cranky but kind bartenders, and, if you're really, really lucky, the hard kernels of popcorn from a machine that hasn't been cleaned since 1971.

I love all those things about dive bars. Tragically, there are few left in the city. Chicago, once the land of a million dives, had gotten glitzy since the years of my childhood. When I first turned twenty-one and was home from college, I was full of disdain for the old neighborhood bars, the ones with the tiny windows that showed nothing from the street, the ones with the sign out front that read only *Pabst,* when everyone in the neighborhood called it Nick's. Back then, I wanted the nightclubs, the glamour, the sleek. And I was glad when the neighborhood bars started closing up, replaced with fake Irish pubs boasting Crab Louie salads. But now, nearing my thirties and carrying a dogged tiredness from the weight of the last six months, I'd fallen in love with the dying breed that was the dive bar. I appreciated the casual and the quiet, punctuated occasionally with a few selections from an old jukebox. I loved the history of them. After so many people in my life had come and gone, I liked that a good dive bar had survived for decades and gave the impression that it would last another fifty years.

Which was why I picked the Old Town Ale House to meet Mayburn on Sunday night.

"How did it go?" he answered without any other greeting when I'd called after leaving the store.

That was one thing I liked about Mayburn—little bullshit and the ability to cut to the chase. "Fine. I guess. I mean, I didn't find anything crazy or suspicious."

"When are you working again at the store?"

"Tuesday."

"Good. We'll talk about it all tonight. Where are we meeting?"

"The Ale House?"

"Fine. Do you mind if Lucy comes?"

I thought about the last time I'd seen Lucy DeSanto—I'd posed as her friend so I could make a copy of her husband's hard drive. The thing was, somewhere along the way my posing had turned into actual friendship. But I hadn't seen her since. "I'd love to see her, but is she okay with me?"

"I told you. She's glad of everything that went down with her ex."

"All right. But this is business, right? Can we talk in front of her?"

"Lucy knows everything." I had never heard Mayburn sound so proud.

"Why do you get to talk about investigations when I don't?"

"A couple of reasons. One, I'm an investigator, and everyone knows that. Two, we've gone over this before."

Mayburn's stipulation was that if I worked with him I couldn't tell anyone. He said I'd be no help if word got around I was a part-time P.I.

"You'll swear them to secrecy," I remember him saying, "but they might let it slip to one person, and that person slips to just one person, and then another and another. The whole reason I need you is because you're a typical, normal North Side Chicago woman. If there's any inkling that's not the case, if anyone knows you do P.I. stuff on the side, it won't work."

"And three," he added, "I'm not working some cover."

"Cover? Do I have a cover? I love that."

"Don't get too excited. P.I. work is grunt work, and you're doing mine. See you at the Ale House."

Now I pulled open the bar door and poked my head inside. A typical night at the Ale House. A guy in his seventies sat near an antique lamp, reading one of the dusty books from the shelf. A pretty woman, probably a mom looking to escape her family, gabbed with the bartender and socked away red wine. A couple about my age, who appeared deep in discussion, sat in the back.

I took a seat at the bar.

"White wine," I said when the bartender reached me. There was no perusing a wine list at the Ale House. White or red, and that was it.

After he gave me the wine, which tasted a little like fermented lemonade, I studied the artwork on the walls—a bizarre mix of Halloween masks, drawings of Second City alumni and paintings of a guy, reputedly the owner, in various compromising positions with some bawdy-looking women.

Ten minutes later the door opened, and in walked Lucy DeSanto, a wispy blonde with a huge smile.

"Izzy!" She launched herself into my arms, squeezing me around the neck. If there were any hard feelings about how we'd left things, Lucy didn't show it. Over her shoulder I saw Mayburn beaming. Love had definitely softened the guy.

"Hey," he said when we finally pulled apart. He gave me a pat on the arm.

"Hey," I said back. With Mayburn, I was definitely one of the guys.

Lucy and Mayburn pulled up bar stools near mine, both of them somehow managing to continually touch each other in the process. A brief discussion about what kind of beer to order ensued. In that little conversation, taking all of twenty seconds, Mayburn and Lucy lost themselves in each other, the warm circle around them almost palpable.

Hon, look, Mayburn said, pointing at the taps, *they have a Hefeweizen.*

Do I like that? Lucy's eyes didn't leave his.

Yes, you know. You had an orange in it one time. The other time you tried a lemon.

And I liked them both.

You liked them both.

This innocuous exchange led to more meaningful gazes and finally a kiss.

And God, did it make me lonely. Theo was sexy. It was fun to date Grady. It was even fun to date Sam after I thought I had lost him. But what I'd really lost was what these two had, the kind of love, infatuation, intimacy—whatever you want to call it, maybe all of the above—that made discussion about fruit in beer seem somehow beautiful.

"Hello!" I waved an arm in front of them.

They smiled, at me, then each other again. "Sorry."

"Izzy, what's been going on with you?" Lucy ran a hand through her blond pixie hair and beamed me a radiant smile.

I told her about my new jobs, the new guys. She told me about her kids, skipped over the topic of Michael and started asking questions about Theo.

Mayburn stopped her when she asked if Theo was a good kisser. "All right, Izzy," he said. "I need to hear about today, and we have to let the sitter go in twenty minutes."

Never had I heard Mayburn utter such a thing. But I decided to let it slide. I gave him the rundown about my day at the Fig Leaf. "So that's it really. I'm not sure what you want me to look for or to do."

"I want you to pay attention to everything. Pay attention to anything that seems off. Even a little bit. I just need you to collect the pieces. Remember what I've told you?"

"Yeah, yeah. The way investigations work," I said as if I was reading the words from a blackboard, "is that you put lots of little pieces together. It's like a puzzle. You have to be patient." He had told me this over and over.

"Right. And I got another bit of advice for you. Like I said, don't plan. Improvise."

"Meaning?"

"Since we don't know what we're looking for, don't hold tight to any set course of action. Don't get freaked out if the way you're doing something doesn't work. Don't plan. Improvise."

Lucy gazed at him with something approaching wonder. "Wise words for life," she said.

He kissed her.

"Okay, you two." I put money on the bar. "I've got the beers, you get out of here and go get the sitter."

They stood and pulled on their coats. Lucy hugged me again. "It was wonderful to see you, Izzy."

"You, too." I squeezed her thin frame.

I watched them through the bar window as they stopped in front and kissed again. For a long, long time.

I turned back to the bar and called Sam from my cell. "I'm at the Ale House. Can you meet me?"

"Mmmph," he said.

"Are you sleeping?"

"Yeah. Exhausted from this morning. I went to bed an hour ago." He breathed in, then moaned the way he did when he rolled over. "Sorry, Red Hot. I'm cashed." He moaned again, and I could almost feel him, the way his body moved under the covers. "Our timing has been bad lately, huh?"

He wasn't just talking about tonight or last night, and we both knew it.

"Yeah," I said simply.

"Good luck at work tomorrow."

"Thanks."

I was about to hang up when I heard, "Hey, Iz?"

I raised the phone to my head. "Yeah?"

"I love you."

"I love you, too."

In the air hung the words, *No matter what happens to us.* I clicked the phone off.

Sipping my wine, I stared at my left hand. I missed my engagement ring. It had been an antique art-deco affair. An emerald-cut diamond surrounded by a frame made of smaller diamonds.

The phone rang again. I smiled, thinking it was Sam. The display read, *Grady, cell.*

"It has come to this," I said as I answered the phone. "I am drinking alone."

He laughed. "Where are you?"

"Old Town Ale House."

"Nice. I'll be there in ten minutes." And he hung up. Because despite the fact that Grady and I were sort of dating now, we had been buddies for years, buddies who didn't have to make small talk.

While I waited, I called Jane. She answered on the first ring.

"How are you?" I asked. "Ready for tomorrow?"

She sighed. "We've been shooting promos all day. But I'm still so freaked out about last night. I threw the flowers and the box away, but I'm jumping out of my skin. I feel like my house isn't mine or something. I keep thinking someone is here."

"Where's Zac?"

Another sigh. "He went back to our house in Long Beach. He's so pissed off at me. More than pissed off. He's furious, and at the same time, he's so detached."

"Do you want me to come over?"

"No. Thanks. I'm going to bed. I have to be at the station at four-thirty. Are you ready?"

"I'll be there at seven." My real new job was about to start.

"See you then, Iz. And thanks for calling."

I hung up with her feeling a distinct unease, a sense of anxiety.

A few minutes later, Grady walked in, edging his wide shoulders through the front door, running his hands through his brown hair. "I'm glad you called." He slipped onto a bar stool next to me.

"You called *me*."

"Only because I knew you wanted me to." Grady ordered a Miller Light from the bartender. "So, what's up?"

I told Grady about my job at the Fig Leaf.

"Are you kidding me?" He gulped his beer. "Stop now. You just gave me enough material to fantasize about for the next four years."

I laughed, then we fell into silence. A heaviness filled the air. After being buddies for years, we'd made out a few times, gone out on a few dates, but nothing between Grady and me was official. We hadn't settled into any kind of pattern, and so the question always floated there—would we or wouldn't we? Would we fool around again? Would we sleep together eventually? Would we keep dating? If we didn't, would we return to the friendship we'd had?

It was the friendship I needed more than anything, and so I forced another laugh. "Tomorrow I've got another new job."

"About time. What is it?"

I told him about Trial TV.

"Nice!" Grady broke into cheers, clapping me on the back. The older man reading a book looked up at us and glared as if he'd just found us in his living room.

"Good for you, Iz." Grady kept thumping me on the shoulder.

"Thanks. You're always such a good friend."

"And I always will be a good friend." But then his grin fell away. "I got to tell you, though, Iz, I'm hanging in there right now, but in terms of me and you…" He motioned between us. "I won't wait forever."

I looked at my wineglass. Empty. I looked back at Grady. "I know that." But I felt a wave of sadness. I'd known, somehow, that Grady wouldn't put up with my waffling forever. Sam probably wouldn't, either. But I didn't want to choose.

I felt another tickle of understanding for Jane. I heard Jane's words from yesterday. *There isn't just one person who can be everything to me. Different people inspire me in different ways, fascinate me in different ways…I just look at my own life differently after I've gotten a taste of someone else's.*

I looked at Grady now, still waiting for me to say something more. In his brown eyes, the color of tree bark turned dark from rain, I saw a friend who would always be there for me, no matter what happened between us now. Which meant we could play at being lovers. We could see where it took us. We didn't have to decide anything.

I opened my mouth, about to tell him about the pearl thong, just waiting in my condo a few blocks away.

But suddenly I pictured it in my mind—me in those racy panties, Grady with me…naked? There was something wrong with that image. Grady, with his bottomless brown eyes, was my friend, first and foremost.

He tilted forward, put his mouth near my ear. "You want to get out of here?" Grady spoke the words low.

We both knew where my condo was. I tried to think of Grady and me in my bed, stripped of clothes, stripped of the remaining walls of friendship.

The thought left me vacant, with a feeling that said, *No, that's not right,* or maybe it was more of a *No, not now.* I wasn't sure which. I wasn't sure why. Would I ever be sure of anything again? God, I longingly remembered the days when I used to be decisive about most everything.

"I should get going." I pulled away from him. "I've got my new job tomorrow."

Grady nodded reluctantly. "Call me tomorrow, all right? Let me know how the job goes."

"I will. I'm sorry, Grady. I'm just a little confused right now."

"Nothing to be sorry for."

I hugged him, and I left fast, my mind swirling—the product, apparently, of too many men, too many jobs, not enough sleep.

Or maybe... a voice inside me said. *Maybe it's just enough.*

I climbed the three flights of stairs to my condo, thinking about starting my new job the next morning, feeling on the precipice of a whole new life. My body tingled with the anticipation of the fall into...what? I didn't know. And that unknown was thrilling me.

I got undressed. I opened my drawer to find the Jeff Beck concert T-shirt of Sam's I liked to sleep in. Slipping it over my head, I expected the shiver of calm and coziness it usually brought me. But for some reason, it felt stifling. I tugged at the neck. Too tight. When I slipped into bed, it felt claustrophobic, as if my body was still jumping, not ready to settle down, no matter how many times I reminded myself that I had to start a new job the next morning.

Sleep wouldn't descend. I kept itching to get out of bed, to do something, but I didn't know what. The responsible Izzy McNeil, that accountable and dependable self I'd always known, was scratching at the walls, sensing that she was onto something new. And wanting to get on with it sooner rather than later.

After half an hour of twisting under my sheets, I got out of bed and found the silver-gray box I'd brought home from the Fig Leaf. Lifting the cover, I pulled open the delicate tissue. In the light that made its way through a crack in my drapes, I stared at the garment. Delicate silver lace, two strands of creamy ivory pearls that ran side by side.

I took off the T-shirt and slipped on the pearl thong. I stood in the dark of my bedroom, naked but for those pearls, sensing a shift in the air, a shift in me.

My cell phone was on my dresser top, the ringer off. I lifted it and saw that I had a text message. From Theo. *Want company?*

I texted back, *Aren't you supposed to be in Mexico?*

Tomorrow. So, are you up for a visit?

I could see him in my kitchen, squeezing blood oranges, the serpent on his forearm slithering with the movement. I started to write back, *Yes*, but then I hesitated. Certainly this behavior was reckless, certainly it meant something.

The thing was, I didn't want to analyze it right now. I just wanted to roll with it.

Door is open, I added to the text. Then I hit Send.

18

I should have been exhausted after Sunday—a day spent panty peddling, a night spent researching the pearl thong. But as I got ready to leave my condo Monday morning, only forty minutes after Theo left, I felt charged up with that same electricity from the night before, an energy I hadn't known since I'd left the law firm.

I put on the suit I used to wear for closing arguments or tough depositions. With its long, clingy skirt and high fitted waist it was professional and sassy, exactly the image I hoped that Trial TV would want in a legal analyst.

Downstairs, I went around my building to the detached garage. Inside, I got my helmet and paused for a second. I used to never wear the helmet, not liking how it smashed my curls and never really believing that I would get in an accident. But I no longer believed I was immune to bad luck, and so I pulled the helmet over my head and fastened the chin strap tight.

As I revved the scooter down Sedgwick, then North Avenue, the traffic was going in the other direction. Most people were headed to the Loop or the Mag Mile, while I was heading to West Webster.

As I buzzed down Clybourn, I raised my face and let the sun beam itself onto my cheeks. When I came to a stop at Racine, I closed my eyes, and I let myself remember the night before. My brain was still assimilating all the images—remembering the way I stood in the shadowy dark of my living room, keen with anticipation as his footsteps pounded, heavier and heavier, up my steps; remembering the old Izzy saying *What are you doing?* while the new Izzy told her to shut up and locked her in a back room of my mind; remembering his face when he walked in and saw me naked except for the thong; remembering the utter lack of words, remembering only the sounds, groans, growls, sighs.

Suddenly the blaring of horns jolted me back to reality. I forced Theo from my mind, locking him in the back room with the old Izzy. I turned left when I got to Webster and drove past Ashland. The neighborhood was populated with a large bank, a Kohl's department store, a huge new building housing a yoga center and a lighting store.

I found the address—a stubby but sprawling brick building with a concrete parking lot. I parked the scooter, and followed the sidewalk to the front door. Inside, the floors were linoleum and the walls unpainted drywall. The hallway was lined with file cabinets topped with large cardboard moving boxes. Jane told me the build out was still happening and that it was typical for a start-up network like this to truly start up without all the pieces in place. Clearly, she wasn't kidding.

I gave my name to a security guard, who issued me a badge and pointed down the hallway. I walked, passing offices. A couple were empty, others used as storage space. Those that were occupied looked like offices you might see at any workplace; each had a computer, phone, notes, photos, knickknacks. The only difference between these offices and those in another industry was that each of these had a minimum of two TVs in them, usually four.

I looked at my watch—6:55 a.m., only a few minutes before Jane's first morning broadcast would begin.

At the end of the hall, I pushed open a heavy door and stopped dead.

If the rest of the building had been slightly shoddy and the construction not complete, the studio was where attention had been lavished. The ceiling was high and covered with lights. Wires wrapped in bright yellow tape crisscrossed the floor and a bevy of cameras stood at the ready, all focused on two sets. In one, an interview area, four royal-blue leather chairs sat in front of a wall of monitors, all showing reporters preparing for stories near courthouses or capitol buildings. Jane had told me this was where expert panelists would come to be questioned and where the morning "Coffee Break" segment would take place. The main set held a large mahogany anchor desk, vaguely resembling a judge's bench. The words *Trial TV* were emblazoned across the front in blue lights edged with white.

Behind the desk, on three large panels, the Trial TV logo was superimposed over moving images displaying shots of famous legal scenes from the last few decades.

Jane sat behind the anchor desk, while a floor director in jeans and a T-shirt read to her from a clipboard. As big as the desk was, Jane had a commanding presence. She wore a suit and a crisp white blouse with a high collar. Her black hair hung on either side of her face, gleaming and smooth. Her makeup was heavy but flawless, drawing out the mauve-blue in her eyes. The only thing that marred her appearance—at least for me—was the scarf. Her red scarf was wound around her neck, its silk ends tucked into the collar of her shirt.

Jane looked up and saw me. "Hi!" she mouthed. She waved me over.

When I got there, she stood and introduced me to another woman who'd walked up at the same time. "Izzy, this is Faith Lowe, litigator turned producer."

"Hi." Faith had black shiny hair in an asymmetrical cut. She looked more avant-garde than most of the litigators I knew.

Jane stepped down from the raised anchor desk then and gave me a quick hug. "How are you?"

"Great," I said. "You look amazing."

"Thanks. My clothes are sponsored on this gig, so I'm all designer now." She made a show of holding up her hands and showing off her suit, which fit her impeccably. Neither of us said anything about the scarf. "How are you feeling about your first day in the news?"

"Good. A little nervous."

"Don't be." She spun me around and pointed to a man at the back of the room. He wore slacks, a gray dress shirt that looked as if it could use some laundering and a yellow tie that was already loosened despite the early hour. He was probably in his late fifties with a ruddy face. His thinning hair, which seemed to be a mix of blond and gray, was messed and stood up in places. He was talking fast and gesturing wildly in front of two guys, who wore chagrined expressions.

"That's Tommy Daley," Jane said. "And no, he's not related to Mayor Daley, so don't ask. He hates that. Tommy is going to be the master of your universe around here. He's the deputy news director. Although he also seems to think he's the managing editor. And the assignment editor. And the executive producer. Anyway, he basically runs this show, so when he gets done chewing out those interns, get over there and introduce yourself."

Tommy's face had gotten very red, nearly purple, and he was leaning in toward one intern, shaking his finger in his face and spewing some kind of speech.

I turned around to Jane. "I'm not sure I want Tommy to be the master of my universe."

She laughed. "His bark is worse than his bite."

"One minute!" someone yelled. "This is it, folks! One minute to airtime."

Jane's smile got larger, her eyes excited.

"Good luck!" I said, squeezing her hand.

"Thanks. Good luck to you, too. Have fun."

She stepped back up on the anchor desk and sat down.

She threaded a tiny microphone under her suit jacket and attached it to the collar, right below her red scarf.

"Ten seconds!" the voice called.

Jane took a big breath and blew it out, glancing around the set with a look that seemed filled with pride. But then her head froze and the expression on her face changed to one of surprise, and then, if I was reading her right, to one of fear.

I followed her sight line to Tommy, who stood toward the back of the room now, speaking to another man. The man had a notepad and seemed to be interviewing Tommy, jotting things on the pad as they spoke. I peered closer and realized the guy making notes was the writer from Friday night. The writer who wrote books. The one Jane had gone home with.

"Five!" the voice called, counting down. Tommy held up a finger to the writer, as if to signal, *Just a minute.* He looked toward the anchor desk and Jane.

I did the same. Jane seemed frozen, staring at the writer. The room went quiet.

"Four!"

"Augustine, you ready?" called the floor director who stood to the right of Jane's anchor desk.

"Three!"

Jane wasn't moving, her eyes unblinking. I glanced back at the writer. He was still jotting notes. But just then, he looked up, right at Jane, and he smiled.

"Two!"

The look from the writer seemed to break Jane's shock. She peered down at the monitor in front of her.

No one yelled "one" but the red lights showed the cameras were rolling.

And then Jane's face rose again, a face that was calm, satisfied, authoritative. "Good morning, I'm Jane Augustine." She gave a smile of pleasure. "Welcome to Trial TV."

Jane turned and faced a different camera. "At Trial TV,

we bring you gavel-to-gavel coverage of the courtrooms that are topping the news. We're revolutionizing the coverage of litigation. Not only will we provide up-to-the-minute reporting, but we'll also give you the real stories of what's happening behind the courtroom doors. We've assembled the best news team in the business along with seasoned lawyers who know what's really going on, and we've got our ears to the ground. If there's breaking legal news, you'll hear it first on Trial TV."

TV monitors flanked both sides of the anchor desk, Jane's beautiful face on each of them.

She turned back to the first camera. She smiled a grin that had a hint of playfulness to it. "So let's get started. Joe Kelley is in Boston, Massachusetts, where the governor has been in hot water and appears in court today."

The monitors changed, now showing a guy in a trench coat in front of a capitol building.

"Joe," Jane said, "what's the story there this morning?"

Joe Kelley began talking. The room started buzzing with activity and conversation. Trial TV was up and running.

Jane's face relaxed for a moment, but I saw her glance toward the back of the room.

I followed her gaze.

The writer was gone.

Because I lost my father when I was eight, you might think I have a daddy-complex, some need to find a father figure in men of his age. Well, Tommy Daley was about the age my dad would have been—fifty-eight—but I wasn't experiencing any kind of daughterlike devotion toward him.

"Why are you here?" he demanded after I'd introduced myself, his voice a series of sharp snaps.

"Jane sent me over." I waved behind me at the anchor desk. "She said you were the master of my universe."

That gave him a pause. He smirked in Jane's direction.

"I friggin' love that girl," he said. "She's the only reason I'm here." He turned his steely gaze back to me. "C'mere."

I followed him through a different door from the one I came in. It led to a large room filled with cubicle desks, each with two computer screens and small TVs. Along the wall was a grid of nine televisions. Two showed Joe Kelley, the current on-air shot, and another showed Jane sitting at the anchor desk, waiting to go back on. The other TVs were tuned to CNN, Fox News, MSNBC and other such stations. Above the TVs hung three clocks. Signs underneath them read *Chicago, New York, Los Angeles.* On another wall was a huge monthly calendar on a dry erase board.

Tommy crossed his arms. "I meant what are *you* doing here on a national television network? Huh? I know we lost what's-her-name last week." He shook his head, muttered something that sounded like *Ivy League, my eye.* "Anyway, I gave the green light to hire you because Jane vouched for you, said you could handle it, but now I want to know, what are you really bringing to the table?"

I flushed a little. On one hand, I'd been asking myself the same question over the weekend. On the other hand, I knew enough guys from the law like Tommy—guys who needed to haze you, to put you through your paces until you could earn their respect. And I understood that. You just couldn't show 'em you were scared.

"I'm a lawyer," I said. "I've got jury trial experience as well as contract negotiations. I worked at Baltimore & Brown—"

Tommy growled and tugged at his yellow tie. "How long did you practice?"

"About five years."

His brown, red-rimmed eyes peered at me, then he actually rolled them toward the ceiling. "Jesus," he muttered. "You're a baby."

I wanted to say, *No, "the baby" was the guy I shoved out of my apartment at five this morning.* Instead, I quickly continued, "For most of the time I practiced, I was head legal counsel for Pickett Enterprises."

That brought his eyes back to me. "You knew Forester?"

"I knew him very well. I miss him every day."

He grunted. "Good guy. So what's your broadcast experience?"

"I used to give statements to the news on behalf of Pickett Enterprises. And Jane said that the trend in news was broadcasters with real life experience."

He winced. "You don't even have a demo, do you?"

"A demo tape? No. Just me." I held out my hands and smiled extra big.

Tommy rubbed the sides of his head, which made his gray-blond hair frizz more. He pointed at the calendar on the far wall. "You know what that is?"

I studied it, read some of the things written there. *Pitello trial. Congressional hearings on athlete enhancement drugs, Mackey appellate argument.* "Looks like different legal stories you're covering."

"Not bad." He gave me a brief nod. "Now listen, you mentioned a trend in the news business, but I don't believe in trends. You know what I believe in?"

I looked at his bloodshot eyes and thought, *Whiskey in your coffee?* I shook my head.

"I believe in smoking at the Billy Goat Tavern. And I believe in newscasters covering the news." He leaned toward me. "*Trained* newscasters. I do not believe in *personalities* in the news." His eyes flicked over my face, and he frowned. "And I don't believe in newscasters and guests sitting on a couch and shouting over each other."

I stayed silent. Once again, I had a feeling that I knew his type—a true professional who went into the business because he had a passion for it, who came up during a certain era, and who needed to bluster about how things have changed before any work could get done. My old law firm was full of such types, and I had been on the receiving end of more bluster than most, since Forester had taken his work away from one of the older, more respected partners and given it all to me. I didn't mind the bluster at all. In fact, I felt I deserved it. I had lucked into that legal work, just as I had lucked into this news job. I liked luck. I wasn't one of those people who would turn my back on it just because I hadn't been striving toward some goal for ten years. But I understood that it made some people crazy, those who *had* strived for a decade. And so I felt it my duty to let myself get called to the mat and to take a little drubbing.

"The other thing I don't believe in," Tommy continued, "is newscasters spouting their opinions or pressing their positions on something." He sighed. "But no one agrees with me on this anymore. So you're here to report, but you're also here to give your opinion, as much as I can't stand that. We need you to get the backstory on everything you cover, and the network wants you to filter the information through your experience in the law." Another up-and-down glance. "However little that might be."

I nodded. "Got it."

Another sigh. "I wanted you to tail another reporter for a few weeks, but this is a start-up network. We've got no time and even less money. So you ready to cover a story today?"

I swallowed hard. "Cover as in on-air?"

"Yeah, you know. Describe the reaction of the defendant—shocked, happy, whatever. Try to talk to the jury. Standard stuff." He looked at his watch. "By the way, in the future, I won't keep giving you this stuff. You have to get your own stories."

I stood there, fairly stupefied. "Jane said I wouldn't be on-air right away."

"I like it about as much as you do, but I just found out that the jury reached a verdict in the Tony Pitello trial, and they're reading it this morning." He looked at the clock on the wall, then looked back at me and scowled more. "You know who Tony Pitello is, right?"

"Sure." I was relieved that Tony Pitello had been all over the news. "Mob lawyer charged with murder-for-hire. He allegedly got someone to knock off a witness who he had been paying to stay out of a case."

Tommy Daley gave me a grudging nod. "I like that you said 'allegedly.' No one in this business seems to remember that word anymore." He clapped his hands together. "All right, so get your shooter."

"Shooter?"

He grimaced. "Your *cameraman*." He pointed across the room to a black guy with a thick mustache. "Now, get the hell out of here."

19

The criminal courthouse at 26th Street and California Avenue, the place lawyers in Chicago refer to simply as "26th and Cal," is not in the nicest location. It isn't too far from some now-gentrified areas on the west side of the city, but such neighborhoods might as well be whole countries apart. A weird airspace seems to exist around 26th and Cal, an air of having seen way, way too much, combined with a bristling, fearful tone as if everyone on the block is looking over their shoulder, certain that something terrible is about to happen again.

The cameraman Tommy assigned to me was a big teddy bear of a guy, and fittingly, his name was Ted. Ted Wheeler was a cheerful man who showed me how to put in my earpiece, called an ISB, and how to work the mike while we were driven in a Trial TV van to the courthouse.

"Cameras aren't allowed in the courthouses in Illinois," Ted said, "so you go inside, watch the verdict and get back outside as fast as you can. We'll pick a spot before you head in, so when you get outside you'll know where we'll be, and you'll need to hit the ground running. We want to broadcast the verdict before any other station or network."

I nodded fast, taking this all down in my head. "Okay, but shouldn't I write what I'm going to say first?"

He nodded.

"When will I do that?"

"While you're running."

I looked at him to see if he would laugh. Nothing. He stroked his mustache in a thoughtful way. Usually I can't stand mustaches, but Ted's suited him.

"We'll be ready to go live whenever you are," Ted said.

"Live?" I squeaked.

"We didn't know until last night that they had a verdict in this case. We need it live. The jury has been sequestered for the weekend. You ever seen a sequestered jury?"

"No, I only did civil cases, and we rarely sequester them for that stuff."

Ted made a whistling sound and chuckled. "They're usually ornery. They don't know when they start deliberating that the judge might sequester them. They don't get to bring a change of clothes or their Ambien or anything. And then the judge sticks them in a crappy hotel and most of them get drunk from the minibar. By the time they get to court, they smell from wearing the same clothes, and they're tired and cranky."

He stopped and peered at my face. "You might want to put on more makeup."

"More?" I'd slathered it on this morning to the point that I felt like a drag queen about to take the stage at the Baton Club.

"The lights and camera suck it out of you." He pointed at my cheeks. "More powder. Blush." Then my eyes. "Lots more mascara."

Thankfully, I'd brought my makeup with me. I grabbed my bag from the floor of the van and began plastering more paint onto my face.

"Anyway," Ted continued, "make sure you memorize what the jurors look like, and we'll try to grab them for interviews when they come out."

I exhaled, mentally scribbling down everything he was telling me. I nodded toward the electronic equipment that filled most of the van. "Do I need to learn any of that stuff?"

"Some of the good reporters learn it eventually, but no." He pointed to the driver, a young guy wearing plaid pants and a bulky black leather jacket. "Ricky will handle it, right, Ricky?"

Ricky raised his chin in the air and kept driving and talking on his cell phone.

Just then we pulled up in front of the courthouse. It was a hodgepodge of a place. The original building was elegant, stately and made of limestone, while the newer section was a utilitarian addition that looked like any other municipal building and had no continuity to the original. A wide swath of concrete stairs ran from the street to the front door and the section where the two sides met.

Trailing up those steps was a huge line of people.

We got out of the van. The day was overcast, wind whipping down the street.

"Aw, crap," Ted said, looking at the line. "It's like this sometimes on Monday morning."

"Is that the security line?" I held my hair back from my face. The wind was blowing it everywhere. I had only been to 26th and Cal once, and that was for a ticket I'd gotten on the Vespa for not signaling a turn. The cop pulled me over, asked me on a date, and when I said, no, thanks, I'm engaged, he gave me a sour look and a citation.

"Yeah," Ted said. "And it's bad. I mean, that kind of line can take an hour." He looked at his watch. "And we don't have an hour."

"There's an attorney line, though, right?" I stood on my toes and craned my neck around the column of disgruntled people.

Ted shrugged. "I've never been here with an attorney before."

I let go of my hair and dug through my bag for the ID I'd previously used to get through security at the Daley Center, the civil courthouse. I flipped it over and read the back. "Yep. It's for the whole county. I can skip this line." I looked back at Ted. "It's legal nirvana."

He beamed.

"What else do I need to know?"

"Room number five hundred. Break a leg."

20

Inside the courthouse, I ran up to a bored-looking sheriff. "Morning. Where's Room five hundred?"

Like an automaton, he pointed to his left, no other movement of his body, no change in his expression.

"Thanks." I sprinted that way, dodging around families, rapper types in baggy jeans, cops. This was definitely not like the civil courthouse, where nearly everyone was a lawyer, and people moved fast and with a purpose.

My heels click-clacked on the floor, but I stopped momentarily when I got to what was obviously the original foyer of the old building. The marble floors, carved stone walls and stained-glass windows were beautiful, but you'd have to look beyond the film of grime that coated them in order to truly appreciate them. No time.

I hurried to the elevator bank and snuck in a packed one as the doors were closing. At the fifth floor, no signs explained where the courtrooms were. I made a few starts and stops in different directions until I found 500.

The courtroom was huge and majestic. At the far end, a judge's bench made of oak sat high above the rest of the room. Next to the bench was an inlaid wood bookshelf full of ancient law texts that looked as if they hadn't been touched in years. A jury box sat on one side of the bench, counsel's tables on the other. Behind the counsel's tables, high oak-trimmed windows lined the wall.

If the courtroom was open and spacious at one end, the gallery was packed. Rows of wooden pews provided seating for probably two hundred people, but the spectators were crammed together, shoulder to shoulder, causing the overflow to stand around the perimeter. I scanned the room and saw a few newscasters I recognized, and others who were obviously news types. Some of them chose to stand near the front, probably to get the best view. I decided to take a different tactic. I muscled my way between a few men at the back, ready to run for the door when the verdict was read.

But we had to wait. And wait. Well, that was one thing that was the same as the civil courthouse—the judges took their sweet time, no matter how many people were wasting away their mornings.

As we waited, my nerves started to ramp up. To distract myself, I texted Grady. I knew he had taken a deposition that morning in a big medical malpractice case.

How did the dep go? I wrote. The text was just like any I would have sent him last year, a question posed by a friend, by another lawyer. But something about it seemed false.

Apparently, Grady felt that, too. *I don't want to talk about depositions,* he texted. *I want to talk about you working at that lingerie store.*

I sat for a second and stared at my phone, thinking. Before I could decide how to respond, I had another text from Grady. *Let's have dinner?*

I waited for an immediate response from deep inside me, something that would tell me either *No, Grady and I are just friends,* or *Hell, yes, tell him you'll meet him tonight.* But no obvious answer appeared. Which frustrated me. Apparently, I was not someone who liked to play on the edge of decision. I had thought that as I got older, I would know sooner, quicker, exactly what I wanted.

Maybe? I wrote Grady.

A pause. I stared at my phone. Finally he replied, *That's the last time you get to use that answer.*

A door behind the judge's bench opened and in walked Tony Pitello with his attorneys. Pitello was a good-looking, if slick, man in his midfifties who, according to the news stories I'd seen, favored silk suits and diamond cuff links. Today was no exception, but the gray silk suit he wore seemed too tight. He'd clearly gained weight during his trial, and his face was red, as if his collar was choking him.

Pitello and his lawyers took a seat at their table, all stone-faced. One of the lawyers leaned toward Pitello and whispered something. Pitello nodded, his eyes fixed on the empty jury box.

The state's attorneys were next to come through the door—two women and one man. They didn't look at the crowd in the courtroom. They joked a little, they cleaned up files on their desks without ever glancing at the spectators or even seeming to feel their presence. It was as though their actions were always watched by a throng of people.

The judge entered the courtroom then. A man in his sixties with wavy gray hair, he stood on his bench, towering over everyone. He said nothing, but the room fell silent. He nodded, then sat.

He clasped his hands on the desk in front of him and looked down at the lawyers. "Any matters to address before I bring in the jury?"

Pitello's lawyers shook their heads no. The lead state's attorney called out, "No, Your Honor."

The judge raised his gaze to the horde of people in his gallery. "There are rules of decorum in this courtroom, especially during the reading of a verdict. I will tolerate no outcries, no emotional displays. Jury service is one of the most important duties any American can provide for his country, and I want this courtroom to remain silent while the verdict is read. I want you to respect this jury and this process. Do you understand?"

Nods from around the courtroom. The judge scrutinized

the faces in the gallery as if he were extracting a tacit agreement from each of us.

The judge looked at his bailiff. "Bring in the jury."

The weight of anticipation hung over the room like a shroud.

The crowd seemed frozen as another door behind the bench opened and twelve jurors filed in. As Ted predicted, the jurors looked exhausted, their clothing rumpled. Seven of them were women, five men.

I tried to make quick notes as they began to take their seats in the jury box. *Asian guy with glasses. Blond woman with birthmark on cheek. Heavyset guy, balding.*

But then I stopped. Because I noticed something about the jury.

None of them were looking at Tony Pitello. Not one.

As lawyers, we always try to read the jury. We watch their facial expressions during testimony to see if they understand the information. We try to divine if they are registering the weight of it. We notice when they nod asleep for a second. We take note when they nudge the person next to them. We take bets on who the foreman will be based on who takes the most notes or who usually comes through the door of the jury room first.

But none of this is a science. Sometimes a jury that seems unmoved by the woes of a plaintiff during a trial comes out of the jury room with a record-breaking verdict for millions of dollars. Other times, it's the woman who seemed to talk to no one, who wrote down not a word during the trial who ends up being the foreman.

But if the jury is about to read their verdict and they don't look at the main participant—the plaintiff in a civil case, the defendant in a criminal one—that's huge.

The opposite isn't always true. If a juror were to glance at Pitello now, it could mean one of many things. They might be sending him a look to say, *Don't worry, you're off the hook,* or a holdout juror might be sending a fleeting apology with their eyes, as if to say *I tried, but I couldn't turn them. You're cooked.*

And yet to not have any juror—not a single member of the twelve—be able to meet Pitello's eyes almost certainly meant one thing. Guilty.

I quickly examined them again. Every juror was looking at the floor, studying their fingernails or staring at the judge.

I looked at Pitello. He'd seen it, too. As a lawyer, he understood exactly what was happening. His mouth hung open a little, as if he was breathing heavily through his mouth. His face grew more florid as he hastily scanned the jury, almost begging them with his gaze to look at him, to send him a message that it was going to be all right.

He got nothing. Not one juror would meet his stare, not even for a nanosecond.

I watched Pitello. He appeared completely panic-stricken. His body seemed to sway.

And then a loud *Crack!* rang through the courtroom.

One of the jurors screamed. The spectators gasped.

Pitello had fainted, his forehead hitting hard against the table in front of him.

The sheriff ran over. He and Pitello's lawyers lifted the man up. He was alert, blinking madly, blood trailing from an open cut above one eyebrow.

"Mr. Pitello, are you all right?" the judge said.

Whispers between Pitello and his lawyers. Pitello touched a hand to his wound, then stared at the blood on his fingers, as if he couldn't comprehend it.

More whispering with his attorneys.

"Mr. Pitello," the judge said in a loud, insistent voice. "Are you all right?"

Pitello nodded.

"Your Honor," one of Pitello's lawyers said, "Mr. Pitello believes he is fine, but if we could have a brief recess to make sure."

The judge frowned. Hushed conversations rolled through the gallery. *What's he doing? Is it a hoax? What's going on?*

The judge directed his scowl toward the onlookers. "Quiet!"

The room fell into silence.

"Ten minutes," the judge said. "And this verdict *will* be read."

He cracked his gavel and the courtroom starting buzzing with conversation.

My body was ramped up with anxiety. What should I do? I looked at the other reporters. No one was moving. Most of them were texting furiously on their phones or looking at their watches.

I felt yanked in two different directions. Stay and wait for the verdict, or run outside and report on what had happened and what I *thought* the verdict would be. There wasn't enough time to do both. It would take nearly five minutes just to get outside.

I heard Tommy Daley in my head then. *You're here to report, but you're also here to give your opinion...The network wants you to filter the information through your experience in the law.*

I bolted from the courtroom and ran to the elevators. It seemed to take an interminable amount of time to get down. As I scurried through the once-grand foyer I began to write my lines in my head. My only experience was from *watching* the news. I really had no idea what I was supposed to say or do. But if the network wanted opinions that were filtered through my legal experience, I had one.

I was panting by the time I reached Ted.

"What's the verdict?" he said.

I shook my head, sucking in breath. "They don't have one yet. Pitello passed out. They took a ten-minute recess, but I think I know what's going to happen, and I want to run with it."

Ted gave me a wary look. "What do you think is going to happen?"

I filled him in on the lack of a single look from the jurors. I told him my opinion that they were going to find Pitello guilty.

"How sure are you?" he said.

"Ninety-nine percent."

We both stared at each other, pondering that one percent.

"Isn't this what Trial TV wants?" I asked. "It's the first day. And if we're the first to report on what we think is expected with this verdict and we get it right, won't that be a good thing?"

Ted nodded. "But if you're wrong…."

"If I'm wrong, I have another job sniffing panties."

Ted's eyebrows furrowed. "What?"

"Nothing. What do you think?"

He shrugged. "Let's do it."

After a minute spent attaching my ISB and setting up the shot, I heard Jane's voice in the earpiece. "Isabel McNeil is at the Criminal Courts Building in Chicago, where the verdict of mob lawyer, Tony Pitello, is about to be announced. Isabel, what's the latest?"

I looked into the camera, the way Ted had told me, and just as he'd told me, I talked to Jane as if she were right in front of me.

"Jane, just minutes ago, the jury in Tony Pitello's case filed into the courtroom, ready to read their verdict. But Pitello fainted, apparently due to the stress of the situation. His head hit the table in front of him, making a small wound on his forehead. Judge Kevin Glenn recessed the court for ten minutes."

"Interesting turn of events," Jane said. "Any idea what's going to happen, Isabel?"

"Yes," I said with authority, peering into the large, reflective eye of the camera. "The jury is going to find him guilty."

21

When I got back to the station, an intern was waiting for me inside the front door. He was the one who had gotten screamed at by Tommy Daley earlier. And he looked even more scared now.

"Tommy wants to see you."

I found Tommy in the studio, standing in front of the interview area with the blue leather chairs. He was waving a clipboard and yelling about getting people miked. Two people sat on the chairs. One was a woman in a brown tweed suit, who looked overwhelmed by her surroundings. "Don't look at the cameras," a floor director was saying to her. "Only look at Jane."

The other person in the interview area was an elegant man in his midsixties with a mass of artfully arranged silver hair. I immediately recognized him as Jackson Prince, Chicago's litigation ruler. He was a multimillionaire lawyer who got all the huge personal injury cases in the city and had now moved on to bigger fish, like the drug companies. Prince didn't seem to notice Tommy's frenetic preparations for what was obviously going to be a guest segment of the show. Instead, he scrolled through his BlackBerry, then when he was done, crossed his legs, sighed a bit and glanced around him, as if he was waiting patiently for someone to deliver him a cup of tea.

Tommy stopped in midrant when he saw me. He stepped

off the set and walked toward me. I smiled a wide, fake grin as I waited.

His face was even ruddier than that morning, his hair electric-looking. "I cannot believe you made a verdict prediction on national TV," he said.

"Isn't that what you said you wanted?"

A snarl formed on his face, and Tommy opened his mouth, but I jumped in before he could respond.

"I mean, what you said *they* wanted," I corrected. "The network wanted me to filter the story through my experience in the law, right? I did that. And I backed it up." On air, I'd explained my reasoning for the opinion—the lack of eye contact from the jurors.

"I was right," I added. I had run back inside the courtroom, found that Pitello had indeed been found guilty, and scuttled back outside to report that the verdict was official.

Tommy Daley shook his head. His features slackened. "I can't believe I still work in this business. I can't believe this is how it works now."

I didn't know how to respond.

"One minute," a voice called out.

A makeup person scampered onto the set and began to dab powder onto Jackson Prince's cheeks.

"Look, let me give you some pointers," Tommy said. "Your cadence is stilted, and you're too tight. You don't have to hold your shoulders like you're facing a firing squad, okay? But yeah, I guess you're right. You *did* give them what they wanted."

Although it wasn't the highest of praise, I nodded. "Thanks."

"Give me a second, and I'll show you how to write it up so we can use the story on a later broadcast."

Tommy stopped and turned as Jane trotted onto the set and settled herself between Prince and the woman in the tweed suit.

The screens around the interview area came to life,

showing two lawyers, one in L.A. and one in New York, both of whom had been placed in front of official-looking bookshelves.

"Three, two…" a voice called out. The lights blazed brighter.

"This is Jane Augustine," Jane said, smiling into the semicircle of cameras surrounding the set. "Welcome back to Trial TV. During our morning Coffee Break today we'll be talking about runaway class action lawsuits."

She quickly introduced her guests, in a way that made it seem like Trial TV had been having a "coffee break" every day for years, and then turned to the woman in tweed. "Professor Carleton, you believe class action suits are abused by overeager lawyers looking to make money, is that right?"

The professor nodded. "Absolutely, Jane. Class actions are supposed to provide closure for victims and pool together resources. But the system is being abused, and packs of lawyers are making off with the cash." She sat up straighter, her face growing animated. "The plaintiffs in these classes usually get very little money, but the lawyers…" She nodded in the direction of Prince. "The lawyers are the victors who make millions and millions in fees."

Jane went next for an opinion from the lawyer in L.A.

When he was finished, she turned away from the professor. "Now to Jackson Prince," Jane said, "one of Chicago's most influential attorneys who currently has liaison-counsel status in a suit against King Pharmaceuticals, the company that makes the arthritis drug, Ladera."

I knew that Jane had interviewed Prince numerous times over the years, and as if there were a secret language between them, she looked at him and raised her eyebrows, as if to say, *What do you think?*

Prince smiled benevolently. "Jane, let me say that billions—literally *billions*—of dollars are ultimately awarded to consumers for restitution. Our class action system is the ultimate watchdog today."

"Mr. Prince," Jane said, putting her notes down, "let's discuss the suit against King Pharmaceuticals."

Prince gave a pleased nod. "We're trying to get reparations from King Pharmaceuticals for injuries caused to millions who took Ladera."

"Let me ask a question about getting into the suit. How do you confirm that people opting into the lawsuit have taken the drug?"

"It's quite simple, actually. Patients provide pharmacy records showing they purchased it."

Jane paused, seemingly very intrigued by something. "How do the patients know to contact you? In this case, for example, do you obtain medical records showing what patients were prescribed Ladera?"

Prince's eyes narrowed, but only for a second. "Of course not. Medical records are confidential. Marketing campaigns are launched to inform patients of their potential case."

"And what about those people who have taken the drug but didn't have any side effects?"

"Generally, they won't become a member of the class."

"Unless they're convinced to testify that they did have such side effects, right?"

Now Prince's eyes squinted and stayed that way. There was a pause during which he and Jane stared at each other. What was going on?

"No dead air, no dead air," Tommy muttered under his breath.

The lawyer from New York, who seemed itching to speak, jumped in. "Jane, if I could say one thing…"

"Of course." Jane introduced the lawyer. The monitors focused on his face. He began to rattle on about pharmaceutical companies pushing these drugs without proper testing. Meanwhile, Prince and Jane continued to stare at each other, as if involved in a silent showdown.

"What's happening?" I whispered to Tommy.

"No fucking idea."

Suddenly, Prince pulled out his BlackBerry and looked at it. Then he pulled off his mike and gestured to a producer. The producer, looking mortified, scampered onto the stage, while the cameras pulled in closer on the New York attorney. Prince and the producer whispered a few words back and forth. Jane asked another question of the remote guest, but continued to stare at Prince.

Tommy cupped his earpiece, listening. "Prince says he's got an emergency in court."

And then Jackson Prince stood and left the set.

22

It's usually only later, after something truly awful happens, that we look back at a certain moment and see that while that moment appeared mundane at the time, it was actually a turning point, the last such moment we would ever have in exactly the same way, with those same people. After we've caught a glimpse of that moment in our life's rearview mirror, it takes on certain crystalline qualities. We view it more clearly than we actually saw it at the time. We give weight to each uttered syllable, to each brief touch.

For me, that moment was when Jane strode up to my desk. The newscasters and production crew who would handle the afternoon and evening broadcasts were coming in now. This was the lull before the next, soon-to-be-arriving storm.

"You were amazing," Jane said. "I knew you would be. You blew it out of the park with that report on Pitello."

I filled with satisfaction at her words. My professional life had been in such a downslide that it was great, even momentarily, to halt that fall.

"*You* were great," I told her. "This is exactly what you're supposed to be doing with your career."

She smiled—a genuine grin, full of pride. "Thanks for saying that. I *do* feel like this is where I'm supposed to be. Did you see the segment with Jackson Prince?"

"Yeah, what happened there?"

Jane smiled. "Tommy wants to kill me, because I won't tell him what's going on, but I'm going to nail Prince to the wall."

"With what?"

"I'm working on a story that will rock him. But I'm still putting the pieces together, and since I'm doing all the writing myself now, it's taking a little longer. I want to make sure I don't run with it before I've got everything nailed down. But Prince knows I'm circling."

I looked at her face. She was clearly excited. "You love this business, don't you?"

"*Love* it," she said without hesitation.

But then her smile faltered. She looked over her shoulder. "Mick was here this morning."

"That writer?"

She nodded, her face stern.

"I saw him. You looked kind of freaked. What was he doing?"

"Interviewing the network president and then some of the other guys. Some book he's writing about the news business."

"You didn't know he'd be here?"

"Hell, no," she said with vehemence. "I don't ever want to see that guy again."

"Why? You two looked like you were having fun the other night."

She peered around, as if to see if anyone was listening. When she turned back to me her face was filled with distaste. "I didn't tell you the other morning, because I was still trying to sort it out in my head, but I think he's been following me."

I stood. "What do you mean?"

Another glance around. "I found some stuff in his apartment, all this information on me—notes, pictures, articles, things like that. He had what grocery store I go to, where I get my hair cut, everything."

"Was it information he could have learned by asking around?"

"He knew my gynecologist."

"Wow. Bizarre."

"Yeah."

"Do you want to call the cops on him?"

"I do, but like I said when you were at my house, I cannot afford bad publicity right now, not with Trial TV just starting. And there's no way the cops would keep this quiet."

"Wait. Jane, why didn't you tell me this when we found the noose? If he was following you, maybe it was him."

She shook her head. "I thought about that, but…" She shrugged. "I don't know how to say this, but I just don't think he would do something like that. He's not the type."

"He was *following* you."

"Yeah, but I think the following thing might have to do with his book. When I found those notes he made about me, he also had stories about other newscasters."

"So? All that says is he's a freak who gets his rocks off stalking newscasters."

"He doesn't know where I keep the key."

"If he really was following you, he might have seen you use it at some point."

She gave a brief nod. "I guess. And I guess I was just hoping the whole thing would blow over, and I'd never see him again. Things have been so rocky with Zac, I haven't wanted to add anything to the mix." She smiled wistfully. "I wish Zac could have been here today."

"Does Zac usually watch your broadcasts in person?"

"No, but today was special, you know? He was supposed to come by this morning, but he's still in Long Beach."

She blinked a few times. Her eyes became tear-filled. "We've got problems."

"What can I do?"

She forced a smile and batted a tear away. "You can go with me to the launch party tonight. You're invited because you're an employee now, and I hate going to these things alone. Zac usually goes with me."

"Of course. I'd love to."

She told me the address for the party and asked me to meet her at a bar down the street beforehand.

I sat down and jotted the name of the place then looked up at Jane. "You sure you don't want to do anything about this Mick guy? I mean, he did show up here today."

"Yeah, but he had an excuse, and he left. He didn't even talk to me. And I haven't heard anything from him since I spent the night there. It's a situation that will go away."

I raised one of my eyebrows and gave her a dubious look.

"And if it doesn't, I'll go to the cops."

"Promise?"

"Promise. Now make sure you wear something fabulous tonight. That's an order from a higher-up at Trial TV."

"Got it. What are you going to do until then?"

"See a friend of mine. I need someone to get my head straight, you know?"

"I know. My friend Maggie does that for me."

"The tough part will be that I have to tell this friend I won't be around much anymore. I need to focus on my marriage."

"That sounds like a good idea."

She put her hand on my shoulder. "And hey, you've been a good friend to me, too. Thank you for that. Really."

I stood and hugged her. "Anytime, Jane."

She squeezed me back. The embrace lasted only for the briefest second. It seemed a mundane moment. But it was one I would return to again and again.

23

When I arrived at the bar at six, there was no sign of Jane.

The place she'd chosen was a Latin bar/restaurant on Illinois Street. Jane said she loved the place, and I could see why. It was a sexy, splashy lounge with sensual drum-based music.

The bar was packed so I stood at the back, behind the crowd. After a while, I checked my watch. Jane was definitely late, which was curious, since her newscaster background usually made her exceptionally punctual. But then again, the day had been a hectic one.

I texted her—*I'm here. Want me to order something for you?*

I shifted back and forth and looked around. Still no Jane. I checked my watch a few times. Had I misunderstood her somehow? I called, but her phone rang and then went to voice mail.

The River East Arts Center, where the party was being held, was on the same block as the bar. Maybe she was already there?

I hustled down Illinois Street, where the Arts Center was lit up and glowing. Located not far from Navy Pier, the gallery was an elegant two-story loft space, which overlooked the river and was decorated with everything from sculptures to oil paintings to pop art. As I walked around, searching for Jane, I peered at some of the discreet stickers at the bottom of the art. Most of the pieces cost as much as I could make in a year at the Fig Leaf.

But Trial TV had spared no expense for their opening party. A band stood in front of the glass wall and belted out jazz numbers. Waiters circled with glasses of sparkling wine. The place was full of elegant people laughing, toasting.

All they needed was a lead newscaster.

I went back to the bar to find it was still packed. I couldn't even make my way to the front. And still no sign of Jane.

By now, she was half an hour late. I called and got her voice mail again. I texted once more—*Are you on your way?*

When she was forty-five minutes late, I went back to the gallery.

Tommy Daley came up to me. He wore the same gray shirt and yellow tie he'd worn to work, but he'd put a shabby tan blazer over it. "Have you seen Jane?"

"I'm looking for her, too. We were supposed to meet up the street, but she didn't show."

"Goddamn it. Ari Adler arrives in five minutes, and Jane was supposed to greet him. Find her, will ya? Find her *now.*"

I called Jane three times, texted her twice and checked the restaurant again. Still no sign.

I thought of her words earlier this afternoon. She was going to see a friend. *I need someone to get my head straight,* she said.

Who was the friend she was meeting? Was it really a friend or one of her flings? Jane said that Zac was gone. Would she have met the person at her place?

Jane's town house wasn't far—just a few minutes by cab ride. I went out front, where a row of cabs waited. A couple minutes later, I was in front of her house. The lights were on, just like the other night. Was Jane still here getting ready? Maybe running late?

I gave the cab cash and asked if he could wait. If Jane was simply late and was ready now, we'd be back in time to greet Ari Adler.

I hurried up the front steps and rang the doorbell. I could hear the sound echoing inside, a vacant sound.

I peered in the window to my right. I saw the chairs where Sam and Charlie and I had sat a few nights before. At the thought of that night, and the scarf shaped like a noose, I felt a chill travel through my body.

I rang the doorbell again. Still no Jane. I called her. "Jane, I'm standing outside your house," I said to her voice mail. "Where are you?"

I waved at the cab driver, signaling for one more minute. He shook his head and yelled out the window, "I go!"

"No, wait!"

But he pulled away.

"Damn," I muttered, then pounded on the door. Even if Jane was home, we'd now have to hunt for a cab, which would take up valuable time.

For lack of anything else to do, I tried the doorknob.

It turned in my hand. The hairs on my arms stood up. Some internal alarm went off inside my body. I pushed the door, and it swung open, making a silent, invisible arc.

What I saw inside formed the basis for another kind of moment. Not a mundane one, certainly not. But it was a moment that would crystallize and freeze in my mind.

And this one would leave a deep, deep stain.

24

"Jane!" I yelled.

She was lying on her side, beneath a hall table. From the position of her body, she looked, almost, as if she'd gotten on the floor to search for something—a dropped earring or a coin—and had lain down for a second. But she was eerily still, her head resting on one arm, the other arm lifeless, draped across the back of her neck.

That arm was covered with blood. And then I noticed more—her hair matted with it; spatters of red over her white suit; a puddle of it underneath her face. For a surreal second, with that pool of maroon and the bright red splashes on the white backdrop of her clothing, she looked like a piece of art from the gallery.

But then reality rushed in with a *whoosh,* and I heard screams of terror in my head.

I dropped my purse and ran to her side. "Jane!"

I knelt next to her, my mind careening, staggering, shrieking.

I touched her waist. As if only a hairline string had held her in that position, her body turned over so that she was lying on her back. A gurgling sound came from her throat. *She's okay,* I thought.

But then blood bubbled from her mouth.

"Oh my God!" I recoiled for a moment, shocked by the blood.

I waited for a second to see if she would cough. Nothing. Her eyes were open. Tiny red flecks dotted the whites of them like bloody pinpricks. Her red scarf was tied tight around her neck, matted with blood.

I felt her wrist. Cold. No pulse. I had to be wrong. I pressed deeper into her flesh. "Oh, God, please. Jane, please!

"Help!" I yelled. My voice seemed to bounce off the taupe walls and lacquered floors and answered me with emptiness.

I kept praying out loud, kept begging in my head to feel the *beat, beat, beat* that would mean Jane Augustine was still alive. Nothing.

I was suddenly freezing cold. Panting with anxiety. Who had done this to her?

It hit me then—whoever it was could still be here. My head jerked back and forth, looking around. But the place looked the same as when I'd been here two nights ago—a lovely town house, everything else in order.

I looked back at Jane.

What should I do? What should I do?

Mouth-to-mouth resuscitation?

I began to lean toward Jane, but that sickening burbling sound arose from her throat again. More blood.

I leapt to my feet and found my purse, my hands shaking violently when I opened it, accidentally hurling its contents over the floor as I searched for the phone.

"No!" My battery was dead. With Theo at my place last night, I'd forgotten to charge it, and with all the calls and texts I'd made to Jane, I'd depleted it.

I bolted to my feet and hurried through the living room. *Where was their house phone?* I couldn't find it.

I darted around the town house—kitchen, dining room, back to the living room. My heart thundered, my eyes were wild. Finally, I spotted a small cordless phone on the book-shelf next to the fireplace.

My fingers felt like unwieldy pieces of wood on the buttons. I panted, moaned. At last I dialed 911.

"Chicago," a man's voice said. "Emergency call center."

"Jane Augustine," I said. "I think she's dead."

25

How unbelievable that someone like Jane, someone who appeared as merely a pretty talking head, was, once you saw behind the exterior, one of the most—okay, *the* most—intensely sexual person anyone could imagine. To be with someone like that was intoxicating. No, intoxicating wasn't a strong enough word. Being with Jane—being in her bed with that body, being in her head—was all-consuming, all-captivating, something you could never, ever get enough of.

And when she asked you to wind that red scarf around her neck, God that was something incredible. First, she would tell you how. Then, when you were doing it, she would sigh and murmur, telling you to keep going. She would tell you to do it harder then, do it faster. *Shoot me out of this world,* she would say. You did it. Happily. Because you wanted to please her, you wanted to blow her mind, because if you did it the right way, if you did it enough, maybe, maybe, maybe she would let you stay in her world forever.

The problem was there was always the sense with Jane that it would end. No, it was more than a sense. Jane had always been clear about her limits. She insisted on saying, *this has to end, this is the last time,* over and over and over. She would never shut up about it.

And despite how badly you wanted it to go on forever, even if you were only let into her world every so often, Jane had been right. It *had* ended. What Jane would not have foreseen was that it was you who ended it, not her. It was you who decided to pull that scarf tighter and tighter around her neck. It was you who, one last time, shot Jane out of this world. In fact, it was you who shot her right to heaven.

26

I can hardly remember the next few hours. When I think of it, I see only bursts of memories—the police lights flashing like blue strobes, the shrieking sirens as the ambulance raced away with Jane's body, the yellow slashes of crime scene tape, the neighbors standing stiffly, arms crossed in front of them as they watched the police swarm the area.

I was questioned by one cop, then another. I know my mouth moved. I know I answered everything, recalling each detail about the night. I know I told them about the break-in Jane had a few days ago, the flowers, the scarf shaped into a noose.

I was driven in the back of a police car to the Belmont station, where a detective asked all the same questions as the others. I gave the same answers. The detective left.

I was in a square windowless room about eight feet around, painted all in white. One wall had a metal bench pushed against it, and above that, a steel ring bolted into the wall. I sat at a fake wood table in the center of the room, one chair on the other side.

Another detective came in. He was a lean guy wearing brown casual pants, a light blue button-down shirt and an empty holster and expensive-looking running shoes. Something about him snapped me out of my fog.

"We've met," I said.

"I'm Detective Vaughn." He sat down across the table.

"You and another detective interviewed me last fall when Forester Pickett passed away." *And you were an asshole,* I wanted to add. Then due to my stop-swearing campaign I amended it. I mean, a total jerk.

"Yep," he said. "If I remember right, your fiancé hit the road, right?" This memory seemed to cause him some pleasure. A little smile played over his mouth and his green eyes crinkled a little. He looked as though he was trying not to laugh, and it made me remember precisely how much I disliked Detective Vaughn.

"Yes," I said. "Sam had to leave town."

"You rope him back in yet?"

"He's back."

"Getting married anytime soon?" His delight in this topic hadn't seemed to wane.

"Not right now. If we could get back to what happened tonight." Suddenly a thought occurred to me. "Has anyone called Zac?"

"The husband? We're trying to find him."

"I think he's in Long Beach."

"California?" His brows, thick and brown, moved closer together. His tone was conversational, as if we weren't here because someone had bludgeoned Jane to death.

Blunt trauma to head and neck, the other detective had said at some point, making it sound clinical, distant. *Strangulation. We're not sure which came first, but from what you said about the body positioning and the scene, it seems she had her back turned. Probably meant she knew the person who did this.*

"Long Beach, Indiana," I said. "They have a house over there." I remembered Jane's words from Saturday after the break-in. "Long Beach is an hour and a half away."

"You have the number for the house there?"

"No."

Detective Vaughn fell quiet, watching my face, then his eyes dropped.

I followed his gaze. "Oh!" I said. My hands were in my lap. There was blood on them. Jane's blood. I turned my hands over. Red-black smears stained the fingers of my left hand, the palm of my right and under the nails.

I stood, really taking in the windowless room for the first time, feeling trapped suddenly, feeling the reality of everything whoosh back in. "I have to wash my hands." I realized that I hadn't been to the bathroom since earlier that night when I got ready for the party.

"Sure." The detective stood with me. "Let's print you while you're out there."

"Print me?"

"Fingerprint you." Again, that casual tone.

"Why do you have to fingerprint me?"

"Gotta figure out whose prints are in that house. Yours are probably all over, huh?" We both looked at my hands.

I felt cold. "I guess."

The woman who fingerprinted me was bored. She yanked at my fingers, pressed them into ink, then a pad. "You're done," she said.

But why did it feel like everything was just starting?

27

"Who hated her?" Detective Vaughn said when I was back in the room. He was sitting, hands clasped on his abdomen, as if he were settling in for a nice, long chat.

"Jane? No one."

He raised one of those thick eyebrows. "What happened to her was a crime of passion."

It was fitting in a way, because Jane was a passionate person. I debated whether to tell Vaughn about her affairs. The last thing I wanted was bad posthumous PR for Jane. She would have been mortified if the final information attached to her name was the fact that she cheated on her husband. She was so much more than that. Plus, I'd promised as a lawyer and a friend that I wouldn't tell anyone about the games she liked to play with the scarf.

I thought of Maggie, too. She was always telling her clients, *Don't speak to the cops. Never talk to them unless they arrest you.*

But I hadn't been given a Miranda warning. I was just a witness to a crime, not a suspect. And yet I had been fingerprinted.

"Is there any reason I need an attorney with me right now?" I asked Vaughn.

"No, we're just talking. I need to hear every possible thing you saw, so we can find out who did this to your friend. Most homicides have to be solved within the first few hours or they won't be solved at all."

Won't be solved… Flashes of Jane's blood-spattered body filled my head again; I could hear my cries bouncing off the hardwood floors as I knelt by her.

I nodded and swallowed down bile from my lurching stomach.

He scratched one finger over his jaw. "So who would do this to her?"

I made my face placid, but in my mind, I struggled. I wanted to say that she thought she was being followed by Mick, the writer. But if I said that, I'd have to explain why—because Jane was, as she had put it, red-blooded.

Red-blooded. It had been almost funny when Jane said it over the weekend. Now, all I could think about was the blood that had covered Jane's head and pooled around her body.

Bile rose in my stomach again. I dropped my head into my hands willing away the image, the horror that went with it.

"You okay?" His voice was resigned, as if he had to ask the question, but he didn't really care about the answer. When I raised my head, I saw that his eyes were keen, studying me.

I couldn't decide what to do. Jane had worked closely with the cops for years, and she had been convinced that if they knew of her affairs, they wouldn't keep quiet about it. "It's been a very long day. I think I need to go home."

"Yeah, sure, just a few more questions, and we'll get you out of here." He clasped his hands on his stomach again. "Who was angry at Jane? She piss anybody off lately?"

I thought of Jackson Prince in the studio that morning. "There was an attorney who was on Trial TV today. He left in the middle of his interview." I shrugged. "He seemed very angry at something Jane said, and she told me later that she was working on a story that could rock him."

"What does that mean, 'rock him'?"

"I don't know. That's just what she said."

"What was the story about?"

"She didn't tell me. And I have to say that this man is a well-respected lawyer. I don't think he'd kill someone over a bad interview or a story."

"His name?"

"Jackson Prince."

"Ambulance chaser, right?"

"He's a plaintiff's attorney, yes."

"Yeah, makes a ton of dough, I heard. He's always giving a press conference for something." Detective Vaughn reached to his right and pulled a stack of forms toward him. He flipped through a few, his hands moving nimbly, clearly something he did on a regular basis. He jotted something down on one page. He asked about Trial TV, about who would have written the story about Jackson Prince.

"Usually broadcasters write their own stories, but in the past Jane operated a little differently." I explained how C. J. Lyons, her producer at the old station, used to do a lot of the writing for Jane. "But now that Jane had become an anchor at Trial TV, she was trying to write her own stuff, and she gave me the impression that this story was hers entirely."

He asked more questions about Jackson Prince. I told him everything I knew, which wasn't much.

"All right, so who else?" the detective said.

"Who else?"

"You know anyone else who was mad at Jane?"

I acted as if I was thinking about the possibilities, but what I was really thinking was that Zac was mad at Jane. She told me that when we met for coffee on Saturday morning and again when I'd gone to her house Saturday night. I'd seen his anger myself when he came home. And Jane had mentioned issues with Zac just today. "Jane and Zac were having some problems," I said, using her words.

"What kind of problems?"

"I don't know the whole story. Like I've told you, Jane and

I were only work colleagues. Well, we were until this week-end when we spent more social time together, but Jane did mention that she and Zac had gone through some tough times."

Detective Vaughn clicked the end of his pen, just looking at me. *Click, click, click.* I could hear nothing else—nothing in the hallway. I wondered if the rooms were soundproofed.

"Was he in town when she found that noose in her house?" the detective asked.

"Jane said that he was at their house in Long Beach on that day, too. He came home after Jane found the flowers and the noose."

Click, click, click.

Detective Vaughn asked me more questions about Zac and Jane. I did everything I could to answer his questions without saying anything explicitly about Jane's extra-marital activity. I couldn't decide whether or not it was the right thing to do, whether I should be more up-front. Every answer seemed like a misstep. Every answer made *me* feel guilty. I wanted to give them every bit of information to catch whoever had killed Jane, but I wanted to protect my friend's reputation, too.

The intensity of it—the questions about who was mad at Jane, the warring in my mind of what I should tell him, all of it piled together with the searing images of Jane's bloodied body—left me depleted.

I felt light-headed, then nauseous again. I hadn't eaten anything, I realized, since lunch, and it was almost eleven.

"I think I need to go home now," I said to Detective Vaughn. I needed to talk to Maggie tomorrow about how much to tell the police. Why hadn't I called her before? It was just that things had happened so fast, and I had nothing to hide.

Detective Vaughn fell quiet, studying me with those keen eyes again.

"Is that okay?" I said, growing claustrophobic.

He tilted his head to one side, then the other. "You're not planning on leaving town, are you?"

"No." Why did I feel so defensive? I was a lawyer, but a civil one. I felt lost in a criminal interrogation, especially when I'd just found a friend dead. "I just want to go home." I felt trapped inside that windowless room. I stood and glanced around. "My coat. I'm not sure where it is."

"We got it," he said. "Evidence. We'll give it back to you after it's been processed."

"Oh."

"Don't worry. We'll drive you home." He stood, too. He was a foot taller and he looked down at me with a powerful gaze. "I'll see you again, though. Soon."

28

That night, the fresh zing of my new life turned to sour despair. Jane, who had been part of that new life, was gone. Murdered.

The delight and adventure I had experienced the last few days—with Theo, with Trial TV—all seemed silly now.

Sam called as I walked in the door. I told him that Jane was killed. That I had found her.

"Jesus, Iz. Are you okay? Where are you?"

"Home."

"I'll be there in ten."

He was there in eight.

It was unlike the last few months, where Sam and I had treaded gingerly around each other, giving the other space, never taking for granted that we would be together for a particular night, much less for a particular lifetime. Now, the fact that he had disappeared on me six months ago didn't matter.

When Sam arrived, it was just us again. No questions. Nothing to figure out. Just Sam and me stripped to the core. Of us. Which had always been good.

Under the halo of my doorway, he held me while I sobbed. We moved into my dark living room. He sat on my favorite yellow chair and pulled me into his lap, tucking my head into the bend of his neck, stroking my hair. I breathed him in—the scent of home after a long trip away—and I waited for the calm and the order that Sam would bring.

But calm and order never arrived.

At 5:00 a.m., my cell phone rang. Somehow I'd managed to sleep by holding tight around Sam's stomach, my head on his chest.

At the sound of the phone, I murmured, tuned back into where I was. I could tell from Sam's breathing that he wasn't sleeping, that he hadn't slept, that he had been pretending to sleep for the last few hours. For me.

I lifted my head off his chest and looked at the phone, which was on top of my dresser.

Sam pulled me back. "Go to sleep."

"What if it's something about Jane?"

He said nothing, and I swung my eyes to meet his. He grimaced.

Sam curled himself around me, creating a nest. "Get some sleep, get some sleep," he murmured.

But the phone wouldn't stop. My house phone started next. I finally lifted the receiver off the nightstand.

"Izzy?" I heard a woman's sharp bark.

"C.J.?" The voice of Jane's ex-producer was unmistakable.

"What time are you getting in this morning?"

I sat up in bed. "What do you mean? Where?"

"To Trial TV," she said, exasperated. "What time will you be here?"

"Uh…" I hadn't even thought about work. To me, Trial TV had been all about Jane, and my new job had been erased somewhere in the horror of last night. But of course, the network would go on. It couldn't stop for Jane's death. She wouldn't want it to.

"I guess seven o'clock," I said. "That's when I'm supposed to show up."

"I need you here now."

"C.J., you know about Jane, right?"

"Yes." Her voice went somber. "Yes," she said again. "And I heard you found her. That must have been hideous. I'm so sorry, Izzy."

It was the first time I'd heard empathy, compassion or anything like it from C. J. Lyons. "Thanks. I'm sorry for you, too. I know you guys were close."

"Yes. This is gut-wrenching."

"I know." I thought for a second. "C.J., I'm confused why you're calling me. You don't even work at Trial TV."

"I do now. As of one this morning. And, like I said, I need you in here. Now."

29

Amid a somber newsroom, C.J. was snarling orders and gesturing with a clipboard when I got there. She had short black hair and dark-rimmed eyeglasses that were pushed up on the top of her head. She was dressed, as she often was, in jeans, a fitted black jacket and no-nonsense shoes. Interns scurried away from her, scribbling notes. Reporters appeared shell-shocked, but they nodded and scattered to cover the stories C.J. was assigning.

She smiled a little when she saw me. "Izzy."

She raised the one arm without the clipboard and gave me a fast embrace with a couple of quick pats on the back. Not the best hug I'd ever gotten, but the only one I'd ever received from C.J.

"Can you believe this?" Her eyes were full of agony. I could tell she hadn't slept, either.

I shook my head. I felt like sobbing again. My eyes darted around the newsroom, and I saw people whispering, pointing. I would always be known as the woman who found Jane Augustine dead.

"Oh, girl," C.J. said, spotting the tears in my eyes. "We're all a mess."

"I know. I'm sorry. And you knew her for so much longer than I did. How are you?"

I saw tears glisten in C.J.'s dark eyes. "I can't talk about it. I feel like I'll never be able to talk about it."

I nodded. "I spent hours with the police yesterday, and it was just…it was just terrible reliving it."

"C.J.!" someone yelled "You want a live shot on the Rivera story?"

She turned around and hollered back at them. Somehow it was a relief to have someone taking charge, doing their job, acting for even a second as if this was just another day at Trial TV.

"Here's the deal," she said when she turned back to me. "I got a call last night from Ari Adler. Tommy Daley quit after he heard about Jane."

"You're kidding."

"No. He said that Jane was the only reason he had come onto the network, and without her he didn't want to be here. So Trial TV lost two of its most important people in one night."

"Jesus."

"I know. The network has only been running for a day, and it's falling apart at the seams. Ari asked me to come on and keep things moving."

"I'm glad. This network was everything to Jane." I thought of Jane this weekend, after she'd found the noose in her house. She wouldn't even call the police because it would have meant bad press for Trial TV. She wanted to do everything she could to make the network a success.

"I'm here to do whatever I can to help," C.J. said. "We're running some taped segments now, but we go live again at seven o'clock." She peered into my eyes. "Can you keep working?"

I glanced over C.J.'s head to the anchor desk. I could see Jane there yesterday, beaming her self-assured smile into the camera, looking pleased and proud and full of life, a new professional life with Trial TV.

"Yeah," I said, but I think there was a waver in my voice. I couldn't stop the warring images of the Jane of yesterday, bursting and alive, and the Jane of last night, the life bled away from her. The two visions battered themselves back and forth in my mind, as if competing for my last memory of her, the way I would remember her.

"Don't fall apart now, Izzy." C.J. grabbed my shoulder and leaned nearer to me. Her brown eyes were bottomless, and yet they seemed all knowing. It seemed as if she could see inside me. "We're all falling apart inside, but we're going to hold it together for Jane, okay?"

I nodded, trying desperately to stick with the image of Jane behind the news desk. But my mind kept snagging on that scarf. The scarf that had choked the life from her.

"Izzy." C.J.'s voice was like a snap. "Are you listening to me?"

I blinked furiously. "Yes. Yes, I'm listening. Tell me what you need."

Her hand on my shoulder tightened. "Ari and I have talked and we want you to do something for us. For Jane."

"Okay."

"We're not going to be able to find a replacement anchor right away," C.J. said. "Everyone in town who might work is under contract. And you know how hard it is to break those contracts." She looked pointedly at me.

I laughed a little. I used to write the contracts for many of the newscasters in town, and I always included solid non-compete clauses and astronomical buyouts, which made it all but impossible for a broadcaster to move quickly from one station to another.

C.J. smiled a little, too. "Thanks to lawyers like you, it's going to take a while before we can get someone on the morning desk. We could have the afternoon people step in, but we don't think it will look good to have newscasters working around the clock, especially since we expect to get even more people tuning in once they've heard Jane is gone, which is why we need you to step up your game."

I threw my hair back and nodded. I was glad that I'd managed to do my makeup and put on the stylish black suit that

I'd bought for Forester's funeral. "Of course." I looked around for Ted, my cameraman from the day prior. How long ago that seemed. "Just tell me where you want me to go."

C.J. paused. Was she worried that I would fall apart?

"I'm fine," I said. "I did okay yesterday at the courthouse."

"I saw it. You did more than okay. Which is why Ari and I want you there."

"Back at the courthouse?"

"No. There."

I noticed then that C.J. was pointing. At the anchor desk.

30

"Let's go over it again," C.J. said. "What's the key to working the prompter?"

"Focus behind it. Look past the words into the iris of the camera, so it doesn't look like you're reading."

"What camera do you look at?"

"The one with the red light. When a new light goes on, I glance down at the script before looking up at the new camera."

"Right. What about the talk-backs today?"

"Try to keep the guests on point. Remember that Senator Hinton will go on forever. Listen for the producer to tell me when to cut him off."

"Great. Opening line?"

"Good morning and welcome to Trial TV. I'm Isabel McNeil."

I had tried to tell C.J. that I wasn't an anchor; I was barely a reporter. But C.J. was relentless. I'd finally caved when she told me that Trial TV wasn't going on the air without me. Did I want to let Jane down?

I didn't. And now here I was fifteen minutes before my first broadcast. And with that realization, it started—a blush that crept up my body, a heat that overtook me.

C.J. pulled back and scrutinized me. "Are you perspiring?"

"Uh-oh."

"Uh-oh?"

"Son of a motherless goat," I said, my working replacement phrase for *son of a bitch.*

"What does that mean?"

"I have this little problem. It hasn't happened in a long time."

"What kind of problem?"

"Um, flop sweating?"

The muscles in her jaw went rigid. "*Flop* sweating? What does that even mean?"

I told her about how occasionally, when I got acutely nervous, usually at the beginning of a trial or some other public speaking, I experienced extreme perspiration. This little problem of mine was unbelievably embarrassing, as if someone had dropped burning embers into my gut and then thrown gasoline on them. And then a truck full of lumber. The waterworks in my body would pour, and my face would get as red as the fire inside me.

"How long?" C.J. barked.

"I don't know. I guess it started in high school. Maybe it's a hormonal thing."

"I mean how long does it last?"

"An hour or so." The more I thought about it, the more I sweated.

"Goddamn it, we don't have an hour! Marissa!"

The makeup artist who had already spent half an hour touching up my face came running out of the dressing room.

"Powder her!" C.J. ordered.

Marissa made a face. "Geez," she said. "That's going to be tough to cover. We should wait until the sweating stops."

"Powder her!" C.J. said again. "And I mean good. I want her spackled."

Marissa stuffed tissue around my collar, pulled a huge powder pad out of her apron and went at me. But I could tell it wasn't working.

"Izzy, stop it!" C.J. said.

"I can't."

"So if you know this is a problem, what's the solution?"

"I've tried a bunch of things."

Once, at the beginning of a trial, I ripped out my shoulder pads and tucked them under my arm. Another time I used the liner notes from a Missy Elliot album I stole off Q's desk. My greatest fear had been that this would happen at my wedding. But since I wasn't getting married anytime soon, I'd stopped thinking about it.

Suddenly I remembered something. "Benadryl!" I yelped. "Does someone have Benadryl?"

C.J. spun around and faced the newsroom. "Who has Benadryl?" she thundered.

Through swipes of the huge powder pad, I could see some people shrug. Faith Lowe, the avant-garde producer I'd met my first day, began to dig in her purse. She held up a triumphant fist. "I've got some." She ran up to C.J. and gave it to her.

C.J. tore the backing from the foil packaging. "Why didn't you bring this out before, Faith?" she asked in an irritated tone.

"Because you didn't ask for it before." Faith turned and stomped away.

"Thanks," I called to Faith's back, but she was weaving her way through the newsroom.

C.J. pulled two tablets out of the foil. "Does this work?"

"I don't know," I said, reaching for them. "A doctor once told me to try it."

C.J. pulled the tablets back toward her. "This stuff makes you tired. Like *really* tired."

I pointed at my pink, burning face. "Do you prefer this?"

"Get her a Red Bull!" she yelled over her shoulder, then put the tablets in my hand. "Take the things. Now!"

I popped the pills. The makeup artist handed me a can of Red Bull.

For the next ten minutes, Marissa kept spackling, while

everyone gathered in the newsroom to watch me. I felt like sweating livestock at a county fair.

"Just keep reading your script," C.J. said. "Get ready to go on-air."

But the sweating wouldn't stop. I was dripping onto my script. "I can't put any more makeup on her," Marissa said.

"Yes, you can," C.J. said.

More blotting with tissues; more swats with a makeup brush and the powder pad.

"Three minutes to air!" someone yelled.

I looked at C.J. with terrified eyes. "I can't do this."

"Yes, you can. That Benadryl will start to work any minute. And remember, you're doing this for Jane."

I closed my eyes. I tried to picture Jane at the anchor desk yesterday, working her magic. But I kept seeing Jane dead last night; Jane rolled out of her house on a gurney.

"One minute to air!" the guy yelled. "Quiet on the set!"

"Izzy," I heard C.J. say.

I opened my eyes. She was peering at my face, and she looked oddly relieved.

"It's working," she said.

She was right. I could feel the heat and the red drain away.

C.J. watched me for another thirty seconds. "Powder once more!" she yelled over her shoulder at Marissa.

This time, the powder felt like cool dust.

Marissa backed away, then C.J., who was nodding at me, staring me in the eyes. "You're all right," she mouthed.

"Ten, nine, eight…"

I closed my eyes again. I didn't try to think of Jane. Instead, I thought of Forester. How he had encouraged me, how he had always told me I could do anything.

"Three, two…"

I opened my eyes. "Good morning and welcome to Trial TV. I'm Isabel McNeil."

As I spoke, looking into the yawning square lens of the

camera, a tranquil, almost eerie composure settled over me. Maybe it was the Benadryl. Maybe it was because this was one last thing I could do for Jane. Whatever it was, I could feel my mouth move, I could hear the words coming out, but it was as if someone else were speaking.

I sank into a hole of detachment that opened in my mind. I thought of all the times I had seen Jane do this, and it was almost as if I was channeling her. Like Jane, when the lead story was over and a red light flashed on a different camera, I glanced down at my script and then turned my body to face it. Like Jane, I read the next story and the next with confidence. Like Jane, I smiled slightly when we went to a commercial.

And when that first segment was over, I finally looked around the room, and I saw people nodding. Ted, the cameraman, gave me a thumbs-up. So did Faith and Ricky, the photographer who had driven the news van.

C.J. rushed up to me. "You've got some kinks, but you're good."

"I am?" I blinked. I felt in a slight stupor from the Benadryl, but I was also buzzing with an energy I had never known before.

"Really good," C.J. said. She rattled off a litany of criticisms and suggestions.

I blinked. How did Jane do this and make it look so effortless?

"Ready?" C.J. asked.

"No."

"Good, because we're back to you in five…four…three…"

31

There was no funeral for Jane, or at least not one open to the public. Instead, her parents, who lived outside of Grand Rapids, Michigan, were holding a private burial there over the weekend. Meanwhile, Zac had a hastily arranged afternoon memorial on Tuesday at the restaurant in the Park Hyatt where she and I had been Friday night; it had always been one of Jane's favorite places.

It seemed early for a memorial service. Didn't such things usually take place a few days after the death? Or maybe that was only when there was a body to be dealt with for the service. I wondered if Jane's parents would have an open casket. I hoped not. Jane should only be remembered for the vivacious, vibrant woman she was.

Spring was still in the air on that Tuesday afternoon, with green buds sprouting from the otherwise bare trees and a fresh scent blowing off the lake. But it was chilly, and so the outside bar, where I'd had drinks with Jane just days before, where she'd asked me to join Trial TV, was closed. Inside, the bar had polished, dark wood and chic furniture. The tall windows overlooked Chicago Avenue, and on the far end, Michigan Avenue and the old Water Tower.

The place was packed. I glanced around and for a second I thought I knew everyone, but realized many were anchors and reporters I'd seen on the news for years. I waved to the few I did know from working at Pickett Enterprises. I saw

C.J. standing near the end of the bar with a producer and assignment editor from Jane's old station. They all appeared distraught. Everybody did.

Q appeared next to me. "Hi," he said simply, somberly. "Thanks for being here."

Sam had offered to come with me, but I wanted to attend the memorial with someone who knew Jane. Q, as my assistant, had worked with her for years, and he had loved her.

Q peered at my face. "TV makeup?"

"Yeah." I told him about anchoring the morning show. And the flop sweat attack. As a result, they'd powdered me in a massive way again that day.

"Wow." Q peered at me some more. "It's going to take an industrial squeegee to get that off."

"And a blowtorch."

Neither of us laughed.

"I can't believe this." Q adjusted his black tie, which he wore with a gray-and-black houndstooth jacket. His new boyfriend had lots of cash, and since they'd gotten together, Q had become a true fashionista. "You okay?"

"No."

He grabbed me around the waist, and we hugged tight.

"Drink?" he said.

"Definitely."

We made our way through the crowd to the bar, said hello to a few people and ordered two glasses of wine.

As we waited for our drinks, I looked around the place. "Oh!" I said, when my eyes landed at the far corner.

A table had been set up there, and on top of it, leaning against the wall, was a blown-up head shot of Jane. In it, she wore a crisp white blouse and a gold braided necklace. She was laughing in the photo, her eyes sparkling. I thought of her, just a few nights ago, outside on the patio, saying, *When someone tells you you're beautiful, you act like it's the first time you've heard that. Because you never know when it'll be the last.*

Tears flooded my eyes.

Q handed me a glass of wine. "Sip this."

I gulped it instead, wanting something to tamp down the emotion that coursed through me as I looked at that photo.

On the table beside the picture were two scrapbooks, filled with what looked to be pictures of Jane. Many, I guessed, taken by Zac.

Q looked from me to the scrapbooks and back. "Let's talk about something else for a second. How's the twenty-one-year-old?"

"In Mexico."

"Oh, honey, is that what he told you? That's the oldest excuse in the book for not calling."

"No, it's not."

"Train wreck. Told you."

I gave him a withering look.

I kept glancing at the table with the scrapbooks, debating whether I could handle looking at them, when I noticed that Zac, grim-faced, hands in his pockets, was standing near the table. He was speaking to a short woman with dark hair who was flipping through the books, dabbing her eyes with a Kleenex.

Zac wore his slim black suit with a white shirt and thin black tie. I could tell the suit was expensive, even from far away. He looked around the crowd, and then his eyes landed on me. For a second, he didn't seem to recognize me, but then he nodded and started walking toward me.

"I'll be right back," I said to Q.

I pushed my way through the crowd until I met up with Zac. Up close I could see his face was ragged, the skin around his eyes more heavily lined than when I had seen him a few days before.

"Zac," I said, "I'm Izzy McNeil. I met you at your house on Saturday when—" I faltered for a second "—when Jane found that stuff. And we talked that morning. And I—"

"I know who you are," Zac interrupted me. He didn't say

anything then, he just looked at me with those anguished eyes. "You found her."

I nodded. I saw Jane again—the white suit spattered red, the pool of blood behind her head. "Yeah, it was…" How to describe? "It was horrible."

He started to say something but his words caught on tears, it sounded like. He shook his head a little and closed his eyes momentarily.

"I'm really sorry for your loss." I hated saying stuff like that at a funeral. Such words always sounded cliché.

Zac shook his head. We were silent for a beat. Then he spoke. "I need to ask you something. When you were out with Jane last week…"

"Yes?" I prompted him to finish.

He shook his head again, as if he'd changed his mind. His eyes narrowed, and I thought I saw his emotion sway from anguish to anger in that one instant.

"What? Please ask me. Say whatever you were going to say, please, because…" My glance drifted over Zac's shoulder and landed on the photo of Jane. I felt those tears leaping into my eyes again.

Zac saw them. "Let's move over here."

We stepped aside into a corner.

"You were out with her Friday night," Zac said. "And when I called you the next day, I mentioned her…" His laugh was harsh. "What did she call them? Her *dalliances,*" he said bitterly. "You know what I mean."

I didn't know what to say. Jane said that she told Zac everything, that he knew everything about her, but what was *everything?* Should I admit I knew what he was talking about?

I simply nodded. I thought about Jane telling me how Zac was sick of her affairs, that he wasn't so understanding anymore. Suddenly, I wanted to ask Zac, *Were you so angry you couldn't take it anymore? Did you kill your wife?*

Within the last six months, I'd developed a suspicious

nature, which had settled inside me and taken up residence. I'd gone from being someone who thought the best of everyone to someone with a wariness that sometimes leapt up and surprised me. I didn't like that about myself. It made me feel much older than my twenty-nine (okay, nearly thirty) years.

"She didn't talk to many people about what she did," Zac said. "Her dalliances. Why you?"

"I'm not sure. Jane and I had always liked each other. And we became closer when she asked me to work for Trial TV."

His eyes moved back and forth, as if they were mining my face for some other meaning behind my words. "Closer. Yeah." He chuckled, but there was no mirth behind it. "You worked for Forester Pickett."

I nodded, surprised at the topic shift. "I did," I said with pride. "Forester was a friend of mine."

"And your fiancé disappeared about the time Forester died, right?" It sounded accusatory somehow.

"Yes."

"And you're a lawyer."

"Yeah." *And I feel like you're taking my deposition.*

"So you know how to evade them?"

"Evade who?"

"The cops. You know how to talk to them, how a murder investigation works." The tone of Zac's words was severe, and again he sounded as if he was accusing me of something.

"I don't do criminal law," I said, as if that explained everything. But really, I had no idea what he was getting at.

He was staring at me so intently now it was disconcerting. "What happened Friday night?"

I felt my grief shift to anxiety. Zac was standing in front of me, my back to the corner of the room, and I suddenly had the feeling of being trapped there. "What do you mean?"

"Where did Jane stay that night?"

I raised my glass and swallowed another gulp of wine. What to tell him? Zac obviously knew about Jane's affairs, but to tell him specifically about Friday, about Jane going home with the writer seemed wrong. A friend's secrets are always a secret. Even if that friend was no longer alive.

"I'm not sure."

"Why were you so evasive when I called Saturday morning?"

He was making this hard. How to tell him that I was trying to cover up for his wife, *and* I was dealing with my first one-night stand, with a guy who was still in my house when he called? I thought of Theo then, and despite the setting, I felt my insides twist with passion. Never had a guy been able to cause such an intense reaction in me. Not even Sam.

"I…I…" I looked over his shoulder at the bar. There was Q. I gave him a look I knew he would read as *Help*.

"I know where Jane stayed," Zac said when I looked back at him.

"You do?"

"Yeah," he said. "She stayed with you."

32

"Jane didn't stay with me that night."

Zac crossed his arms, looking self-satisfied. "Don't play with me."

"I'm not playing. Why would you say that?"

He scoffed. "No, let me ask you a question. Why were you and Jane hanging out so much lately?"

"Because we were becoming friends. Because she asked me to be on Trial TV."

"Friends." Another bitter laugh. "I bet you were good friends."

"What are you implying?"

"That you and Jane were more than friends."

"That's ridiculous."

"Then why were you being so evasive when I called Saturday morning?"

I paused. Fine, I would come out with it. "If I sounded evasive, it was because I thought your wife had probably gone home with a man she was talking to Friday night." I wasn't sure how much to say. I had promised Jane I wouldn't say anything about the scarfing, given her my word as an attorney, too. But I could say anything I wanted about myself. "And also…" This was embarrassing. "*I* went home with a man, a kid really. I went home with this guy, and he was with me when you called, and the whole situation was making me nervous, and…" I held my free hand up in a shrug. "And that's why I probably sounded evasive, but Jane was *not* with me."

Zac looked unimpressed. "She wouldn't tell me who she was with that night. She usually did, but not on that night."

"She was with some writer."

"Some writer?" His question was laced with sarcasm.

"Yes, Mick is his name."

"Mick what?"

"Mick…uh…actually I never did learn it." Again, I experienced that feeling I'd had the night before at the police station—a feeling of guilt. It was irrational. There was no reason to feel guilty about anything. And if anyone should feel guilt, shouldn't it be Zac? His anger was palpable now but contained. What had he been like in the private moments with Jane, who he knew cheated on him, and frequently? Had he been so contained with her?

Zac shook his head, his mouth tightening. "It was the same thing with you that it was with all the guys she was with—all of a sudden she's out one night, and it's just business or it's just friends, and then I can't find her. It was the same shit with you." His voice was getting louder. "The exact same shit!"

I looked around, embarrassed. People were starting to stare. This was bizarre. Six months ago I'd been at Forester's funeral and had been pulled into a confrontation. The same thing was happening here.

I leaned toward him and dropped my voice. "Zac, it was *just* business. We were *just* friends."

Q arrived at my side then. He put a hand on my elbow. "Everything okay here?"

I took a breath, inhaling air that seemed foul, tinged with accusations. "Q, this is Zac, Jane's husband."

They shook hands, Q murmuring words of condolence. Those kind, soft-spoken words made me remember that we were at a funeral, and the man in front of me had lost his wife, and that man had probably not slept last night and was most likely just shooting his mouth off out of exhaustion.

"Look, Zac," I said calmly. "Not that it matters, but Jane really wasn't with me Friday night."

"Not that it matters?" Zac's tone was mocking now. "The way I see it, you were with Jane a lot this weekend—she stayed at your place Friday night, she ran back to meet you for coffee the next morning so you could get your stories straight, you came over when she found that shit in the house. And now that I think about it, maybe you left those flowers and that noose. You probably knew where she kept the key."

My mouth opened. Wide. But no sounds came from it. I looked at Q, whose face was surprised and confused. As my assistant, Q had always known what to do to get me out of trouble, but neither of us knew what to do here.

Two men came up to Zac then. "We're so sorry," one said. Zac shook their hands. He patted one on the shoulder with his left hand.

And I saw then that on Zac's left hand was a massive bruise. It covered the base of his thumb, the knuckles of his first two fingers. Its blue-black color seeped toward the center of his hand.

I felt my eyebrows knit together as I stared at it.

Zac must have seen my look. When the men left, he glanced down at his hand. "I had an accident at our house in Long Beach," he said. "I was cutting up the dead wood that fell during the winter. The whole stack fell on my hand."

I wanted to say, *The dog ate my homework once, too.* He just happened to get a bruised hand at the same time his wife was beaten and killed?

"Look," he said, his voice laced with undisguised frustration. "The cops have already seen this, all right?" He lifted his hand then, holding it, clenched, in front of my face.

I drew back instinctively.

"Jesus, *you're* scared of *me?*" he said, his voice raised. Over his shoulder I saw a couple of people turn and stare.

"I'm not scared, Zac." I made my tone soothing. But

truthfully, I *was* scared. This whole situation was spiraling out of control, and seeing Zac's raised fist made me think how terrified Jane must have felt on the night of her death. I was sick at the thought, sick with the realization that Jane had died, not in a bed surrounded by relatives, but facedown on the floor of her house, her skull bashed and bleeding. Someone raising a fist, or some other object, over and over. Someone wrapping that scarf around her neck.

Zac dropped his fist and breathed out hard. The anger disappeared from his features, and for a moment anguish returned, like a bird landing on a familiar branch. I wondered if he would cry. "I loved Jane. More than anyone. More than anything."

"I'm sure you did." That was the truth. I didn't doubt for a second that Zac had loved Jane. Probably immensely. But had he loved her so much that he could no longer tolerate her stepping-out behavior? Had it made him a little crazy?

I looked around to see if anyone had been watching our conversation. A few people nearby turned away. Elsewhere, people talked in muted voices and drank fast.

A tall man came up behind Zac then. His silver hair was coifed, and he had a strong body that looked like something you'd see on a thirty-five-year-old, rather than the sixty-five years he probably had seen. Jackson Prince.

Prince gave me a sad smile, clearly not recognizing me from the station, then touched Zac lightly on the arm. "I have to leave," he said in his signature melodic voice. I'd heard he could woo a jury in two sentences.

"I just wanted to say how much I adored Jane," Prince said. "I respected her work immensely. She was one of the best."

She was one of the best who was about to bust you for something big.

Zac shook his hand. "Thanks, Jack. That means a lot."

Prince murmured a few more words about Jane and promised to check in with Zac to see if he needed anything, then he turned and made his way through the multitude of mourners, moving lightly on his feet, nodding hello to people at every turn.

Zac stared at Prince's retreating back, then at one of the windows overlooking Chicago Avenue, as if he was looking for his wife, who might any minute be running, late, up the street.

He turned back to me, his eyes lasering onto mine. "You should know, I told the cops I thought you were with Jane Friday night."

Again, that irrational guilt rippled through me. I felt my throat tightening. "Zac, that's not true. Even if it were, what are you trying to imply? That *I* was the one who hurt Jane? That's ludicrous."

"Is it? Guys were always getting intense about Jane. I've seen it more than once. So why should you be any different? And Jane was always up-front about how she didn't want to leave her marriage. I wondered when someone would get too intense and not be able to take it. As far as I know, you've been seeing her for a while. As far as I know, she was breaking up with you."

I groaned with frustration. "Zac, I told you I was with someone Friday night." I looked at Q. "Please tell him."

Q grinned. "Her first one-night stand," he said to Zac. "I'm so proud."

He turned to Q. "You meet this one-night stand?"

"No, but I got all the gory details."

Right then, I saw him standing near the front door. Mick. The writer. His gray hair and tanned youthful face made him stand out from the crowd.

"That's him!" I said.

I looked back and saw that Zac's eyes hadn't left mine.

"Zac," I said, insistently, "*that* is the writer who Jane was with the other night."

I pointed. We all looked in the direction of the door.

But Mick had disappeared.

33

I dodged mourners as I hurried toward the door, trying to catch up with Mick.

C.J. was suddenly in front of me. "Iz, you were great today. Really."

"Thanks, C.J." I stood on my toes to see over her shoulder. I couldn't see Mick.

C.J. kept talking. "You do need to adjust a lot of things. Tomorrow let's get you in the editing bay to watch the tape. You'll be able to see issues that need working out."

"Great. I'll come in early and stay late. Look, I've got to run."

"Don't forget to look over your scripts tonight."

"Got it." I didn't tell her that I also had to work at the Fig Leaf tonight.

I dashed around her, heading fast toward the entrance. I came out into a marbled foyer. A hostess stood behind a podium, a vacant smile on her face.

"Did you see a guy with a tan and gray hair come out here?" I asked her.

"A guy…? Um, now who were you looking for?"

He must have left. The elevator to the lobby was right there. I hit the button, then looked at the display. The elevator was stopping in the lobby now.

"Are there stairs to the street?" I asked the hostess.

I wanted to catch up to Mick. I wanted to find out his

last name so I could give it to Zac and prove to him I wasn't the one with Jane that night. I wanted to ask Mick why in the hell he'd been following her, whether it was really for a story or something more sinister. I wanted to give his answers to the police and let them decide if he was telling the truth.

The hostess gestured with a game-show wave toward the elevator. "This will take you *right* downstairs."

"Yes, but are there actual stairs?" I couldn't hide the impatience in my voice, causing her smooth brow to crinkle.

"There is an emergency exit."

"Where's that?"

But then the elevator dinged behind me. The doors opened and people flooded out, most of them heading to the memorial.

I dove inside. When the elevator reached the lobby I swiveled my head around, searching for Mick. No sign of him. I ran out into the street, crossing my arms against the late-afternoon chill. And then I saw him—I recognized the gray hair and the blazer he'd been wearing—walking west on Chicago, then taking a right onto Wabash.

Tucking my purse under my arm, I sprinted after him as fast as my high heels would let me. I'd gotten used to heels over the years. I was one of those freaks who said, *I actually prefer high heels,* and mostly meant it. But running in them was a different story. You simply couldn't run *heel-toe, heel-toe*, the way you would with normal shoes. Instead, you had to do a ridiculously silly flat-footed, bouncy jog. And in his flat shoes, Mick was moving much quicker than me.

I turned the same way as him when I got to Wabash. I saw an open door to a bar called Pippins. Was that the arm of his coat, the flash of his gray hair entering the place? I bounced/jogged to Pippins like a lame deer and stepped inside. A bunch of college-age students with about ten pitchers of beer on their table were almost the only patrons. An older man, a professor type in a blazer, was taking a seat at the bar. Definitely not Mick.

I bolted outside, looking both ways. I ran back toward the hotel. I stood in front of the entrance spinning around, hunting for Mick. He was nowhere to be seen.

Just then Q came outside. "Okay, what happened back there?"

I kept looking around. Where had Mick gone? "I don't know. Zac seems to think I had a thing with Jane."

"Did you?"

I turned to face him. "Are you joking? You're questioning me, too?"

He gave an innocent shrug. "Hey, you're in a free-to-be-you-and-me mood these days. Maybe you tried out some girl-on-girl action, too. Ooh! If you turn gay, you have to give me credit for it. We keep track of that stuff. There's a point system."

I smacked him on the arm then spun around, still half hunting for Mick, although he was clearly gone.

Q stopped me with a hand on my shoulder. "Let me drive you home. I think you've had enough for a few days."

I looked at my friend, at his gray eyes the color of ash. Neither of us said anything for a moment. We didn't have to. In that look, I saw the sympathy. Sometimes it isn't what you see in yourself, but what you see reflected in the eyes of a good friend. That gaze Q was giving me—one of concern, of compassion, even a little pity—stopped me cold and took all the fire out of me.

"Let me take you home," he said. "Do you have a coat?"

I realized that I was standing with my arms crossed over my chest, shivering a little. I shook my head. I had stopped off at home and accidentally left it there.

Q flagged a cab and tucked me into the back then climbed in beside me. He directed the driver down Chicago, turning onto State Street. The quiet in the back of that musty cab allowed my grief and exhaustion to return. But I couldn't go home and sleep. For one thing, I had to work tonight at the Fig Leaf. I thought of calling Mayburn and canceling, but when Sam was missing, Mayburn went above and beyond to help me. I wouldn't let him down.

I looked at my watch. I had time before I had to punch the clock, and there was someone I suddenly very much wanted to see. As we passed Division, I turned to Q. "I need to see my mom."

Victoria McNeil and I didn't have the symbiotic relationship that some mothers and daughters did. She was beautiful in a willowy, reserved, strawberry-blond kind of way, a way that radiated both melancholy and mystery, while I was simply brassy and flashy. She spoke quietly, gracefully, and only when her words were necessary, so we weren't exactly kindred spirits.

I'd found out a lot about my mom in the recent year, skeletons she never thought another living soul would see. Those secrets had initially separated us, but oddly, over the last few months as we tentatively dipped our toes back in the waters of our relationship, the secrets had bonded us. We never spoke of them, but the fact that I knew, and that I wasn't judging her for them, brought us closer.

That recent bond was one of the reasons I wanted to see her. The other was that no matter how old you are, sometimes you just need your mom.

The cab pulled up in front of her house on State Street, the one she shared with Spencer, her real estate developer husband. Their turn-of-the-century graystone near the corner of Goethe Street was tall and graceful with a large arched front door. Lights were on inside.

"If it's okay, I'm coming with you," Q said.

I smiled at him. "Absolutely. I miss seeing you every day."

We hadn't even rung the bell before the door opened. There was my mom, beautiful in cream slacks and a silver raw-silk blouse. "Hi, Boo," she said.

It was a nickname given to me by my father. After he

died, my mother started using it, as if it kept him a little bit alive.

"How was the memorial?" she asked.

I had called her a few hours ago and told her the whole story—finding Jane yesterday, anchoring Trial TV and the fact that the memorial was this afternoon.

"Sad," I answered. "Awful."

"Oh, baby." She looked over my head. "Hi, Q."

"Hi, Victoria."

My mother stepped back, and the sound of jazz from inside her house trickled out and enveloped me, relaxing me. I moved inside, and she pulled me into her arms, stroked my hair.

Their front living room was wide with ivory couches and subdued oriental rugs over big-planked, glossy wood floors. It was a beautiful room, but my mother, who suffered bouts of depression, didn't like how it grew dark in the late afternoon. And so when the living room fell into shadow, like now, everyone headed for the back of the house. By the time my mother and I pulled apart, I could hear Q already in the kitchen, talking with Spence and someone else.

My mother led me to the kitchen. "Sheets!" I said, seeing my brother.

"Hey, Iz." He hugged me.

Spence, my sweet stepfather, did the same. He was a pleasant-looking man with brown hair streaked with gray. At least that's how I always thought of him, but I looked closer now and noticed that his hair was mostly white. Funny how people close to you can grow older without you ever noticing.

"C'mere, darling girl." Spence wore khaki pants and a white shirt over his barrel chest. He guided me toward the round breakfast nook built into a paneled bay window.

On the table was a plate of prosciutto, dried fruit and a parmesan-type cheese next to a half-full bottle of red. Spence and my mom were old school—the cocktails and snacks always came out at five sharp, especially now that Spence was mostly retired. But the red wine, I was sure, was courtesy of my brother, who thought that life should be spent sipping a glass of Barolo or Bordeaux or Merlot.

Charlie poured a glass for Q, then started to pour one for me.

I held out my hand. "I can't. I already had one today at the memorial, and I have to work tonight at the lingerie store."

My mom gave me a disapproving glance. "You're going to run yourself into the ground, Izzy."

"I took this job, and I promised to be there." My promise, and my loyalty, were to Mayburn, not the store, but I left that unsaid.

"But you don't need this job at the store now," my mom said. "You've got Trial TV. You're an *anchor*."

"I'm just the fill-in anchor." The truth was, once the flop sweating had stopped, and despite the way I'd gotten the job, I loved it. Somewhere over the course of the day, a tiny, furtive hope had grown that they might keep me on in that position.

We tucked ourselves into the breakfast nook, the others sipping their wine.

Charlie studied me. "Not doing so good, huh?"

"Nope."

I told them about Zac being so weird around me at the memorial, so suspicious.

"I don't know what to do or what to think," I admitted. "He even said he thought Jane and I were together, like a couple, last weekend. He told the police that."

"Whoa." Charlie made a face.

Spence waved a hand. "Hey, this is the Chicago PD. They're not going to be swayed by the outlandish statements of a grief-stricken husband."

"But what if they are? The detective, this guy named Vaughn, already seems to dislike me and be suspicious of me for some reason."

Spence shook his head. "You know I'm friends with the police chief, right? Went to school with him. I've got his cell. I'll call him right now and find out the story. I'm sure there's nothing to worry about."

"You don't have to do that." But my protest was weak. The situation with Jane's death was starting to feel as if it was twisting out of control and just beyond my grasp.

"Call him, Spence," my mother said in her smooth voice.

Spence rubbed his hands together, then pulled his cell phone out of his pocket. Spence was the kind of guy who loved a good task. He'd started his own company—real estate developing—when he was young. He'd grown it into a successful business that now provided consulting for developments around the country. The company had been bought by a larger one, and then another company, and slowly Spence had stepped out, becoming mostly a figurehead. He was happy being retired, being wealthy, but if you gave him a good task that had immediacy to it, especially one for Charlie or me, he was giddy.

Spence got out of the banquette, dialing his cell phone. A second later, he was booming into it. "George! Spence Calloway calling. How are you?"

He moved into the living room, his voice trailing off. I asked Charlie how his back was doing.

"Hurts all the time," he said cheerfully.

Charlie had been seriously injured in an accident involving a construction truck shortly after he graduated from college. He was still in physical therapy and still living off the comp settlement, which he viewed, with his bizarrely optimistic attitude, as a lucky break. He had this innate belief that life would work out, one way or another, and it wasn't worth worrying about. So the back injury, which physically troubled him all the time, wasn't seen as something to stress over.

We talked about Charlie's current physical therapy regimen. I asked my mom about the Victoria Project, a charity she had started. Q asked her if he could volunteer, since he had time on his hands now. When Spence came back in the room, we were having a moment that felt blessedly normal, a moment filled with family chat.

And so it wasn't until my mother stopped talking and instead looked at her husband with a concerned expression that we all stopped.

"Spence?" she said. "Is everything all right?"

Spence gave me a painful look, one of those looks that said, *This is going to hurt.* "George knew the case, of course," he said. "Knew you." He pointed with his head in my direction. He didn't say anything for a second.

"And?" my mother prompted.

"He said you'll be hearing from them soon." Another pause during which I could hear the passing *whoosh* of a car on the street, the scrape of a tree branch along the side of the house. "You've been named a person of interest."

34

Mick Grenier sat at his desk, staring at the photos of Jane, the news clippings, the notes he'd made.

He arranged the photos on his desktop in a vertical row, starting at the top with photos where Jane appeared youngest. The photos climbed down his desk—Jane over the passage of time, her stunning looks surviving that journey well.

He had left the memorial abruptly. It had been harder than he thought. He would miss Jane Augustine. He hadn't imagined that would be the case. If you had told him what was going to happen and asked him if he would care that she was gone, he would have said no. He would have looked at the situation calmly, in a cool, detached way (the ability to do so was one worthwhile thing his father had taught him), and he would have said that her death could only be good for him. He still believed that to be true, but staring at the pictures, he had to admit that he'd gotten somewhat emotionally involved.

He placed the final photo on his desk. It was a head shot that Trial TV sent out with its press kit. In the photo, she wore the red scarf.

Jane had also worn the scarf in the photo that appeared in *Chicago Magazine*. He found that article and placed it at the bottom of a new row. Moving upward, he created another vertical row, this time of news clippings, oldest at the top. One more row then—his notes about Jane. He always dated his notes, so it was easy enough to put those in order.

His father, Beaumont Grenier, the novelist, would have hated the project he was working on. Mick's father particularly despised "celebrity journalism," which, when Mick looked back on it, was probably why he had worked for a celebrity magazine in L.A. after college.

He didn't know exactly why he had always wanted to be different from his father. Maybe it was just typical kid stuff, or maybe it was because his father was in love only with his work, and he never pretended otherwise, not to his wife, not to his kids. Taking the celeb magazine job to spite his father was surely a large part of the reason Mick did it, but as with everything in life, it had a cause and effect.

Because of that celebrity magazine, Mick ended up having a quickie marriage to an actress he fell in love with. And it was because that actress shot a film in Chicago for a couple of months that he moved there with her. The marriage didn't survive the two months, but Mick got his first book out of it—a tell-all about the ex. And Mick got Chicago, too, which he liked a lot more than the East Coast and a hell of a lot more than L.A. He found it honest and unpretentious.

So he'd stayed, and so it was really all because of his father that he was in Chicago. And if he looked at it now, his latest project was yet another attempt to distinguish himself from Beaumont Grenier. He was a different kind of creative than his father. Reality was his medium. People today were crazier, more fucked up, than any character a mere novelist like his father could create. And it was pure skill to be able to use that reality—all the pretty, gory truth of it—to tell the perfect story; to edit out the commonplace and spit-shine the salacious.

He paused now and looked at the grid of information he'd created about Jane Augustine. This grid was always what he did when he was nearing the end of a research period. This time it was different, of course. This time his subject was dead.

35

The doorbell rang. Hearing it, my mother stood. "That's Maggie," she said.

If I'd been a jealous person, I might have been envious of my mother's absolute adoration of my friend Maggie. She was delighted by her, charmed by her and impressed with the fact that Maggie was a criminal defense lawyer—a tiny, sweet girl who rumbled with the scary kids and held her own.

As soon as Spence delivered his news that I was a "person of interest," my mother had opened her eyes wide and murmured, "We must call Maggie."

As luck would have it, Maggie and her sort-of boyfriend, Wyatt, had been on their way to drinks and dinner downtown and agreed to stop by.

"Let's adjourn to the living room," my mother said. "There's no room in here for all of us." She really did like Maggie if she was suggesting the living room.

We trooped through the kitchen and dining room, my mother turning on bright lights along the way.

Maggie opened the front door on her own, calling, "Anybody home?" Her wavy, light brown hair with its natural streaks of gold swung away from her face.

My mother, so much taller than Maggie's short, little frame, swooped her into a hug.

Maggie introduced Wyatt to everyone. He was an undeniably handsome guy in his midforties, almost fifteen years older than Maggie, and a high-ranking exec at a biotech firm. The two originally met when Maggie was in law school, back when she thought she should choose an area of law different from her grandfather, a famous prosecutor turned defense lawyer. Even though she had no apparent affinity for it, she picked labor and employment work. She got a summer associate position at a big firm, and there she met one of the firm's clients, Wyatt Bluestone, who was getting sued for sexual harassment. Maggie was asked to conduct the intake interviews with Wyatt, and so they had to spend a fair amount of time together. He told her what a bunch of crap the claim was. He talked to her about how hard it was to be in his position and to bring your employees along without crossing any lines. Maggie believed him, and they started dating.

They were together for seven months back then. Wyatt was charismatic, but I never trusted him. And yet Maggie was in love. Finally, though, she began to realize that they spent all their time at restaurants eating fabulous dinners or in his bed having fabulous sex. While this wasn't necessarily bad, it became clear that Wyatt wasn't interested in spending time with her friends and family, nor was he interested in introducing her to his. One day, Maggie went to his place in the middle of the day to retrieve the cell phone she'd left there, and she found him having sex with his assistant. It hit her then that the sexual harassment thing was probably true. It hit her that, as one of Wyatt's attorneys, *she* might have a claim against him. Technically, his assistant certainly did. Technically, Maggie was heartbroken. After that, I had spent many nights watching Maggie cry into a large glass of vodka to get her through the breakup with Wyatt.

But now Wyatt was back. They'd reconnected on Facebook. He was older but still gorgeous—a full head of black hair, big shoulders cloaked with only the most expensive designer clothes.

I shook his hand. "Good to see you." I tried hard to sound genuine.

Maggie swore that she wasn't being stupid. She swore Wyatt had changed his dastardly ways. And as they took a seat on my mother's silk couch, with the streetlights through the front window making halos around their heads, I had to admit that Wyatt seemed more devoted, more calm. He helped Maggie off with her coat; he stroked her arm; he smiled while looking deeply into her eyes.

I was dying to ask Maggie what I was supposed to do now that I was a person of interest, but my mother believed strongly in small talk before anything else. "Where are you two going to dinner?" she asked, settling onto an ivory-colored chair.

"Les Nomades," Wyatt said.

"Les Nomades on a Tuesday?" My mother was clearly impressed.

"I'm friends with the head chef."

Maggie and I exchanged looks. Her eyes said, *Please shut up. Please don't even think it.*

What I was thinking was what I'd told Maggie once— that Wyatt was allegedly friends with *everyone*. If you said you were going to a bar, it was likely Wyatt would tell you he was tight with the manager. If you mentioned a Cubs game, he was buddies with the first baseman.

Les Nomades was a French restaurant, one of the fanciest in the city. The fact that Wyatt and Maggie were headed there reminded me of the Wyatt of old—all the snazzy restaurants and the glitzy nights out—and yet the fact that he was here, that he'd veered away from his evening plans to bring his girlfriend to see her train-wreck best friend and her family, was promising.

My mother told a brief story about the last time she had been at Les Nomades. Q described a disastrous date he'd had there once, and then my mom segued into the topic at hand. "We need your help, Maggie. Spence just had a disturbing phone conference with the chief of police."

Spence, his brow furrowed, related his conversation. After being on the anchor desk all morning, I found it a balm to let someone else do the talking. Spence finished with, "He says Izzy has been named as a person of interest."

Maggie made a disapproving tsk.

"What do you think?" I said.

"I think that "person of interest" is bullshit. On one hand, it doesn't mean anything except that the cops have some *Law and Order*–style hunch about you, but they don't want to call you a suspect and risk a lawsuit. The term has no legal significance."

"Seriously?" I felt optimism trickle into the room. "That's good, right?"

"In a sense, yes. It doesn't even mean you're a witness. All it means is that you're someone the police want to talk to again. The problem is that if it leaks out, the media will pick it up and splash it everywhere. Your reputation could be damaged forever. Think about Richard Jewell, the guy who was a person of interest in the Olympic bombings in the '90s. They dragged that guy through the mud."

"The Chicago police haven't announced this yet," Spence said.

"That just means they don't think they need help from the community right now."

"There must be a way to stop the police from mentioning it in the future," my mom said.

Maggie shrugged. "They do what they want to do."

My mother leaned forward. "Certainly, we can do *something*. Izzy has been through enough. This person of interest thing is ridiculous, and I won't have her go through hell for the whims of the cops. I won't have her name tarnished by this."

I blinked, looking at my mom. Her protective, den-mother attitude was not something she showed often. Even though she was a restrained person, she was someone who exuded energy, who made everyone want to be close to her.

But her depression had led her to spend most of my child-hood in pajamas, silently wandering the house, her thin frame like a mannequin I'd seen in the windows of Marshall Field's.

"All right, let's think of something…" Maggie glanced around the room. "Let's really think about this…." You could tell she was excited by the way her eyes darted past all of our faces and then back again. This was the same way Maggie looked at a jury when a closing argument really started to roll—as if she was letting every one of them in on a secret.

"The cops don't usually make deals," Maggie said, "and I wouldn't normally suggest you talk to them, because we have a little history with forced confessions in this town. But I'm thinking that I can call in some favors. We could tell them you'll agree to be questioned, as long as they keep it quiet."

"Izzy is a lawyer," my mom said. "She can handle being questioned. And you would be with her, right, Maggie?"

"Of course." Maggie nodded. "Let's just think about this some more, and see what happens. I'll put in some calls tomorrow and see if I can find out anything."

My mother gave a small exhale of relief. "Thank you, Maggie. Thank you."

When I walked Maggie and Wyatt to the door, Maggie pulled me aside. "How are you doing with all this? I mean losing Jane, finding her."

"I'm messed up."

"I can't imagine." She shook her head.

I gestured at Wyatt. "How's it going?"

A sweet grin turned up her mouth. "It's great. It's sexy."

"It was always sexy, right?"

She made a sound of exasperation. "Please, don't judge him because of last time. We're good. *I'm* good."

"Okay. No judging." It was the least I could do. "And hey," I said, "if you need any lingerie, let me know. I have to work at the store tonight."

She scoffed. "You're the lingerie girl, not me. I can barely muster up something other than my cotton undies to go out with him."

"I've got something to get you out of those old cotton scraps." I whispered to her about the pearl thong.

When I pulled away, her eyes were wide, her mouth O-shaped. "Where can I get it?"

"I'll get you one tonight."

A half hour later I was off to peddle some panties.

36

I took a cab to my place to get my Vespa, the only thing I could think of that might clear my head. But as I drove down Sedgwick toward the Fig Leaf, the cool air, instead of being invigorating, only made me shiver. Or maybe it was the phrase that kept circling my mind. *Person of interest.* *Person of interest.* I tried to focus on tonight. On the job that I had to do—pretending I was someone named Lexi Hammond, a law student who worked part-time in a lingerie store.

In the last year alone, I'd been a lawyer, a fiancée, a jilted lover, a mourner, a broadcaster, a moonlighting P.I., a witness. And now a person of interest. It made me feel fragmented, all parts entirely separate, almost ephemeral.

But then I remembered Forester. He had given me a mountain of legal work for reasons no one understood at first. And even though I now understood more why he'd done it, none of it changed the fact that he had believed utterly in me. Sometimes remembering that was just the kick in the ass I needed. It made me pull hard on the gas. It got me there with five minutes to spare.

But I pulled over a block away and called Mayburn. "What if the manager, Josie, has seen me on Trial TV?"

"She seem like the type to watch a legal channel?"

"No."

"Any PR on you yet?"

"No."

"Then I'd say it's fine. Just watch her in case she's look-ing at you suspiciously."

"She looks at everyone suspiciously."

"You know what I mean. And hopefully I just need you for a week or two more."

The door to the Fig Leaf chimed when I walked in a minute later. Josie was behind the counter, squinting at her faux-antique register, a pen tucked behind her bobbed hair. She peered over her glasses at me, but said nothing.

"Hi!" I hurried through the store. There was nothing that made me try harder than someone who clearly didn't like me.

But then Josie surprised me. "I'm glad you're here," she said, although without changing her bland expression. "We've got a bride and a pack of bridesmaids coming in an hour. The bride wants everyone to wear matching under-wear."

I unbuttoned my coat. "Are you serious?"

"Can you believe that? She's actually making everyone wear the same bras and the same panties."

"What a Nazi."

"I know." I saw the first full and genuine smile ever from Josie. "I can't handle it," she said. "I need you to help them."

"Sure."

"Thanks." The smile disappeared. "I got dumped last year by the guy I thought I was going to marry."

Suddenly, I truly wanted to make her feel better. I couldn't offer up my exact story. *My fiancé took off, and he allegedly stole a bunch of money from my client, who was also my father figure.* But I sure as hell could talk generally about it. And convincingly.

"I was engaged," I said. "He left town two months before our wedding."

She took off the glasses. "Are you freaking kidding me?" She sounded oddly excited.

"Yep. Had the dress, the hall, the ring." I looked at my hand and didn't have an ounce of trouble mustering up a sigh. "I miss that ring."

"Holy shit." Her tone was full of grudging admiration.

I shrugged. "These things happen for a reason." Best to get off this topic before it depressed me more than I already was.

"Yeah, well…" She turned back toward the register. "If these things happen for a reason, the reason in my case is my ex is a self-righteous, pigheaded child with mommy issues."

I laughed, then went into the back room to hang up my coat. I looked around the other storerooms, finding most of them piled with boxes of product. If Josie was up to something, as the owner thought she was, it was not a failure to stock the store.

Josie came in back. She gestured at the boxes. "Until the Nazi bride and her SS officers get here I need you to unpack this. I try to schedule all our deliveries for Tuesday, and we got a ton today."

"No problem." Then I thought of Maggie. "Oh, and can I get a pearl thong for my friend?"

Josie stopped and studied me with an expression I couldn't read. "Did you try yours?"

I blushed a little. "Yeah."

"Hot, huh?"

"That's an understatement."

She grinned. "What size is your girlfriend?"

"Small. Or extra small. About the size of that girl, Nina, the other night."

Josie pulled out a step stool and used it to reach a metal box on a high shelf. She took keys from a ring in her pocket and unlocked the box. "I keep the thongs in here because they're so expensive."

They weren't more expensive than some of the peignoirs she carried, and those weren't locked up, but I said nothing.

Josie reached in and drew out a silver box, the same as she'd given me the other night. I started to say that I thought she only had size smalls in black. That was what she had said the other day to her customer, Nina. But maybe she'd gotten more stock today. And it didn't sound as if Maggie cared what color it was.

Josie handed the box to me. "I can't give you the discount on that since it's for your friend. Now, get to work on this stock, okay? It's all got to be on the floor by the end of the night."

For the next hour, I sliced cardboard with a box cutter, I steamed, I hung, I tagged. At first, I found the work soothing. I ran my finger over purple velvet straps as I smoothed them; I stopped and appreciated the embroidered swirls on pieces of slick silk. After each item was hung, I had to find it on a list of expected inventory that Josie had prepared. I had to note the price and then create a handwritten ticket on a small linen card. The card was then threaded with yellow ribbon and attached to the garment.

I knew Mayburn needed information about the products and the pricing to determine whether Josie was involved in anything shady. I looked over my shoulder to make sure Josie was still in the front, took a notebook out of my purse and then scribbled as fast as I could the names of lingerie items, the makers, the cost, the markup.

I heard the front door chime once or twice, followed by the sound of Josie's voice greeting a customer, the murmur of conversation as she helped them.

But now the door chimed again and the store was soon filled with the loud chatter of women who had obviously stopped for drinks on their way over. The bridal party, I thought. I straightened my suit and headed out of the back room.

There were eight women buzzing about the place, all shrieking and pointing and holding up negligees. Their joy was palpable and innocent, and I felt a kind of envy I hadn't experienced before—a feeling that I might never again have such unencumbered joy.

I'm the same Izzy I always was, I told myself. But as I stood in the doorway, gazing at a bunch of women a few years younger than me, I knew that no matter what happened from here on—with the cops, with Jane's death, with Trial TV, with Sam, with Theo, with Grady—I was different because of what I'd done and seen over the last year; because of what I'd done and seen over the last week.

Still, I was there for a job. I put on my anchorwoman face—the calm, confident one that I'd learned from watching Jane—and I began to walk toward the pack of women.

But then I froze. I could tell who the bride was now— she was at the center of a knot of women who were holding out every piece of white lingerie we had. "Look at this one!" they were saying. "No, this one is perfect!"

The bride laughed and swung around, gazing at everything with big eyes. "I can't decide, you guys. My wedding night will be the most important night of my life."

Josie stood to the side, and I could see her hiding a grimace. She turned and looked at me, giving me a glance that said, *Can you believe this piece of work?*

The good employee in me wanted to charge in and take over, helping the bride the way I'd been asked to do. But there was one very big problem. I knew the bride. I knew the asymmetrical cut of her shiny black hair. It was Faith Lowe, the producer from Trial TV.

37

Josie found me in the back, furiously steaming cashmere pajamas, trying to hide behind a cloud of vapor.

"What do you think you're doing?" she said in a fierce whisper. "I need you out there."

I struggled for something to say. I couldn't exactly tell her that I knew Faith from Trial TV.

"I know that girl," I said.

"Who?"

"Faith. The bride. She's a lawyer, right?" I remembered that Jane told me Faith was one of the Trial TV employees who also had legal experience.

"I don't know," Josie said, irritated. "I'm just trying to sell her a lot of merchandise, and I told you to handle her. *I* run this store, Lexi."

"I know." I bit my lip, trying to come up with something to sway her, some reason I could stay hidden in the back. I quickly reviewed all my dealings with Josie. The only time I'd seen her frosty exterior melt even a little bit was earlier tonight when I'd told her about my fiancé taking off.

"She's the one," I said, at the same time sending a silent apology to Faith for the fact that I was about to trash her name.

"The one what?"

"The one who my fiancé was involved with when he dumped me."

Josie drew in a quick breath. "Are you serious?" But then she made a face. "I thought you said he left town."

"He did. With her."

A gasp. "So she's here because she's about to marry *your* fiancé?"

Hmm. Tricky. "Well, no. She dumped my fiancé and then she got with someone else. So really she broke two hearts."

"The bitch!"

"I know." *Sorry, Faith.* "So, I really can't help her."

Josie huffed and looked at me sympathetically. "*Of course* you can't."

I gestured at the stock. "I'm going to get all this done, though."

Josie nodded. "I'll handle the bridal party." She grunted. "And all those negligees that were on sale up front? They are *not* on sale any longer. Not for that girl."

"Thanks, Josie." I felt the first bond with her, and then guilt for having engineered it.

She stomped back to the front, and I could hear her addressing Faith in a saccharine voice.

I pulled the notebook from my purse again and wrote for Mayburn, *Will raise prices when doesn't like a customer.* Then I went back to work on the stock, attacking it with a vengeance, determined, at least, to do a good job for Josie.

A minute later—*bam, bam, bam*—a knock came from the door that led to the alley.

There was a little window cut into the door. I peered out and saw a guy in a black baseball cap holding a large cardboard box, almost like a big pizza box. Behind him was a white van. More stock?

I was about to open the door, when Josie rushed into the back room. "Got it," she said breathlessly.

She opened the door. "Hey, Steve."

Steve, a mean-looking guy with black oily hair and a meager beard, grunted and held out the cardboard box. He stopped short for a second when he saw me. He dragged his eyes up and down my body, smiled slightly. He was probably my age, in his late twenties, but he was one of those people who looked as if life had treated him hard. Or maybe *he* had treated life hard.

"This is my new clerk," Josie said.

Steve nodded, leered in my direction.

Josie took the box and held the door open so he could leave. But Steve wasn't moving. He was still staring at me, a weird, twisted kind of smirk on his face.

"Thanks, Steve." Josie's words were loud. "See you later." She shut the door so he had no choice but to step back. When he was outside, she locked it. Then she opened the box. Inside were smaller black boxes, like the one she'd sold to Nina a few days ago.

"More pearl thongs?" I said.

"Yeah."

"If you want to give me the key, I'll put them up there." I gestured to the locked box on the high shelf. "That way you can get back out front."

"No, I've got it." She sighed. "That evil woman has her girls trying on fifteen different nude bras. They're never going to get out of here."

Out came the step stool and the keys. She quickly arranged the pearl-thong boxes in the lockbox, tucked her keys in her pocket and then shot back into the front room.

I stood there for a moment, thinking. Why not just let me take the delivery of the pearl thongs? Why not let me put them away? She trusted me with the rest of the merchandise, even the more pricey pieces. And then there was the fact that she kept the thongs locked up.

I hustled to the back door and peered through the window. Steve was sitting in his van, using his steering wheel as a writing desk, making some kind of notation. Then he started the van and pulled down the alley. I opened the door and watched his taillights trail away in the dark night. He kept heading down the alleyway, clearly one of those Chicagoans who knew how to avoid the traffic on the main streets. Just like I did.

My scooter was sitting right there. I watched that van, still making its way down the long alley that ran perpendicular to Racine Avenue.

I thought of what Mayburn had told me when he'd gotten me on this case. *Pay attention to everything. Pay attention to anything that seems off. Even a little bit. I just need you to collect the pieces.*

And then I thought of another thing Mayburn had said to me—*Don't plan. Improvise.*

I rushed to my coat and put it on with my helmet. Then I grabbed my scooter keys and phone from my purse and tucked them in a pocket. It sounded as though Josie would be with Faith and her friends for at least another fifteen to twenty minutes, maybe longer.

I opened the back door and wedged a small piece of Styrofoam into the base of it, then I jumped on my scooter and followed the van.

38

I saw the van's lights—at least I hoped it was the van—nearly two blocks ahead of me, still in the alley. I pulled back on the gas, trying to catch up.

I decided I would tail the van for just a little while, to see where it went. It would be a piece I could collect for Mayburn.

A barely there spring rain dotted the visor of my helmet with mist. *Be careful,* I told myself. Scooters were the fastest way to get around the city, but they didn't take well to bad weather.

I gained on the van, coming within a block of it, then only half a block, so I could almost make out the license plate. Z2…There were four more characters, but I couldn't read them. As gently as possible, I pulled back harder on the gas.

But just then the van reached Armitage Avenue and turned right. By the time I caught up, three cars were between us. I curved around one of them at a stop sign and kept an eye on the van. It went left at Racine, where Armitage dead-ended, then took a quick right where Armitage started again. I followed him on the bridge over the Chicago River, the grates of the metal making my scooter feel wobbly, the slick rain not helping.

Once over the bridge, the car in front of me turned, and I could see the van under the streetlights. I tried again to see the plate number, but the misting rain obscured my view.

When the van turned onto Cortland Avenue and I followed, the third car continued onward, removing the barrier between me and Steve, whoever he was. I pulled over to the side of the road, putting a little distance between us, then resumed following him. The van made its way through Wicker Park, taking a few turns and finally heading into another alley.

I slowed, waited, then turned down the alley myself. *Damn*. It was gone.

I zipped down the alley, my eyes scanning either side. Nothing. The houses here were a mix of brick three-flat apartments and older bungalows, all with garages behind them.

I was about to turn around and head back to the store, when I saw it. About a block down the alley, behind a tan-painted bungalow, the van was parked next to a garage. I sped toward it. As I reached it, the van's interior lights suddenly went on, and Steve got out of the driver's seat. He looked at the scooter as it passed, and it seemed he stared right through the visor of my helmet.

I looked away, and pulled back hard on the gas, causing my back tire to fishtail a little.

Half a block later, I stopped and glanced behind me. No sign of Steve. I parked in an empty spot by a garage. A sign on the garage screamed *No Parking!!!!*, replete with small print practically threatening a gangland-style shooting. I parked there anyway, squinting at my watch. I'd been gone eight minutes. I could only spare a few more before I had to hightail it back to the store.

I got off the Vespa and peered around the garage.

The alley here was darker than those in Lincoln Park. Only one streetlight blinked anemically. The rain began to fall harder, making a soft but ominous rattle on my helmet. I tucked my hair under the collar of my coat, but left the helmet on. Walking around, I must have looked like a Martian. The helmet killed my peripheral vision, but it protected me from the rain and from being identified.

I tiptoed in my high heels toward the van. Between the shoes and my black suit, I wasn't able to move fast. Which gave me enough time to wonder what on earth I was doing. Why was I tailing a van and creeping around an alley for a part-time job? Was this really what I was supposed to be doing with my life? Not to mention the fact that a friend of mine had died—had been *murdered*—and I found her. I could sense layers upon layers of sorrow and fatigue, bewilderment and shock, deep inside me. Why wasn't I tuning into those and just falling apart? Why wasn't I telling Mayburn I couldn't possibly work at a lingerie store and sneak around at night, looking for who knew what?

But I kept tiptoeing, and as I did, I came upon the answer. I didn't want to tap in to those emotions that lay heavy inside me. I didn't want to sink into them and let them overwhelm me. And so, going on with everyday life, despite its absurdity, felt good. It felt exciting, even, and I liked that excitement a hell of a lot more than those intimidating emotions.

When I got to Steve's van, I saw that the garage he had parked next to was lit up now, while the house in front of it was dark. It seemed clear he'd gone in the garage, which was big enough to hold two cars. I wondered why he wouldn't use it to park the van. But then maybe multiple tenants lived in the house, sharing the garage?

Whatever was in the garage, though, couldn't be seen from the alley. All the windows were covered with newspaper. I tiptoed around the entire structure. Two small windows on either side of the stand-alone garage. All four blocked out. I stood still, listening, but there were no sounds from within. Maybe he lived there? A garage apartment?

I glanced at my watch. I'd been gone ten minutes. I had to get back. I looked around for the address, then memorized it for Mayburn.

As a last ditch-effort, I tried to study the newsprint in one of the windows. Maybe the date on the papers would tell

Mayburn something. We'd know, at least, how long ago Steve had hung them there. It seemed a miniscule bit of information, but I came back again to Mayburn's persistent metaphor about investigations being made up of puzzle pieces.

I couldn't quite see the date on the newspaper, so I took out my cell phone and flipped it open so the light came on. I held it up to the newspaper—the *Chicago Tribune,* dated about one year ago.

Then I noticed something. I slipped my phone back in my pocket and bent down. There was a small space, maybe half a centimeter wide, at the bottom of the window that the newspaper didn't cover.

I peered through the space, making out a wooden bench of some sort. There were materials strewn across it. Was this where the pearl thongs were made? Suddenly, I worried about the cleanliness of the one I'd worn.

Wham! I felt a smack on the side of my helmet. It caught me off guard, pitching me forward.

The helmet cracked hard against the side of the garage, my head rattling around inside, and I fell to my knees.

39

Detective Vaughn walked the hallway at the Belmont police station. Everyone hated when he did this—paced the halls—but he wasn't a sitter. He couldn't just sit and ponder like some detectives; he needed to be moving. Plus, the area around the station wasn't the most scenic, to say the least, certainly not at night. The problem was that all he had to ponder on this case, at least right now was supposition and gut feelings.

Like the one he had about Izzy McNeil. He hadn't liked her when he first met her—after her fiancé took off. He couldn't say why, because he got the feeling that just about *everyone* liked Izzy McNeil. Which might have been why he didn't like her. It irritated him to no end when beautiful women had everything handed to them, and from what he could tell that's exactly what had happened with her. That Forester Pickett had given her all her work and now she'd somehow landed a network news job. People like that frustrated someone like him, to whom nothing had been easy—not his mom's death when he was twelve, or his dad's three months later; not the series of foster homes he got shuffled around to; not the five years it took him to graduate high school; not the five years it took him to get into the CPD police academy; not the nights he'd worked as a bouncer at a bar on Division while going to the academy; not the decade that it had taken him to rise to the rank of detective.

But then again, now that he was here, Vaughn was a good detective because he knew that gut instincts, while often right, weren't everything, and he knew that just because he didn't like someone like Izzy McNeil didn't mean she was a perpetrator. There was just something off about this Jane Augustine case, and his questions kept circling back to McNeil, the time the two had spent before Jane's death, the way she'd slipped right into her "friend's" anchor chair not even twenty-four hours after her death. Then there was the fact that just six months ago, her fiancé took off with thirty million dollars' worth of her boss's property, and she'd claimed not to be involved then, as well. It was too coincidental. And he didn't believe in coincidences.

"Hey, Vaughn!"

He stopped pacing and looked up the hall to see Erin Cutter, the forensics person on the Augustine case. He'd specifically asked for her because she was the best. She never acted on gut instinct or supposition, and the way things were going for Chicago detectives these days—with accusations flying around about forced confessions and arrests without probable cause—he needed Cutter's hard-core factual approach to balance his own.

Back in the day, Vaughn used to be able to roll with his gut instincts in this job. Maybe pull in a witness, maybe scare the shit of him, maybe ice him for a while by letting him sit for a day or four in a windowless room. But now, ever since a few detectives had taken it too far, they'd fucked it up for the rest of them. And so Vaughn needed people like Cutter to make sure that he had the backup he required to roll with those gut instincts. Or to get him rolling in another direction.

Cutter came bustling down the hall at him. She was Northern Irish, with white skin and black hair, and she did the bustling thing really well. The skirt of the suit she wore, an olive-green one he'd seen at least fifty times, swished against her legs as she came toward him.

"You got the lab report?" he asked her.

She grinned. "You'll have it this afternoon."

"Christ, you're the best."

DNA lab reports on the average murder case took at least a week, often much longer, but when you had a high-profile case like Augustine's, and a ballbuster like Cutter, you might be able to get it in a day or two.

She stopped when she reached him. "I hope you've got something to show for making me rush it."

He gave her a wicked grin. "*You've* definitely got something to show."

She punched him in the shoulder. They laughed. Both of them were married, and neither fooled around on the side, but this was the way they worked.

"This case is fucked up," he said. "I can feel it. You did DNA sequencing for the bedroom fluids, right?"

"Right," Cutter said. "Full results aren't back yet, but when the ET took the samples, they were wet. Augustine had sex the day she was killed."

"The day her husband was supposedly out of town," Vaughn mused.

"You know what Nietzsche said about cheating?"

"God, I love a woman who quotes Nietzsche."

She smacked him again, but he wasn't kidding. He and his wife had gone stale years ago. He'd never been unfaithful, but he'd thought about it. A lot. And if he were to stray, it would be with someone like Cutter, someone both sexy and smart as hell.

"Let's see, how does that quote go?" Cutter screwed up her face and looked at the ceiling as if reading the quotation there. "I remember now." She looked back at him. "The quality of a marriage is proven by its ability to tolerate an occasional exception."

"You think that's true?" Cutter had just had her third kid six months ago. From what he could tell she was one of the lucky ones who enjoyed marriage and kids.

"I wouldn't know. And I hope I never have to test the theory."

Cutter turned and swished down the hallway, while Vaughn headed toward his desk, his thoughts soon returning to another woman. Izzy McNeil.

40

Every cell in my body went on high alert. *Get up, get up!* a voice yelled in my head.

But my terrified body wasn't reacting as fast as it normally would. Everything seemed tilted, slanted. I couldn't tell if it was the angle of the helmet or the blow to the head. My knees screamed. I felt blood trickling from them.

I sensed someone behind me, and as I looked down, trying to focus on the ground, telling myself to stand, I caught a glimpse of shoes behind me. Men's athletic shoes. I tried to notice what kind they were. I heard Mayburn telling me to take note of any details. I got to my feet, but then I felt a massive shove from behind. My hands flew out, catching myself on the garage. I sensed other blows coming. I cowered, covering my head.

"Stop!" I yelled. "I called the cops! They're already on their way." I had no idea why I was saying this, but it was the only thing I could think of.

It must have worked because suddenly the only sound was the faint trickle of rain on my helmet. I stood and spun around, the lack of peripheral vision in the helmet making me feel as if I was stoned.

Hit him back, the voice said. *Kick him.*

But no one was there.

* * *

My hands shook so much I could hardly drive the scooter. I felt the air drying the blood on my knees. Finally, I was almost back to the Fig Leaf. As fast as I could manage with my quivering hands, I headed down the alley behind the store. Luckily, the rain had stopped.

Parking the scooter and pulling off my helmet, I tried very hard not to whimper. My brain felt discombobulated. Fear rang inside me like a loud gong, steady and loud.

My hands shook as I looked at my watch. I'd been gone almost twenty minutes.

I had wanted to call Mayburn but it was hard to talk on the cell phone and drive the scooter at the same time. I had wanted to call the cops, but now that I was a person of interest, it seemed fishy somehow for me to have found a dead body and then been smacked around in an alley all in the span of twenty-four hours.

When Zac said he told the cops I'd been with Jane, I'd felt irrationally guilty. I had done nothing wrong when it came to Jane. I had done nothing wrong tonight. And yet I knew as a lawyer that little jagged pieces didn't just make up the puzzle of an investigation, they could make someone innocent look very, very suspicious.

Somehow, I would finish work, I decided, and then I would call Mayburn. And he would help me decide what to do.

As I put down the kickstand and took off my helmet, it struck me as odd that I hadn't even thought to call Sam. A short time ago, he was the only one I called with any kind of crisis—large or small. And yet now, even after the comfort he had provided last night, he wasn't my first gut response. He wasn't even the second. I looked down at my knees. They were only minimally scraped. A few streaks of blood ran from them. I licked my fingers and tried to rub it off.

I glanced at the door to the Fig Leaf. The Styrofoam was

still in there. *Thank you, God.* I pushed open the door, stepping gingerly inside.

"Where the hell did you go?" Josie stood in the center of the room, hand on her hip, angry eyes peering from behind her silver glasses.

"Um…I was going to run to Starbucks." I glanced down at the helmet in my hands. "But I came back to see if you wanted anything."

Her eyes narrowed further, then dragged down my body, stopping at my knees.

"And I fell," I added. "Accidentally."

She stalked toward me. "There is no leaving the store while you're working."

"Right. Won't happen again."

"Ever."

"Of course."

"And we don't prop open this back door. That's a security risk. Do you understand?"

"Absolutely. I'm sorry."

She was close to me now, and I could detect the smell of talcum powder and something beneath it, an exotic scent. For the first time, I noticed that her light green eyes were flecked with spots of brown.

"You're on thin ice," she said.

I wasn't sure precisely what she meant but I nodded.

"So you'd better be careful."

41

Later that night my cell phone rang. *Mayburn,* the display read.

"It's cleaned out," he said.

"What is?"

"The garage. I just went over there."

"Are you kidding me?" I padded over the wood floor of my living room in pajamas and socks.

"There's some basic stuff there, like a bench, newspapers, but nothing personal. I tracked down the owner of the place. He rents out the bungalow to a family and rented the garage on a month-by-month basis to some guy from the neighborhood."

"Is the guy named Steve?"

"He says the name he gave him was Tobias Minter. He never ran a credit check because it was just the garage and it was month to month."

"Did you look up Tobias Minter?"

"Yep, and the only one I could find with that name died in 1670." He sighed. "How's your head?"

"Killing me."

"Did you take some Advil?"

"Is ten too many?"

"You're kidding, right?"

"I wanted to take ten. I scaled it back to three."

"Are you sure you don't want to go to the hospital?"

"No, I don't think I have a concussion, just a whopping headache. There's not even a bump. The helmet saved me. Plus, I'm too tired. If I go to Northwestern, I'll be there all night, and I have to go on-air in about seven hours."

"I'm really sorry, Iz."

"Aw, don't be," I said, trying to make light of the situation. "Everybody needs to get smacked around once in a while." But really, the fear was still ringing inside me. I couldn't stop thinking about Jane. About what she'd gone through. About me being a person of interest.

I told Mayburn about it.

"Oh, Jesus Christ," Mayburn said. "A person of interest is not a good thing."

"Thank you. I think I know that."

"You gotta get the cops not to talk. They'll smear you with this stuff if you let them."

"Maggie is working on it." *Please, please, please let Maggie be able to do something.*

"When can I pick up that pearl thong you bought tonight? I want to check it out."

"Hey, no sharing Maggie's pearl thong with Lucy."

"Oh, she's going to be getting her own, trust me."

"I don't know what's with these thongs, but the odd thing is Josie seems to have two kinds—one that comes in a black box and one, like mine and Maggie's, that comes in silver boxes. I'm not sure if they're just different colors, but they seem to be from different manufacturers.

"Another odd thing is she keeps them locked up."

"And the guy who delivered them was probably the one who smacked the hell out of me."

He grunted. I could tell he was thinking. "We need to get both kinds of these thongs—the black and the silver—if I'm going to really check them out. When are you supposed to work again?"

"Sunday. But please don't make me go back there. I'm even more scared of Josie than I am of Steve. Or whoever he is." I leaned against the kitchen counter and rubbed my forehead with my hands.

"I don't know if I want you going back there, either. Look, let's take it one thing at a time. When can I get the thong you got for your friend?"

"I can bring it tomorrow to Trial TV." I gave him the address.

"Got it. Call me if you don't feel good."

"I will." Again, I thought of Sam and how I hadn't called him earlier. It bothered me deeply. I told myself I shouldn't place too much significance on it. After all, I was working on a case for Mayburn, and I'd promised him that I wouldn't tell anyone. So it was natural that I'd think to call Mayburn.

But how natural was it that when Sam had called an hour later, I told him I wanted to be alone tonight?

Despite the connection we'd had last night, and the one we'd probably always have, that connection was no longer permeating our daily lives.

Something had come between Sam and me. And that something—that feeling of a gap, a vacancy where we used to be sealed tight—couldn't be denied.

I went to bed by myself.

42

On Wednesday morning, two days after Jane's death, I sat in the studio's interview area.

"This morning for our Coffee Break," I read from the prompter, "we're discussing a recent ruling on behalf of the plaintiffs in a lawsuit against King Pharmaceuticals. King is the target of a class action suit filed by famed Chicago lawyer Jackson Prince on behalf of patients he claims were injured or killed by the arthritis drug Ladera. Yesterday, a U.S. District Court denied a request by King to dismiss the suit."

I glanced down at the written script and squeezed my knees together tight, just like C.J. told me. I heard her other instructions in my head—*shift a little toward your guest then turn your torso slightly back to the camera*. I did so, and out of the corner of my eye, I saw her giving me a thumbs-up.

I looked up at the prompter. "Joining us today is Jackson Prince himself. Good morning, Mr. Prince."

I turned my body farther to face Prince, whose slate-gray suit complemented the blue leather of the chair behind him. He looked both casual and elegant, both scholarly and handsome. "Good morning. Thanks for having me, Isabel." He beamed a megawatt smile full of perfect, white teeth.

"Can you tell us the impact of the judge's ruling?"

Prince gave a nod of his head. "Judge Wainright's ruling

will finally put an end to the stalling tactics employed by
King Pharmaceuticals, so that the many patients who died
or were harmed by their drug can be compensated." Prince
went on, describing the lawsuit and the conduct of King
Pharmaceuticals in more detail.

I nodded and smiled and occasionally furrowed my
brows at the alleged wrongdoing of King Pharmaceuticals,
but really I was thinking about Jane.

If Prince had been anxious and on guard when she had
interviewed him two days ago, he certainly wasn't now.

"He's ready," I heard in my ISB. "Go to satellite."

"Joining us via satellite," I read from the script, "is
Howard Lemmon, attorney for King Pharmaceuticals. Mr.
Lemmon, how does King respond to these allegations?" I
looked at the monitor, trying not to squint at the sharp lines
of light that beamed across the set, and watched as the
attorney gave the standard corporation-being-sued statements, similar to those I used to give when defending
Pickett Enterprises. "Thanks, Isabel. Although we believe
the motion to dismiss should have been granted, we look
forward to a trial on the merits…" Blah, blah, blah… "We
want to show America and our stockholders that we have
nothing to hide…." More blah. "We are proud of our
research and the drugs that help to save millions of lives."

I asked each lawyer a few more questions, then read,
"Stay tuned to Trial TV, where we'll be closely following
the King Pharmaceuticals lawsuit. Thanks to our guests for
joining us." I turned to a different camera. "Coming up…"
I read from the list of stories that would follow.

The monitors showing the King Pharmaceuticals attorney went blank. The lights over the leather chair grouping
went dark. Jackson Prince stood and extended his hand to
me, then grasped my hand with both of his, meeting my eyes
and smiling in a way that appeared warm and friendly.
Prince was used to connecting with people, I could tell, and
under normal circumstances, I, too, would have been

swayed by that gaze and that grasp. But there was something going on with Prince, according to Jane, something she had been about to reveal. And yet with her gone, he seemed very much at ease.

I hated, suddenly, that Jane was dead, that I was essentially standing in her shoes and yet neither Prince nor I was mentioning her.

"I saw you at Jane's memorial," I said.

Something crossed Prince's eyes. I couldn't tell what. "Ah, yes. A tragedy." He dropped my hand. "I was very fond of Jane. We had worked together for years."

"Worked together? How do you mean?" I'm not sure why, but I wondered for the first time if Prince had been one of Jane's dalliances.

"I frequently gave interviews to Jane before anyone else."

"You trusted her to cover your stories well."

"I did indeed." His eyes flicked around the newsroom. "Well, I must be going. It was a pleasure."

"Izzy," I heard C.J. call from behind me. "I need you on the desk in one minute."

"Got it," I called over my shoulder. I turned back to Prince and moved a little in front of him so he couldn't walk away. "Were you and Jane working on any stories recently? I mean, other than the King Pharmaceuticals lawsuit?"

"No, not recently. And this case has been in a holding pattern for some time. I would have called Jane about this recent ruling, but we didn't even know when the judge was going to issue it, and by then, of course, Jane was…"

"Killed."

"Yes."

Did you do it? Did you need to keep her from the story she said was going to nail you the wall?

"What was the last story you gave Jane to break?"

"Izzy," C.J. called. "Let's go."

I held up one finger and began backing toward the desk, but my eyes were still on Prince, waiting for his answer.

"I can't recall," he said. "Possibly a fire case I had at the end of last year. Anyway, good luck with your broadcast." He turned and left, but after a step or two he looked back, as if to see that I was still there. And he gave me that charming and warm smile again. One that left me cold.

43

As soon as the morning shift of Trial TV was over and the afternoon anchors and producers started taking over the set, C. J. Lyons held a meeting to recap the show and quickly summarize the stories for the next day.

When everyone left, I stopped C.J. "Can I ask a question? Do you know about a story Jane was working on that involved Jackson Prince?"

"Just this King case."

"What about the case exactly?"

"You know—the motion to dismiss, whether the lawsuit would go forward."

I frowned. It didn't seem like anything that would make Prince stalk off the set a few days ago. "What about the members of the class action and how they got to become members? On the first broadcast of Trial TV, Jane was asking Prince about that."

C.J. nodded. "I saw it. She was just asking basic questions to get the audience up and running."

I bit my lip. "It sounded like something bigger. Something involving Prince himself."

C.J. squinted a little behind her black glasses. "Prince is squeaky clean. I mean, he's at the top of his game. I can't imagine a story about him personally."

"You used to write most of Jane's stories, right?"

She nodded. "Used to. That's not how it usually works—

most newscasters write their own stories—but somehow we fell into this pattern where Jane did the interviews, but I wrote the pieces and put them together."

"Were there any stories about Prince?"

She shook her head. "But I don't know what she was working on recently." C.J. flipped her glasses up on top of her short black hair. "Now that we're on this topic, we should talk about you starting to work your own stories. Not that it's absolutely required when you're riding the anchor desk, but it would be good if you had experience pulling in your own stuff. Especially if you want to stay in this business."

I thought about this for a second. *This business* was nothing I'd ever envisioned for myself, nothing I'd ever considered even for a second. But I liked it. More than liked it. The minute-to-minute nature of it thrilled me. I loved how working in the news put me so squarely in the present, unable to think, at least for a while, about Sam, or Theo, or Zac's accusations, or even Jane.

I wondered if Jane could somehow see me now. I wanted her to be proud of me. "If Jane was working on a story about Prince, would she have taken notes?" I asked C.J.

"Sure."

"Where would those be? I'd like to pick up the stories where Jane left off. Would that be okay?"

"That's great. But we might have a problem with the notes."

"What do you mean?"

"Follow me. I'll show you her desk."

C.J. and I walked through the set. The afternoon people were scurrying around, their anticipation ramped up. We crossed through the newsroom, making our way through the obstacle course of reporter and producer desks.

Finally we came to Jane's. As lead anchor she had been allotted one of the nicer desks—large and tucked slightly behind a curving wall.

And it was a mess.

"The cops went through it last night," C.J. said. "I came here after the memorial, and they were here."

"Was it Detective Vaughn?"

"That's the guy. He's a bundle of fun, huh?"

"Yeah." I looked at Jane's desk. "Did he find anything?"

"No idea. Took a few things, like notebooks and her computer. Made me sign some chain of custody sheet. Then he left."

"Is it okay to go through it now?"

"I don't see why not. We didn't get any instructions not to touch it, and to be honest, I'd love to know if Jane had any good stories that we could finish up for her." She exhaled. "Except…"

"What?"

C.J. crossed her arms over her clipboard and glanced at the desk. "Maybe I should do it. Jane had some…well, some personal issues, and I just wouldn't want them to come to light now. You know, now that she's…"

She and I studied each other. I thought I knew what she was talking about—Jane's affairs. And her issues with Zac. I knew C.J. and Jane had been close. She probably knew about these things, but I didn't want to blow any confidences Jane had trusted me with.

"I mean…" C.J. shrugged. "I guess the cops might have taken anything like that, but in case there is something…"

"I'm just looking for stories on Prince," I said, "or other good leads Jane had. If I find anything personal, I'll…" I'll what?

C.J. shook her head. "It should be fine. Jane didn't keep diaries. She never wanted a record of her personal thoughts or actions."

Again, C.J. and I studied each other, and again, I think we both knew that we were talking about, without mentioning, Jane's affairs.

"But if you find anything," C.J. continued, "let me know, okay?"

"I will." We gazed at the handwritten notes, newspaper clippings and printouts of Web pages that littered the desk.

"Find a story if it's there," she said. "Do it for her legacy."

I spent the next four hours at Jane's desk. At first I read everything—magazine articles on a missing person's case in Tahoe, lists of people to interview in a large product liability case. But even after the cops had picked through her research, there still wasn't enough time to read it all in one sitting. Jane might not have been writing her own stories for years, but she had clearly put in a lot of work in the last few months.

I decided instead to organize piles based on topics—the Tahoe case, the product liability one, the trial of a celeb in L.A. for domestic assault. No mention of Jackson Prince. Had the cops confiscated anything like that?

I managed to shape the desktop into a field of small piles based on general topics. As I did so, I unearthed a large number of pages printed from Web sites, all of them about class action cases and how plaintiffs opted into certain lawsuits, particularly medical cases. This was the same topic Jane had been questioning Jackson Prince about. I felt a flicker of excitement as I found more and more material on the topic, most of it about how advertisements would target potential plaintiffs. But then I got frustrated. There was nothing specific about the King Pharmaceuticals case or about Prince. Again, I wondered if the cops had taken that stuff. Or maybe Jane had kept such notes in her computer. The one the cops had.

I opened the desk drawers and looked inside. In the top left drawer, I found a small photo of Jane and Zac. She was looking at him, her eyes adoring, while he was looking at the camera, his hand around her shoulder. The photo was encapsulated in a tiny red alligator frame.

I went through the other drawers, finding some cosmetics, an extra pair of shoes, some hair products, office supplies. But there was no more research. No notebooks telling me Prince had done something wrong. I decided to take home the information on class action cases and read it over.

I pulled open the drawer with office supplies, found a manila file folder and started putting the class action material in there. As I did so, I noticed some notes in Jane's handwriting on the back of one of the pages.

I turned the sheet over. Fifteen names were written there in a list, toward the bottom of the page. The first was *Carina Fariello*. The next ones were *Rick Dexter, Jerry Hay, Trace Ritson, Angela Hamilton-Wood*. The list went on.

I took it with me to the cubicle Tommy Daley assigned me on Monday. Compared to Jane's desk, it was barren except for the computer and TV monitors.

I looked up the names on the list on Google. I got nothing for Carina Fariello. I found entries for a number of different men named Rick Dexter. Jerry Hay was a physician. Same for Trace Ritson, who appeared to be a rheumatologist from South Carolina. Hamilton-Wood was also a rheumatologist. As I typed in the rest of the names, most appeared to be doctors. I found a physician locator Web site and typed in all fifteen names, one by one. With the exception of Carina Faricllo, whose name I didn't find, all were physicians. All rheumatologists.

I used the computer to look up rheumatology. *Rheumatism is a term used to describe any painful disorder affecting the loco-motor system including joints, muscles, connective tissues, and soft tissues around the joints and bones.* Basically rheumatologists, the site said, dealt frequently with arthritis and prescribed treatment for the disease—like the drug Ladera, the one made by King Pharmaceuticals.

I thought of Jane questioning Prince about whether he obtained medical records to learn if certain patients had taken the drug Ladera and, therefore, could be members of a class.

But there was nothing about Jackson Prince on this list.

I went back to Jane's desk, picked up her phone and started to dial Grady's number. Grady worked in the medical malpractice department of Baltimore & Brown, my old firm. He defended doctors and had represented some physicians as part of class action cases. He was the perfect person to ask about the topic.

But then there was the last time I'd seen Grady—at the Old Town Ale House. I felt strange now, calling only because I needed something.

Before I could decide whether to call, an intern came up to me. "Izzy, you have a visitor," he said. "Some guy named John Mayburn. He's outside."

"Thanks." I had forgotten he was coming by to pick up Maggie's pearl thong. I put it in my purse, along with my cell phone and the list of names from Jane's research.

Outside, Mayburn was standing on the cracked front sidewalk, his hands in the pockets of a leather jacket.

"I thought this was some big news outfit," he said, glancing with disdain at the building.

"Nice to see you, too. Here's your thong." I handed him the box.

"How's your head?"

"Fine. I took a couple of Advil. And I've got bigger things to worry about other than a headache." I told Mayburn about seeing Jackson Prince, about his stalking off the set a few days ago. I showed him the paper and the names I'd found in Jane's desk, which all appeared to be doctors. "The list is probably nothing. I think I'm grasping at straws. But tell me—what would you do if you'd found that list and you were working on a case like this?"

He squinted at the names. "Lots of ways you can go. I'd get all the addresses and phone numbers of everyone here and start by calling them. See if they'll talk to you. That Carina Fariello is probably a doctor, too, from the sound of it. I'd check her out." He paused. "Look, I wanted to talk to you about this person of interest thing. I was talking to Lucy and we're…well, we're kind of worried about you."

"You are?" For some reason, this struck me as unbelievably sweet.

"Well, *I'm* not worried," he said. "If I was I wouldn't have you work for me. You're a cool customer."

"I was."

"Why do you say that in the past tense?"

"You sure you're not worried about me?"

He nodded. "Maybe a little. But not because of my case or anything. We just want to know if you're all right."

"'We,' as in you and Lucy, right?"

"Yeah."

Suddenly I liked the fact that Mayburn had known me only recently. Sure, he'd met me while I was a lawyer, but in general Mayburn didn't seem to think of me as Izzy McNeil, star attorney, or Izzy McNeil, fiancée, or Izzy McNeil…anything. He just saw the Izzy I was now— tougher in some ways than she'd thought, but also struggling after the murder of a friend and the fact that she was now a "person of interest."

So, I just came out with it. "I'm afraid that if I think about it too much, I'll fall apart."

"Yeah." He nodded, like he expected that answer. "What do you usually do when you fall apart?"

"Talk to my friends. My family. Sam." There was Sam, showing up last again, even though he'd been sending texts all day—*Are you okay, Red Hot? I love you.*

"Have you done that yet?" Mayburn said. "Seen your friends and family?"

"Yesterday after the memorial. And Sam the night before."

He peered into my eyes. "Seems like you could use some more of that. Got any other friends you can talk to?"

I almost said, *I've got you, right?*

But we weren't quite there yet. And then I thought of

someone who was there. "I've got to go," I said, "but tell me. How should I check into Carina Fariello?"

"Let me copy that list. I'll run her name for you, and I'll check out the docs, too. I've got some time after I drop off this thong at the lab." He grinned. "The guys there are going to love this." He put the box under his arm, took out his phone and typed in the names from the list.

I gestured to the box. "Don't you want to check it out?"

He opened it, looked inside the tissue. "Holy mother of God."

"I know."

He looked back up at me. "Get one of these for Lucy, and give me an hour on the docs," Mayburn said.

"Got it."

He turned and left.

I looked up at the clear, sun-soaked sky. I raised my face, trying to feel a breeze that might blow off the lake. But back here, on the west side, the breeze was barely a tickle.

I thought about Mayburn's questions about seeing my friends.

Then I lifted my phone and called Grady.

44

"She finally calls," Grady said, answering.

"How are you?"

"Trying not to be wounded. You know, every other woman I date calls me too much. You never call."

"I have a decent excuse." I told him about Jane.

"Shit, Izzy. You were the one that found her?"

The blood…that scarf…Jane's lifeless eyes. "Yeah."

"What can I do?"

"Talk to me about something else for a second? Something I'm researching?"

"Shoot."

"I've got these names." I told him about finding the list among Jane's research. I read the names. "Know any of these docs?"

"I took a dep of that Ritson guy once. And I've seen Dr. Hay's name. He's a Chicago doc. So is Hamilton-Wood. She's supposed to be good."

I felt a little piece of disappointment cut into me. "So they might just be the names of expert witnesses? Like maybe on a class action case?"

"Well, probably not just one case. If they're all rheumatologists, that's too many for one case. I mean, when you're hunting for experts, you might blow through a few of them, looking for someone who will give you the right testimony."

"But in a class action case, with so many plaintiffs, wouldn't you need this many docs to testify?"

"Right. That's the point of class actions. They pool all the plaintiffs, so you can pool all the resources, all the experts. By the way, what class action case are we talking about?"

"Ladera."

"Jackson Prince's case?" Everyone in Chicago knew Prince. He won the biggest verdicts, and he scored more PR than any attorney in the city. "On a case like that, where Prince is the liaison-counsel, he would end up with a panel of experts, maybe one or two rheumatologists, maybe a cardiologist to testify how the drug caused heart attacks or whatever, a rehab doc to testify about the plight of the injured plaintiffs, maybe some neurologists if the drug affects the brain. That kind of thing."

"So maybe the list is the group of doctors Prince was *considering* as expert witnesses?"

"Where did you say you found the list?"

"I found it in Jane's stuff."

"I don't know why a newscaster would have a list of Prince's proposed experts. That stuff is protected by the work-product privilege."

The sun shifted around the building and felt hot, as if spring was really here. And yet I couldn't get in touch with that spring feeling, that infusion of renewal. I wondered for a bleak moment if I would ever feel that again. "Ever heard of Carina Fariello?"

"Nope. Another doc?"

"I'm not sure." My cell phone buzzed. I looked at it. Mayburn on the other line. "Grady, can I call you back in a second?"

He laughed. "I think we both know you're not going to call."

"No, I am. I just have to—"

"You don't have to call me. You don't have to do anything. It's okay, Iz. Really. Let me know if you need me."

* * *

"I've got something," Mayburn said.

"Already?"

"My place isn't far from Trial TV, and hey, I'm good. So, you got a pen to write this down?"

"Hold on." I hurried inside the Trial TV building.

C.J. stood inside the newsroom, a pen behind her ear, and seemed about to speak.

One second, I mouthed as I hurried past her.

I skirted the Trial TV sets where the afternoon anchors were in full swing and went to my desk. I found a pen and cradled the phone with my ear. "Ready."

"Carina is actually Margaret Fariello. I think Carina is her middle name. Address…" He read off a location. "That's north of Lawrence."

"Is she a doctor?"

"No, an accountant. She works as an overnight book-keeper at O'Hare for one of the airlines."

"Weird that Jane would have her name on the list with the doctors."

"Maybe not. You know who she used to work for?"

"One of the docs?"

"Prince & Associates."

"Jackson Prince's firm."

"Yeah. Here's her home phone number." He rattled off some digits.

"This is great. Thanks." But my words were quickly followed by a sense of deflation. Really, what had I learned? That Jane was doing research on Jackson Prince? I already had that information. That Jane had questioned some doctors about the Ladera case? That maybe she'd called some people at Prince's law firm? Didn't add up to anything. Certainly nothing I'd learned would give Prince a reason to kill Jane.

Plus, there was the scarf. The way Jane had been strangled with it. That seemed to suggest that whoever had done that to her had known about Jane's predilection for erotic asphyxiation.

Was it possible that Jane and Prince had had an affair? He was easily twenty years older than her, and he didn't seem like Jane's type. But then wasn't that Jane's main point? Her affairs brought her into another world, another life, one that she would otherwise have little access to.

But then again, maybe Prince and Jane hadn't had an affair. Maybe Jane had been killed with the scarf because it was her signature, her way of highlighting a big story. She'd been wearing it on the day she questioned Prince on Trial TV. And if the story about Prince had been big, and he'd known about it, then maybe strangling her with it was his way of truly shutting her up.

"Iz, I've to run," Mayburn said on the phone. "I told Lucy I'd pick up dinner for the kids."

"Dinner for the kids? You did not just say that."

"Shut it. I'll talk to you later."

C.J. came up to my desk. In her jeans and blazer, she took a wide stance and gave me a sour face. "I've been looking for you. You need to take a call in my office."

"Sorry. I had to talk to someone outside."

"Whatever. The police have been calling the station."

"On a case we're covering?"

"On *Jane's* case. They're looking for you." She jerked a thumb. "Let's go."

C.J. had taken over Tommy Daley's office. It was a real office with a door that closed, but the only things in it now were a desk and a bunch of boxes C.J. had brought from her old station. Most were open and overflowing with what looked like office stuff—old scripts, reference books and manuals, broadcast plaques and awards, notebooks, coffee mugs.

C.J. nodded tersely at the phone. I stared at it a moment, with its three rows of lights, many solid and bright, others dark, one lone light blinking at the top.

I lifted the receiver with trepidation. My arm seemed to tingle with the movement. I gulped hard at something bitter that rose in my throat. "Hello?"

"Isabel McNeil." It was a statement, not a question. And I knew that voice. Detective Vaughn.

I glanced up at C.J., who stood in the doorway, her arms still crossed. I put my hand over the receiver. "Can I get a minute on my own?"

She pursed her lips, nodded reluctantly, then left.

I gripped the phone. "Can I help you?"

"You've been named a person of interest," he said in a somber voice.

"I know that." I raised my other hand to my mouth. For a second, I felt as if I might throw up. My fingers were icy cold as they touched my lips. Sometimes my hands went cold like that when I hadn't eaten (and I hadn't since early this morning), but somehow I knew it was more than that. It was fear.

"And I hear you've got yourself a lawyer," Vaughn said, "and that she'll bring you in if we don't announce this to the public."

"Yes."

"Good, because we need to see you at the station. We need an alibi for Monday night before you found Jane. And for late Friday night after you two were out."

I knew I should welcome the opportunity to speak to them, to clear this up, because I wasn't guilty of *anything*. But still my stomach curled into a tight fist.

"Tomorrow work for you?" Vaughn said, like we were meeting up for coffee.

"In the afternoon." After Trial TV. I named a time.

And then, despite the fact that I knew it was stupid to piss off the cops, even if this cop in particular was a complete jerk, no, a complete *asshole,* I hung up.

45

Lincoln Park is a massive garden in the middle of the city, a great place to stroll, to lose yourself. Or maybe to find yourself.

When I'd gotten home after my talk with Vaughn, I hadn't known what to do. I called Theo a few times, silently begging him to be home already, so he could tell the cops I was with him on Friday night, not Jane. But over and over and over I only got his voice mail. And it was starting to mess with my mind. Was he really in Mexico? Was he really who he said he was? I became anxious, suspicious and generally freaked out by the way everything seemed to be spiraling, and in a direction I hadn't charted for myself.

And so I worked myself into something resembling a panic attack. I stood in my kitchen, hand on the counter as if to hold myself there, my breath coming in ragged gulps. I'd heard about people having anxiety attacks. Q, for example, had always claimed to have them when he stepped on the scale at the gym. But was *this* what he was talking about? Did he feel as if he might choke, might faint? *Breathe,* I ordered myself. It seemed so simple—*breathe.* But I couldn't get my lungs to cooperate.

I called Maggie. "I'm going to the Belmont station tomorrow."

"Remember, you don't *have* to talk to them," she said. "I told them you would talk if they kept quiet about the 'person of interest' thing, but we can always pull the plug."

"But then they'll tell everyone I'm a person of interest."

"Maybe."

"Probably, right? I mean, if I don't talk to them."

A pause. "Yeah, probably."

I thought about Jane's affairs and the "scarfing." I'd promised Jane I wouldn't mention the scarfing, but I was going to have to talk about her affairs, at least her night with the writer, in order to show Vaughn I wasn't with her late that night. I told Maggie about Theo then.

"Mmm, he sounds hot."

"You have no idea." Then I told her about Jane's writer, and after reminding her of our own attorney-client privilege, about Jane's affairs. "I need to tell the cops all this, right?"

"On the one hand, if it could help find who did this to her, yes. But on the other hand, it doesn't mean they'll stop looking at you…."

"But it will explain that she wasn't with me Friday night. She was with the writer."

"The problem is you don't even know that writer's name."

"Mick."

"Mick what? Is that short for Michael?"

I started panting again. "I don't know! But if I can just explain who Jane was with that night and who I was with…"

She exhaled loud. "Iz, just because you tell the cops X and Y doesn't mean they get to Z."

Pant, pant, pant. "I…have…to do *something*."

"Okay, okay. We're going to the station tomorrow, and we're going to figure this out," she said. "I'll pick you up and take you there."

My breathing slowed. A bit of fresh air seeped its way into my lungs. "*Thank* you. Thank you."

"No problem." She was quiet for a minute. "When was the last time you worked out?"

My mind knotted. "Can't remember."

"Put on your running shoes and take a walk along the

lake. That's an order from your attorney and your best friend. It's gorgeous out."

Maggie knew I wasn't a runner, like her. She knew I didn't like to work out at all. Sweating in public reminded me too much of my flop sweat spells. But Mags also knew I always felt better when I did some kind of exercise.

And so I went to Lincoln Park, and now, I walked fast with my iPod loud, playing a song by the Kooks—"She Moves in Her Own Way." I loved that song. It was Sam who used to blare it while he waited for me to get ready for an evening out. But it seemed too upbeat. I stopped, pulled out the iPod and scrolled backwards, looking for something different. The Killers came up. I almost clicked on it, but then I registered the word—*Killers*—and it chilled me, made me think of Jane's battered body.

I started walking again, scrolling through my iPod, and landed on a hard-edged song from Liz Phair. I clicked on it and headed for the North Avenue bridge that would take me to Lake Michigan.

When I reached it, I trotted up the stairs and ran across the bridge, and right then I felt something release inside my body, breath finally flooding into my lungs.

I wanted to harness the feeling, to let it consume me, and so I went to the middle of the bridge, suspended a hundred feet over Lake Shore Drive, and I hung over it, playing my music loud, watching the cars zip by in the south lanes, sucking in breath after breath after breath, letting the heat of the sun sink into me. I don't know how long I stood there, and I was only aware of time passing when the cars began to slow. Rush hour. I looked up at the stately apartments that hugged the curve on Lake Shore Drive, as if clinging to their views. I raised my face farther and looked at the skyline. I *loved* that skyline. Always had. Even when I was a kid, it reminded me that the city had been there for so much longer than me. And now it reminded me that people in this city had survived worse than what I was experiencing.

But, unfortunately, Jane hadn't survived at all. Jane, who loved this city, too.

My eyes filled with the tears I hadn't let myself cry at the memorial. I thought about the fact that Jane would never again see this skyline; never again sit on a rooftop deck of a Chicago restaurant and drink wine, gazing at the lights glittering around her; never again roast in the sun on the bleachers at Wrigley, slurping a yeasty beer; never again jostle through crowds at Taste of Chicago or Jazz Fest or Old Town Art Fair; never again see the symphony play at Millennium Park on a crisp summer evening; never watch the tulips magically appear in the mid-lane boxes of LaSalle Street; never again witness the massive Christmas tree at Daley Plaza next to a two-story menorah.

I wasn't even sure Jane had loved all those things. They were things I loved about Chicago. Jane probably had her own list. But that list was gone with her.

So, on behalf of Jane, who couldn't do it, I raised my hand, and just for one second, I waved goodbye to the city.

46

Jackson Prince walked the underground tunnel that led from his office to Trattoria No. 10.

Technically, this tunnel was called the Pedway. Its official purpose was to link various El trains with various downtown buildings. Not that Prince ever rode the El train. Each morning, a driver picked him up from his East Erie apartment, where he owned the penthouse, and dropped him off at his office building. To Prince, the best thing about that building was not his massive corner office or the fact that it had a view of Daley Plaza. No, the best thing about his building was that he could access the tunnel and take it right to court, where he pitied the other lawyers who arrived flushed from the summer heat or shivering from the arctic winter and who had to juggle trench coats and umbrellas when they stepped up to the bench.

The next best thing about the tunnel was that it led him to Trattoria No. 10, a subterranean Italian restaurant and bar that was a favorite among Chicago's legal crowd.

But tonight, he wasn't meeting a lawyer. Tonight was about Jerry Hay and thanking the good doctor. Now that no one was looking over Prince's shoulder on this matter, he could enjoy it again. He could properly show Dr. Hay his appreciation, which would make them both very happy.

Dr. Hay was already at the bar, a highball in front of him. Hay was an average-looking guy—medium height and a nondescript face that was probably similar to many of the guys Hay grew up with in Bridgeport. Prince had done his research on Hay, and he knew that Hay had done better than many of the guys in his neighborhood, most of whom had gone the cop or fireman route. At thirty-five, Hay operated his own rheumatology practice. Yes, Hay was successful. Or at least he appeared so to the outside observer. But Prince knew that the early, external success of a young doctor like Hay didn't translate immediately to financial success. There were the astronomical student loans, the ever-soaring malpractice premiums and the ever-dwindling Medicare payments on behalf of older patients, which made up most of Hay's practice. Which all meant that Hay's life-style with his Northbrook home, his Lake Geneva summer house, three kids, his stay-at-home wife and his three expensive cars became harder and harder to afford.

And that was where Prince stepped in.

He stepped up beside the doctor now and stretched out his hand. "Jerry." He shook the man's hand, warmly patting his shoulder.

Prince liked to call doctors like Hay by their first names. He thought it helped to let Hay know he was above him, that his J.D. had brought many more riches than Hay's M.D. Not that Prince liked to gloat. He just liked people to know their place in his world.

"You ready for your trip next week?" he asked Hay.

The doctor smiled, one of the first lighthearted grins Prince had seen from him. "Very ready. Betsy is already packed. And of course she's told everyone in the neighborhood that we're taking a private plane. I can't thank you enough."

Prince patted him on the shoulder again. "I'm happy to do it. It's nothing."

That wasn't exactly true. Technically he'd already paid Hay for services rendered, and a week at Prince's home in Palm Springs for Hay's family, along with the use of Prince's plane to take them there, wasn't exactly cheap. But compared to what he'd gained from the assistance Hay and the other docs gave him, it was a drop in a very, very big bucket.

47

When I rounded the corner, the band O.A.R. on my iPod, I saw him.

He was on my stoop, leaning against the doorjamb. He looked at his phone, typing something with the thumb of one hand. The sight of him stopped me and at first I felt only elation. But that feeling was short-lived. I stood just looking at him, trying to sort out combative thoughts. One said, *I love him. I'll always love him,* while the other said, *You can love someone and still not have it be right for you, for right now.*

I didn't know which was stronger. I called out to him.

He didn't hear me, and for some reason, this seemed like a portent. I walked toward him. Still, he didn't look up. Finally, when I was nearly next to him, he saw me, and his face split into a grin, teeth gleaming.

"Sam," I said simply. We hugged tight. "I didn't even know you were coming."

"You would have if you'd checked your messages in the last hour."

"I've been walking by the lake."

"Good." His olive-green eyes took in my face. "You needed that, huh?"

"I did." I stuck my keys in the front door. "What are you doing on the street?"

He followed me up the stairs, smacking me playfully on the ass like he usually did. "I didn't have your keys with me."

I stopped and turned. "Since when did you stop carrying my keys?"

He shrugged, the shoulders of his suit lifting up. "I took them off my key ring once when I was going to rugby practice and had too much stuff in my pockets. You know how it is."

I didn't. And this sounded significant—this not carrying his set of my keys. Because, as far as I'd known, Sam had carried my keys every day since I gave them to him five months after we started dating.

Sam and I had met at the summer picnic of Forester Pickett. I would never forget that day in the June sun, on a lush lawn in Lake Forest, when I first saw Sam. His blond hair shone in the sunlight, and a shy grin pulled at the corners of his wide mouth. Right then, I had the random but distinct thought—*I could kiss that mouth. Forever.*

Sam and I started that moment in the sun, and five months later, we were solidly into the era of Us with a capital U—a time when we scarcely remembered what came before each other, when we no longer envisioned a time that we would exist without the other.

Back then, one of the other condo owners in my building was a woman who often traveled for her job. Her newspapers would collect and litter the stoop, making Sam crazy.

"It's such a waste of paper," he'd say, picking them up.

So I'd taken one of those old papers one day and wrapped a set of my keys in them. It was waiting by his orange coffee mug when he got up in the morning. He opened it. He beamed. Sam said it was the greatest gift he'd ever received. He had never complained about those papers again. But now here he was, without those keys, unsure when he'd even stopped carrying them.

Sam looked up at me, standing in the stairway, unmoving. "What?"

"Nothing. It's probably nothing." I turned and kept climbing. As I'd told Mayburn earlier, I had bigger things to worry about.

"I came to take you to dinner," Sam said. "North Pond Café."

I stopped again, this time for a good reason, and spun around. "Really?" I asked, my spirits returning.

North Pond Café was a high-end eatery tucked at the other end of Lincoln Park. To reach it, you had to walk through at least part of the park, and as a result, it was closed during the winter months. Sam and I loved it.

Sam nodded.

"Is it open?"

"Just reopened last week. So get ready."

I wrapped my arms around his neck. "What's the occasion?"

"Us." He smacked me on the ass again. "Go."

An hour later, the cab dropped us off on Lakeview Avenue at Deming. The sky was a splashy mix of dark blue from the east and a mustard gold from the west behind us. We walked on a sidewalk leading away from the street and under a fieldstone footbridge. On the other side of the bridge, lit by discreetly-placed lights, was a long pond that stretched into the distance and was capped at the end by a snippet of the Chicago skyline. Unlike Lake Michigan, with its unprotected shore and its tendency to turn tumultuous, the pond was buffeted by trees—all popping with buds— and was always flat, always smooth. It was what made the café, which sat at one end, so soothing.

The café was in a Frank Lloyd Wright-ish building. Inside, the dark wood was set off by golden lights, the sparkle of stained glass, white tablecloths and gleaming glassware.

We were seated at a table that overlooked the pond. I slipped into my chair and gazed across the table at Sam. "How did you land the best table?"

"Not important."

"Well, then what is?"

"Me and you, Iz." His hand slipped across the cloth and offered itself to me.

I took it, and we looked at each other, grinning, and despite the disastrous week I'd had, I felt the wheels of Sam and me moving and clicking and snapping themselves into place.

Sam ordered a bottle of French white. As the waiter poured it, Sam looked at me. "I want to hear what's going on. Everything," he said. "But nothing serious until we've got one glass under our belt. Okay with you?"

I sighed with happiness. "Great." As much as I knew myself capable of handling my life, sometimes it felt damned good to have someone else call even the smallest of shots.

For the next half hour, we talked about the things we used to talk about—Sam's job, our families, the rugby team, the wedding of a friend that was coming up that summer.

And when the waiter came back to pour more wine, Sam said, "All right. Tell me."

He didn't have to say about what. I told him about Jane's memorial, finding I was a *person of interest,* interviewing Prince and the fact that I would be interviewed by the police the next day. I left out my run-in with Steve (or Tobias or whoever had been driving that van), since I'd promised Mayburn complete secrecy this time around. Ultimately, my omission about Mayburn didn't matter. Sam and I sipped our wine and ate distractedly, and while we did, we reconnected and we talked and we interrupted each other the way we used to and we finished stories for each other, just like we used to.

We were biting into a whiskey bread pudding and sipping a glass of dessert wine when a group of professionals in suits passed our table, trailing behind the hostess.

One of them, a woman, stopped suddenly and pointed at me. "My gosh, are you Isabel? Isabel McDonald or something like that?"

"Izzy McNeil. Hi." I held out my hand. "I'm sorry. I don't remember you."

"Oh, we haven't met. I've seen you on Trial TV. I've been watching it this week, and I *love* it."

"Thank you!" I had yet to speak to someone who had actually seen the programming and who wasn't a friend or relation.

Her face turned stricken. "I can't believe what happened to Jane Augustine."

"I know." I didn't mention that I had seen, up close and too personally, exactly what had happened to Jane.

"I'm sure it must be hard for all of you, but the network is great. You guys are fantastic." She looked over her shoulder at a younger guy. "Don't I always say that Trial TV is fantastic?" She gestured at him. "He's my associate."

The guy laughed. "She does. She has you on in her office all day."

The woman threw up her hands. "What can I say? I'm one of those lawyers who love the law, and so I love Trial TV." She pointed at me again. "But you. You're my favorite."

I felt unbelievably flattered. I remembered, again, Jane on the patio, talking about graciously accepting compliments. *Because you never know when it'll be the last.*

"Thank you," I said. "Thank you very much."

"Okay." The woman crossed her arms. "So tell me, how do you decide what cases to cover? Because I have an *insane* case for you."

She was a U.S. Attorney, she told us. The others were her colleagues. She spoke for a minute, the others jumping in here and there, all telling the story of a conspiracy they'd uncovered on a case.

Finally, she stopped and said, "I'm sorry. I didn't even introduce myself. I'm Duffy Carey."

We shook hands again, and I pointed across the table. "This is Sam, my fia—" I coughed. I looked at Sam. We both laughed. It was impossible to know what to call each other these days.

Duffy Carey didn't seem to notice. She shook Sam's hand effusively, introduced her colleagues and launched into another story about an organized crime case she was working on. But every two seconds, she stopped to tell me how I was the perfect person to cover the case. "With your brains and your looks," she said, waving a hand at my head, "you can take on any case you want."

Thinking of Jane again, I smiled and thanked her once more. I glanced at Sam. He was smiling, too, but it was a stiff kind of smile, the *I'm-barely-putting-up-with-this* type of smile. The type he gave when one of his sisters thought she was Annie Leibovitz because she had a digital camera in her hand.

"I'm sorry," I said, gently interrupting Duffy. "We were just finishing dinner, and—"

"My gosh, *I'm* sorry. We'll let you go. It was so nice to meet you." She pumped my hand one more time and moved away.

I turned back to Sam, laughing a little. "Wow, that was funny."

"Yeah." That stiff smile hadn't budged.

"What's up?"

"What do you mean?"

"You look miserable."

He shook his head, as if shaking off a mood he hadn't realized he had. "Sorry."

We fell into a weird silence. We went back to our desserts.

"So have you been playing a lot?" I asked, meaning his guitar.

At the same time, Sam was speaking. "Do you think you're going to be in that business for a while?"

We both stopped. Laughed awkwardly. "You go," I said.

He made a face I didn't recognize. "I guess I was just wondering how long you're planning on doing this TV thing."

I sat back. "I'm not sure. I took the job because I couldn't find anything else, but I have to say I like it. The news is exciting. It's always minute to minute, and it makes you forget everything else except what you're doing."

Sam nodded, frowned. "That's great. It really is. Sometimes I wish my job was more like that."

More silence. He was in some kind of mood, but I seemed to have lost the ability to read him at any second, a realization which sent a hollow pang of dread through me.

"So…" Sam said, his brow creasing the way it did when he was thinking hard. "If you stay in the news business, then that kind of thing—" he nodded in the direction of Duffy Carey's table, "—is going to happen all the time. You know, people coming up to you, telling you how much they like you."

I shrugged. "Or more likely they'll come up to me and tell me what a fool I look like, and how I should try harder to control the flop sweating."

We both laughed, a natural laugh at last.

But Sam's frown returned.

"What is it?" I asked.

"Nothing. Let's enjoy the night."

"Sam, you can't say nothing. Clearly there's *something*."

A shake of his head. "It really is nothing. And there's enough going on in your world."

"Yeah, but you are my world." It was what I used to say. Saying it now, reflexively, felt a little bit off. "Tell me," I said. "Please. Even if it's nothing."

He sighed, looked at me. "I'm just not sure how I like all that." He gestured again toward Duffy Carey's table. "People coming up to us, to you."

This surprised me. Sam was one of the most laid-back, friendly people I knew. He could meet anyone, talk to anyone. "Did you not like her?"

"No, no. She seems cool. Sounds like she's got an interesting job, and I like that she thinks you're fantastic. Because you are, by the way. Have I told you that?"

"No."

He grabbed my hand again. Squeezed it. "Well, you are." He let my hand go. "But I'm not sure I like the public-eye thing."

I nodded, slowly, trying to process what he was saying. "I'm not even sure I do, either. I mean, even though I've been on TV for a few days, I don't feel like I'm in the public eye yet." I waved at Duffy's table. "That's the first time something like that has happened."

"But it won't be the last."

"It might."

"No, it won't."

"What if it's not? What are you saying?"

"I'm not sure. It's just occurring to me, but I guess…"

I waited for what he had to say, and it felt like waiting for a guillotine to drop.

"I guess," he said, "that I just don't like it."

"But you'll get used to it?"

He shrugged. "Could you ever get used to that?"

"I think so. Are you saying you couldn't?"

"No." A pause. "Maybe." Another stop. "I guess we'll have to see."

Those words pulled me into something resembling despair. "Sam, you and I have been waiting to see for a while now."

"Yeah," he said, his voice irritated, "we've been waiting to see if you can get over what happened six months ago."

I said nothing. "And so now there's something else we have to wait on, this public-eye thing?"

"I guess there is."

"And that's because of me, too."

His lips pressed firmly together. The quiet wound its way around us, feeling like a stalemate. The night of Sam and I snapping back into place had snapped us apart again.

We paid the bill, walked past the pond and under the fieldstone bridge. The city was dark now, with only the low hum of electricity, the random passing car.

"My place?" Sam said.

"I have to be on set at six. Let's go to my place." I looked for a cab. I stopped when I realized Sam hadn't answered. "You can go home before work in the morning, right?"

"Or we can go to my place now and get my stuff for tomorrow, and then go to your place."

My temples started to ache. But this time it wasn't just from being hit on the head, it was from too many layers of emotions—the fear of losing Sam; despondency at losing Jane; anger that Zac had turned the cops on me in his misplaced rage.

"Yeah, okay," I said to Sam. There was defeat in my voice.

We looked at our watches, started figuring out how long it would take. Meanwhile, it grew chillier on the street, and my headache throbbed. "Sam, what if we just do it tomorrow night? I'll come to your place or you come to mine, whatever you want."

I expected him to protest. I guess I hoped he would. But he just craned his neck to look for a cab. "Yeah, tomorrow," he said. Then, "Shit, I've got rugby practice."

"Well, after that. Or Friday." We used to feel an urgency to be together. Where had it gone?

We both seemed to sense the change. He looked at me with a face suddenly torn, anguished, surprised. He reached out his arms and pulled me close. I put my head on his chest, smelling a hint of the tea tree aftershave he wore, smelling something deeper, something pure Sam.

"This is stupid," he said. "I'm coming home with you now."

"No, it's okay. I know it's difficult, and you have to be at work early, too. If not tomorrow, we'll get together soon."

"Okay." I hated that he had given in so easily. That we both had.

Still we clung to each other. Still I breathed him in. That scent brought tears to my eyes, pain to my belly.

"What's happening?" I said, my words muffled.

He squeezed me tighter. "Nothing," he murmured. "Nothing."

That was exactly what I feared.

48

The city was a blur outside my cab window. I couldn't focus on anything, couldn't see past the haze in my brain, the ache of Sam and me skidding to some new form of us, or maybe no form at all, or some form that would exist on a plane we'd never even known was out there. How fast it had changed, twisted, turned.

The same could be said of Jane's murder investigation, with how quickly I'd gone from friend and coworker to a person of interest. None of it made any sense to me, and the longer I thought about it, the angrier it made me. The city outside the cab window became a violent composite of hazy smudges, of dark and then of glaring electric light.

Who did Zac Ellis think he was, accusing me? I understood that his suspicion of me had started Saturday morning when I was spouting off possible explanations for her absence, when I really suspected that she'd gone home with Mick. I was trying so hard not to get her in trouble, and trying so hard to contain the fact that I had gone home with someone myself, that I probably sounded as if I had something much bigger to hide. *But still.* Still, it was Zac's crazy suspicions that had gotten caught in the lens of the cops' radar. As far as I could tell, it was because of *him* that everything was spinning so quickly out of control right now.

When the cab neared my house, I leaned forward. "I'm going somewhere different," I said. I gave him Jane's address.

49

When the cab pulled up in front of Jane's house—correction, it was solely Zac's house now—I saw the lights were on, and all the drapes in the front closed tight. Two news vans were parked on the street, lights on, but there were no reporters or cameramen outside. The night's quiet had a temporary feel to it, as if the calm had died down, but everyone knew the storm would erupt again tomorrow.

And then that night came back to me in a flash. I couldn't walk in that front door again.

"Can you take me around to the other side, please?" I asked the cabbie, remembering the rear entrance that Jane had showed me.

The back of their house faced the alley—familiar territory for a photographer like Zac, who featured such alleys in his work. But for me, the barely lit dark and the eerie silence made me remember another terrifying time—last night, those hands shoving me against the garage.

I asked the cabbie to drive a few houses past Zac's, then gave him a twenty. "Will you wait for me, please?"

"What do you mean wait for ya?" He was a huge man who looked as if he'd been poured into his cab ten years ago and hadn't gotten out yet. I doubted whether he could be responsive enough to help me if I needed it.

"Just wait, and call the cops if I don't come back, okay? I'm going to that house right there." I pointed.

"I'm not calling the cops."

I gave him a ten. "You can drive away if you want, but call the cops if I don't come back in ten minutes. Please." Ten minutes was enough to confront Zac, to ask him a few questions, to get him to see that I had nothing to do with his wife's love life, certainly nothing to do with her death.

I hurried down the alley, looking every which way, my heels feeling unstable on the uneven brick. I thought of how I would talk to Zac in a simple way, assuring him I wasn't involved with Jane. I knew that, as a new widower, he had to be struggling through circles of hell I hadn't even glimpsed yet.

A gate protected the rear of the house, with a swinging door cut into it. Locked. I looked up at the house. Like the front, all the lights appeared to be on but the drapes and blinds were closed. I looked around for a buzzer. There didn't seem to be one. I walked down a ways, trying to see into the house from another angle, but again all the curtains were closed. Then the back door of the house opened. I saw Zac and another person. A woman. She was wearing a plaid coat and a white beret. She stepped out of the house first. Zac was behind her, not wearing a coat. He looked up and down the alley. His eyes seemed to miss me in a dark corner of the property. His gaze stopped when he saw the cab up the street, but then the woman in the beret put her arms around him. He hugged her back. Tight. And for a long time. They kissed on the lips once, then again, then once more. Zac closed the door, and she trotted down the stairs. She was pretty in a quirky way. She walked through the gate, and I remembered I'd seen her before at Jane's funeral, the dark-haired woman looking through the photo book of Jane, dabbing at her eyes.

I stepped back quickly, against the side of a neighboring garage. When I poked my head out, I saw that the woman had spied my cab. She hurried that way, waving at it. And then my thirty-dollar cabbie let her in and drove away.

The loss of my cab was one thing. The fact that Zac had been accusing me of something when he'd clearly had his own secrets pissed me off even more. I marched to the back gate. It had closed but hadn't locked when the woman left. I was inside and heading up the back stairs in a second.

I pounded on the door. It opened, and Zac poked his head out.

"How long have you had a girlfriend?" I said.

His eyes narrowed. He opened the door farther and gestured at me to come in.

50

Zac and I stood in his big kitchen, both of us leaning against the countertops, both of us with our arms crossed tight over our chest. Between us, the granite island, marbled in tan and black, held an assortment of sympathy cards and baked goods.

"Her name is Zoey," Zac said.

Zac and Zoey. It was actually a cute name for a couple, but now probably wasn't the time to point that out.

"How long have you been together?" I asked.

"We're not together. She was helping me move back into my house for the first time since Jane died. It's been a crime scene until now."

"From what I saw, she looked like more than a friend."

"Fuck you," Zac said. "You have no idea what my life has been like." He leaned forward, arms squeezed tight around himself, the veins on his neck standing up. "And you have no idea what it was like to be married to Jane. She cheated. You know about her *dalliances,* right? And she probably also told you that I let her do it. And you know why? Because I loved her. I fucking *loved* her. So that's it. Now, what do you want?"

He stopped short and took a breath. His energy and the intensity seemed to drain away then, as if he were a sponge pressed hard, everything seeping out.

I spoke up. "I can't imagine how tough that would

have been. You know, being with Jane, while she was… doing whatever."

"Doing *whom*ever."

"So you turned to Zoey. It's understandable."

"Look, I don't have to explain anything to you. But the fact is I've got nothing to hide, so I'll tell you. Zoey and I picked up again just this past weekend."

The weekend before your wife died, I thought. *Kind of an interesting coincidence.*

Zac sighed. "We dated years ago. We broke up right before I met Jane, and we stayed friends. And that was all it was. But on Saturday, when Jane wasn't home, I was about at the end of my rope." Zac was looking at the floor now, almost as though he was talking to himself. "After that, I just couldn't stand being in the city. I went to our house in Long Beach. I was trying to sort out what to do. And then Jane found that noose in the house."

I stayed quiet. Jane had said that Zac could have driven to Chicago from Long Beach and left the scarf in that noose shape when she was at the gym. As her husband, he would certainly have known where she kept it.

He was shaking his head, emotion taking over his face. And then he looked at me, his eyes boring into mine. "Can you see why I loved Jane?"

"Of course," I answered softly. "She was dynamic. Smart. Beautiful."

"And sexy," he added matter-of-factly. "And that was what brought her down."

"What do you mean?"

"She was beaten and then strangled with her scarf." He shook his head. "That scarf."

That scarf. Zac and I just looked at each other.

"This whole thing is so surreal," he said.

Was it surreal because he had killed his wife? I couldn't get a read on him.

"But Zoey has helped me," he continued. "That's what

I'm trying to tell you. I called her to talk on Sunday, and we met and…"

I wanted to say, *And the next day your wife was dead.* But Zac appeared to be telling the truth. And he seemed tortured by it.

"Is it wise to be hanging out with her, Zac," I asked. "While the cops are still investigating?" Why I was willing to help this guy when all he'd been doing was trying to bring me down, I didn't know. There was something about him that touched me. And if he hadn't killed his wife, he would be going crazy trying to figure out who did. Just like me.

"I don't care if the cops see me with her. Don't you get that? I told you I don't have anything to hide."

"I don't, either, Zac. That's what I wanted to talk to you about."

His face hardened. "You seemed like you had something to hide Saturday morning."

"I explained that."

"So where is he? This guy you went home with? Have you introduced him to the cops?"

I bit my lip. "He's still out of town."

"Right."

"Look, what makes you think Jane went home with *me* on Friday?"

"I told you earlier. I'm not stupid. I know Jane's pattern and the way it went when she was fucking around. She'd go out one night, and she would always have an excuse. It's networking, she would say. It's a friend of a friend. In this case it's 'someone I want to bring into Trial TV.' And then— boom—I can't find her, but then she turns up the next morning. It was the same shit with you."

"When you saw her on Saturday, did you ask who she'd been with?"

"I asked her if she was with 'some guy,' because that's what she always said."

"Fine. *Some guy,* Zac. Not some *girl.*"

He shook his head, peering at me. "She didn't say that this time, though. I've thought about this a lot since she was killed. I asked her if it was some guy, and she said, 'Something like that.'"

"It's the same thing."

"It's not. She was all hopped up and freaky that morning, like she was trying out something new. Trust me, I know Jane's moods. Something different had happened, or *someone* different."

"That someone different wasn't me!"

"So you say."

"I told you. She was with a writer named Mick. And he was at Trial TV on the day it launched. And Jane said that he had been following her. She'd figured it out that morning. That's why she was acting so strange."

He peered at me, eyes squinting. "You didn't tell me that before."

"I didn't *get* to say that before. We were at the memorial, and then I saw him."

"Yeah, you saw him. And then you took off. You find him?"

"No."

He made a face like, *Uh-huh. Sure.*

I looked down and waved a hand at myself. I was still in the dress, ivory coat and heels that I'd worn to dinner. "Look at me! Do I look like I would kill someone?"

"I'm not saying you killed her. Not necessarily. I'm just saying I think you were together. I think you hid that, and I think you're still hiding something. It's Vaughn who says you did it, and man, he seems really sure."

"This is insane!"

Zac uncrossed his arms, and his face distorted. "You know what's insane? That someone killed Jane! And if you did kill her, I'll hurt you. I'm not kidding. If you've got a soft spot, I'll find it. I'll fuck you up."

I exhaled loud, suddenly terrified. "I should leave." But

then suddenly I thought of something. "Years ago, when you and Zoey split up, did you break up with her or was it the other way around?"

His forehead furrowed. "What does it matter?"

"Just curious."

"You should mind your own goddamned business."

"It's odd you won't tell me."

"I've got nothing to hide. Unlike you. I broke up with Zoey, okay? But we stayed friends."

"And being friends with her, did you tell Zoey about Jane's affairs?"

"Yeah. Eventually. So what? She was one of the few people I told. She's that good of a friend."

"Did Jane know you were friends?"

"Of course. And she was fine with it. Jane was not the jealous type."

"So Jane knew Zoey." I was thinking of how the detective had said that it appeared Jane had let someone in, someone she knew, and that she had turned her back.

"Of course. In fact, they liked each other. They were friends, sort of."

"I'm sure it would have been hard for Zoey to be friends with the woman who replaced her."

Zac lifted his shoulders and dropped them again. "They didn't see each other very often."

"You said Jane wasn't the jealous type, but was Zoey?"

His forehead creased deeper. "Are you implying that Zoey did this to Jane?"

"I have no idea. I'm just asking."

"You are a crazy bitch!" The veins in his neck were prominent now. "Zoey is a sweet person, a person who was there to listen to me when I needed it."

"And maybe someone who wanted you back? Maybe she was angry at having to watch you struggle so much with Jane?"

"No." He shook his head, irritated. "Just shut up, okay? Because you have no idea what you're talking about."

"No more than you know what you're talking about when you throw around allegations about Jane and me. I want to figure out who did this to Jane."

"It sounds like you want to figure out someone else to pin it on. And you saw Zoey. She's about an inch over five feet. Jane was almost a foot taller." He looked me up and down. "Meanwhile, *you're* pretty tall. Not as tall as Jane, but it wouldn't have been a problem for you to do something about her, especially if you wanted her job."

"Zac, I *didn't* want her job. I'd never even thought about being on the news until Friday when Jane brought it up."

"I don't want to hear it." Zac stalked to his back door and opened it. "Get out."

I walked to the door. I stepped outside, trying to think fast, think of some way to derail this train of thought that Zac had about me. I opened my mouth, but before I could say another thing, he slammed it, and I heard the lock click into place.

51

After I went off the air on Thursday, Maggie called to say she was picking me up at Trial TV.

I stood out front under an umbrella, the earlier sunshine having given way to a looming dust-colored sky that leaked a continual drizzle. It was one of those rains that seemed as if it would go on forever.

Maggie's little black Honda splashed into the parking lot and pulled up front. Maggie had bought this car when we were in law school, and although she made enough now to afford better, she said she didn't want to drive an expensive car to the neighborhoods she had to visit as a criminal defense attorney.

"How are you?" she asked, when I was in the car. She pulled out of the parking lot and headed toward Belmont.

"Nervous."

Her face scrunched the way it did when she was thinking hard. She tapped her top and bottom teeth together, something she did when she was nervous, too.

"What's going on with you?" I said. "Are you all right?"

"I've been better."

"Wyatt?"

"No, he's cool." She smiled briefly. "He's great actually." The scrunched expression returned. "It's this case I had this morning. A woman busted with heroin. She's our age. A mom with four kids, and she's raising all of them by herself."

"How much heroin?" I'd learned something from being friends with Maggie. You could get caught with just about any kind of drug, but what really mattered was how *much* you had on you, and whether you had intent to sell it.

"Enough. It's her third felony." She grimaced, turned right. "The problem is she's had two other felony drug convictions. And under the sentencing guidelines, three convictions can get you life."

"Life in prison?" I asked, shocked.

"Yep. I just had to tell this woman that she might never see her kids again outside of visitation days, never go to their graduations or their weddings." Maggie looked as if she was on the point of tears, then they cleared and her face became full of anger. "The *war* on drugs," she scoffed. "Nice war, putting away moms for life. I've had clients who got less— way less—for raping a kid or kidnapping someone." She scoffed again. "Hell, I've had clients get less for murder one."

I fell silent. All this talk of sentencing was starting to mess with my head.

Maggie shot me a look. "Sorry. We're onto your case now."

"Yeah, my case. Murder one."

"Ignore me. What I meant to say is that Jane Augustine has a case, and you're just here to talk about it."

The Belmont police station sat under the bypass of a highway entrance, as if the city had found its presence distasteful and had dumped it there to keep it out of sight. Its exterior was brown and squat, almost blending in with the concrete parking lot that surrounded it.

Maggie pulled into a parking space marked *CPD Only*. I pointed at the sign. "It's for police officers."

"They never tow."

We got out of the car and huddled under my umbrella as we walked toward the building. Maggie wore a long wool coat that was too warm for the weather and too big for her— she was so tiny that most of her clothes seemed too large.

Suddenly, both of Maggie's cell phones started ringing. She juggled them, shooting orders to her staff, texting clients back. I'd often thought that there should be a reality TV show where contestants compete on who can multitask the best. Maggie would kick ass.

"I've got a jail visit in two hours," she said. "But luckily, those kind of clients can wait. They aren't going anywhere soon." She dumped one cell phone back in her bag, kept listening to messages on another and kept talking to me all the while. "Okay, let's review, Iz. Just listen to their questions, and answer only what they ask. Don't let them lead you into saying anything you don't think is true. They have video cameras in the rooms, but they don't usually turn them on unless you want to confess."

"I've got nothing to confess!"

Maggie stopped. She put the other phone in her purse and brushed her hair away from her eyes. She rarely had time to doctor her hair with product, and so it generally blew around in the Chicago wind, like now. Her forehead creased as she stared at me.

"What is that look?" I said.

"There's no reason for me to be nervous here, is there?"

"What do you mean?"

"You didn't have anything to do with what happened to Jane, right?"

My mouth dropped open, mortified. "How can you ask that? You're supposed to be my friend! What kind of a question—"

"Hey, hey, hey." She reached out and squeezed my forearm. "It's a lawyer question, not a friend question."

"Well, the answer is no! Of course I didn't have anything to do with Jane's death." Suddenly, I felt those tears in my eyes again. "Jane and I weren't friends like you and I are, but she *was* a friend. And you know I would never kill anyone!"

Maggie reached her arms around my neck and embraced

me. Since I was five inches taller than her, I had to lean down. She was a fierce hugger, something I loved. As usual, I was struck with how much better those strong embraces made me feel.

"Of course you wouldn't. And I know she was a friend," Maggie said, her words muffled by our coats. "I just had to ask, because I don't want to take you in there if there's even the slightest chance this could all come back around to bite you."

"No way," I said.

She pulled back, peered in my eyes and smiled. "Let's do it then."

Inside, at a square desk in the center of the lobby, were four uniformed police officers. Three were standing together and laughing at something in the newspaper. The other, a dark-skinned man whose uniform was immaculate, and who looked uncomfortable at the jovial nature of his partners, squinted at us when we entered.

Then he recognized Maggie. "Hey, Bristol!" His face cracked into a smile. "What are you doing here? Got another client you're trying to get off on a Miranda technicality?"

"Hey, Munoz," Maggie called back in a lighthearted tone. She gestured at me. "This is my client."

"Oh." He dropped his grin. "Thought you were a lawyer."

"I am," I said.

"Oh," he said again. Now he appeared confused.

"I'm here about the Jane Augustine case."

Officer Munoz nodded, squinting once more, as if he was trying to figure me out.

The other officers put down the newspaper and came forward. "I loved Jane Augustine," the female police officer said.

"Yeah, she always got the stories right," another said. "Especially the legal stuff."

"Who would do that to her?"

All the officers turned to me. I felt a blush creeping over

my face. "I don't know," I said. "I'm just here to help. I found her—"

Maggie put her hand on my arm, cutting me off, and she shook her head. I could hear her unspoken words. *Shut up.* "Detective Vaughn," she said, looking at Officer Munoz. "I guess he's got the case."

"Yeah, he's upstairs." Munoz raised a clipboard from behind the desk. "Just got to have you log in."

Munoz came around the desk and searched us, then ran our bags through a metal detector.

He pointed at the stairs. "You know where you're going."

Maggie thanked him again, and led me up the stairs. She stopped halfway up and turned. "Remember to listen to what he says, what he's actually asking, and be careful. I didn't get a good vibe from this guy last time." After Sam had disappeared and Forester died, Maggie was the one who helped us sort everything out, and she'd met Vaughn.

"Me, either," I said.

We kept climbing the stairs and stopped when we got to the top. We walked down a sterile hallway. As we did, I could hear a voice speaking. The words weren't quite audible but something about the voice sounded familiar. Maggie heard it too. She stopped. We both stood there, listening. Maggie's face scrunched in confusion.

"Is that...?" she said.

"It sounds like me," I said. By now, I could clearly recognize my own voice.

Maggie and I looked at each other, puzzled. We kept walking.

I could make out the words now. And then I realized what it was—my broadcast yesterday on Trial TV.

We reached a windowless square room that looked just like the one I'd been in the other night. Except that the table inside had a phone and a small TV on top of it, three chairs around it.

And in one of those chairs was Detective Vaughn. He

wore brown pants, a white shirt, an empty holster. He turned when he saw us.

"Just watching you on TV here." He pointed to the screen. "You're good." He stood and his eyes bolted onto mine. "You're really good."

52

He shook Maggie's hand. "Nice to see you again." Ignoring any kind of greeting for me, he pointed to the side of the table with the two chairs.

"Nice to see you, too," I said.

He continued to ignore me.

Maggie took a seat. I followed her lead.

Vaughn closed the door, sealing the room into silence.

As we took our seats, I looked at Vaughn. His brownish hair with shots of gray seemed newly cut and stood up straight like the bristles of a brush. When he caught my eyes on him, he smiled with one side of his mouth. He had sharp eyes that made no excuses for studying me.

I gave as calm a smile as I could, as if to say, *Go ahead, I'm ready.* But he just kept dissecting me with his eyes. The silence in the room grew oppressive.

"You had some questions for my client?" Maggie's tone was congenial, but matter-of-fact.

"Yeah, one sec." Detective Vaughn opened a manila folder and pushed his chair back, balancing the folder on a crossed knee so we couldn't see what was there. He grabbed a pen clipped to his belt. *Click, click, click* with the end of his pen. He glanced up at me, grinned. It was as if he knew that the sound drove me crazy. He made some notes.

"Okay." He sighed. "They make us write all this stuff down when we interrogate a suspect."

I glanced at Maggie with a silent question—*Did he just call me a suspect?*

Maggie stared at him hard. "Can we get moving, please?"

"Yeah, hold on." He scribbled something. "Isabel McNeil…" he said, almost under his breath. More scribbling. "Represented by Maggie Bristol…"

He looked up. "You related to Marty Bristol?"

Maggie nodded. "He's my grandfather." Then she added, "He's also my law partner."

Detective Vaughn gave an appreciative nod. "I remember when he had the Keith Lee Baker case."

Maggie nodded again. Her grandfather, Martin Bristol, now a wealthy criminal defense lawyer, had started out his career on the state side and prosecuted the infamous serial killer, Keith Lee Baker. Far from being intimidated by her grandfather's reputation, or feeling like she had to take a backseat to it, Maggie had no qualms using that reputation to open doors. She'd always said that in business, everyone got a leg up for one reason or another—maybe it was your connections, maybe it was your looks, or maybe it was the fact that your grandpa put away a particularly nasty serial killer.

"Hey," Maggie said to Vaughn. "Someone told me you worked the Kenny Paris case. Is that right?

"Yeah."

"Heard it was a crazy one," Maggie said.

I had no idea what they were talking about, but Detective Vaughn laughed. "Oh, man, it was fucking nuts." He shook his head.

He and Maggie bantered for a few more minutes, their tone sounding more as if they were gossiping about a neighbor's lawn rather than the prosecution of a man who had killed ten people in a robbery gone awry.

"Okay." Vaughn gazed at me with that laserlike focus. "Have you wanted to do that for a long time?"

I was taken by surprise. "Do what?"

He pointed at the TV, now off. "Be a newscaster."

"It never occurred to me until Jane offered me a job at Trial TV."

He smirked, as if he didn't believe it. "You've got Zac Ellis all revved up."

"*I've* got him all revved up? I haven't done anything to that guy. In fact, you should know that he's already dating someone else."

He nodded, his expression unfazed. "He thinks you were dating his wife."

"That's nuts." I glanced at Maggie, who was wearing her focused but unflappable lawyer look.

"Is it? I've got a witness who says they saw you and Jane having coffee Saturday."

"We did."

"That person also said you two looked very cozy."

"We were friends. If that's cozy-looking…" I trailed off, shrugged.

He said nothing.

"I don't know what you want from me," I said.

"I want you to tell me the truth."

"I *am*."

Another smirk. "Good. Then tell me the truth about this. Did you kiss Jane when you were having coffee that day?"

"No!"

"That same witness who saw you having coffee said that they saw you kissing."

"That's absurd!" But then I remembered Jane leaning close to me. I remembered thinking she might be going to kiss me. I blushed now at the thought.

Vaughn noticed. I could tell, because the smirk suddenly involved both sides of his mouth.

"Jane and I were talking about the night before," I explained, "and Jane was trying to make a point by leaning close to me. We did *not* kiss."

"Where were you the night before?"

"I told you this on Monday. Jane and I were out that night at the hotel bar and then the place on Damen. I should have also told you that Jane went home with someone that night. A guy." I looked at Maggie, who nodded at me to go ahead. "And so did I."

"Why didn't you tell me that before?"

I swallowed hard. "I didn't know if it was an okay thing to talk about. Jane and I were friends—*just* friends—but since she's married and a public figure, I thought it would look bad if this information came out."

I thought about one other thing I hadn't told them—the sex game Jane liked to play, the scarfing. I'd promised her I wouldn't. Because I was the attorney she had consulted on that matter, I *couldn't*. But I'd already told them about the noose made from her scarf that she found in her house. They didn't need to know that Jane had that sexual habit, that predilection, did they? I hated it when people, usually celebrities, became better remembered for how they had died rather than the life they had lived. The actor who accidentally overdoses, the politician who dies while visiting a prostitute. Their legend becomes about the circumstance of their death and the building of evidence by the press as to how they got to that point. The great work they did slides away in the collective consciousness of society, replaced by the reports that the celeb was a drug addict, a sex addict, a cheater. Jane won an Emmy Award. She broke huge stories and lived her life with passion. *That* was what she should be remembered for, not a minor sexual preference.

Maggie cleared her throat. I realized I'd trailed off in thought, and Vaughn had said nothing.

I looked at him expectantly, but he just sat quietly. The silence, started out like a trickle of water, but then it began to pool and grow. Like the other night, I could hear nothing outside the room.

Vaughn stared intensely at me. Mute.

Maggie had told me to only answer the questions he asked. And if he asked, I would answer.

But he wasn't saying anything.

The room grew more and more uncomfortable. Suddenly the silence seemed like an ocean crashing over us. I heard Maggie clear her throat. Still, Vaughn and I gazed at each other relentlessly, a showdown. I remember he'd been like this the day he questioned me after Sam disappeared. But then I didn't feel so afraid of what he was thinking.

And the more he stared at me, the more the silence expanded, taking up all the air in the room. I grew more and more terrified, because swimming in that sea of silence, I could suddenly tell exactly what he was thinking. *You* killed Jane Augustine.

"You all done, Detective?" Maggie said, breaking the awful quiet.

He didn't even glance at her, but he finally spoke. "So on Friday night, you and Jane didn't go home together from this place on Damen?"

It had the feel of a question, but Detective Vaughn's tone made it clear he thought he knew the answer.

"No. I went home with a guy I met that night." It sounded so seedy.

"A guy."

"Yes. His name is Theo Jameson."

Vaughn pulled the file folder in front of him closer. He opened it, picked up his pen. *Click, click, click, click, click.* "Theodore..." he said, trailing off.

"Theo," I said, loudly, firmly. "That's how he introduced himself. Theo Jameson."

He wrote the name down. "Got his number?"

"Yes." I leaned over, took my phone from my bag, read the number to him.

Vaughn wrote it down, closed his folder again. "So if I

call this Theodore guy, he'll tell me he was at your house that night?"

"Yes, he's in Mexico right now. Some place that doesn't have cell service. But I believe he'll be back shortly."

"Huh. Interesting timing."

I gritted my teeth. I'd had enough. "You should also be looking for the guy Jane went home with that night. Mick." He wasn't writing it down.

"Last name?" he said.

I exhaled. "I don't know his last name. I saw him at Jane's memorial for a second, then he disappeared."

"He disappeared." He shook his head, as if he couldn't believe anything coming from my mouth.

"Look, Detective," Maggie said, "my client wanted to come here and be open about her whereabouts, and Jane's, on Friday night. But *I'd* like to know why Friday night is so important. This woman was killed on Monday night."

"I'll tell you why I'm asking her questions about Friday. Because I think she's lying to me about it."

"I'm not!" I couldn't keep my cool. I pounded a fist on the table. "Give me a lie detector test or something!"

"Great. Let's do that."

"Izzy," Maggie barked, putting a hand out and sending me a warning look. "You are *not* taking a polygraph."

"Why not?"

"Yeah," Vaughn said with a cool smile. "Why not?"

"Detective Vaughn knows as well as I do," Maggie said, "that there are false positives with polygraphs and false negatives, which is why they're not admissible. They only create more problems. I think it's time to leave."

"I don't want to leave," I said. "I want to hash this out. *Now.*" I'd never been the patient type and there was no way I was leaving now and walking around the city, knowing a cop thought I was lying, thought maybe I had something to do with Jane's death.

Maggie gave a grunt. "Detective, if you continue to be aggressive, we're out of here. I can promise you that. I don't usually tell you guys how to do your job, but I think you should be concentrating on Monday. On the day Jane was killed."

"Let's do that." He gestured with his head at me. "Where were you that day, before the Trial TV party?"

"I told you this Monday night. I told a bunch of other cops, too."

"That's right, you did tell me." He made a show of looking at some notes, but I could tell from his eyes he wasn't reading them. "You went home that afternoon after you left the station, right?"

"Right," I said, annoyed. Then I checked myself. He was riling me up. He was hoping I'd get riled up enough that I'd say something stupid. But I knew that trick. I'd used it when I took depositions of people. "Right," I said again, in an almost bored tone now. "I went home. I cleaned up my place and did a few things around my house. Then I got ready for the party."

"You call anybody that afternoon?"

I thought about it. "No."

"You e-mail anybody?"

"No. I was exhausted from my first day at Trial TV. I didn't even turn on my home computer."

"You got any neighbors who you maybe talked to?"

The other condo owners in my building were guys who worked until late every day. "No," I answered. "But I texted Jane from the Latin place. A bunch of times."

"You texted her *saying* you were there. Doesn't mean you were."

"I saw Tommy Daley at the party."

Vaughn didn't even blink. "Yep. He says he saw you. For about ten seconds. No one else remembers seeing you at the restaurant or the gallery. Sounds to me like you ran in and ran out of the party so you'd have an alibi. But that still leaves you a lot of time. More than enough."

My nerves started to fray. I sent Maggie an anxious look.

"Got a weapon?" Maggie asked.

He turned to her. "Excuse me?"

"Got a murder weapon?"

"Yeah. She was choked with her scarf. No prints on it."

"She was beaten, too, right? On the head? You find the weapon that did that?"

Vaughn looked uncomfortable for the first time that day. He scratched the side of his head. "Not yet."

"Got a time of death?"

"Sometime between three and six p.m. on Monday. Same time that your client has no alibi."

"Uh-huh." Maggie closed the legal pad on the table in front of her. "Got any more questions, Detective?" she said.

He looked at her with a mildly amused expression. "I've got a lot. Because from what we can tell, from all the evidence we collected and the fact that there was no sign of a chase, a fight or a struggle, Jane Augustine was probably killed by someone she knew. The only thing that shows she might have fought back at the last minute was the stuff scattered all over the floor near her body."

"What stuff?" Maggie asked.

He looked pointedly at me. "Your client's lipstick, her credit cards, her checkbook—stuff she had in her purse that went flying when Jane realized what was happening and fought back."

"I dropped my purse when I was trying to call for help!" I said. "After I found her lying there…"

Vaughn directed his gaze back at Maggie and continued on in a calm voice. "From what your client tells us about the scene and from what we found, Jane let someone into the house. Probably, from her positioning, she turned her back to someone because she trusted that person."

"If you believe my client's recollections about the scene, why didn't you believe her when she says she didn't do it?"

"Wait," I interrupted, remembering something. "Jane

told me on Monday that she was getting together with a friend before the party."

Vaughn glanced at me. "Sure. That friend was you."

"No, earlier. Like in the afternoon."

Again, his attention went back to Maggie. "It seems to me that your girl here—" he jerked his head at me "—was one of the last people to see Jane that day, certainly the last person to talk to her in detail, and she was the person that Jane had made plans with before the party. She was very close with Jane that weekend. And that means that she had the opportunity and the means and hey, would you look at that? She just happens to land in Augustine's anchor chair the next day." He grinned and held up his hands. "Sounds like motive to me."

I was trembling inside. I wanted to scream, *Shut up! That's crazy!*

Maggie stood. "We're done."

"You're pulling her out?"

"I'm pulling her." She looked pointedly at me, and I got to my feet.

Vaughn gave Maggie a cold smile. "Sure, take her out. Doesn't matter to me. Because I'm real sure you'll be bringing her back sometime soon." He stood along with her. "By the way, that little deal you struck with someone at headquarters in order to keep us quiet about the person of interest thing? It's over."

53

I could feel someone watching me. I could feel it even before I opened my eyes. I kept my eyes closed, trying to wake up, trying to make sense of the jumbled, jagged images in my dreams, all of them red—the blood on Jane's body, her scarf. And the fear that tinged my sleep—that had an alarming red hue to it, too. And now someone was watching me. I knew it. I opened my eyes.

I yelped. "Sam!" I sucked in a lungful of refreshing air.

I was exhausted last night, and sleep had finally come so hard that I'd forgotten that Sam had skipped rugby practice and come to my place. Or maybe I'd forgotten because I was accustomed now to sleeping without him. Or maybe it was because I didn't want to remember how odd it had been between us last night. Sam came over, and he'd listened to my tale of being questioned. We'd analyzed the situation from every angle possible. He comforted me. But there was a distance between us, as if we'd stumbled over something that night at North Pond Café, and we hadn't been able to get to our feet yet.

Now, he scooped me into him, and I curled against his warm chest. "I was waiting until the last minute to wake you up," he said.

"What time is it?"

"Five after five."

"I have to go. I have to get to the studio for makeup."

"Call in sick."

"I'm not sick."

"You've got an unbelievable amount going on in your life, and you're going to make yourself sick if you keep going like this."

And he didn't even know about Theo, about the fact that he was my alibi for the night the cops thought I was with Jane, about the fact that I still couldn't reach him. "I have to keep going," I said. "And this is my job, Sam. I really like it. And I'm also doing it for Jane, despite the fact that the cops seem to think that I killed her to get it."

"I can't believe they'll stick with that theory for long. You're the least violent person in the country."

"I know!" I sat up. "Remember that bug in our room in Mexico?"

He laughed. "That wasn't a bug. It was a small aircraft masquerading as a bug. And you still wanted me to get it out of the room instead of killing it."

"Exactly. It's crazy that they think I did something to Jane."

Sam shook his head. "You know what? I've been thinking about this. You said Detective Vaughn was a jerk to you when he questioned you last year."

I nodded. Neither of us mentioned that the reason I was questioned was because Sam had disappeared. We were both so tired of talking about it, of analyzing it, that somewhere along the way we'd both started pretending it hadn't happened.

"He's probably just being a jerk now," Sam continued. "I mean, he hasn't told anyone you're a person of interest. Maybe you're not. Maybe he's doing this to a bunch of people. He's just a jerk."

I went with that sentiment. I got ready for work, and because it was still raining, I took a cab to Trial TV. All the while, I repeated in my mind, *He's just a jerk. He's just a jerk. He's just a jerk.*

Meanwhile, I had to talk to *someone* about the guy I'd taken home Friday night, the guy who was my alibi for that night. I needed to talk to someone who would never judge me.

I called Q from my cell phone. "So, you remember Theo?"

"The twenty-one-year-old?"

"Yeah."

"I think the brakes on the train might be screeching and I'm heading for a crash."

"Oh, Jesus, tell me."

"Promise not to say I told you so?"

"Never."

I sighed. I told him about Vaughn's questions about Friday night, how Theo was in Mexico and unreachable.

I expected Q to laugh, to be delighted, to hoot and holler and give me hell and somehow make me feel better.

Instead, I heard silence, then a soft, "Yeesh."

"Yeesh? What's that mean?"

"Yeesh, like this might not be the fun train wreck I expected. This sounds like a full-on plane crash. With two-hundred and fifty people on board. Into the Indian Ocean. Everyone dead."

"Is that supposed to be funny?"

"No. I mean, I'm sorry, but this detective could get you in some serious trouble here."

"He's just an asshole." It felt good to swear.

Q said nothing—no quip words, no mocking jest.

I blinked. I looked out the cab window at a vacant lot on Clybourn, Q's reaction making me feel even more vacant. And terrified.

The cab turned onto Webster. "I have to go."

"Can I do anything?"

"Go to Mexico and find the train wreck?"

Still no laugh from him. Just a "Let me know."

I walked through the halls of Trial TV, trying to focus on the day, trying not to think about Jane or Vaughn. I had nearly gotten myself out of the twist in my head when C.J. came running into the makeup room. We were only minutes from going on-air with the morning broadcast, and I'd been reading my script. I'd finally gotten the hang of reading it beforehand, making it sound fresh when I read it again on air.

C.J. wore dark jeans and a white blazer today. Her expression was stern under her dark glasses.

"I just wanted to give you the heads-up," she said. "New script." She handed it to me. "And one of the stories is about Jane."

My breath caught in my lungs and seemed to come back up so that I felt as if I had choked on something invisible. "What about Jane?"

"We don't know. The cops have called a press conference."

"To say what?"

"They won't give us anything." C.J.'s stern expression turned to anguish. "Maybe they have a lead."

Or maybe they have a person of interest.

"Izzy, we need you on set!" I heard someone call from outside the room.

C.J. followed me out while I left the room, the makeup artist scampering beside me, patting me with more powder. No one could forget my flop sweat attack a few days ago, and as a result, I was the most thoroughly powdered newscaster in the city.

I got settled on the desk—Jane's desk, I always thought of it—my eyes reading over the new script. There was a notation I didn't recognize in front of the story about the press conference.

"What does this mean?" I asked C.J., pointing to it.

"Means you'll cut to that story whenever the cops start the meat of the conference. We don't know exactly what time that will be. Just listen for your cue."

Should I tell C.J. that the press conference might be about me?

"Clear set," I heard. "Izzy, ready?"

"Uh…" There was no time.

They started the countdown.

"Good luck," C.J. said, stepping away from the anchor desk.

I arranged my suit so I was sitting on the jacket to pull it straight. I arranged my face so it didn't give the impression of utter panic. I tried to keep positive. I kept repeating my mantra, *He's just an asshole. He's just an asshole.*

And then we were on.

I read and I turned and I smiled and I cut to field reporters, but the whole time, I felt as if my skin was zinging with anticipation. I was almost relieved when I heard in my ear, "Go to the Augustine story," and I spoke the words, "Let's go live to Tom Bennett at Police Headquarters on South Michigan Avenue here in Chicago. Tom has the latest on the murder of our colleague, Jane Augustine."

54

At first it wasn't as bad as I thought. There was Vaughn, in a sport coat and yellow tie, looking like the picture of efficiency, a flag to one side of him, the Chicago Police logo behind him. Mikes from at least fifteen different stations and networks were set up on the podium.

"We're here today to ask the community for assistance," he said. "We need that assistance to help find who is responsible for the murder of Jane Augustine. First we would like any information about the identity of a man named Mick, who might have spent time in the company of Ms. Augustine on Friday night. This man is believed to be a writer, living in the Chicago area."

I took in a huge breath, sucking in air as if I'd been drowning for the last minute and had just noticed it.

But then Vaughn shuffled some papers, cleared his throat, and I felt the water flood over my head again.

"We'd also like to discuss today a person of interest," he said.

At the anchor desk, I clutched the script in my hands, which had grown damp with sweat, watching Vaughn with growing terror. And because all the monitors—those behind my desk, those in the interview area, those for the producers—were showing Vaughn's face, it felt as if he were surrounding me. His voice boomed into my earpiece.

I waited for Vaughn to say my name. I hoped to hear

someone else's. But instead he summarized the investigation—how they had sealed the Augustine residence for days; how they had collected evidence; how the Chicago Crime Lab had finished some analysis and was rushing to complete the rest.

"In terms of the person of interest…." He looked down, as if searching for the correct name. He paused. "Let me say that this person had been cooperative with the police until recently, which leads us to release her name in case anyone in the community can provide additional information which we haven't been able to collect."

Her. I'd heard it.

My eyes shot across the room to C.J., whose expression was stern, rapt.

My breath felt shallow. Why did I feel so guilty once again, when I'd done nothing?

"The person of interest," Vaughn said, "is Isabel McNeil, a local attorney and now a newscaster on Trial TV, where Ms. Augustine had also worked."

Every pair of eyes in the newsroom shot to mine. I felt a ferocious blush creeping over me.

"I've talked to them twice," I said, with as much authority as I could muster. "I had nothing to do with it, and I've told them everything I know."

C.J.'s mouth was hanging agape. She shook her head fiercely, then turned and stormed from the set.

I heard a producer in my ear. "They're not taking questions. We're going back to you in one…. Uh, I guess."

I saw Vaughn end the press conference. The reporters erupted with questions, but Vaughn shook his head and held up his hand, then left. The monitors shifted to a shot of Tom Bennett trying to hide his surprise while he wrapped up what had been said.

And then it was back to me. The person of interest.

I went to that spot I'd found a few days ago, when I'd first sat in the anchor chair. I saw the script in front of me.

I heard words leaving my mouth. But it was as if some-one else was speaking. I sank once again into a detached space in my mind, while I talked and read and talked some more.

No one looked at me during commercial breaks. No one seemed to know what to say. C.J. was gone from the set for the rest of the broadcast.

The minute it was over, she was next to the anchor desk, her face grim. "I need you in my office. Immediately."

"I've been on the phone with Ari Adler," C.J. said. "Dis-cussing the fact that you're a suspect in Jane's death."

"I am not a suspect! I'm a person of interest." For some reason, the term came out with some pride. "It's very dif-ferent," I rushed to explain. "It doesn't mean anything. I'm *not* a suspect. I'm not even a witness except for after the fact."

She straightened the lapel of her white jacket and squirmed a bit in her chair. "Tom Bennett has a source inside the CPD. It's not official, and they don't have enough yet to arrest you, but they're looking at you as someone who could have killed Jane."

I actually felt a falling sensation, as if I were tumbling backward into a gaping black hole. "C.J., I did not hurt Jane."

"Of course you didn't." She didn't sound convincing.

"I didn't!" I said.

She held up two hands. "Izzy, we love you. You stepped up when this network needed you, when Jane needed you. And none of us will ever forget it. We think you're great. You could have a career in broadcasting ahead of you. But it's not at Trial TV."

"What are you saying?"

"Look, for better or for worse, our ratings will probably skyrocket after this. From a business standpoint, I'd love to keep you, even for a few days. But from a human standpoint, we can't have someone who's a potential suspect in Jane's murder sitting in Jane's chair. Vanessa Bock, the afternoon anchor, is going to start headlining the morning, and we're pulling a reporter in to cover afternoons and evenings on the desk." C.J. shook her head, as if she could barely get the words out. But she got them out all right. "Izzy, we have to let you go."

My eyes swam around her office, looking for solid ground. Like yesterday, the place was still packed with boxes filled with office stuff, personal items, coffee mugs, awards.

"Izzy, I believe you," C.J. said. "And I believe in whatever you want to do with yourself and your career."

What *would* I do with my career now? With myself? Then I realized it didn't matter. Little mattered compared to what had happened to Jane. And the fact that I was being questioned about it.

My eyes finally settled on one of C.J.'s boxes stuffed with broadcast awards, plaques, trophies. I pointed at them. "I guess I won't get a chance to win any of those."

C.J.'s eyes stayed on me. "You might be able to find another gig in the business. But I won't kid you. It'll be tough to get someone to take you on after this. I'll be a reference, of course."

There was a knock on C.J.'s door. One of the interns stuck his head in. "We've got a crowd outside."

"Other press?" C.J. asked.

He nodded. "Lots."

"Damn." She stood. "Izzy, I don't want to usher you out, but you should go. It will only get worse."

I stood with her. I extended my hand to C.J. and shook hers. "By the way, this is freaking baloney." Nope, the swear replacement campaign wasn't going to cut it today. "No, let me tell you, this is fucking bullshit."

55

Outside Trial TV, a small crowd of photographers sprang into action, their *click, click, click* reminding me of Vaughn's ballpoint pen.

"Izzy!" a reporter yelled. "How are you?"

I recognized him as Andrew Trammel, whose contract I had negotiated two years ago. It was so strange to see him in this environment, to be on the other side of the microphone—not as an attorney or a reporter but as the *story*.

Andy put his mike close to my face. "What's your reaction to the news that you've been named a person of interest in the Augustine case?"

I knew that if Maggie could see me now, she would be yelling, *No comment!*

But I really wasn't a no-comment kind of girl.

The rest of the reporters shoved their mikes forward.

"I was," I said, "the one who found Jane Augustine on the night she died. I adored Jane. I know nothing other than what I've already told the police."

Except about Jane's scarfing games.

The reporters surged forward, blocking me in, yelling more questions. Video and TV cameras surrounded me.

"Izzy, over here!" The voice that cut through the others was familiar. I looked to the right. Mayburn. He pushed through the reporters, grabbed my arm and propelled me through the throng to a navy-blue Mercedes. "Get in!"

He opened the passenger door, practically shoved me inside and slammed it behind me.

Lucy was in the driver's seat, her ivory-gold sweater matching her blond hair. "Hi, Iz," she said with a smile.

Mayburn jumped in the backseat. "Go!" he yelled.

Lucy's face set in a determined line, and she floored the car and squealed out of the Trial TV parking lot.

"Thank you!" I said. "How did you know to get me?"

"I've been watching you on Trial TV around the clock," Lucy said. "When I saw the press conference, I told Mayburn you needed help."

"Something else, too," Mayburn said from behind. "I tailed Carina Fariello today—that accountant who used to work for Jackson Prince? She's at home right now. And considering the press conference about you this morning, I think we better get over there and talk to her. Now."

As we drove, I told them Trial TV had fired me.

"What?" Lucy was outraged. "You were great on that station."

"Thanks. They said they had to let me go because of this person of interest thing and the fact that I happened to take over Jane's job after she died."

Mayburn grunted. "Yeah, that doesn't look good."

I shivered as a chill of fear raced through my body. "I'm scared."

"You didn't do anything wrong," Lucy said.

"I know that, but the cops don't."

Silence in the car.

"The upside is…" I trailed off. I always could find an upside to just about any scenario, but what was the upside here? "Okay, new topic. How do we approach Carina Fariello?"

We batted around a few ways to speak with her. Although Mayburn rarely shied away from subterfuge or a little creative license with the facts, we decided that we would be up-front with her and conversational. More than anything we wanted to get her talking.

I turned around and looked at Mayburn. "Hey," I said, "what's going on with the Fig Leaf case?"

"I need you to get a pearl thong."

"I already gave you a pearl thong. Maggie's. And by the way, I want it back."

He pulled at the collar of his brown leather jacket and shifted in the seat. "Uh, yeah, it's kind of been dismantled."

"Dismantled? Why?"

"I told you I had to have it analyzed. Those pearls are plastic, by the way."

"Did you really think they were going to be real pearls?"

"Hey, I want one of those thongs." Lucy stopped at a light and shot a sultry smile over her shoulder at Mayburn.

"Oh, trust me, I'm getting you one in every color."

"Okay, no sex talk," I said. "And, Mayburn, now that I'm out of a full-time job, *again,* I not only expect to be reimbursed for that thong, but I want another one for my friend."

"I need the other kind of thong. One of the black boxed ones that the guy in the van delivered. From what you told me, Josie is guarding the pearl thongs. And the owner of the store says she only knew about one kind of pearl thong — the silver, like the one you gave me."

"Why don't you just get a key from the owner and you go in there and get it?"

"Because she's in Palm Beach and won't be back in town anytime soon. Plus she says she didn't know Josie was keeping things locked up. She doesn't have a key to that box. Only Josie does apparently.

"I'd have to either steal the lock box where she keeps them, or borrow the key from her when she's not looking."

"There's got to be a way."

More silence, all of us thinking. Compared to shaking a murder rap, getting my hands on a piece of lingerie didn't sound that challenging. "I'll figure it out," I said.

"Here we are." Lucy pulled over to the side of the street, pointing.

Carina Fariello's house was light blue, a single-story family home in a neighborhood where there was lots of parking and moms strolled by with their kids.

We rang the doorbell. A heavyset woman with black curly hair, probably in her late forties, opened the door and peered at us through the screen. She looked at us in the same tense way that I would if three strange people showed up on my doorstep. "Yes?"

"Ms. Fariello, I'm Isabel McNeil. We wanted to see if we could talk to you about Jane Augustine."

Her face sagged. "I can't believe what happened to her."

"I know. We're trying to find anything we can about her murder. Your name was found on a piece of paper in Jane's desk. Can we speak with you?"

"Are you the police?" She glanced at our clothing.

"Private detective," Mayburn said.

"Private detective," not "private investigator," was the official term utilized in Illinois statutes, but most people still used the term *investigator* or *P.I.* Mayburn threw around the *detective* word when he wanted to sound more official.

It seemed to do the trick. "Yeah, sure." Carina Fariello unlocked and opened her screened door. "I don't have a lot of time, though. I have to get ready for work."

"We just have a few questions."

She led us down a narrow foyer covered in fake wood flooring to a living room that looked generally unused. The light blue of the furniture cushions probably had once matched the house paint, but had since been bleached to a light gray.

Carina Fariello pointed to the couch and took a seat on a nearby chair. As Mayburn, Lucy and I sat on the couch, she stood again. "I'm sorry. I should have asked. Can I get you something to drink?"

We all declined. "Ms. Fariello…" I said.

"Call me Carina." She took her seat again.

"Thanks. Carina, as I mentioned, your name was on a paper in Jane Augustine's desk. There were also about fourteen other names. All were doctors." I lifted my purse from the floor and rooted around until I found the list. I read a few of them. "Do you know these doctors?"

Carina's face was grim, her eyes jumping around now. "Who are you working for?"

Mayburn spoke up. "We're working on this case for free. We—" he gestured at himself and me "—We don't believe that the police are doing enough to find out what happened to Jane."

I was relieved he didn't mention the term "person of interest."

"I don't understand. Why would those names be related to her death?"

"We're not sure, either," I said. "We're just going over some of the stories she was working on. One was about Jackson Prince. Something possibly about class action lawsuits. These names were on the back of research she had. You used to work for Prince, right?"

Somewhere during my explanation, Carina's eyes had slipped to the floor. They stayed there, and she said nothing for a few seconds.

Then her eyes came back to mine. "I did work for him. Until he fired me. I was the one who called Jane with those names."

A beat went by. "That's great," Mayburn said. His face was bland, almost bored, but I could see an excited glimmer in his eyes. "What kind of work did you do for him?"

Carina's jaw moved into a firm line. "I was his office manager and bookkeeper. I'm a CPA. I worked for him for years, but he fired me five months ago." Her eyes grew a little wet. "I have a job out at O'Hare now."

"Why did Mr. Prince fire you?" I asked.

"He said it was because he had to lay off some staff. He

did have a bad couple of years recently—only a few big verdicts or settlements—but no one else got fired, and the firm was starting to do great again. Especially with the Ladera cases."

"What's Prince's role with those cases?"

"He's liaison-counsel. He oversees the entire lawsuit and the other lawyers working on it. If the plaintiffs get any settlements or judgments, he'll get about a third of everything."

"Did the doctors on the list have anything to do with Ladera?"

"Well, that's what Prince said, but I don't know… Do you know anything about class action suits or how they work with the experts?"

"They pool their experts," I said, remembering what Grady had told me. "Usually, they just have a few for the whole class."

"Exactly." Carina nodded emphatically. "We already had a panel of experts for the Ladera, and yet the firm kept paying the doctors on the list, too. Prince told me the doctors were additional experts. I kept asking him about it, because it seemed weird. Each doctor was someone that Jackson had consulted with before the lawsuit went into class action status, but there was no reason to keep them on after that."

"Is it possible he was just keeping them on the payroll in case they needed additional guidance with the case?"

"That's what I thought at first. But usually if a doctor acts as an expert—maybe they review records or summarize research—then they submit bills to us. They tell us how many hours they spent. So the bills are always for different amounts. But with these doctors, even before the cases got class action status, Jackson would create an invoice for them, rather than the other way around, and the invoices were always the exact same amount."

"You said you kept asking him about the payments," Mayburn prodded.

"I did. He told me the doctors were experts. And he told

me to remember what my job was at the firm. And then he told me to pay them." Her face went stiff. "And I don't know if you know Mr. Prince, but you really don't say no to him."

"Because he's charming?" I asked.

She laughed, but it had a sour edge. "He's not that charming when there's no jury or a camera. He's a screamer."

I grimaced. In the legal profession, certain lawyers, despite their perfect suits and their gentleman's attitude in court, had the reputation of being a "screamer" in the comfort of their law-firm walls.

"He yells at the staff all the time," Carina said. "That's one thing I don't miss about that job." She pulled nervously at a strand of hair, then seemed to notice and clasped her hands tight in her lap. "It was bugging me, though, those payments, and I felt like it was part of my job to speak up, you know? When I kept asking about them, he wasn't happy. Then when he started flying those same doctors around on his private plane, and I asked him about that, too, he fired me a few days afterward."

"Where were the doctors going on the plane?" Mayburn asked.

"They used it individually to go to different places. From what I could tell from the passenger lists we had to provide to the pilots, it was the doctors and their friends or the doctors and their families. And they almost always stayed at one of Prince's vacation houses."

"Did Prince always treat his experts this well?" Mayburn asked.

She laughed with that brittle edge again. "Are you kidding? He treats them like they're paralegals."

"So why the special treatment here?" I asked. "Why those doctors?"

Carina shrugged. "He would never tell me. Then he fired me."

"And is that when you called Jane?"

She nodded. "I've watched her every night for years, and I know she likes legal stories." Her mouth pursed. "I guess I should say she *liked* legal stories. Anyway, there was an ad on her old station. It was Jane asking people to call the station with any legal news. I didn't know if there was much of a story with Jackson Prince, but I thought I'd try. I was so mad about being fired. I left a message on the tip line. It took a while, but then she called me back." The tightness to her mouth left, and she smiled. "Jane called me herself, can you believe that?"

I smiled, too. "That sounds like Jane. What did she say?"

"She just asked me some questions. I told her about the lump payments to the doctors, the plane trips, how they were all supposedly on the Ladera case."

"What did Jane do then?"

"She asked me for the phone numbers of the doctors. I didn't have them anymore, but I told her where each doctor lived—they're in different places around the country. She must have found their information because she phoned me back and said she'd called them. Most wouldn't talk to her, but then she found someone she'd met before, Dr. Hamilton-Wood. And Jane had spoken to her one-on-one."

"Do you know what the doctor told her?"

"I'm not sure. Jane told me that she was moving to Trial TV, but she was still looking into the story. She said that she was close to putting something together. She asked if I would be interviewed on the air when she was ready, and I told her, yes. Prince didn't even give me severance pay, and he told the unemployment office that I was fired for cause, so I couldn't get unemployment. I called a couple of lawyers, but no one seems to think it's a great employment case. Or maybe they just don't want to sue Jackson Prince."

She looked at her watch. "I don't know anything else. I hadn't talked to Jane in a while." She shuddered. "And then she was dead."

56

Rush hour in Chicago is never fun. Years ago, afternoon traffic used to head northbound, cars full of refugees fleeing the Loop. But now, people worked in every neighborhood in Chicago, and rush hour no longer discriminated against North, South, East or West. It was everywhere.

So there I was, heading home in a cab at rush hour with lots of time to turn over and over in my mind what Carina Fariello had told me. What was going on with Jackson Prince and the doctors he was paying? Did it have anything to do with what happened to Jane? I *had* to find out. Because not only was Jane dead, and not only was I out of a job, but I could be out of a life if I didn't stop this person of interest craziness from spinning out of control.

The best place to start, it seemed, was with Dr. Hamilton-Wood, the one doctor Jane apparently had some success with.

The cabbie grunted as he got into another lane and got stopped by a long line of barely crawling cars. Normally the traffic would have made me grit my teeth, but today, I didn't mind so much. I needed to simply sit and decompress and get my mind around the fact that in the span of a week I'd gone from unemployed to news reporter to anchor and back to unemployed again. I'd gone from upstanding citizen to person of interest. So, in a way, it was good to be alone in a sticky, grungy cab littered with Red Eye newspapers, all of which were at least a week old, none of which had articles about Jane. Or me.

My cell phone rang. Sam.

"Are you all right?" he said. "I'm at O'Hare, about to get on my plane to Cinci."

"I forgot you were going." Sam had a meeting with a big client in Cincinnati the next morning.

"Well, I'm not now. I've been working all day, but I just saw the news. And heard your name. Iz, this is insane."

"I know."

"Where are you?"

"In a cab going home."

"Good. I'm leaving the airport. I'm walking back down the terminal right now."

"No, don't change your trip."

"Are you kidding? I'm coming to your place. Are you all right?"

"Yeah. Except that I got fired."

"Trial TV *fired* you?"

"They did."

"That's bullshit!"

"That's what I told them." The cab changed lanes again, but the traffic slowed even more. And yet it felt nice to be barely inching along. "Look, Sam, don't cancel your trip. You're already at the airport, and you're only going for a night and there's nothing you can do. And the truth is I could use a little time to myself. Last night was…" I didn't know how to put it—awkward, lacking, not "us"?

"Yeah. I know what you're saying."

At least we still had the ability to communicate without words. At least we both agreed that last night had not been so wonderful, even if we couldn't agree on, or even figure out, why.

"When does your flight board?" I asked.

"Five minutes."

"Just go. Nothing is going to happen. I'm going to hole up at home."

"I don't know, Red Hot. I think you need someone with you right now. Even if you don't want it to be me."

"I'm fine by myself."

"Are you sure?"

The cab got off at North Avenue. "I'm almost home. I'm sure."

He sighed. I could hear the frustration there. "I'll call you as soon as I land."

"Perfect. Love you."

"I love you, Red Hot."

Twenty minutes later, the cab was turning onto Sedgwick, and I was breathing deeper with relief. But as the taxi approached my condo, things started swirling very fast again.

News vans littered my street. Two of them were from Trial TV. Others were NBC, CBS, even CNN. Reporters stood on my front lawn, chatting amiably. Waiting.

"Shazzer," I said, under my breath. Then, when the swear replacement didn't have the right feel I said, "Shit." How did they get my address? My number and address were unlisted. But then I remembered that as an employee of Trial TV, at least until today, the station had my address. And I knew from working around the news industry for a while that once a certain network or station finds a good shot or a good witness or a good anything, it doesn't stay secret for long.

"I need to go somewhere else," I told the cab driver.

"Where to?"

"Um…"

Sam was probably on his plane right now. Q had already left that morning for a trip to Miami with his boyfriend.

I dialed Maggie's cell phone but got a message. She might be in a late meeting with a client. Or maybe with Wyatt.

"I gotta get going," the cabbie said. "I've got a pickup at O'Hare."

A pickup at O'Hare—the Holy Grail of Chicago cabbies. They'll throw you in front of a bus going fifty on Lake Shore if they get a call for a pickup at O'Hare.

I tried to remember what my mom was doing today. I didn't have a key to her place on me.

Just then one of the reporters saw me in the cab. He pointed, and they all started surging toward me.

"Whoa," the cabbie said. "I'm out of here. You have to go."

"Wait, wait, please. I have to figure out…" My mind raced about. I could get out and run for the Sedgwick El train. I could get out and run for my front door, but they'd never leave. All night they would be out there.

"Damn it," I said.

"Seriously," the driver said. "You have to get going."

Just then I saw someone else move toward the cab, even faster than the reporters or cameramen.

Grady.

He yanked the cab door open, his face worried. "My car is right here." He pointed to the curb.

"Thank God."

Grady threw a twenty at the driver, pulled me from the cab and hustled me to the car. Cameras whirred and clicked. Reporters pushed toward me and shouted questions. One question I heard over and over again—*Did you kill Jane Augustine?*—and it terrified me.

I knew what Maggie would tell me to say, and I finally listened to her.

"No comment!"

57

Grady's place was a haven, although you wouldn't know it from the outside. He lived in a nondescript condo building off State Street, where a lot of the late-twenties and early-thirties crowd lived until they could afford better. Grady couldn't yet, not on what an associate made. But inside, Grady's condo was decorated with care.

"I forgot how great your apartment is." I looked around the front room with its chocolate walls, white-framed photos, leather couches and golden drum lamps.

"Yeah, well, don't forget I got help from my sister. Hey, I'm going to change out of this suit. You want something to wear?" He glanced at my own suit.

"Maybe just a sweatshirt or something."

He gestured at me to follow him into the bedroom. The walls there were charcoal, the bedding stark white.

"You're so neat," I said.

"My cleaning woman is neat. She came today." He opened his closet, pulled out a red hooded sweatshirt that read *Galena Fire Department.*

I pointed at the sweatshirt. "Have you been home lately?"

"Nah. Too busy. Just like you."

There was a subtle edge to his words. I ignored it. I slipped out of my suit jacket. "Well, now that I've been fired I won't be so busy." I pulled the sweatshirt over the silk camisole I wore underneath. "Man, that feels better."

I tugged my hair from the collar, pushed the sleeves up. I realized Grady hadn't said anything.

He stood in front of his closet. He took off his suit coat. "So what does that mean? You're going to have more time for me now?"

I shrugged. "Yeah." *Once I get the cops off my back; once I find out who killed Jane.*

Grady unbuttoned the cuffs of his shirt. He had strong forearms, long fingers. "You sure?"

"Sure, I'm sure." I wanted to be sure. I wanted my life to be as simplistic as this.

His eyes weren't moving from mine. The condo seemed quiet suddenly, the buzz of the city, of the last week, disappearing.

He took a step toward me. Then another. He lifted one of the strings from the hood on the sweatshirt I wore, twirled it in his hand. "You look good in this." Then he was closer, within inches. He had a faint freckle on the right side of his bottom lip. I stared at it. He leaned in. He nudged my cheekbone with his lips, then bent and put his face in my neck and inhaled.

"God," he said. "You smell good."

So did he—more earthy than Sam, more familiar than Theo.

He pulled his face back, looked at me again, brushed a lock of hair from my forehead.

And then he kissed me. I pushed back into his lips. Both of his hands went to my face. We kept kissing. Fifteen seconds went by, maybe twenty.

Then suddenly he stopped and moved his face away, his eyes searching mine. "You're not into it, are you?"

"Into what?"

"Me and you."

"Sure I am." I wanted to be. I wanted to think—*to feel*—anything except reality.

He took a step back. My face felt cold without his hands there.

"I shouldn't be asking questions now," he said. "You have too much going on already."

My brain was a scramble. There *was* too much inside it—too many questions, too many worries, maybe too many men. I opened my mouth, tried to put into words the jumble of thoughts. I started and stopped a few times.

And then suddenly there was one thing that seemed clear, one thing that I wasn't questioning. "I'm into us as friends."

His face was impassive. A beat went by. Then another. "So you're into us as friends, huh? Nothing more."

"Yeah." Saying it out loud made me realize how true it was. But I felt awful at the resigned look on Grady's face. "Maybe it's just what's going on right now. All this stuff with Jane."

"It's not that stuff." His face was hard now. "You've been trying to see us differently, but…"

He was right. And he deserved to know it. "I don't know what's wrong with me, Grady. You're amazing. And adorable." I looked at those forearms. "And sexy."

"But not to you. Not really."

I said nothing.

"Is it you and Sam? Are you guys back together?"

"It's not that."

My cell phone rang from my purse, sitting on Grady's bed. I didn't answer it. Grady and I just stared at each other, some kind of understanding settling between us.

"It's okay, Iz," he said. "We're friends."

The phone rang again. It stopped. Then started again.

I finally broke our gaze and found my cell phone. *Sam, cell.* He'd called three times.

"Sorry," I said to Grady. I raised the phone to my ear. "Hello?"

"Jesus, Izzy, I can't believe you," he said. "I can't believe you're with Grady."

Out on Grady's balcony, the sky was gray and misty. Clutching the phone to my ear, I shivered. But it didn't matter. The conversation was short.

"Jesus." Sam's voice was full of irritation. "My flight got delayed, I went to the bar, and there you are on CNN, getting in Grady's goddamned car!"

"I didn't know there was going to be media crawling around my house. I didn't know what to do."

"So you called Grady."

"No! I didn't call him. He was there, and he helped me."

"Yeah, he's been really fucking helpful for a while now."

"Grady is a friend of mine."

"He's more than that, and you know it."

I thought of what had just gone on between Grady and me. "We're friends."

"Some friend. You waved me off, Iz. *Me*. When I wanted to help you. You let him rescue you."

My mouth fell open. Wordless for a moment, I looked down at the street, fifteen floors below, the cars zipping by. "He did *not* rescue me."

"Yeah, he did. And if it's not him, it'll be someone else. You'll always be one of those people who's got someone."

"What the hell are you talking about?"

"I'm talking about the fact that when everything happened six months ago, I wasn't even gone for more than a week before you moved on to Grady."

"You *disappeared*. You were *gone*. And I didn't move on!"

"You did. You let him save you."

Sam's harsh words somehow disintegrated the confusion in my head. "You know what, Sam? No one is going to save me. No one except myself."

This time I hung up on him.

I yanked open the balcony door. Grady stood in his kitchen, leaning against a counter, his arms crossed over his chest.

"Grady, I'm sorry. I've got to go."

"To Sam's?"

"No. To find Dr. Hamilton-Wood."

58

I drove south on Lake Shore Drive in Grady's car, heading toward Hyde Park. Rush hour was over now, and I zipped past the Loop, the Shedd Aquarium and the Field Museum. I got off at 42nd Street. I pulled over to the side of the road and glanced at the MapQuest directions. A minute later, I was in an older, stately neighborhood, some houses brick, others stone, all majestic. A few were in need of repair, but generally the street was impressive. According to the newspapers, this South Side neighborhood had undergone a resurgence lately, and it wasn't hard to see why—it was close to the lake, near the University of Chicago and the Museum of Science & Industry, and it retained an architectural flavor that spoke of Chicago in days gone by.

I glanced at the directions again, searching for Dr. Hamilton-Wood's place. The fact that Grady had lent me his car and looked up these directions made me love him. But that love was, I saw now, springing from the earth of our friendship. It wasn't a bloom of romance.

Sam, of course, was a different story. Sam and I had the friendship and definitely the romance, but something was off and now wasn't the time to figure it out. Now was the time for action.

I put both Sam and Grady from my mind and turned down Blackstone Avenue. I drove around the block a few times until I found Dr. Hamilton-Wood's house. Kids played in the front yard as dusk settled over the city. A woman sat on the front steps. I drove past, parked a few houses down and watched her. She was African-American, her hair straightened and curled up gently at the ends. She wore a white blouse and jeans. Her legs were crossed, her expression blank as she watched the kids kicking two balls—one huge and yellow, one pink.

I got out of the car and walked toward the house. It was older, like the rest of the block, but Dr. Hamilton-Wood's house was lovely, made of white stone with a turret at the upper left and stained glass in the front door. That stained glass sparkled as the streetlights replaced the last remnants of daylight.

The kids stopped as I walked up the front sidewalk. I must have looked harmless because they picked up their game just as quickly.

The woman uncrossed her legs, sat up straighter and put a pleasant smile on her face.

"Hi, I'm Izzy McNeil." I extended my hand.

She stood and shook it. "Angela Hamilton. Are you new in the neighborhood?"

"No. I'm here because of Jane Augustine."

The smile swept away. "It's so sad what happened to her. I admired Jane immensely."

"How did you know her?"

She walked down the few stairs to ground level. She could have been anywhere in age from twenty-five to forty-five, although her medical degree probably put her toward the latter.

"My brother was shot seven years ago," she said. "They didn't catch who did it for the longest time, and only then because of Jane. She was the only one who kept asking questions and digging around. The cops had long stopped caring."

"Yeah, that sounds like Jane. She liked the tough stories."

"Are you collecting for some kind of charity in her

name?" The doctor gestured toward the house. "I can get my checkbook."

"No, I'm here to ask some questions. I'm trying to figure out how Jane died."

"I heard she was beaten."

"And strangled." I saw Jane's eyes, permanently open, the pinpricks of blood dotting the whites of those eyes. "I'm trying to find out who did that to her. I understand you spoke to Jane recently about a story she was working on?"

A flicker of something—caution, perhaps?—registered on her face, then disappeared. "Yes. She was working on a story about class actions. I gave her some information."

"What kind of information?"

Something closed in the doctor's face. "It's fairly technical."

"Did it have anything to do with Jackson Prince?"

She blinked a few times. "Possibly. We talked about a lot of things. But look, I should go. I have to get the kids to bed." She glanced at her children, still tearing around the lawn. "Brady! Thomas! In the house and get ready for a bath."

The children grumbled but pattered up the front stone steps.

"Good night." She gave me a polite smile, similar to the one she'd had when I first walked up. She started to turn away.

"Dr. Hamilton-Wood," I said. "I just have a few questions."

She grimaced. "It's Dr. Hamilton now. My husband and I split. I'm using my maiden name." She shook her head. "Anyway…"

"Dr. Hamilton—"

"Look, I spoke to Jane only because I knew her from my brother's shooting, and to be honest, I felt like I owed her, but really I don't have any interest in discussing this any further. Okay?" Her face was determined. She started to turn again.

"Dr. Hamilton, what if Jane died because of that story?"

She froze, cocked her head. "How is that possible?"

"I need to know if the story had to do with Jackson Prince in particular. He was angry with Jane. I saw that myself at Trial TV on the day she died, and he—"

"Wait, what did you say your name was?"

I swallowed hard. Never had I felt so hesitant to say my own name. Finally, I did.

"Izzy," she said. "Isabel. You're the person the police were talking about."

"I'm a person of interest, yes," I said through a clenched jaw. "I'm not a suspect. I'm the one who found Jane, and now I need to find out who hurt her."

"Shouldn't the cops be doing that?"

"They should. I think they're looking in the wrong places."

She held up a hand. "Look, I really need to go."

"Dr. Hamilton, please."

"No, really." She started to walk away.

I followed. "Dr. Hamilton, I saw Jackson Prince on the day she died." I was talking fast now, afraid to lose her. "He was a guest at the network, and she interviewed him and asked some very pointed questions about class actions and how members of the class were located. He was angry at her. Obviously very angry. She told me that she was about to break a story that could rock him. That night she was dead."

Dr. Hamilton stopped, her body half turned back toward mine. She closed her eyes for a moment, then opened them again.

I kept talking. "Was the story big enough that Prince might have harmed Jane to prevent it from coming out? Or maybe he hired someone to do it?"

She opened her mouth but said nothing.

"Mom!" one of her kids yelled from the house.

"I'm sorry," she said. "I've really got to go. I can't talk to you. Good luck."

I fished an old business card from my purse and ran after her. "If you'd like, you can call me later. Anytime, really." She stopped, and I found a pen. Scribbled down my cell phone. As I handed the card to her, I looked into her eyes. "Jane was a friend of mine. She didn't deserve to die the way she did. If there's any chance Jackson Prince had anything to do with it, you need to say so. *Please*."

The sun had finally slipped away, hooding the neighborhood in a blue-black darkness. But in the light of the street lamps I could see Dr. Hamilton clearly. We said nothing for a moment, just two women, eyes meeting.

"Mom!" one of her kids yelled again.

She turned and walked toward the house, the crisp white of her shirt contrasting against the new night.

I walked back to the car, drove in silence. Fifteen minutes later, as I got off on North Avenue, she called.

59

The exterior of Dr. Hamilton's house might have been old Chicago, but the inside had been gutted and redone to perfection.

Dr. Hamilton looked as if she had been crying since I turned around and drove back to her house. She had put the kids to bed. The two of us sat at her kitchen table—big, made of a deep maple that shone luminously.

"Do you see all this?" She gestured at the delicate lights dangling over the island. They looked like hand-blown Italian glass. She pointed at the large, shiny appliances. "See that stove? That's Le Corneau. It cost twenty-five thousand dollars. And my whole house is like that. Everyone thinks doctors make so much money. Are you kidding me? That's what *I* thought too when I was in medical school and then in residency and then in my fellowship, and the whole time I'm just taking on loans and loans and loans. My husband and I have kids, and he stops working because *I'm* the doctor, right? I'm making so much money." She stopped and put her head in her hands. Then she raised her face and looked at me, eyes tormented. "Do you really think Jackson Prince had anything to do with Jane's murder?"

"I don't know. I just know that I didn't do it." I took a breath. "Look, here's the thing. I'm a lawyer." I laughed. "Or I was. And I know you doctors don't love lawyers, but it was…it is…a great profession. And I was a part of that until it went away last year, and I thought I had it bad then. But now I'm about to lose a hell of a lot more than my profession. I could lose my life here." I hadn't said that out loud before, hadn't even really thought it. But it was true. And it was terrifying.

Dr. Hamilton must have seen the panic in my face. She dropped her head in her hands again. "I never should have told Jane anything. I should have kept my mouth shut." She sat up and crossed her arms, then tugged at the collar of her white blouse. "I'm putting my license at risk if I talk about what I did. I mean, I didn't kill anyone or anything, but..." She shook her head. "The thing is my husband is gone. And I don't really want to practice medicine anymore. I really don't."

I said nothing. I wasn't sure what she was talking about. But then the whole story poured out.

When she had been accepted into a rheumatology practice after her residency, she thought her life of bills and student loans was over. She was making enough not just to pay those loans back but to save and to put her kids in Ivy League colleges. Her children wouldn't have to hustle and piece together scholarships and grants like she had. Dr. Hamilton and her husband bought the house. They put her kids in the University of Chicago Lab School, and they lived well, she said. They lived big.

But Medicare payments got cut, and then insurance companies slashed the amounts for which they would reimburse physicians. Meanwhile, her own insurance premiums skyrocketed. Her two partners at her small practice were getting older, and they asked her to step in as managing partner. She did, but sometimes she had to take a cut in monthly pay, just to pay her partners their salaries. Then one of her partners got sued, and the verdict was outside his insurance coverage. The attorneys for the patient went after the doctor's practice group, and because of some legal loophole due to a shoddy limited liability corporation (set up before Dr. Hamilton was even on board) the practice took a hit, and then none of the doctors got paid for a while.

The result, Dr. Hamilton said, was that she found herself in dire financial straits. As she talked, her face looked stricken under the soft light that emanated from the Italian glass. She couldn't admit it to anyone. She was a *doctor,* after all. She was the star of her family and her friends. And yet because her husband was staying home with the kids and not working, she found herself in a worse financial position than anyone she knew.

"And then I met Jackson Prince." Her eyes stared up at the Italian glass, as if to stop tears from falling. "I can't stand it when doctors testify against other doctors, especially in the same city. I said I'd never do it, but I started putting feelers out there, saying that I would review some medical malpractice cases. I needed to figure out some way to make money. Prince calls. Asks me to consult on one case. I gave a deposition for him. He said the other attorneys were blown out of the water because I was so cool under pressure. And I liked hearing that, you know? Because personally I was under so much pressure. I thought maybe I'd testify some more. But there aren't a lot of rheumatology malpractice cases. I asked Prince a couple of times if he had any more work for me. He said not yet. And then he asked if I prescribed Ladera."

She stopped, exhaling as if she'd just remembered to do so.

"And had you recommended that drug to your patients?" I asked.

She smiled bitterly. "That was another kick in the pants. The drug reps who pushed Ladera were persuasive. I mean, they can't wine and dine doctors the way they used to back in the pharmaceutical heyday, but they would ask you to give talks for them and they paid you for the talks. The more you prescribed the drug, the more they liked you and asked you to do these talks and pay you for it. So I made Ladera my preferred arthritis drug. I prescribed it for ninety-five percent of my arthritis patients."

"Did any of them have heart complications like the lawsuit alleges?"

"Some. Two died. I referred the cases to Jackson Prince's office. And then he called one day. I remember it because I was in my office and our lawyers had just told me that we'd lost another lawsuit. One of my partners had really gotten sloppy in his old age. And so I get this call, and I can feel it all swooping away from me, and I was so scared. And then Prince calls and we talked and I thought, 'How funny. One lawyer sinks me, another one saves me.'"

"What did he say?"

She pressed her lips together hard. "He said I must have other patients who had heart problems. He was looking for more plaintiffs."

"Was this after the class action suit was filed?"

"Before. There were a smattering of isolated Ladera cases, but Prince wanted to get more and get them certified for class action status. He told me that's where all the money is."

"But if you personally didn't have any other patients who had problems from Ladera, there was no one to refer to Prince, right?"

She sighed. "He didn't just want referrals. He wanted me to go through my records and find anybody who'd developed the tiniest heart condition or wheezing or shortness of breath, or anything like that. I'll give you an example. A large number of women over fifty develop mitral valve prolapse, okay? It's a minor condition where the chambers of the heart don't exactly close perfectly. It's usually harmless, and it isn't normally caused by anything specific. But it *is* a heart condition, and if that patient had taken Ladera, even if there was only a small chance the drug could have caused it, Prince could file a lawsuit for them."

"And increase the numbers of plaintiffs," I said. "And get lead-counsel status. And get a lot of money if the lawsuit brings settlements or verdicts."

She shrugged. "I don't know how all that legal stuff works. I didn't *want* to know. I just heard Prince tell me that if I gave him the names of these patients and their contact information, he'd never say he got the names from me. He'd just contact them and ask if they'd ever taken Ladera, whether they'd ever had a condition like mitral valve prolapse—or whatever condition I told him they had—and he'd tell them he'd file a lawsuit for them. Patients don't say no to that, right? It's potential free money." Tears welled up in her eyes. "And that's what his offer was like for me, too."

"He paid you for the information?"

Her eyes were closed, as if she couldn't bear to see what was in front of her. She nodded. "A lot. For every name, I got a lump sum. Each patient I could think of that had anything even resembling a heart condition, he'd take. And each time I got paid. And for a while I could breathe again."

"I'm sure you know this, but it's highly unethical for lawyers to pay doctors for referrals or for that kind of information."

She gave me a withering look. "Are you kidding me? It's highly unethical for *me* to *give* that kind of information. I violated physician-patient privilege. I went against everything I've been taught, everything I believe in. Like I said before, I could lose my license."

"And yet you told Jane all this?"

She nodded.

"Why?"

"Because the more money I took from Prince, the guiltier I felt. If I thought I was an emotional wreck before, it got even worse. And it took its toll on my marriage. My husband cheated on me." She scoffed. "He left me for some *girl* who lives in Pittsburgh!" She pointed at the ceiling. "I'm left here to raise my kids on my own. And I keep thinking, God, what kind of an example am I?"

Dr. Hamilton stopped and looked at me, her eyes beseeching, as if I could answer the question. When I said nothing, she slumped a little in her chair. "When Jane called me, saying she was doing a story on Prince, it was like a sign. It was like someone saying, 'Stop this madness. Admit what you did and move on.' And I trusted Jane, because she had done so much to find who killed my brother. She said she would keep my name out of it. So I told her."

She sat up again and pushed her shoulders back. "And now Jane is gone. And if Jackson Prince did anything to her, I could never live with myself. I'm having a hard enough time living with myself anyway."

The suffering in her eyes was painful. "Now that Jane has been killed," I said, "would you be willing to tell the cops what you've told me?"

She nodded. A small, rueful smile broke through the gloom of her expression. "Yeah. Yeah, I would. Because I'm coming clean. I'm starting over." She lifted her shoulders then let them fall again. "Whatever happens, from now on, I'm going to be the person my kids think I am."

60

Detective Vaughn wasn't at the station when I called. I knew Maggie would tell me to never contact him but I didn't care. I got his voice mail as I whizzed down Lake Shore Drive in Grady's car, speeding past the skyline, the city lights blurring in crazy streaks in the car window. I left a message, summarizing in a rush what I learned from Dr. Hamilton. Then I called Mayburn and told him the long version.

"I can't believe this," I said when I came to the end of the story. "Jackson Prince is one of the most respected trial lawyers in the city. In the country, even."

"Respect doesn't buy them anything. And class actions? Hell, I knew a P.I. who worked on a class action case. He got paid $150 an hour, which seems good, right? But those lawyers? Even after the plaintiffs got paid, they got fifty, maybe sixty million."

"I know. Wait until Vaughn hears this."

Mayburn grunted. "Don't expect him to change his mind. When these cops get it in their head you did something, it's hard as hell to get them off it. They're dogs with a bone. And for some reason, from what you've told me, you're looking like a damn good one right now."

Anxiety hit my stomach. "Did you find the contact information for those doctors that were on that list? Like phone numbers and e-mails?"

"Yeah. What do you want them for?"

"I'm going to rattle their cages. See if I can get them to say anything about Prince and whether he had the same arrangement with them that he had with Dr. Hamilton."

"I think you're going to have to talk to Prince, too. You're good at reading people. See what his reaction is."

"But if he killed Jane because she knew this, or he had someone kill her, would he do the same to me?"

"What are you more scared of? That he's going to come after you? Or that you could spend your life in prison?"

61

I drove fast down Sedgwick, speeding by Eugenie to see if the media was still on my front lawn. Not as many as before, but a few were camped out.

I turned around before they saw me and drove to my mom's house on State Street. She'd been calling all day since the police press conference.

When I got there, the lights of her house were on, thank God.

"Oh, honey," my mom said when she opened the door. She stepped outside and gripped me in a tight hug. This was unlike my mother—open and fierce displays of affection. But then again, having a daughter named a person of interest in a murder case would probably bring out the affection in any parent.

"The media is at my place," I said, my words muffled by her shoulder, which was cloaked in a pale green blouse. "I've been gone all day, but I don't want to go home."

"This is your home, too, Izzy. C'mon." My mother led me inside and upstairs to her bedroom. It was a serene place decorated with pale silk walls and a white chaise lounge in the corner. She pulled me into her closet. It had once been the maid's quarters in this house, but now it held my mother's expansive and expensive wardrobe. "We have to get you out of that suit." She poked through her shelves, rifled through hangers. "Let's see…"

Finally she placed a light pink sweater on the center dresser. "I know you don't like pink, but I promise you this sweater is the most comfortable one I own." She flipped through a few more hangers, pulling out a pair of ivory trousers.

"Mom, you're thinner than me. Those will never fit."

"Of course they will. They're a size larger than I normally wear because I got them to wear on the flight to South Africa." Mom and Spence had recently taken a trip to Capetown. My mother still believed that one should dress up for a flight. The fact that people wore sweats, or even pajamas, on a flight horrified her.

"We'll be downstairs," she said. "Charlie brought over some wine."

We looked at each other and, without saying anything, laughed. Charlie was always bringing over wine.

She left the closet, and as I started to strip off my suit, I thought about the fact that Charlie spent so much time here. He was a regular in this house, while I was only an occasional visitor.

After I changed into my mother's clothes, the difference in my mood was palpable. Baby-pink and ivory were my mother's colors, not mine. The trousers, lined with heavy silk, were wide legged, made for the very tall and the very thin, not the style I would usually wear. I had to cuff the bottoms. Yet it was nice, for a moment, to not only slip out of my suit but out of myself.

When I got downstairs, Spence, Charlie and my mom were tucked into the table by the kitchen bay window. Charlie lifted his chin in greeting. Spence jumped up to hug me.

I looked around. A few bottles of wine sat on the counter, along with wedges of cheese wrapped in red-and-white paper.

I slid into the banquette next to Charlie.

"You all right?" he said.

"No." I shrugged. "I don't know."

He nodded then shifted around in the booth, wincing a bit.

"Is your back still bothering you?" I asked.

"Yeah."

"See the doctor lately?"

"Can't afford it," he said in a low voice. "The settlement money is almost gone."

I looked at my mom and Spence. They were arguing about how much cheese to put on a plate. "Ask Mom and Spence. They'll help you."

"I know, but I don't want them to. They help me enough. I just have to figure out what I should do. What I want to do."

"Wow."

"I know. The guy known as Sheets might actually have to spend less time in bed and more time looking for a job."

"It's the end of an era."

He shoved me playfully. "Don't worry. I'm not going to start competing with you for overachiever status."

My mom put a plate of cheese, prosciutto and bread in front of us. I looked up and noticed that the TV was on low in a corner above the cabinets. Spence and my mother so rarely watched TV that I couldn't ever recall seeing it on. When I looked closer, I saw why they were watching it.

"CNN," I said. "Has there been anything about Jane?" It was easier to say *about Jane* than *about me*.

Spence and my mother exchanged glances.

"A story earlier," my mom said. "Just a short piece."

"What did it say?"

"Nothing really."

"They were reporting rumors," my brother said. "They're like a bunch of eighth-grade girls."

Until today, I had been part of that bunch. "They're just doing their job."

Spence poured me a glass of wine.

"Tell me about the story," I said. "I want to know everything."

Earlier, I had no interest in seeing what the media was churning out. I thought I'd be too freaked out. But ever since I told Sam that I was saving myself, I no longer wanted to hide. Not from anything. Not from rumors or lies or half-truths. I was in a battle, and I needed as much intel as I could get.

Spence and my brother stayed silent, but my mom looked at me and nodded. "They're just hashing and rehashing. They showed the press conference. They said you were a person of interest. They showed you leaving Trial TV. They showed you coming home and then leaving again." She looked at her watch. "We've been waiting for the nine-o'clock local news."

I glanced at the clock on the kitchen wall. It was just about nine now. "Let's put it on."

My mom and Spence sat down, and my mom changed the channel to WGN.

We silently sipped our wine, while we waited for the news at the top of the hour. And finally there it was. My mother picked up the remote again and turned it louder.

"Good evening," the newscaster was saying. "Once again, our leading story is the murder of local newscaster Jane Augustine. And we have breaking news."

"Oh, boy," my brother said.

My stomach tensed.

"Earlier today the police asked the community for help in identifying a man known only as 'Mick,' a man who had possibly spent time with Augustine over the weekend. And now, that man is speaking out." The shot changed to a guy standing in front of a bookshelf. A handsome guy. Gray hair, tanned face. It was Mick, all right. I grabbed the remote, dialed up the volume even more.

A banner across the bottom of the screen read *Mick Grenier,* and below that, *Writer. Spent time with Jane Augus-*

tine. There were three news mikes set up in front of him. He began speaking. "I invited the press into my home today in order to let the authorities know that I was the person who spent time with Jane Augustine on the Friday before her death. We were friends. And I had nothing to do with her murder."

"Oh, really?" I jumped up from the table. "That guy was stalking Jane!"

I grabbed the phone from the counter and dialed the number for the Belmont police station, a number I'd just dialed. I asked for Vaughn. He wasn't in. Yet again his voice mail.

"Hey, Vaughn," I said. "The guy I told you about, the one who was stalking Jane Augustine? He's giving a press conference right now on WGN, in case you care."

I slammed the phone down. I looked at my family. Charlie was making a face like *Uh-oh.* My mother's eyes were riveted to the TV. Spence gave me a little smile and a nod, and I could just hear him thinking something like, *Nice spunk.*

On TV, Mick was still going on about his friendship with Jane, how she was a lovely woman, how he'd met her because he was covering her for some story.

"Oh, that's bullshit!" I said.

Just then they showed the outside of Grenier's house. "Hey!" I pointed to it. "I know that house." It was on Goethe Street, only a few blocks from my mom's.

"Gotta go," I said. Without grabbing a coat or even my purse, I strode through the living room, stepping into a pair of my mother's shoes, and dashed out the front door.

62

It took me five minutes to find Mick's place. It wasn't hard. Three news trucks were parked on the street, men loading stuff into them. Clearly, Mick's little press conference was over. I waited down the block, watching the cameramen pack their vehicles then a few reporters leave the house, which was small, well-tended and tucked between two larger buildings.

When it looked as if everyone was gone, I trotted up the steps. I was about to knock on the front door—an old one made of carved wood and painted a deep cabernet—but I decided instead to just try it. The knob turned, opening onto a small, sophisticated living room lined with books. And there, in front of a bookshelf, was Mick. He was picking up chairs, obviously tidying up after the conference.

"Did you tell them you were stalking her?" I asked.

He turned. He was wearing dark jeans and a brown shirt that matched his eyes. If he was startled by my presence, he didn't say so. In fact, he grinned. "Isabel McNeil," he said, ignoring my question. "How are you? I only met you that once on Friday night, but I've seen a lot of your face on the news today."

"Yeah, you, too. Why did you call a press conference to announce you were the one the police were looking for? Why not just go to the cops with it?"

He shrugged. "You know the saying. There's no such

thing as bad PR. Plus, I'm a writer. I learned a long time ago to never trust the police. And part of my next book is about Jane." He looked me up and down. "And maybe about you."

"Who are you kidding about this 'book'? You'd been following her. Were you the one who killed her?"

He laughed. "I didn't do anything to Jane."

"You slept with her, right?"

"Good point."

"She told me you had a collection of articles about her and pictures of her."

"I do."

"You were *stalking* her."

He didn't react defensively. He didn't respond at all. He just cocked his head. Only a tiny fraction. And if I'd been in a nightclub, talking to a guy like Mick, I would have seen that as a playful move, something inviting discussion. But now, his freakish calm chilled me.

"Ever been a writer?" he said.

"I'm a lawyer." I bit my lip. "Was. I was a lawyer."

"And a newscaster."

"They fired me."

"Whoa, are you serious? God, this story keeps getting better." He bent toward a brass-topped table and grabbed a notebook, scribbling something inside.

He looked back at me, giving me a peculiar stare. I wondered, for a weird second, if he'd done research on me, too, if perhaps there was a picture of Izzy McNeil somewhere in his desk, mixed in with the photos of Jane Augustine, who was no longer alive, who hadn't realized on Friday night that her time was tick, tick, ticking away.

I glanced behind me at the door. I was only a foot from it. It was still a crack open.

"I wasn't stalking her," Mick said. "I was writing about her."

"What were you writing?"

A pause. "Do you want to sit down?" He gestured at a brocaded sofa under the front window.

"No." I took a step toward the door.

"Well, I'm going to sit." He sank onto the sofa. "Look, I don't usually talk about what I'm working on with anyone but my agent and my editor, but I'm going to talk to you. So let me ask you something. Have you read Norman Mailer?"

I stopped for a second, surprised by the shift in topic, disconcerted by the intensity in those eyes. I thought about the question. "I prefer less misogynistic writers."

"You've heard that, right?"

"Heard what?"

"That he hated women."

"I read one of his books."

"But mostly you've heard that he was a misogynist?"

"I don't want to talk about Norman Mailer!" I couldn't help but raise my voice. But then I tried to swallow down the anger. Emotions had never helped me before when I was questioning people—in a deposition or on the stand. They certainly wouldn't help now. "I want to know why you were stalking Jane."

"You know what Norman Mailer believed?"

I wanted to scream in frustration. I said nothing.

"Mailer told me once that writing was a heroic enterprise, and writers were heroic figures."

"Wait, Mailer told *you* once? I know you've got the gray hair, but aren't you a little young to have been buddies with Mailer?"

"He was buddies with people I knew."

"Who? Oh, wait…" Suddenly, his last name made sense. "Are you related to Beaumont Grenier?" Beaumont Grenier was a contemporary of Mailer's, considered one of the best of his generation. My client, Forester, had loved his work.

"Something like that." For the first time, Mick looked uncomfortable.

I thought about what I knew of Beaumont Grenier. After a few bestselling books, he'd left the literary limelight in

New York and moved to Maine, where he had a summer house. He stayed there all year-round, even during the most frozen winter days, with only his wife and his son for company, because it was the only place he could write.

"Are you Beaumont Grenier's kid?" I asked.

"Something like that," he said again in a dry tone. "Look, what I was saying about Mailer was—"

"You were saying something about heroism. Are you sitting here telling me you're heroic?" The anger of my earlier tone had been replaced by incredulity.

He shrugged minimally, as if to say he couldn't change the things that were true. "Mailer also said that every woman was a culture unto herself, with all the roots and tendrils that make up a culture."

"And?"

"He didn't hate women. He just thought that being with a woman was like being in a new country."

"I can't even imagine why you're telling me this. Is it because you thought Jane was a culture? A country?"

He smiled. "I think of it in broader terms than Mailer did. I think of all the subjects I write about as being their own enigmas, their own cultures. And as a writer covering those puzzling cultures, I have to find out everything I can about them."

It reminded me of something Jane had said—that she stepped outside her marriage because every person she was with brought her something new.

But Mick was still talking. "When I get the chance," he said, "I like to live in their skin."

I recoiled. "'Live in their skin,'" I repeated. *"Live in their skin?* Is that a reference to sex with Jane? You're sick."

"Why am I sick? She's a beautiful woman." His head dipped to one side. "She *was* a beautiful woman. And I was writing about her. I wanted to see any side of her I could. I wanted to be inside her, sure. I've always said that every writer would fuck some of his characters if he got a chance."

I couldn't hide my distaste. "You saw her as a character? And that's how you justify stalking her and sleeping with her?"

"It wasn't stalking. It was research."

"So let's see if I'm getting this straight—first, you were following her."

Another bob of his head in a silent acknowledgement. No remorse on his face.

"And you've been scouring the Web for any references to her."

Another nod.

"You cut out pictures and articles from magazines about her."

"Right."

"Did you get into her house somehow and leave those flowers and that noose?"

His eyes went a little wide. "No, but that's brilliant. Did that happen?" He grabbed the notebook. More scribbling.

"You're psychotic. You were at Trial TV on that Monday, the day she died."

"Absolutely. I was doing background research on her. That network wants PR so bad, the president of Trial TV himself invited me right in."

"Jane said she found notes you kept about what grocery stores she went to and where she got her hair cut."

He was nodding. Still he looked unperturbed. In fact, he seemed quite proud of himself. "Let me save you a little time. I also hung out wherever I thought she would be. When she was shooting a promo for Trial TV in front of the courthouse, I was in that crowd. And I've been paying bouncers and bar workers to let me know when she was out in the city. And when a bouncer called on Friday saying you guys were at that place on Damen, I called my buddy and I was there in ten minutes. And yes, I slept with her, in part for research, and in part because what man wouldn't?"

"She was married."

"Not my problem." Again, he looked so undisturbed by all this.

"What are you writing?"

He thought about it. He shrugged.

He sat back and crossed his legs. He looked over me for a second. "I'm writing about the news media, and in particular what happens when broadcasters become the news or when they become celebrities in their own right."

"Jane wasn't 'the news' until she was killed."

"That's not exactly true. She was a celebrity who people gossiped about. People in the biz have been talking about her affairs for the last few years. And recently, word got to the streets, and trust me, it was going to hit the public's attention sooner rather than later. She was about to become news because of her personal life. I pride myself on being able to see those stories before they happen. She isn't the only broadcaster I'm covering for this book." A little smile, almost wistful, played over his mouth. "But she sure was the most entertaining." The eyes shot back to mine. "So that's it, counselor." That maddening shrug again.

"If all this is true, why aren't you more upset about Jane being dead?"

"Are you kidding me? With her dead, she's even a bigger story."

Again, I felt myself recoil. I crossed my arms over my chest, my mother's thin cashmere sweater in that delicate pink making me feel even more vulnerable. "You're a sociopath."

"No. I just want to write the best stories, and now with Jane gone and everything I've already put into place for this story, I'll come out on top. That's all I care about. My publisher is pushing up the release of the book. I'll work on it around the clock, and they'll put it out." He shrugged. "I'll probably make a bestseller list."

"Nice. And then maybe you can get over your complex about your famous father."

Zing. I'd hit a sore spot. I could see the muscles in Mick's neck tighten.

While I had him off-kilter, I kept going. "Have you heard about something called scarfing?"

He didn't look confused at the term. Or surprised. "I've heard of it."

"Did you do it with Jane?"

A little shrug. "She asked. And I like to give a girl what she wants."

"Where were you Monday? After you left Trial TV?"

"You mean when Jane died? You want to know if I have an alibi?"

I nodded.

"You're learning a lot from the police, huh? God, if you *did* kill her, it would be great for my book."

"I didn't kill her! Where were you that day?"

"What time did she die?"

"Sometime between three and six."

"I was writing."

"Here?"

"No. A place called Uncommon Ground. It's up near Wrigley. I'm there all the time, and yes, I'm sure someone there will tell you they saw me that afternoon."

There was a banging on the front door.

It opened with a slow creak.

And there was Vaughn.

He looked from Mick to me and back again, and I could see his eyes jumping, his mind leaping to connections even more absurd than the ones he already had.

"I came over when I saw his press conference," I said before he could even open his mouth. "This is the guy who Jane was with on Friday night."

Two uniformed cops stepped inside, behind Vaughn. Mick looked amused by the police inhabiting his place. He stood up and offered his hand to Vaughn. "Mick Grenier. Nice to meet you."

"We need to take you in for questioning."

A wave of relief fell over me. This would all get straight-ened out now.

"Sure," Mick said. "Just let me get a jacket."

He left the room.

Vaughn gestured at one of the uniformed cops. "Go with him." He turned back to me.

"So you'll ask him where he was on Friday night?" I demanded. "And you're going to confirm that he was with Jane?"

"I'll ask him, Izzy."

I hated the sound of my name coming from his lips. "You should confirm that he was stalking her, too."

"Don't worry, Izzy." He said it in such a tone that it sounded like *Don't worry your pretty little head.*

"And when you finally realize I wasn't with Jane that night, then this…this calling me a person of interest, it's over, right?"

"For you?" He actually laughed. "For you, this whole thing is a long way from over."

63

The minute I woke up in my mother's guest room the next morning, fear was waiting—sitting calmly in a corner of my mind, legs crossed, filing her nails. She was waiting, like someone who officially lived in my brain now, who didn't intend to leave anytime soon. I realized then that I'd seen her before. Fear had been with me for a while, long before Jane died.

I tried to remember when fear hadn't been a resident. I dialed my mind back and back, reviewing clip reels of my life, searching and searching, and I finally landed on last autumn, a time when Sam and I were still *Sam and Izzy,* when our wedding was only a few months away. I *thought* I was busy then. I thought life was crazy. I thought that I had been pushed to my limits with work and wedding plans. And yet, every morning when I woke up back then, I was, I realized now, content.

I found the phone in the room and took it back to bed with me, curling myself tight under the covers. In the dim morning light seeping through the ivory curtains, I called Sam. He would just be waking up in Cincinnati, I figured. "It's me. I'm calling from my mom's."

"Hey, Red Hot," he said.

"Didn't sleep last night, huh?" I could tell. Sam had problems sleeping when he was upset, and his voice was always different in the morning after he tossed and turned.

"No."

I waited for him to say he was sorry about last night, about blowing up at me about Grady, but neither of us said anything.

Finally, I broke the silence. "Remember the song you were going to sing for me on our wedding night?"

Silence for a minute, then, "Of course."

"I was just thinking that I never heard it. What did it say?"

"I can't sing it now."

"No, don't sing, but tell me a couple of lines. Maybe the refrain?"

He exhaled, as though it hurt to remember the song. "It was called 'We've Come to It.' The song was about how everything was culminating on that night, how everything that we'd done led us there, but the song was also about how we would keep coming to it every day, even after that night."

I pulled the covers tighter around me, missing him, missing *Us*. "What did you think of when you wrote 'come to it.' I mean, what was *It?*"

"It. You know. It was us. Settled. Happy."

"No secrets." I couldn't help it.

"I don't have any secrets, Izzy! Jesus, we're back to this again."

I threw off the covers and sat up. "You're right. I do keep bringing it up, and I'm sorry, but I guess the thing is…" What was the *thing?* "This thing is…" I felt on the edge of some revelation, some small, quiet, truthful revelation. "The thing is, I don't know. I don't know why it's not right. I just feel it in my bones. Something keeps telling me it's not right between us."

"I don't know what else I can do." He said this simply. Not annoyed. Just resigned.

"I don't, either. I think it needs time."

"We've given it a lot of time."

"Maybe we need more."

"I don't know if I have more."

The fear sitting in the corner of my mind leapt to her feet, danced around. "What do you mean?"

"I don't know. But I know this isn't the time to make any decisions." A pause. "What's going on with Jane's case?"

I sat up and looked around the room at the tasteful furniture, the impressionistic painting, trying to ground myself, but everything seemed to swing around crazily. "What does that mean? For you and me?"

"It doesn't mean anything. Not right now. I shouldn't have said that about not having time. I do. I'll always have time for you. C'mon. Let's not go over this again. Tell me what's happening with Jane's case."

I felt short of breath.

Sam seemed to know. "Izzy. We'll be okay. One way or another. I promise you that. Let's get you through this right now, this thing with Jane."

I sucked in air. I liked the take-control tone of his voice. "Okay, here's what happened last night." I gave him all the details. I told him that I was going to try and check out Mick's alibi.

"You're going to be fine, Izzy. Really. This will all work out the way it's supposed to. And you can rely on me, okay? You *can*. Whatever you need. Just let me know."

I said, *okay*. I said, *I love you*. And we got off the phone.

I sat there in the silence of the guest room, thinking that what I really needed was to somehow return myself to the place I'd been last fall. If I could go back, I would appreciate it more. I would be more cautious with life.

But then fear started filing her nails again in the corner of my mind, reminding me there was no going back.

And so I made myself get out of bed; I opened the window and looked down onto a sun-dappled State Street, and made myself register the warmth, the fact that it would probably be a sunny spring day in the sixties; I made myself leave the room, made myself read the note my mother left outside the door, saying she'd chosen a few dresses for me in her closet, that she would be back in a few hours; I made myself get dressed in a linen spring dress that wasn't as tight as I thought and cinched it with the wide black belt my mother had laid out; I made myself walk down the street to find Grady's car, and I pointed it in the direction of Wrigleyville.

64

I called information and got the address for Uncommon Ground, the place where Mick said he'd been writing when Jane was killed.

I drove north on Lincoln Avenue, the traffic was surprisingly slow for midmorning on a Saturday. And the sidewalks were crowded with people, mostly my age and younger, all of them strolling, all looking really, really happy. I saw a bunch of Cubs hats and realized there was a game today. In Chicago, when there's a Cubs game at 1:20 in the afternoon, you don't get there at 1:00 p.m., you get there as early as your liver will allow you to start drinking. I couldn't have been more jealous of those fans at that minute.

Finally I reached Racine and took a right, taking that to Clark and then Grace. Uncommon Ground was a funky little place with a fireplace, wood tables and local art on the walls. It was, apparently, a coffee shop during the day, a bar at night. It was crowded now with Cubs fans prepping themselves with omelets and bloodies.

I walked up to the hostess.

"Just one?" She looked for an empty table.

"Actually, I'm trying to find information about whether someone was here earlier this week. Apparently he's one of your regulars."

"Who's that?"

"Mick Grenier?"

She nodded. "Oh, Mick. Yeah. That weird writer dude."

"Do you know if he was here Monday afternoon, between three and six?"

"I wasn't here then, but Brian was." She looked over my shoulder. "Hey, Brian." A guy with blond dreadlocks and arms laden with food paused with an expectant look. "You worked Monday afternoon, right?"

The guy nodded.

"Did you see Mick Grenier in here that day, the writer?"

He looked up at the ceiling. "Uh…I don't know. Probably. He's here a few times a week."

"Do you know if he was here that day in particular?" I asked.

Another glance at the ceiling. A little shift of the plates on his arms. "Yeah…yeah. He was. I remember now because he asked me how my weekend was."

So maybe Mick was telling the truth.

"Just one more question. How long was he here?"

"He left right before my shift ended, so he was here a few hours. He left right about four."

"Thanks," I said.

Jane died between three and six, and Mick had given me the impression he'd been at Uncommon Ground the whole time.

Maybe Mick wasn't telling the truth at all.

Outside the coffee shop, fans in Cubs gear were sauntering toward the stadium, beers in hand.

I got in Grady's car and tried to figure out what to do next. I called Mayburn, told him about Uncommon Ground.

"Hmm." I could almost hear him thinking. Then, "I've got phone numbers and addresses for all those doctors. I'll e-mail them to you right now. I'd try the home phone numbers since it's the weekend. Easier than getting past their office staff, too."

"You're the best."

"I know. How are you doing?"

"I'm wearing my mother's clothes."

"Ouch."

"Yeah. What do you think about this Mick guy?"

"Well, you should tell the police his alibi is shaky, but it doesn't sound like the cops want to let you go just yet." Mayburn grunted. "It sounds like you need to visit Jackson Prince."

"Got it."

I hung up with Mayburn, then called information and got the number for Prince & Associates. I needed to see Prince face-to-face, but how to get in front of him and fast *and* on a weekend? The service answered.

With firms like Prince & Associates, there is always a way to get a hold of someone because they're all about flash and cash. Attorneys like them love big, tragic situations that allow them to sue a boatload of people. They want people calling them around the clock with possible cases, tipping them off when there's a bus crash or a catastrophic mishap at a hospital. If I could pretend I had a huge case, they might see me. If, for example, I could say I was a pregnant woman who'd eaten a contaminated Pop-Tart that burned the roof of my mouth, and that my Pulitzer-prize-winning husband drove me to the hospital and died in a car accident on the way, and that at the hospital the doctor screwed up and I lost my baby because the doctor was watching a rerun of the series finale of *Buffy the Vampire Slayer,* Prince might see me. Alas, I wasn't that great of a liar.

But maybe my real story, and Jane's name, were good enough.

"I'd like to make an appointment to see Jackson Prince about a case."

"Are you an existing client?"

"No, I got Mr. Prince's name from a friend. I worked with Jane Augustine at Trial TV. They fired me yesterday, and I want to talk to Mr. Prince about a wrongful termination suit."

"An associate of Mr. Prince's could probably see you on Monday."

"I'd like to see him today. I'm considering other attorneys and I'm going to sign with someone by the end of the day."

"Well, let me see if I can get an associate to call you."

"Actually, I need to see Jackson Prince. In person. And tell him that I also need to talk to him about Jane Augustine."

"Mr. Prince doesn't see people on the weekends, generally."

"If you could just contact him, I'd appreciate it."

She was silent for a moment. I could imagine her debating calling Prince and pissing him off versus not letting him know about my call until Monday and possibly pissing him off even more if it turned out to be a big case.

"Hold, please," she said grumpily. A minute later, she was back on the line. "Mr. Prince will see you today if you can be at the office in one hour."

65

Prince's law firm was on the fifteenth floor of a building at Dearborn and Washington. A cranky secretary who had probably had to interrupt her weekend brought me into Prince's office and pointed sternly to forest-green bucket leather chairs in front of a desk large enough to play hockey on.

Instead of sitting, I walked toward the two walls of glass windows that overlooked the Daley Plaza—the civil courthouse—and the steel Picasso sculpture that stood in front of it. Visible in the distance was a hint of the rounded, mirrored Thompson Center, where state business was conducted, and the funky black-and-white sculpture that graced its facade. From a legal standpoint, this was one of the best views in the city.

A minute went by, then another. I took a seat and stared at Prince's wall of fame—his diplomas from Yale Law School, a plethora of plaques from various bar associations. I checked my watch. It had been five minutes. He was icing me. An old trial lawyer technique—*Make 'em wait. Keep people sitting long enough to get them pissed but not long enough to get them to leave.*

Finally, Prince strode in. He was wearing a light gray suit that matched his hair and set off his clear, sharp eyes. I wonder if he'd put the suit on for me or whether he just lived in them all the time. It was hard to imagine him in anything but a suit.

"Ms. McNeil, a pleasure to see you again." He extended

his hand the way the Pope does, as if I should bow and kiss his ring. I gave his hand a firm shake.

He walked around his desk, moved a few objects—his paper blotter and a silver pen holder—an inch or so to the left, then sat down. "I understand you might have a wrongful termination suit?" He didn't sound at all put out that he'd been called in to see me on a weekend.

"Yes. Until yesterday, I worked at Trial TV."

He nodded.

"They fired me," I continued, "because I was named a person of interest in Jane Augustine's murder."

No reaction. "Tell me about your position there."

I told him how Jane had offered me the position, how I'd been an on-air analyst but that I'd been promoted when Jane died. I told him that they had fired me yesterday, after the police press conference. He asked me a few questions about my background, about Trial TV.

"Hmm." He moved the silver pen holder again. Just a fraction of an inch. His eyes zeroed in on mine again. "Do you have any kids?"

"No."

"Anyone you're supporting?"

"Just myself."

"And in the course of firing you, did anyone at the firm mention the fact that you are a woman?"

"No."

"Well, Ms. McNeil, you should probably consult an employment lawyer, but it doesn't sound to me like you have a strong termination suit. As a woman you're a member of a commonly protected class, but it doesn't seem that played a part in your firing. And you don't have a large amount of damages. You'd only been there a few days, and you're clearly capable of mitigating your damages by getting another job—whether it's in the law or in broadcasting." He gave me a *tough break* kind of face. "My secretary said you also wanted to talk about Jane Augustine."

I nodded. "I wanted to ask you about Monday, when Jane interviewed you the first time. You seemed to be upset at something she said to you."

He pursed his mouth a little and tilted his head. "Not at all. I'm used to dealing with the press, and that is simply how those interviews go—sometimes they're softball questions, other times they're more in depth. I respected Jane immensely, and I knew she never asked the easy questions. But I certainly wasn't upset by anything she said that day."

"You left rather abruptly. While the segment was still on-air."

Prince sat back. He put his hands in front of his chest and made a crown with his fingers. "Did you tell the police that I was angry with Jane? That I might have been angry enough to kill her?"

I felt a little blush flooding into my cheeks. There was no reason to be embarrassed, but I felt as if I'd been caught at something. "They asked if anyone had been mad at Jane. I told them about you leaving the segment early."

"I had a court emergency."

"What kind of emergency? When I was practicing law, I don't remember any type of 'court' emergencies that would come up. I mean, court appearances, even trials, are well scheduled."

"You never did personal injury work, I take it."

"A little, but mostly entertainment law. I used to represent Forester Pickett." I hated to use Forester posthumously to get cred, but Prince would have known him, and I knew Forester would have said, *Go for it. Trot my name out there all you want.*

"I knew Forester well." Prince gave me an impressed nod. "And I'll tell you, as a personal injury lawyer, I often have settlement conferences in the judge's chambers, and I'll bring in our clients and the representatives of the defendants, sometimes from around the country. In this case, one of my associates was handling the matter, but the judge was pushing him to settle for much less than we had anticipated, and he needed my counsel."

It didn't sound like much of an emergency to me, and I'd handled such settlement cases before, but I decided to move on. "Can I ask where you were on Monday afternoon?"

He frowned at me, the expression causing two deep lines between his eyes. "I don't like your implication, Ms. McNeil. For your information, I've already talked to the police about this, and as I told them, I had a meeting with an expert witness in Highland Park at three Monday afternoon. I left my office at two that day. I met with my expert. His deposition started at four. It went until about six."

"I met with Dr. Hamilton-Wood recently."

Prince didn't flinch, didn't blink, didn't make any kind of response. But then again, he was one of the best trial lawyers in the nation. It was his bread and butter to never, never let anyone see him sweat.

"Do you know Dr. Hamilton?" I asked.

"She's acted as an expert of mine on occasion."

"Well, Jane Augustine had spoken to Dr. Hamilton about a story," I said. "It was one of the last stories she worked on before she died."

He raised his silver eyebrows, adjusted the cuffs of his suit. "Interesting. What story was it?"

"I believe it was about the nature of class action suits and the way that plaintiffs are contacted, particularly in cases like Ladera."

I wasn't sure how much to reveal to Prince. On the one hand, I wanted to confront him with what Dr. Hamilton had told me, but on the other hand, I was hoping he would give me something before I scared him off. If I said too much, accused him of too much, he was sure to show me the door.

"I'm sorry." He clasped his hands and leaned his elbows on the desktop. "I'm not sure why you're telling me all this."

"Had Jane contacted you about this story?"

"Not that I recall."

I paused a beat, then two, my gaze never veering from Jackson Prince. Confronting him would have scared the crap out of me a month ago, but it was funny how much courage one could get from a potential murder rap. I wanted to ask him outright—*Did you pay Dr. Hamilton to refer patients to you? Patients who had even minor heart conditions so you could represent them and make them part of the class action? Did your fear of being exposed cause you to do something about it?*

But I knew from just sitting there with Prince that he was never going to admit anything. Why should he? I might have a better chance contacting the other doctors. And so it wasn't fear that prevented me from asking. It was a calculated decision, and it felt good to be so clear-headed about something.

"So you're not aware exactly what the story was about?" I asked.

"I have no idea. I certainly would have helped her if I knew. Jane was one of my favorite members of the media." He said this last phrase like, *She was one of my favorite pets.*

I said nothing for a moment. Prince, neither. You could tell he was good at drawing out silences, waiting for moves he could react to. It was what made him a great trial lawyer.

The next thing I knew the secretary was back in the office. "Mr. Prince, don't you need to leave for the golf course?"

"I do." He stood and held out his hand. I had no choice but to follow suit. Prince clasped my hand a moment longer than he had on the way in. I tried to pull away, but still he grasped it, peering into my eyes and searching them, his own flicking back and forth. "Good luck to you on your employment situation," he said. "Times like these can be very, very—" He gripped my hand slightly harder. "—challenging."

A flash of Jane crossed my mind—her eyes wide-open

and lifeless, that scarf too tight around her neck, the blood, the blood.

I yanked my hand away. "Thank you." And I left Prince's office.

66

I couldn't go home and deal with the media. I drove, instead, to a Starbucks on Wells Street and lucked out by finding a sunny table by the front window.

I called Mayburn and told him about my meeting with Prince. "He says he has an alibi." I explained about Prince's meeting and deposition on Monday afternoon.

"Assuming the meeting with his expert happened and it started on time," Mayburn said, "he had an hour to drive to Highland Park. An hour is enough time to stop by Jane's house on his way. If you think Prince really did it, we should get the name of that expert and check out exactly what time he arrived there. But don't forget, from what you've told me, Prince might not be the type to get his own hands dirty. He might have hired someone to pay Jane her last visit."

The whole thing sickened me. Exhausted me. But I couldn't slow down.

"Call you later," I said to Mayburn.

I pulled out my BlackBerry and pulled up the contact information that Mayburn sent me for the doctors. I started with the first one. Dr. Trace Ritson in Charleston, South Carolina.

"May I ask who's calling?" his wife said when I asked to speak with him.

"Isabel McNeil."

"Are you a patient?"

"No, I'm calling from Chicago. I'm with Trial TV." *Used to be* with Trial TV. It seemed a very white lie at this point. "I'd like to talk to him about some work he did for Jackson Prince."

"I think it's best if you call him at the office on Monday."

"Could you please tell Dr. Ritson that Jane Augustine was killed a few days ago, and it might have been because of Jackson Prince?"

Silence. Then, "One minute, please."

But it wasn't a minute. Only thirty seconds later, Dr. Ritson was on the phone.

I managed to speak with not only Dr. Ritson, but four other doctors. I called Mayburn, told him what I'd learned and asked if he could contact the other doctors. Then I called C.J.'s cell phone and told her I had a story I wanted to work on, a story Jane had been working on before she died.

"Izzy, why are you doing this? We fired you."

"I'm working on it for Jane. Because I think it might tell us who killed her. Because I know *I* didn't. And most importantly, it was one of Jane's last stories. I want to do this for her."

Silence.

"Do you want me to take it to another station?"

A pause. "I'll meet you at the station."

When I pulled into the parking lot of Trial TV, I was as nervous as I had been my first day.

No news trucks, except for Trial TV's own, sat outside. But then again, the news stations covering Jane's murder probably had more than enough exterior shots of the place by now. And certainly no one expected me to come back.

The security guard frowned when he saw me, but my badge still worked. They hadn't deactivated it yet. I walked down the linoleum hallway. The walls had been painted sometime this week, and although the smell of fresh paint lingered, file cabinets were pushed against the walls, white cardboard boxes on top.

The first person I ran into was Ted, the cameraman who worked with me that first day.

He stopped, raised his eyebrows. "How are you doing, Izzy?"

"Been better."

"I bet." He said it kindly. "I've got to tell you, I think it's ridiculous that they're looking at you for Jane's murder."

"Thanks, I appreciate that."

He pulled at his mustache. "I thought you really had some natural talent for this business. I'm sorry about what happened. Is there anything I can do?"

I thought about it. "Would you be my shooter on something if I get the go-ahead from C.J.? It's something to do for Jane."

"Hell, yes. Let me know."

I thanked him and kept walking down the hallway, passing the sets. Eventually I came to the newsroom. There weren't as many people as there were during the week, and the reception I got wasn't as warm as the one from Ted. There were a few half waves. A couple of surprised looks. One or two people said hello but didn't stop to talk. Maybe no one knew exactly how to react. For that matter, I hardly knew what to do myself.

I found C.J. in the green room, talking to a man in a pinstripe suit who looked like a lawyer, probably a guest in an upcoming segment.

C.J. stepped out of the green room when she saw me, closing the door behind her. "How are you doing, Izzy?" She frowned, and without waiting for an answer, said, "What's the story?"

I told her about the list of names, what Carina Fariello had told us, what Dr. Hamilton had confessed to me. I told her about confronting Jackson Prince.

She pushed her glasses up on the top of her head. "So it's Prince's word against this doctor?"

"Maybe Prince's word against a lot of doctors." I told her

how I'd called Dr. Ritson, and then Dr. Hay and Dr. Dexter and a few others. I had gotten through half of Jane's list. Mayburn promised to tackle the rest for me. "At first I hit the same wall Jane did with the doctors. No one would talk. Some of them had heard about Jane's death, a few hadn't, but when I told them that her death might have been linked to this story, a few started talking. Most were vague, not exactly giving me as much as Dr. Hamilton did, and some said they would only talk off the record."

C.J.'s brown eyes were entirely focused on me now. "Will any of these doctors give an interview?"

"I know Dr. Hamilton will. She feels terrible about Jane. I'm pretty sure that Carina Fariello, the accountant for Prince, will speak about it, too."

C.J. took the glasses off her head and chewed on one of the ends. She kept looking at me, slightly nodding, clearly thinking over everything I'd told her. "Let's do it," she said finally. "I'll be the producer for you."

"Really?"

"Yeah. We've got to do it for Jane. And this story has to be told. It's the kind of thing that could win an Emmy."

"Are you serious?"

She smiled. "I am."

I smiled a little, too, but it felt wistful. "Jane had an Emmy."

"Yeah. She won it for a great story about a vice cop who was dealing heroin. I worked that story with her. Did you ever see it?"

I shook my head.

"Jane was amazing. Absolutely at the top of her form." She sighed, stared over my shoulder for a moment, her eyes full of grief for Jane. But then her expression shifted, and she looked back at me with something that seemed like pleasure. "Jane would be proud of you," she said.

"Really?"

"Yeah. And I'm proud of you, too."

"That's one of the best compliments you could give me."

For the first time I felt a kinship with C.J. My cell phone rang then. I took it from my purse and looked at it. *Theo Jameson.*

67

"I can't believe Jane is dead," Theo said.

"I can't believe you're just calling me back now." I put my hand over the phone and gestured to C.J. that I had to take the call. *Thank you,* I mouthed to her.

She gave me a thumbs-up. "Go get 'em."

"I'm really sorry," Theo was saying. "I didn't check messages at all while I was gone. Really no way to do it. Anyway, I just got back. I'm still on our plane."

I walked through the studio, back down the main hallway. "*Our* plane, like your own private plane?" Despite my fear, who was cracking her knuckles now, ready to get back into high gear, I was impressed.

"It's just a corporate share. Anyway, we're just pulling into Midway. Man, I'm in shock about Jane. What happened?"

I went outside, got in Grady's car and poured out the whole story to Theo, my words tripping over themselves. Finally I got to the end.

"I feel sick," he said. "I can't believe someone would do that to her."

"I know. The thing that's nuts is that the cops seem to think *I* might have done that to her."

"What? Why?"

"I don't really understand it, but part of it has to do with the fact that the cops think I'm lying about where I was last

Friday night. That guy Mick that we met admitted yesterday that he was with Jane Friday night, and I thought that
would put me in the clear, but the detective on the case
seems to be saying it didn't matter and that I'm still a possible suspect."

"That's intense, Izzy."

"I know."

"You could be in some serious trouble." He didn't say it
in a threatening way, or even in a *holy-cow-get-away-from-
this-girl* kind of way. He said it matter-of-factly, and my
whole body welcomed it. Nearly everyone— Sam, Q, my
mom, Spence—had been trying to tell me not to worry.
They believed in me so much, which was amazing. But
their utter belief led them to think that the situation was
going to go away. And it wasn't. To hear someone say the
real truth—that I could be in deep trouble—was refreshing.
Almost as if I could stop hoping that it was going to go away
and just deal with the fact that it was *here*.

"I know," I said again. "Want to hear something else?"

"Yeah." And I could tell he did.

I told him how the day after Jane died, I'd gone on-air
as the host of Trial TV. "And then they fired me," I said.

"Because you might be a suspect in Jane's murder?"

"Yeah."

"Damn, girl. I can't get over this. Where are you?"

"I'm about to go home. The press might be there, but I
don't care anymore. I have nothing to hide. And I need to
be in my own house and think about what I should do next.
And I really need you to tell people that we were together
that night."

"I'll meet you there in half an hour."

68

The press must have thought I would never return. A few news trucks were still parked in front of my place, but the masses were gone. Luckily, my garage was behind the building. I drove around the block and down the alley. I got out, moved my scooter and then parked Grady's car. The problem with the garage, however, was that it was detached. The only way to enter the main building was to walk around the garage to the front door. I knew the minute the people in the news vans saw me, they would be out of their vehicles. Fast.

My heart racing a little, I left the garage and crept along the side wall of the building. It made me remember the other night in Bucktown, when I was creeping along the alley, looking for that van. I could feel those hands shoving me, could feel myself going down onto the cobblestones. The thought made my heart pound faster.

When I got to the corner of my building I paused. I would have to step out into the open and walk the twenty or so feet to the front door.

Or run.

"Hey!" I heard a shout. The doors of a news van opened, then another and another. Cameramen leapt out of each. They were running even faster than me, and by the time I reached the door they were right behind me. A reporter must have been in one of the vans, too. "Izzy," he yelled.

"Did you kill Jane Augustine? How do you feel about being fired from Trial TV?"

My hands fumbled with my keys.

"Where were you Monday afternoon when Jane Augustine was killed?"

It was so hard not to answer. It was so hard not to turn and yell, "Of course I didn't kill Jane!" But I could hear Maggie repeating in my brain—*Say nothing!*

Finally I got my key in the door. The cameramen jostled themselves on either side of me, practically pushing their lenses into my face. They felt like big snouts sniffing for a story. I opened the door, pushed it open and fell inside.

The cameramen tried to stick the lenses in the door, but I managed to shove it closed. I was panting so hard that I had to stop and catch my breath before I could climb the three flights.

When I got upstairs, I had never been so happy to see my little condo, my old marble fireplace, my favorite yellow-and-white chair. I opened every blind and curtain in my house, wanting as much light as possible, except for those that might allow the news guys to see in from the street.

I pulled out my phone and texted Theo—*Just a warning. The press is outside my house.*

Not a problem, he wrote back.

And apparently it wasn't. By the time I could change into jeans and a T-shirt, he was buzzing from downstairs, and then there he was, unfazed, taking up all the space in the frame of my door.

"Girl, how are you?" Without waiting for an answer, he stepped into my house and he pulled me into his arms. He was so tall that I could lay my face on his chest, against the soft cotton of his black T-shirt, pushing aside the army jacket he wore over it. He wrapped his arms around me and stroked my hair. Then he led me to the couch and sat me down. He pushed up the sleeves of his jacket, and I stared at the ribbons of the red tattoo that trailed down one forearm, the black pointed serpent's tail that snaked down the other. They made me think of the other tattoos he had—the one on his left hip, the one on his collarbone.

"This thing that happened to Jane," he said, "it's got me rattled." His eyes were sad, and for the first time, he looked older than his twenty-one years, like someone who had seen something haunting. "What can I do to help?"

"I want you to talk to the detective and tell him we were together Friday night."

"Sure."

I called the Belmont police station. Again, Vaughn wasn't there. Again, I left a message. "Maybe he'll call back," I said hopefully. I couldn't believe I actually wanted to talk to Vaughn.

We waited, making chitchat about Theo's trip, ignoring the sexual tension that, even now, was ripe.

Theo took my hand and, very simply, stroked it. It was an old-fashioned gesture, and coming from someone like him, it touched me more than I would have imagined.

"So how was the surfing?" I asked.

"Forget the surfing," he said. "This is about you. What else can I do?"

"I don't know." I was overwhelmed suddenly by a sense of helplessness.

Theo seemed to sense it. "Anything," he said. "I'll do anything."

I thought for a moment. "You know, as far as I can tell, I got pulled into this initially because Zac, Jane's husband, thought I was involved with his wife, especially on Friday night. I kept telling him that *you* were with me that night, not Jane, but he doesn't believe me. I'm still not sure he does. Would you talk to him?" I thought of what Mayburn had told me. "If I can finally get Zac off my back, it might help with the police."

Theo looked into my eyes, not saying anything for a second. "If that's what you need."

I picked up my cell phone and called Zac. Voice mail. I left a message saying I had something to talk to him about.

When he didn't call back, I called again. Then I texted him—*Zac, I need to talk to you urgently. It will just take a minute.*

The phone rang. Zac. "What?" he said, when I answered.

"Hi. Listen, Zac, I have someone who wants to talk to you." I handed the phone to Theo.

"Hi, this is Theo," he said, "I just wanted to tell you that I spent the night with Izzy on Friday and—" He looked at the phone then handed it back to me. "He hung up."

I called Zac again.

"I don't think I want to hear anything from you," he said, "or from anyone you're involved with."

"Zac, c'mon! This is about Jane."

"I am well aware of *that.*"

"And I didn't kill her. No matter what you think or what the cops are saying." I left off, *And I think there's a chance you did.* "And I was not with Jane Friday night. You heard him say that."

"You could have any guy call me and say that."

"Then meet us in person. We'll come to you."

"I'm at our house in Indiana."

I still had Grady's car. I remembered Jane telling me their lake house was only a sixty-five mile drive.

"How about this?" I said. "Tell me a coffee shop, someplace public, someplace near your house, and we'll meet you there." I looked at Theo, whose brow was creased with concern.

"It takes more than an hour to get here," Zac said.

"That's fine. When we get there, we just need five minutes. That's all."

Another pause.

"Please," I said simply.

Another pause, then, "There's a place called Lakeshore Coffee. It's in Michigan City."

I hunted for a pen and wrote down the address and directions.

"Call me when you get close," he said, "and I'll meet you there."

I turned and gave Theo a thumbs-up.

69

We took the Dan Ryan to the Skyway, flying past the steel mills that hulked in front of Lake Michigan, which was choppy today, an icy denim-blue. In Indiana, we got off on a rural highway. At first it was all truck stops and car washes, but soon the road began to bend and curve, skimming by golden grass as high as my thighs and outcroppings of trees just starting to bloom with spring's new green. Every so often there was a burst of yellow daffodils on the side of the road.

Theo looked at the directions. "It's only a couple more miles."

I dialed Zac's phone. He answered right away.

"Hi, Zac. We're only a few miles away."

"Already? I'm up on Mount Baldy."

"What's that?"

"A state park in the dunes. It's where Jane and I used to come a lot." He coughed, and I wondered for a second if he might cry. I felt a war of emotions for him—sympathy for the fact that he'd lost his wife and yet also distrust, wondering if he had caused that loss.

Zac cleared his throat. "Where are you guys now?"

I peered at the street and told him the name of the gas station we had just passed.

"You're actually almost here. Do you see a brown sign that says Mount Baldy?"

We went around a bend in the road. "Yeah, I see it."

"You might as well just come here," Zac said. "Follow the signs to the summit. You'll see us."

"Us?"

"Zoey and me."

I opened my mouth to say something about how fast he'd moved on from Jane, but I didn't want to make him angry. "See you soon."

I turned up a sharply angled driveway for Mount Baldy, wooded on both sides, and drove into a parking lot. Through the not-quite blooming trees you could see massive sand dunes and hear the crashing of the waves of Lake Michigan beyond.

There was only one other car in the parking lot, a black Jeep. Theo and I looked around and then back at each other.

"Does it seem weird that we're meeting him in a forest preserve or whatever this is?" I said.

"Yeah."

We were both silent. My nerves started to zing a little.

"But then again," Theo said, "you're the one that called him. It's not like he lured you here."

"I know, but he's here with his new girlfriend. Or old girlfriend. Whatever. And I've been wondering about this woman. I mean, it sounds like she's always been in love with Zac. He broke up with her and then moved on to Jane. Then she and Jane were friends, or so Zac claims."

"You think she was jealous enough to do something to Jane?"

I shrugged. "I have no idea. Maybe Zac and Zoey worked together to get rid of Jane?"

More silence. "Why don't we just leave?" Theo said. "You don't need any more trouble."

"I know."

I tried to breathe deep, tried to think. Then I remembered, again, how I told Sam that I was going to save myself. "I have to do something. *Anything*. I want to take you to see

Zac, and I want him to hear that we were together, that I wasn't with Jane."

Theo nodded, but he seemed a little reluctant.

"I know this is a weird situation," I said. "Are you okay?"

"I guess. If you think this is the right thing, we'll do it."

I looked around, saw signs with arrows pointing the way to the summit. "He said to follow those signs."

Theo and I got out of the car. He grabbed my hand as we walked. "Are *you* okay?"

I nodded and squeezed his hand. He was as sweet as he was smoking hot.

He stopped and pulled me tight to him. He even *smelled* sexy.

"Izzy," he said. "I just want you to know…I'm into you."

I laughed. "You're into me?"

"Yeah."

"Even with all this crap going on?"

"Yeah."

"Then I feel bad for you. You're just a kid, and you should be doing kid things."

"I'm not a kid."

"You're twenty-one."

He pulled back and looked at me, raised his eyebrows. "I won't deny my age. All I can do is tell you what I feel. That's how I operate—I say what I feel. And what I feel is…" He shook his head a little. "I'm *into* you."

"I'm a mess," I said.

"You're a mess I want to get dirty in."

How was it possible that he made every utterance sexy?

In that moment, I forgot that Detective Vaughn was after me. I forgot that Jane had died. I forgot that I had found her. I forgot the fact that my life, at that moment, was nothing like what I thought it would be.

Because what my life was like at that moment was… oddly…exquisite. I stood in a wooded lot with Theo; with his square jaw and his soft lips framed by his chin-length hair. And beyond him I could see a forest of barely blooming trees, the pale blue sky shimmering between the branches.

Lately, I felt like someone scarred. My fiancé had disappeared a few months before our wedding; my client had been killed and I'd lost most of my work. And now this thing with Jane—to be questioned by the police, to be, apparently, a suspect in a murder investigation. It just scarred me more, and somewhere a largely unconscious thought had crept into my brain, and it was this—*You're different now.*

And yet this person—this youthful, sexy, intellectual being—was standing in front of me and telling me that he liked my messiness, something that Sam seemed to dislike greatly. Even better, Theo wanted to get dirty in it.

Theo took my hand. "Let's go find Zac."

We walked through the parking lot, following the summit signs to a dirt path, edged by wood planks and an occasional bush bursting with yellow buds. The path coursed through the forest, the ceiling a high canopy of crisscrossed trees— a mixture of oaks, pines, birches.

Inside those trees now, the sound of the lake was buffeted, so we only heard our softly thudding footfalls, a distant branch breaking, the chirping exchange of a few birds.

We stopped along the path and read a sign that explained that the dunes had been created centuries ago by glaciers, moving and carving the land in their wake.

The path turned and began to incline. So did my anxiety. We seemed in the middle of nowhere.

When we got to the top, I gasped. We were at the highest crest of a sand dune, probably a few hundred feet up. The dune swooped down on the other side, creating a broad face of smooth sand leading right up to Lake Michigan, glittering in the spring sun, crashing with foamy waves onto the beach. It was bright, beautiful, and for a moment it cleansed my anxiousness.

Theo took his sunglasses from his pocket and put them on. He looked like a model. "Damn," he said. "I had no idea there was anything like this on the other side of the lake. I've never been here."

"Me, either, but I already want to come back." Some tiny voice said, *As long as I don't end up in jail.*

Theo turned and hugged me. "I want to come back here with you," he murmured into my hair. "When all this is over." He hugged me tighter. "And it will all be over soon."

I wanted to say, *Promise?* but the truth was, I didn't know if I believed in promises anymore. I just hugged him tighter and prayed he was right.

As I was pulling back, I saw someone. "I think that's them."

Theo and I turned and saw two figures about halfway down the face of the dune, sitting close enough that their shoulders touched, although both had their arms wrapped around their knees, staring at the blue waves. Then one figure looked up. Zac. He saw us, gave a terse wave.

We walked toward them. Zac and Zoey stood and walked to meet us. As we crossed the expanse of dune, I felt as if I was in the Sahara, and I had the odd feeling of being in a showdown.

As they got closer, I could see that Zac was wearing jeans and the beat-up but stylish leather jacket he'd worn when I first met him with Jane. Zoey, also in jeans, was as lean as Zac. She had olive skin tone and eyes so dark they looked almost black. She wore another beret, this one black, but both she and Zac were squinting in the bright sun. Zac's face was creased down his cheeks. His eyes looked red, strained.

"Zac—" I gestured between the two men "—this is Theo."

Theo offered his hand. Zac looked at it, ignored it.

Zoey didn't offer her hand, either. She looked at me, her eyes passing over my face with no emotion. There was something disconcerting about those eyes. Then she looked at Zac, and I could see an expression in them, one of adoration. He looked back at her. "Can you give us a second?"

She nodded, still silent, and walked away, over the side of the sand dune, disappearing from sight. Not knowing where she was made me nervous.

"Where is she going?" My eyes lingered on the spot I'd last seen her.

"I thought you wanted to talk to me," Zac said, his tone brusque. "So talk."

"Uh…" I dragged my eyes back. I glanced at Theo. He gave me a small nod, as if to say, *Go ahead.* I turned to Zac. "It was Theo who I was with Friday night."

Zac looked at Theo, as if for confirmation. He had to look up, because he was slightly below us on the dune, and because Zac was a relatively small guy.

Theo nodded. "Yeah, man. Sorry if I caused any problems, being out of town. Sorry about Jane."

Zac pursed his lips as if he could barely stand the conversation.

Theo seemed to sense it. "Anyway, I met Izzy on Friday night, and we went to her place together. I'm going to tell this to the cops, too. So…" He shrugged.

Zac looked at me. "You guys have anything else to say?"

"I just hope you believe me now, Zac. I adored Jane. I wouldn't have done anything to hurt her." *But I'm not so sure that you didn't.* I glanced around to see if Zoey had reappeared. Why did I feel as if she was going to creep up on us? There was no sign of anyone. The three of us were seemingly alone.

Zac looked at Theo. "Take your sunglasses off," he demanded.

What the hell?

I looked back and forth between him and Zac. Some kind of weird energy had surrounded us and the sand below me seemed to shift.

"Take them off," Zac said.

Theo's eyes went to me. I shrugged. His hand was slow in rising to his face, and I noticed that he paused in touching the arm of his glasses, that in finally pulling them off, again slowly, he seemed to be trying to give himself some time.

When his glasses were finally off and his arm at his side, the two men stared at each other. And stared. And stared.

"Yeah, I thought so," Zac said. He looked at me. "Is he good in bed?"

"Zac, don't be an ass. We just came here to tell you—"

He cut me off. "I bet you think he's good in bed." He looked at Theo and scoffed. "I know Jane did."

Zac Ellis turned and walked down the slope of sand, and then he, too, disappeared over the dune.

70

"You used to sleep with Jane?" The waves of the lake seemed bigger, sounded louder.

Theo's eyes were full of something—pain, maybe?—but what did I know? He said nothing.

"You had an affair with Jane?"

"Affair. Whatever."

"Whatever? How can you be so cavalier about this?" I didn't wait for an answer. "How long were you together?"

"A couple of months."

"You and Jane dated—cheated—for a couple of months, and you didn't mention that?"

He shrugged. "I don't kiss and tell."

"Even *after* the person you kissed was murdered?" My voice was rising. "Even after I told you *I* was being investigated for her murder? You didn't think that was information you should mention?"

He stayed silent. He looked angry now as he stared down at me. His hair fell in his face, shrouding it.

"Why did she even introduce us?" I asked.

Another shrug. "After she ended things, we stayed friends. She was always trying to introduce me to women. She wanted me to be happy. But I was never into any of those women. Not until you."

My eyes searched his face. "You were never into anyone because you were still into Jane, right?"

He said nothing.

"Were you in love with her?"

He shrugged. "Once. I guess. And I was pissed at her when she dumped me, but—"

"But what? Was sleeping with me some messed-up way to get back at her?"

He paused, looking even more irritated, then he muttered an unconvincing, "No." His hair fell farther in his face. He leaned toward me a bit, and I felt irrationally cornered.

"I'm leaving." I turned and started walking toward the car. When I stepped from the dune and onto the forested path, shadows fell around me. I started walking faster. As I did, I heard a voice in my head, my logical, intuitive voice saying, *Run. Get out of here.*

Theo jogged past, stood in front of me.

"Don't," I said, feeling panicked now. We were out here in the middle of nowhere.

I tried to move around him, but he put his hands on my shoulders and held me firm. Still he wasn't saying anything.

"Why did you even come here with me?" I asked, my words fast, a little panicked now. "Didn't you know Zac would recognize you?"

"I only met him once. I figured if he did recognize me, and it came out, then it was meant to." His hands were still on my shoulders. He stared at me intently. I was scared of him suddenly. Found myself, ironically, wishing Zac was here, wishing anyone else was here. I swiveled my head around, saw no one.

"Who *are* you?" I tried to shake his hands from my shoulders, but he was too strong. "I mean, where is your apartment? Why have we never been there?"

"My place sucks. I'm in the same place I had three years ago when I started my business. I've been too busy to move."

I looked at him, stared at those lips, the same lips that had done so many great things to me, and then I looked back into his eyes. I didn't know this guy, I realized. Not at all.

"Are you lying? Maybe you lied to Jane about who you were, too. You're probably not some young hotshot, you're probably a player. Someone who preys on people."

"No. Everything I've told you is true."

"Except that you dated Jane." I shoved him aside finally. "What other secrets do you have?" And then I thought of one. "Did you and Jane play any games together?"

"What do you mean?"

I looked around, wondering if Zac and Zoey were somewhere near. Maybe listening. I stood closer to him and dropped my voice. "Like scarfing?"

He paused, but I saw the recognition in his eyes.

"You did. You did that to her."

He gave a little nod, lips pursed together tight.

"Why don't you say something?" My loud voice echoed through the forest.

"What do you want me to say?" he yelled.

I saw Jane's body—the blood, that scarf around her neck. "Oh my God, did you kill her? You have this story about Mexico, but you could have been in Chicago the whole time."

"What are you babbling about?"

He hadn't denied it. I shoved him hard now and hurled myself down the path. My pulse started racing as fast as my legs. He ran behind me, calling my name, chasing me.

I ignored him, making my feet move faster, my pulse bang harder. The whole time I was aware that he could outrun me; he could pounce on me from behind; he could do anything to me he wanted. And where were Zoey and Zac? My mind reeled around like an animal trapped in a cage. Was this some kind of bizarre setup? Were Zoey and Zac *and* Theo all in this together?

Finally, the parking lot came into view. I whimpered with relief and broke into a final sprint toward the car.

"Stop!" he said.

I clicked the driver's door open with the remote. When

I reached the door, I yanked it open. He was standing on the other side of the car.

I got in and started the car, making sure the passenger door was still locked.

"Izzy!" I heard through the windows. He pounded on the side of the car. "You can't leave me here!"

But I floored the car into Reverse, and that's exactly what I did.

71

After thirty minutes in the car, when I was breathing normally again, I wondered if I should go back and get Theo, if I shouldn't have left him there. But my mind was still a swirl of worries and one big question—had he killed Jane?

I went over and over that moment in my head when Zac said, *I bet you think he's good in bed...I know Jane did.*

Theo had slept with Jane, and he never mentioned it to me. He wanted to make her jealous. He wanted to make her angry. So clearly, he must have been angry himself. Enough to kill her? And was he lying about going to Mexico? It was, as Detective Vaughn had pointed out, *interesting timing,* and then there was the scarfing thing. He *knew* about it. He'd done it to Jane, and that's how she'd been killed.

I tried to imagine Theo hitting Jane, winding that scarf around her neck in the last moments of her life. My stomach felt as if it were filling with bile.

It could have been Zac, too. Then there was Zoey, and her creepy, silent presence. There was Jackson Prince. Which reminded me about the doctors Mayburn was contacting.

I called him, told him that Theo was back and that he used to have a relationship with Jane.

He whistled. "This thing just keeps getting more messed up by the moment. At least you have an alibi for Friday night."

"Yeah. Now if I could just get one for Monday, the day she died. Any luck with the doctors?"

"I just got one of them to talk."

"Are you serious? What did he say?"

"It's a she. Dr. Holly Wallace. I guess it's the ladies who are going to sink Prince. Wallace had a similar story to Dr. Hamilton's. She wouldn't quite go the whole way and admit she'd referred any cases or taken payments, but it was obvious she knew what I was talking about, and she was on the phone with me for almost forty-five minutes."

"You think she'll talk on camera? I got clearance from Trial TV to work on this story."

"The Trial TV that fired you?"

"Yeah. I guess it's sort of a freelance thing." Traffic slowed at Sheffield with a horde of people heading into Whole Foods. I glanced in my rearview mirror. I don't know what I was looking for. Zac following me? Or maybe Theo? Should I call and make sure he had gotten out of there okay? I saw that image again, him hitting Jane, winding that scarf around her neck.

"Is Trial TV paying you for this story?" Mayburn said.

"I don't know. I didn't ask. I'm basically picking up on Jane's last story. I'm doing it for Jane, not the money." I hadn't even thought about my financial situation with everything else going on. Weird how things that seemed so serious, so emergent, became wisps, barely concerns, when dwarfed by something bigger.

"Give me one more talk with Dr. Wallace," Mayburn said, "and I think I can get her. And hey, you're going back to the Fig Leaf tomorrow, right? You're supposed to get paid once a week."

I groaned. That was another thing I hadn't thought about. "You're not going to make me go back there after what happened?"

"I'm already working on getting a van that will look like a utility truck. It'll sit outside the store. I'll be watching you guys through the front windows, and all you have to do, if you can, is get one of the black pearl thongs. Once you've got it, run out, and we're out of there."

"Don't you think Josie might have seen me on the news by now?"

"Not everybody is dialed in. Some people never watch the news. You walk in and you'll be able to tell right away if she recognizes you. If she does, turn right around and walk out."

I reached Clybourn Avenue. I saw Uncle Julio's Hacienda, a Mexican restaurant where Sam and I used to go for brunch on Sunday mornings.

Sam. Was he home yet? It seemed long ago since I had talked to him this morning. It seemed long ago since all was right with us. And something about that gap felt weighty, different.

"C'mon, you have to do this for me," Mayburn was saying. "Josie has something going on at the Fig Leaf, and we're close to finding out what. Just get me one of those thongs."

I groaned again. "I guess since you're helping me."

"Great. And I'm going to keep helping you. Dr. Ismael up next." He clicked off.

I pulled my mind away from Sam. But that only left Jane. And Zac and Zoey and Theo and Prince. And then there was Mick. He'd admitted to following her. Essentially, he'd admitted to stalking her. And now the creep planned to write a tell-all book about Jane, something that infuriated me.

I called information for Mick's home number. No listing.

I got off the phone and drove to his house, parking in front, punching the hazard lights on Grady's car. There were no reporters or TV cameramen around. Maybe they'd decided Mick's part of the story was done. But I knew there was another story—the one he was working on about Jane. The thought that his book could slaughter Jane's memory, the same way she'd been slaughtered, sickened me further.

I stormed up the front stairs and pounded on his maroon door, really, really hoping he was home.

He was. He opened the door, blinked a few times when he saw me, then looked over my shoulders and peered around me.

"There's no press here." I crossed my arms over my chest. "I'm here to tell you that you can't…" I took a breath, tried to calm down. I would likely get nowhere if I unleashed my anger on this guy. "I'm here to ask you a favor."

"Uh, okay." He wore a white T-shirt and old jeans. His gray hair was messed in places as if he'd been in the house and napping all day.

"Don't write this story about Jane."

He studied me, said nothing. Then, "Are you saying that because you don't want to be part of the story yourself?"

"No! I just don't want anyone to forget Jane."

He squinted. "Well, then I better write this book."

"But it's going to be about Jane's affairs, not who Jane really was."

"I think you're making a philosophical distinction. Maybe what she did off-air defined who she was."

"No," I said again, frustrated. "Look, have you told the press about your book?"

"Not yet. The timing isn't right. I don't want the PR until it hits the shelves."

"Why is everything about PR and your book?"

He laughed. "Are you kidding? Because that's my world. That's what I do. Norman Mailer once said…"

"Shut up about Norman Mailer! Why do you always quote Norman Mailer?"

He looked amused at my outburst. He peered over my shoulder again. This time I followed his gaze and saw that a few people were standing on the street, watching us. They didn't look like media.

"Come inside," Mick said.

I stepped into his small foyer so we were out of earshot,

but I wouldn't go any farther. The other night I'd been emboldened by the fact that the press was outside. I'd felt relatively protected. But now it was only Mick and me.

I crossed my arms again. "This is not going to be a long conversation. Just tell me you'll consider forgetting this story."

"No way. Mailer said—"

"Jesus!" I interrupted. "Why are you so fascinated by Norman Mailer?"

"Because *he* knew what it was like to be a writer. He ran for Mayor of New York. He was married six times. He had all these mistresses."

"So what? I don't get it. Do you have some kind of fascination with people who cheat?"

"No, I have a fascination for people who *live* their lives. Really live them. For the most part, Mailer was like that. He jumped in, and he gobbled up life. He didn't hole up in the woods."

"Ah." I actually felt a little sympathy for Mick then.

"What's that mean, that 'ah'?"

"Well, it's not that hard to figure out, is it? I'm sure some therapist has told you already, but clearly you're looking to idealize a male figure who wasn't like your father."

His amused expression turned solemn with an underlying edge of anger. "You don't know anything about my father."

"I just know what I've read. That he moved you and your mom to some tiny town in Maine and lived out his years there."

Mick shook his head, but only minutely, as if he was trying to hold back his movements. "I looked up to Norman because he was different than my dad, sure. And I *choose* not to be like my father. It's not as subconscious as you might think."

"So then you are able to choose. You can choose whether to be a—" I searched for a replacement word and came up with none "—a dickhead," I said, "and slander Jane's good name or not."

"It's not slander or libel if it's true. You're a lawyer, you should know that."

"No, it's still slander and libel. It's just that you have a defense to it if it's true. As a lawyer, I'll tell you that you'd also have a defense because of the fact that Jane is dead. But as a human being I'm asking you not to *use* those defenses."

"Are you saying I'm inhumane?" He seemed to find this funny.

"Look, you clearly have daddy issues, and I can see why…"

Apparently, that comment was not so funny. His eyes narrowed, jaw muscles tensed.

"Look," I pointed at him. "You're getting pissed. I don't even know why, and really I don't care. I mean, I know it's about your dad, and I'm guessing you're annoyed because I don't know the whole story. I just *read* something and now I'm spouting it back. And that's exactly what you're doing to Jane if you write this stuff about her or let it get out. Two wrongs don't make a right, Mick. Don't turn around and do to Jane what was done to your family."

He said nothing.

"And if you did anything to Jane," I said, "then you should talk about it. You should tell *that* story."

His face relaxed. "From what I hear, *you're* the one they think should come clean."

I felt him study me. What was I doing trying to talk this guy, this investigative journalist, out of writing about Jane? He was probably analyzing me right now so he could write about me. I uncrossed my arms. "I should go."

He said nothing. He was looking at me with some expression I couldn't read. A curiosity, certainly, but not the salacious curiosity that I would have expected.

I turned and walked down the steps and onto Goethe Street, unsure what to do next.

Traffic whizzed by on LaSalle Street. I heard shouts from Wells Street in the other direction. It was almost Saturday night. I thought about how just over a week ago, I didn't know I would be a news reporter, an anchor, a suspect. Now my skin tingled with a weird kind of energy, my body twitched with a premonitory buzz. And a question occurred to me—if it had all changed so much in only one week, what could happen next?

72

The media were outside my condo when I got home, and they were still camped out when I left for the store Sunday morning. Jittery from a night of little sleep, I stopped and took a breath before I pushed open the front door of my condo building.

If Sam was back in Chicago, he hadn't called the night before to let me know, and some combination of pride and caution made me not call him. I wasn't sure what I would say. I wasn't sure what I wanted to happen. I wasn't sure how I felt about him right now, or, maybe more importantly, how he felt about me, about us. The lingering uncertainty from the last few months had only increased, not gone away as I'd hoped. And so, last night, I had lain in my bed, thinking of Sam, thinking of Grady, thinking of Theo, and most of all thinking of the fact that earlier this week I had all of them, and now, for one reason or another, they were gone.

That was fine, really. Honestly, I'm not the kind of girl who needs someone—a guy or a friend or a family member— around all the time. I *like* being with myself. But the rapidity with which people had come and gone from my life lately was freaking me out. Not just Sam, Grady and Theo, but Jane, and the people at Trial TV, too, and Forester, and everyone at my old law firm of Baltimore & Brown.

When I stepped outside my building, the reporters and cameramen leapt into action, shoving microphones, yelling questions. One cameraman pulled his face from behind the lens and smiled sheepishly at me.

"Ricky?" I said. It was the guy who'd worked the equipment in the van on my first day at Trial TV.

"Hey," he said simply, then went back to filming me.

They surrounded me like a swarm of bees, following me as I hurried to the garage.

Suddenly, I heard a *thump, thump* behind me, then shouting. "Get away from her. You leave her alone! Now!"

I swirled around. Then I couldn't help it. I burst out laughing. "Bunny?"

Bunny Loveland was the housekeeper my mother hired when we first moved to Chicago following my dad's death. With her once-a-week beauty-shop hair that lay in rounded, gray rows, she looked the part of a kind grandmother, which was probably what my mother was hoping for. But Bunny turned out to be a cranky, fairly mean-spirited person who cracked a smile only when she saw a Polish sausage from Vienna Beef. And yet, she was honest as hell. She became my go-to person whenever I needed a swift slap in the face.

Except that now, she was trying to slap a reporter. "Go home!" she shouted, elbowing another reporter, then cracking yet another over the head with a faux-leather purse.

"Bunny?" I said again, louder this time.

She paused from her beating and looked at me. "I'm trying to help ya, kid. Now get out of here!"

She swung the purse in an arc, hitting a camera with surprising force. Meanwhile, I yelled thanks and took off in a sprint for the garage.

I thought about taking Grady's car, but I realized that the reporters would follow me, and even if Bunny could keep a few of them back, I had no idea how to lose the others behind the wheel of a big automobile.

I got on my Vespa and secured my helmet, tightening the chin strap to the point where it was almost cutting into my skin. I opened the garage door and sped forward, nearly hitting one of the cameramen. I saw Ricky behind him. Bunny was still dueling with a few reporters.

"Sorry!" I called to Ricky over my shoulder and pulled back hard on the gas, lurching over the cobblestones.

Two cars and a van were sitting at the end of the alley, cameramen hanging from the windows. I was about to turn onto a main street when I realized that the alleys might be the best way to shake them. I crisscrossed from alley to alley, darting glances over my shoulder at the news people doggedly trailing me, the Vespa shaking and bumping from the cobblestones. One of the alleys was ultranarrow, and the van behind me had to stop. The cars kept up with me, though, and their hulking presence began to get scary.

"Son of a motherless goat," I muttered, my new replacement attempt for "son of a bitch." I would have to try something different.

I got onto Sheffield and floored the scooter. Every time there was a left-turn lane, I got in it, shot ahead of the cars going straight and then veered back into the main lane, leaving behind a trail of honks and bleats. I could see one of the news cars, about six cars behind me now, but still keeping up with me.

I steered the scooter into another alley. Two SUVs were parked behind an apartment building. I drove the scooter between them and stopped at the back of the largest SUV, hoping it would obscure the Vespa from the alley. I jumped off and crouched down. I hadn't been doing anything physical, but my heart was racing. The feeling of being chased was not one I enjoyed.

Five seconds later, the car with the cameraman turned into the alley. And blew right by me. I dropped my head and sucked in the dirty, exhaust-filled air from the alley, grateful for it, before I got back on my scooter and steered it toward the Fig Leaf.

My alley adventure made me late. I didn't even have time to look for Mayburn's van as I ran in.

Josie glared at me. Was it because she'd seen me on TV? My heart started tripping around again.

She looked pointedly at her watch.

"I'm really sorry I'm late," I said to Josie, "I—"

She drew her finger and thumb across her mouth, as if to say, *Zip it,* and pointed at the back room. "Five boxes of stock. Go."

So she hadn't seen me on TV. Thank God. And I needed to be in the stockroom anyway, near those black thongs. The problem was—how to get Josie's keys and get into that locked box, high on the shelf? Josie either kept the keys on her or left them near the register at the front desk.

I sliced open the first box and went to work on the contents—bustiers in three different colors, pink, white, black. Reflexively, I thought of how Sam would love me in the black one. Then I shook the thought away. Immediately, Theo popped into my mind. Had everything we'd shared been some kind of game to him, some sick way to get back at Jane? Nope, I wasn't going to go there, either.

I turned back to the bustiers, steaming and folding them, making the handwritten price tags and attaching them. But the whole time, my eyes kept dodging to the locked box up on the shelf, where Josie kept the thongs.

Once I got the bustiers steamed, I opened the second box of stock—push-up bras with blue gingham ribbons threaded through the top.

I went out into the front of the store. "Josie," I said, holding aloft one of the bras. "Do these need to be steamed?"

I knew the answer. According to Josie, everything needed to be steamed, if only to loosen up the fabric and make it softer. But I needed an excuse to see if her keys were in plain view.

They were. Right next to her at the register.

"Yes, of *course.*" She began lecturing me about the importance of steaming, while I nodded and nodded. It was both tragic and fascinating that this stuff meant so much to Josie.

I couldn't think how to get her away from the register or the keys, so I went into the back room and kept attacking the stock, shooting glances up at the metal box every minute or so.

At ten, the store opened, and Josie ordered me to the front. It was a sunny, crisp spring day, everyone giddy with the weather, and the place was soon crowded. I opened the door at one point, ostensibly to let in some fresh air, but really I wanted to check on Mayburn. And just as he'd said, a white van was parked across the street with the words *Midwest Gas* stenciled on the side in red. The window of the driver's seat slid down a few inches. Mayburn gave me a quick nod, then the window slid back up.

The hours passed quickly, me manning the front, Josie ringing up customers and showing them to the dressing room.

At about three o'clock two women walked in. "Welcome to the Fig Leaf," I said, then went back to refolding pajamas that had been messed up by someone's toddler.

I could feel one of the women looking at me, just staring. She whispered something to her friend, who turned to look at me. I met their eyes and smiled. "Can I help you find anything?"

"No," the first woman said. "We're just trying to figure out where we've seen you. On TV maybe?"

I shot a look over my shoulder at Josie. Thankfully, she was behind the counter with a small line of people in front of her. I peered through the front window and saw Mayburn's van, still parked across the street.

What to do? What to do?

I decided to go for the blatant lie. "Not me," I said. "But I've heard there's some woman who looks like me…." I trailed off and tried to keep my head down, staring at the table of pajamas with an intensity I usually reserved for court appearances.

"Yeah, that girl who killed the newscaster!" the woman said. "That's who you look like!"

"Oh, you're right," her friend said. "Exactly!"

"She didn't *kill* the newscaster," I objected.

"I heard she did," said the first women.

Another woman, wearing a spring sundress, came forward. "Are you talking about Jane Augustine's murder?"

"Yeah."

"Isabel McNeil," the woman in the dress confirmed. "That's the woman who they think did it."

I froze. I started blushing. I could feel the pulse in my neck rat-a-tat-tat. "She did *not* do it."

"She took over her job," the woman said.

"And she's the only one who was supposed to be with Jane Augustine that afternoon," the first woman added.

"Jane was supposed to be with a friend," I said. "Not m…" I started to say *not me* but I caught myself. Everyone looked at me funny.

Another glance over my shoulder. Josie was done ringing up the sales and was now headed toward us. I had to get out of this conversation. *Fast.*

"Ladies, we've got some great underwear on sale over there." I pointed to the side of the store, then spun around and started walking. "Be right back," I said to Josie. "Bathroom." I patted my stomach vaguely and made a face as if to imply female difficulties or a tapeworm complication.

Josie frowned but gave me a quick nod.

I hurried to the back. As I passed the counter, I saw her keys. Right there by the register. I threw a look behind me and saw Josie was talking to the ladies. Was she talking about the redhead on TV who'd supposedly killed Jane Augustine? The one I looked like? Should I pull the plug now, run out the door to Mayburn's van?

My eyes darted to the keys again. I thought of how much Mayburn had helped me over the last six months. Now it was my turn to help him again on one of his cases. If I could get in the metal box right now, Josie probably wouldn't leave the front anytime soon. But if she saw me grabbing the keys, she'd lose it.

I veered toward the register and stopped behind it, pretending to move around the gift boxes. I looked at Josie and she gave me a *What are you doing?* frown, then glanced toward the back room as if to say, *Are you going or not?*

I nodded, smiled. "Be right back," I mouthed. I started moving in the direction of the storeroom, but I kept my eyes on Josie, and as soon as she turned back to the women, I shot my arm out and snatched the keys.

By the time I got in the back room, I was shaking from anticipation. My eyes swung around wildly. Where was that step stool that Josie had used to reach the locked box? I dodged from room to room, searching for it, finally finding it in a closet.

I dragged the stool and placed it right under the box. Before I climbed up, I stuck my head out of the back room. Josie was still in front, but she was backing up as she talked to a customer, headed for the register, where she'd probably see that her keys were gone.

Go, I told myself. *Now or never.*

I climbed on to the step stool. The keys jingled as I tried to stick one, then another and another in the small slot in the metal box.

"Damn it," I muttered. Why did Josie have so many freaking keys?

I held my breath for a second, listening for Josie's approaching footsteps. But instead I heard the sound of the register ringing a sale.

I stared at the key ring. She had a monogrammed brass plate hanging from the ring and about nine keys. I studied them, looking for the smallest one, looking at the front plate of the metal box to see if any of them seemed to match. Maybe I should just grab the whole box and take off with it?

I pushed up on the box. It was heavier than I thought. And

it was already bad enough I was trying to steal a single thong.

"C'mon," I muttered, my hands trembling as I tried another key and another one.

The last key slid in and turned smoothly.

"I might have a 34B in the back," I heard Josie say from the front of the store. She was talking loud, giving me a signal to get my ass back out there, I could tell. Was she heading here at the same time?

Hurry, Izzy.

I opened it and reached inside. I pulled out a few thong boxes, each of them gray, like the one I already had and the one I'd bought for Maggie. I shoved them back and rummaged around inside. This time I yanked out one of the black ones.

"Yes!" I whispered.

I locked the box, jumped down from the step stool and stashed the stool back in the closet.

"Just one moment," I heard Josie saying in her First Lady voice, then the sound of her clicking heels coming closer and closer to the back room.

"Shit, shit, shit," I muttered, not even trying for one of my swear replacements. She was steps away, and here I was with her keys and a black-boxed thong. My purse was in one of the other storerooms. I didn't have time to reach it and stash the thong inside before she would be here.

I squeezed the box. It was thin. I managed to squash it into a V-shape. Now, where to put it? I looked down at myself. I was wearing straight-legged black pants and a black blouse. The pants were so fitted that the pockets were useless, but the blouse was loose and full. I stuck the rolled-up box between my breasts, anchored by my bra. Now what to do with the keys?

Josie was just outside. I could hear the angry clack of her shoes. Lacking anything else to do, I stuck the keys under one armpit and clamped down my arm, holding them there.

"What are you doing?" she hissed. Josie stood, a hand on her hip, a snarl on her face.

"I had to use the restroom. I'll get back out there."

I hustled toward her, pressing my arm down harder.

"Have you seen my keys?" Her eyes, narrowed and suspicious behind her silver-framed glasses, darted around the back room. I prayed that I had pushed the metal box back into place, just like it had been.

"They're by the register, aren't they? Let me look." I scurried past her before she could say anything, rushed to the register and bent down, dropping the keys from underneath my arm. I stood back up. "Here they are!" I said.

A customer came to the register, and I rang up her purchases, trying to breathe, trying not to move too fast, trying to squeeze my breasts together to hold the thong box in place. Never had a greater pectoral exercise been performed.

Josie came up behind me. "Where were they?" she said when the customer was gone. She picked up the keys that I'd placed by the register.

"On the floor."

"How would they have gotten on the floor?" Her tone was now cold, cool. It was much more nerve-racking than her irritated voice.

"I don't know." I peered through the front window again. The Midwest Gas truck was still there.

The customer left the store, and suddenly there was a lull. Josie and I were alone. I moved around the register, trying to act nonchalant, straightening some robes that had slipped from their hangers.

Meanwhile, Josie watched me. Just watched me. Had she heard what the women had been saying, that I looked like the newscaster accused of killing Jane? Did she know I *was* the newscaster accused of killing Jane? Or was she staring at me because of the key incident?

"Lexi, I'd like to talk to you," I heard her say.

I turned, nodded as casually as possible.

"Please come here."

I walked to the register, trying to make my face bored. But the damn thong box started to slip. I clenched the muscles of my neck and chest, trying to hold it in place.

"I don't trust you." She said it like that, no lead-in, no explanation. Just laid it out.

"Uh…why?" *Because I just stole one of your thongs and I'm holding it between my boobs?*

"I'm not sure." Her eyes searched my face. "I'm not sure what we should do about you."

It was that word—*we*—that scared me. Did she mean her and "Steve"? Or was she just using the royal "we"?

Josie and I stood there, just the two of us in the store, her gaze unflinching. Outside, I could hear cars streaming by, then occasional laughter from people walking past. But inside the store, it was silent. Meanwhile, I was starting to sweat, and the thong box slid lower.

Josie glanced at my chest, frowned deeper.

I tried to give a breezy smile, but with the energy I was exerting to hold the box, I'm sure it came out like a grimace.

"What are you doing?" She glanced up and down my body.

The sweating continued; the box slithered lower. Any minute now, it was going to fall, right onto the floor.

I let myself grimace again. "I'm not feeling so good. I need to use the restroom again."

Before Josie could respond, I headed toward the back, putting a hand on my chest as soon as I passed her. When I got to the back, I ran to grab my purse and stuffed the box inside.

"Lexi!" I heard her call, and once again I heard the *snap, snap* of her heels.

I stood, frozen for a second.

"Lexi!" I heard again. She stepped into the back room and glared.

"My stomach feels awful," I said. "Something is wrong with me." I put a hand on my stomach. "Sorry."

She stared at me suspiciously. She took a step toward me, then another.

Suddenly, there was a pounding at the back door. We both jumped a little.

Josie marched past me and opened it. "Hey, Steve," she said in a distracted tone.

But Steve didn't look too distracted. In fact, he was looking right at me, his bearded face twisted not so much into a leer this time, but a hard, pensive expression, as if he was trying to remember something. He ran a hand through his oily black hair. I got a flash of that night in the alley— the brutal *crack* on the side of my helmet, falling into the garage, a massive shove from behind, blood trickling from my knees. Had he told her about the prowler in the helmet the other night or did they not have that kind of relationship?

Steve held out a box to Josie, although his eyes didn't leave mine.

Blast, it was more pearl thongs. Which meant Josie was about to get that stool, unlock that box and see that one was missing.

Josie took the box from him, moving away and mumbling *thanks*.

Steve stood there, grimacing at me now, some kind of intensity lighting his eyes.

My stomach started to churn then. I really did feel sick.

Josie stopped, looked at him. "Okay, thanks, Steve," she said, obviously trying to get him to leave.

But he didn't budge. Instead, he stood, and he stared, and his eyes narrowed further.

My heart rate tripled. I was trapped. Josie was blocking the door to the store. Steve stood in front of the door to the alley.

I glanced behind me. It was time to bolt, but neither of them moved. Josie glanced at Steve, then at me, as if she was trying to figure out what was going on. Steve remained still.

The front door trilled as someone opened it.

We all looked toward the sound.

"Hello?" I heard a male voice say. I knew that voice.

"Hello?" the man said again.

Mayburn. *Thank you, thank you.* He must have been watching. He must have sensed I was in trouble.

"I'm looking for a present for my girlfriend?" he called.

Josie huffed, then shook her head. "Get out there and help him," she said tersely to me.

She didn't have to tell me twice. "Sure, sure." Holding my purse, I dashed into the front room.

The sunlight from the front window hit me in the face.

Mayburn stood, hand holding open the front door. "Did you get it?" he mouthed.

I nodded fast and walked right toward him. "Go!"

Outside, we rushed across the street. Mayburn yanked open the driver's door of the van and gestured with a hurried hand toward the other side.

"Wait," I said. "What about my scooter?"

"We'll come back for it," Mayburn said. "Get in!"

73

My phone kept ringing as Mayburn and I drove through Lincoln Park. I ignored it, instead telling him the whole story and handing over the black thong.

Finally, I looked at the phone as Mayburn stopped at a light at Armitage and Sheffield. It was Maggie. She'd called four times.

I didn't have to fake a stomach illness now. I felt my insides diving and twisting. Was there some news from Vaughn, some rumor on TV, the declaration of Izzy McNeil as official suspect?

I called her back. "It's me." I waited for the worst.

I heard Maggie sniffle. Bad sign. It must be truly awful. Maggie never cried about work. But then again, it was hard to represent your best friend in a murder investigation.

"Mags, what is it?" I watched a group of high school guys come out of the 7-Eleven, glugging Slurpees and smacking each other around. I had never wanted to be a seventeen-year-old, Slurpee-glugging guy until that moment.

More sniffling. "It's Wyatt."

I hate to say it, but I felt relief. "What did he do?"

"You mean *who* did he do?"

"Oh, no."

"Oh, yeah. Where are you?"

"Armitage and Sheffield."

"By the Twisted Lizard?"

I glanced across the street and saw the underground Mexican place. "Yeah."

"Perfect. I need a dark bar and something with a lot of tequila. Can you meet me there?"

"Of course." I gestured for Mayburn to pull over and told Maggie I'd be waiting.

Mayburn drew over to the curb and opened the black thong box. Using a pen, he lifted it, grinning.

"What is it? Why do you look so happy?" I asked.

"Are you kidding? Eighty-five percent of my job usually involves surveillance. I sit for hours in a fricking car outside a fricking apartment building with a fricking camera pointed at the front door. This—" he raised the thong higher "—is the highlight of my week."

"Men are so weird. I wouldn't be getting all excited if you gave me a pair of boxers."

He held the thong toward me. "This is not the same thing as boxers. *This* is something different."

I remembered putting my thong on, sharing it with Theo. "Good point."

"Anyway," Mayburn said, "I'll drop this off at the lab. And I'll get your scooter. Either I'll have someone help me get it in the van or we'll drive it for you. Give me the keys."

I handed them over. For some reason, I didn't want to leave the van, which seemed like a little container of quasi-normalcy. Joking with Mayburn about thongs was as far away from a murder investigation as I could get.

"What are you doing the rest of the day?" I asked Mayburn.

"I have to meet Lucy at her kid's soccer game in ten minutes."

"Wow. The soccer games now, huh?"

"Shut it."

"I'm happy for you," I said.

"Don't get all sentimental."

I opened the door. "See ya."

Fifteen minutes later, Maggie was tiptoeing down the stairs of the Twisted Lizard into the dimly lit bar. She wore dark jeans cuffed at the bottom, her little feet in pink loafers. Her golden hair was a mess, as was her face.

I hugged her, then grabbed a napkin from the bar and wiped the mascara from under her eyes. "What do you want to drink?"

Maggie ordered a margarita. "On the rocks. With double tequila."

"What happened?" I said when her drink was delivered.

"It was just like last time." She sniffled, started to cry. "I mean, you told me it would be the same thing. You *told* me."

"I was just guessing. And hey, he looked devoted to you the other night at my mom's house."

"Yeah, exactly. He *looked* devoted. And he acted devoted to me at his house after dinner. It was amazing. I was actually thinking we might get engaged this summer."

"Really?"

"Yeah, and then..." She trailed off, gulped her drink, and glanced at me. "Why aren't you drinking?"

"Didn't sleep well last night."

"Yeah, I'm sure." More sniffling. "But you have to drink with me!"

She began to cry, so I quickly waved at the bartender and ordered a Corona.

"Okay, Mags," I said. "What happened?"

"Like I said, same thing. I mean, almost exactly the same thing. We went out last night. Had an amazing time. Today, I left around noon to work on your case. I wanted to do some research about the term 'person of interest' and how often those persons are converted to suspects."

At the thought, my stomach gripped.

"When I got to the office, I worked for a while," Maggie said, "and then I decided to work out. My gym bag was at his place, because I've been staying there so much. I knew he didn't have anything going on today, so I just dodged over there."

"Don't tell me."

"Yep. He was with someone. I mean, they weren't having sex. It wasn't *exactly* like last time, but they were getting ready to go out to lunch. She was clearly picking him up for a lunch date, like no big deal, like I hadn't been there just an hour before." Her face crumpled and more tears streamed down her face.

"Well, maybe it was a friend of his. I mean, did you stop to ask who it was or did you just storm out?"

"I didn't have to ask!" Her voice rose. "This was the woman he dated last year, the woman who broke his heart. I knew because of the pictures that are still around his house. And when I came in, you should have seen his face. It said everything. When I took him outside and asked, 'Is this what it seems?' he said, 'Yes.' Just like that. He said yes!"

"What a total jerk."

This only made her cry more. "He's not! He's actually a good guy. He's just not in love with me."

I pushed her drink away and turned her so that she was facing me. "Mags."

She searched my eyes. "I know. Don't defend him. I know." She sagged forward, crying.

I held her, gesturing over her back at the bartender that we were fine, just a little crying jag. And honestly, it felt good to be the one propping someone else up for a change.

When she was done, she wiped her eyes on her cocktail napkin and sucked down the rest of her drink. "What's going on with you?"

I looked at the festive colored lights above the bar. "Well, let's see. Theo came back from Mexico."

Her face brightened. "Excellent! And will he tell the cops he was with you Friday night?"

"We called and left Vaughn a message. Theo says he'll explain."

"So why do you look miserable?"

"Because I found out that he used to sleep with Jane."

"No fricking way."

"Yep. He flirted with me when we met to get back at her." I shrugged.

"Iz, I have to tell you no matter what his motivation was, this isn't good."

"What do you mean?"

She grimaced. Glanced down, then back at me. "Think of how this is going to look to the cops. After Jane died, you got Jane's anchor chair *and* her ex-boyfriend."

74

Reporters and cameramen littered my lawn. I felt immediate sympathy for my downstairs neighbors for putting up with this.

Unfortunately, it looked like Bunny Loveland had put her media beatings on hold. I paid the cabbie, then pushed past them all, shoving blindly at those who surged around me. As I hurried toward the building, I kept my head down, ignoring the calls of "Izzy! Izzy!", deliberately tuning out the questions, although snippets of them permeated my resolve—
...kill Jane?...wanted her job?

I fumbled at the door, trying to get my keys in the lock. I could feel the reporters behind me, could hear the whir of shooters with their video cameras, could hear the snapping of the photographers. I felt trapped there, in front of my door, my fingers groping to get the right key, reminding me of my struggle to get in that metal box only a few hours ago.

Finally, I got the key in the lock, swung the door open, jumped inside. I slammed the door against the melee. Panting, I stood inside, letting the cool dark of the hallway wash over me. When I'd caught my breath, I started up the stairs.

But something seemed wrong, felt awry. As if I wasn't the only person in the stairwell. I froze, listening for any sounds. Nothing. Just my crazy imagination. I took slow steps, seeing nothing, hearing nothing. And yet I felt *something*.

Calm down, I told myself. *Calm down.* I kept climbing, and my breath became short again, partly from the exertion and partly because my nerves were singing from the crush of reporters outside.

I was about to turn the landing and go up the last flight of steps when I heard a man's voice. "Izzy."

It came from above. It came from my place.

I halted on the landing, a chill slinking into my bones. "Sam?"

It didn't sound like Sam but no one else had keys to my place. No response.

"Tom? Bill?" I said, mentioning the names of my neighbors, even though the voice hadn't sounded like either of them.

Again, nothing.

My heart started pounding harder in my chest.

I headed back downstairs, my pulse tapping against my throat. But I stopped. I realized I would have to face the media again. I could understand for the first time why celebrities complained about press and paparazzi. I stood, unmoving, unable to decide what to do.

Then that man's voice again… "Izzy." Then the *pound, pound, pound* of footsteps coming down the stairs, coming down from my condo. "Izzy?" I heard. The voice was familiar, but I could barely concentrate with the hammering of blood in my ears.

Pound, pound, pound. The footsteps were coming closer.

Press or no, I was getting out of there. I started running down the stairs. The footsteps above me were coming faster now. I was being chased. I held on to the banister, went down as fast as I could, nearly tripping.

"Izzy, stop!" I heard above me. "Where are you going?"

I finally recognized the voice. I halted, turned.

Theo. His face was twisted with irritation. He wore the same jeans, black T-shirt and army jacket that he'd had on yesterday. I had thought the outfit cute then, but now it seemed severe, militant. His long hair hung around his face, nearly hiding his features as he looked down at me.

"How did you get in here?" I asked.

"Well, I had to take the train back to the city yesterday. And then the cops picked me up, because I'd called them on the way. I spent the night with that guy Vaughn. The dude is a prick, but I told him everything. Told him we were together Friday night. After the police station, I went home, and I got something to show you, and I came right here."

"How did you get in here?" I demanded.

He shrugged. "I saw all the press, so I waited near the door. I said I was your brother. Your neighbor or somebody left, and I caught the door. I came in and made sure those dudes—" he gestured with his chin toward the front of the building "—stayed out."

"And you've just been sitting in my stairwell? For how long?"

He shrugged again. "A couple of hours."

I took one slow step back. Then another. He was freaking me out. I didn't trust him anymore. I couldn't believe I ever had. "I think you should leave. Right now."

"Jeez, girl, I just wanted to show you something." His face grew more irritated, angry. It scared me to see him like that.

"You know there are a mass of reporters right out that door?" But even I could hear that the threat was lame. He could get down the steps and grab me in a second.

"I'm about to leave," he said. "But I told you I have to show you something first."

Pound, pound, pound. He came down the steps, growing closer to me. My heart thumped even louder against my ribs.

"Stop," I said, holding up my hand. "Just stop. What do you want to show me?"

He reached into the breast pocket of his jacket.

My breath stopped. *What was he doing?*

He pulled something from the jacket. It was square. Blue.

"It's my passport," he said. "It says I was in Mexico on Monday, just like I told you." He bent down and tossed the passport. It bounced and skidded to a step above me.

I picked it up, looked at his photo—admittedly adorable, a sexy twist to his mouth. I flipped through the pages. And there it was—an entry stamp for Mexico on Monday. An exit stamp for yesterday.

I looked up at him, my brain reeling with the surreal of him, of this situation. For a second, I craved the calm familiarity that I used to have with Sam, missed the days when we were together, when he understood every notion my mind seemed to register, every little twinge my body felt and I understood his.

Theo sat down on a step and put his arms on his knees. He seemed to realize that my thoughts and my emotions were spinning, whirling, that they were having a very hard time landing.

"I was going to tell you, you know," he said.

"Tell me what?"

"About Jane. And me. Izzy, I've only known you for a week." He no longer looked anxious or irritated but rather wistful and compassionate and something else I couldn't read. He tucked a lock of hair behind his ears. "But it feels like I've known you longer." He took a breath, then exhaled loud. "Look, inside my head, I'm older than twenty-one. But I'm still learning things—about relationships, about sex, about work. I'm changing all the time. And I'm different now than I was when I was with Jane. I'm into you in a whole different way." He seemed earnest. He seemed as if he was telling me the truth. But it was obvious to me I had absolutely no fricking clue what the truth was anymore.

"And yet the only reason you hit on me," I said, "the only reason you slept with me, was to get back at Jane. Because you were in love with her."

"No, I'm over Jane. I have been for a while, and I hadn't seen her in forever before that night. When I ran into you guys, and she introduced us, I was just playing at first, hitting on you to try to make her crazy, but she didn't care, and then I realized I did. About *you*. There's just something about you."

I looked at his passport again, and thought about everything I'd learned about Theo in that week. He had never lied to me, I realized. He had omitted information, certainly, but I understood what he was saying. We'd only known each other such a short time, just a weekend, really. When I thought about it, he had never really done anything wrong, not that I could tell. And his passport proved that he couldn't have killed Jane.

"I'm sorry I accused you," I said.

He smiled. "You didn't accuse. You asked."

"I guess I was surprised. To hear about the Jane thing. And I think I felt stupid."

He nodded. "That's not fun."

I shrugged. "It wasn't. But it's also not fun to be accused. I know that. So I'm…I'm sorry I accused you."

He gazed at me. "What can I do? I want to help you." He was so big physically, and there was also the presence of *him*, which took up so much space. Yet right now, he looked helpless. And young.

The stairwell was growing warm, stifling almost. Outside I could hear muted chatter from the media.

"C'mere," Theo said, standing.

I stood, silent. Finally, I took a step up, then another and another until I was one above him and our faces were even, until I could breathe in that Theo scent that had made me crazy all last weekend. And it still worked. The human, sexual part of me that couldn't be turned off was turned on. But my brain wouldn't let me go there.

"What can I do?" he said again. His voice was soft. I stared at his cushioned lips. "What can I do?" He put his hands on my waist.

"Theo, I can't," I said, pulling back a little.

"Shh," he said. "We're not… We're just…" Slowly, his hands still on my waist, he drew me closer; slowly he wrapped his big arms around me, pulling me into him, curling me against his body, stroking my hair, holding me.

I shuddered with comfort. And finally, I clung to him.

We stayed like that for minutes. Five, maybe, then time stretched. It must have been ten minutes and then fifteen. Neither of us moved. Something about being there soothed me, restored me, almost.

But then the calm of the moment was shattered by a banging sound, then a buzzing noise, then loud knocking. I could hear the buzzer reverberate upstairs in my apartment.

"Do you want to answer it?" Theo asked.

I shook my head. "It's just the press." I curled myself into him for another moment. But the banging got louder, and the buzzing didn't let up. Every few seconds or so, *buzz, buzz, buzz.* And then finally, whoever it was started laying on the buzzer, so that a long screech filled the stairwell.

Theo stood straighter. "I'll get rid of them."

"No, don't. Don't do anything."

More pounding, more buzzing.

"Look, Theo," I said, trying to ignore it. "You asked what you could do, and I think the only thing you can really do right now is stay away from me." I thought of Maggie's comments. "It doesn't look good that you dated Jane and then me, and then Jane ended up dead, and I ended up with her job. And really, I'm in no shape to spend time with anyone."

He shrugged. "I want you however you are. Wherever you are." He touched my jaw with the fingers of his left hand. He pulled my face toward him. He kissed me with those lips, that tongue. And for that moment, the world was vaporized, gone, nothing lingering except us.

But then more banging, the buzzing. Whoever it was, they weren't going to stop.

I groaned, blinked a few times, pulled my face away. "I

should get that. And you should go. Maybe when this is over…" I trailed off, struck with fear that it might never be over. But I shook that fear away. *Enough with the fear,* I thought. It would get me absolutely nowhere.

Once more, his fingers on my jaw; once more, a kiss, this one quick. Too quick. "When this is over," he said, nodding, as if he was very sure of something.

Thumping, buzzing from the front door.

I groaned. I turned and stormed down the stairs. "Who is it?" I shouted through the door.

"Detective Vaughn."

I looked up at Theo, heard Maggie's words—*this doesn't look good.* Should I take him up to my apartment and leave down the back stairs? But that would look like I was hiding something. And I had nothing to hide.

"McNeil," I heard Vaughn yell, "I have a warrant."

75

When I opened the door, Vaughn stood with two uniformed cops behind him. The cameras and reporters formed a half circle around them, clicking and shooting like mad.

Oh God, what was happening? I zeroed in on Vaughn's face, which bore his usual self-satisfied half grin.

"Izzy! Izzy!" the reporters yelled. They were a pulsing mass.

Vaughn's eyes shot over my head to Theo. And he grinned. "How about that?"

"He was here to show me his passport," I said. "He's leaving."

Theo touched the small of my back—a gentle, lingering touch that said so many things—and then he stepped outside, moved around Vaughn and the officers and walked right across my lawn. I watched him until he reached the street. A few of the reporters followed him. He said nothing to them. He kept walking.

And then he stopped for one minute, turned around and met my eyes. He raised his arm. He gave a wave, and then Theo kept walking away from me, just as I'd asked him to do.

"You better let me in," Vaughn said with a full, cold grin, "or I'm going to make a statement to these guys."

Damn it. I didn't know what to do. I needed to call Maggie.

He glanced over his shoulder at the retreating figure of Theo. "The press *love* a good sex triangle. It won't just make the headlines here. You'll probably get international coverage when I tell them this one."

Vaughn turned around and held up a hand. The media went silent. I felt the situation spiraling away from me. I had no idea what he was going to say or do. All I knew was that the last time he made a statement I got fired.

"No," I said, before he could start.

He threw a glance at me over his shoulder. I gestured for him to step inside the door.

He did so with a smirk, and then it was just the two of us in the dark stairwell, the door shutting, bringing a relative silence.

For a weird second, it felt as if we had gone on a date, and we were saying goodbye. I'd never been that close to him before.

And I didn't want to be. "What do you want?"

"To come into your apartment."

"No way."

He smiled again. "Like I said, I've got a warrant."

"An—" I could hardly get myself to say it "—an arrest warrant?"

"Not yet. That's next."

He reached into his pocket and pulled out a few folded sheets of paper. He opened them up and handed them to me. The top of the first sheet read, *Search Warrant*. I tried to read it, but my breath was short and the words seemed to skitter around. I could see that it listed my name and address, as well as the address for Trial TV, and it was signed by a judge. I flipped to the other sheets. There was an affidavit and a complaint requesting the warrant.

"I didn't get a copy of this," I said. "In order for this to be valid, I should have received notice."

Vaughn smiled. "You're not so good of a lawyer, are you? We don't have to give you notice of anything."

My mind whirled over conversations I'd had with Maggie and realized he was right—they didn't have to give notice for a *request* of a search warrant. They just had to tell you when they got it.

"Ever seen an Emmy Award?" he asked.

"What?" I said, irritated.

"An Emmy Award."

"I've seen the show."

"I mean the award. The trophy. Ever seen one?"

I shook my head. What was he going on about? Then I remembered something. "I guess I saw Jane's."

"Really?" He cocked his head to the side. "When did you see that?"

"The Saturday before she died. When she found the flowers in her house and asked me to come over. I told you about that."

"You told me you went there. You didn't tell me you'd looked at the Emmy, picked it up, whatever."

"I didn't pick it up. My brother did."

"Your brother? Really?" His eyebrows shot up. "What's your brother's name?"

I hesitated. Should I tell him? But he could easily find it out. "Charlie. Charlie McNeil."

"Charles McNeil." He seemed to be saying it as though he was memorizing the name. "And what about the day Jane died, when you were there that day. You see the Emmy then?"

"Enough," I said. "I'm not answering any questions without my lawyer."

He looked at me and blinked. Then blinked again. Then once more. The blinking was making me think of the way he clicked his pen. Instead of *click, click, click,* it was now *blink, blink, blink.*

"Let me ask you a question," I said. "What did you tell a judge in order to get this warrant?"

He guffawed. "Are you kidding me? What didn't we tell

them? You were the one who was supposed to see Jane before the party. You took over her job the next day. You were seen kissing Jane a few days before she died."

"We did *not* kiss. I told you that. Just like I told you I wasn't with her on Friday."

He cocked his head. "I'll give you that one. Your boyfriend, Theodore, came in." He gave me a mocking look. "Isn't he a little young for you?"

Ignoring the crack, I said, "He told you everything."

"Yeah, yeah he did. Boy, that was fun." Vaughn, the jerk, really looked as if he meant it, as though questioning Theo had been a party for him. What was wrong with this guy? Why did he dislike me so much?

I said nothing. I could feel myself scowl. And then a thought occurred to me—maybe it wasn't so simple as Vaughn not liking me. Maybe he really thought I was guilty. The feeling of being wrongfully accused was a terrible one, an unbelievably vulnerable one. And to have someone truly believe something horrible about you—that you killed someone—was even worse than the accusation.

Vaughn kept talking. "And boy, then what does Theodore tell me? He says that he used to sleep with Jane. And now *you two* are together."

I swallowed hard. "We're not together."

He laughed. "Yeah, whatever. You were obsessed with Jane. You had some weird love triangle going on."

I pictured Maggie screaming at me, and I finally clamped my mouth shut.

"Look," Vaughn said, "the point is, we didn't have a problem getting this warrant, even before I heard from Theodore. We told the judge everything about you, and we told her some other interesting tidbits about Jane and the crime scene, too."

"Like what?" I couldn't help it. It shot out of my mouth. *Interesting tidbits about the crime scene.* What did that mean?

"Don't worry. All I'm saying is we had way, *way* more

than we needed to get this." He held up the warrant again. "So it has been issued, and now you and I and those guys outside…" He jerked a thumb at the door. "We're going upstairs to your apartment."

I felt terrified suddenly. "You're not going in my condo until my lawyer gets here."

Again that cold smile. "Doesn't work like that. We don't have to wait for anything. And under Illinois law, we can force you to be there while we conduct the search." He opened the front door. "Let's do it," he said to the two cops.

76

Everything I owned was pawed through, shaken, opened, poked at.

Initially, Vaughn mostly stood around while his uniformed cops did the dirty work, and somehow that was worse. He walked back and forth from cop to cop, looking over their shoulders as they rifled through my shelves, ran their fingers over my clothes, dug their hands deep into the drawer where I kept my underwear. Vaughn watched it all—a voyeur who seemed to get off not from the act of the search but from my reaction to it. I could tell that he read my face, that he saw my mortification, my sense of violation.

I kept calling and texting Maggie. Where *was* she?

I walked, arms crossed, from room to room, helpless, watching them.

I stopped in my living room and over the bar top saw a cop paw through my kitchen drawers.

My phone rang. Mayburn.

"You did it!" he was saying as I answered. His voice was loud and happy.

"I did what?"

The officer closed the utensil drawer and started on my cabinets.

"You nailed Josie."

"What do you mean?"

"I just got off the phone with the lab who analyzed the thong."

"You got them to do it on a weekend?"

"They owed me one. So guess what they found? The pearls on the black thong you lifted—you know what they're made of?"

"Plastic?"

"Cocaine!"

"Are you kidding me?" My mind shot to my own pearl thong. "But mine… The one I had…?" When I wore that thing, did I have eight-balls lining my ass?

"No, I told you this week—the kind you had was made of plastic. Anyway, this is great. I mean, it's not great for my client to find out that her manager was selling cocaine out of her store in the form of a pearl thong, but she knew something was wrong, and it turns out, she was right. Now she's got to decide how to deal with it. But the thing is we did our job. Or I should say *you* did."

"Thanks." At least I hadn't been fired from this gig. I was about to tell him the cops were at my house when my phone beeped. Maggie. "Mayburn, gotta go."

I answered the phone. "Mags!" I turned my back and dropped my voice. "The police are here."

"Got your messages. Sorry. I've been with Wyatt."

"With Wyatt, like *with* Wyatt?"

"With Wyatt, like breaking up with Wyatt. What's happening over there?"

"I'm standing in my living room, watching a cop go through my kitchen."

Over the bar top, I could see the cop bending down, digging through the drawers next to the stove. He was a burly black guy. When he heard me mention him, he stood up and gave me a *just-my-job* kind of a look, then bent down again. He seemed like the nicer one of the two. The other one I could hear guffawing with Vaughn in my bedroom. They'd probably found the pearl thong.

"Did they show you the warrant?" Maggie asked. "They have to have it in their hand and show it to you."

"Yeah, he showed it to me."

"Okay, and you haven't said anything, have you? Anything that could be construed as a statement?"

"Well…" I said again.

"Oh, no."

"He asked me whether I'd ever seen the Emmy Awards." I thought about it. "No, I take that back. He asked me if I had ever seen *an* Emmy Award."

"What? Look, don't say anything else. *Nothing,* okay? I'm on my way."

Maggie arrived fifteen minutes later. She was still wearing jeans. With her lack of makeup and her red eyes, she looked like a forlorn teenager. But she didn't act like one.

She gave me a quick hug. "Jesus, those newspeople are tenacious," she said, standing on her tiny tiptoes to grab me tight around the neck. "Is Vaughn here?"

"Yeah." Gratitude filled me. No matter what happened here, I wasn't alone.

She let me go. "Vaughn!" she bellowed. Maggie can be surprisingly loud for such a small person.

Vaughn came out of my bedroom, wearing one of his patented smug looks.

"Where's the warrant?" she demanded.

He reached in his pocket, handed it to her.

She flipped through the pages. "How did you establish probable cause?"

"Easy. I already told your friend here."

"Well, her attorney is here, so tell me."

"Nah. You know as well as I do, the only person I've got to explain something to is the judge. And I already did that." He nodded at the warrant. "It's all there." He turned and walked toward my office.

I drew Maggie toward the door. "Isn't there anything we can do?"

She looked at the warrant, reading. She flipped to the complaint and affidavit attached to the back. "It says here they're looking for any evidence of a relationship, romantic or sexual, between you and Jane Augustine. They can take any information or data stored in the form of electronic or magnetic coding."

"What does that mean?"

"It means they can take your…"

Right then the not-so-nice cop walked by. Carrying my computer.

"…Computer," Maggie finished, watching him, her eyes dropping back to the affidavit. "And any correspondence or communications between you and Jane, including chat logs, e-mails, letters. And they're also looking for awards or trophies," she said, still reading, "specifically, an Emmy Award, described as a gold statuette depicting a winged woman holding a globe."

"What is that about?" I said.

"I don't know." More squinting as Maggie kept reading. "Why is the address for Trial TV listed on there?"

"Probably because they started working on this when you were still employed there, and it got thrown into the order." She flipped another page and bit her lip. "Huh."

"Huh, what?"

"The warrant also allows them to take secondary standards."

"What are standards?"

"Fingerprints, hair samples, stuff where they can get your DNA." Maggie's head snapped up. "What else have they taken out of here other than the computer?"

"Nothing that I know of." Right then, the not-so-nice cop came back inside and headed for the office.

"Have they been in your bathroom?"

"Yeah."

"Did you see them looking at anything like your toothbrush or hairbrush?"

"Yes."

She took off running. "Vaughn!" she yelled.

I followed her. He and one of the cops were in my office, going through file folders—copies of work documents I used to keep at home when I still represented Pickett Enterprises. "Those are privileged," I said.

Vaughn pointed at something in a manila file. "These are communications between you and Jane Augustine."

I stepped forward and looked at what he was holding. "Yeah, I was negotiating her contract with Pickett Enterprises. And most of those communications were between her attorney and me. Those are privileged. You can't take them. Or look at them for that matter." I snatched them from his hand.

He snatched them back. Looked at Maggie. "You better tell your client not to touch a police officer. Or come even close."

I glanced at Mags. She gave me a little nod and made a face like, *Careful.*

Vaughn handed the file to the uniformed cop, who dropped it in a plastic bag and took it from the room.

"Vaughn," Maggie said. "I'd like to know why you're looking for DNA from my client."

"Why do you think?"

"Her fingerprints were at Jane's place. We all know that."

"So maybe we want more than prints."

"Did you remove anything from her bathroom?" Maggie demanded.

"Not yet, but hey, we're not done."

Maggie studied Vaughn. She took me by the arm and led me outside the apartment into the dim stairwell. "I wish I knew why they wanted your DNA. It might tell us more about why they're looking at you as a potential suspect. I mean, we already know that your fingerprints are in Jane's house. You were there. But they probably want standards to match with something else."

"Like what?"

She lifted her shoulders and let them fall. "It could be blood at the scene that wasn't Jane's, something like that."

"Maybe Spence can call his friend at the police department and see if they know something?"

"Excellent! Call him."

I scrolled fast through my speed dial. Spence had no kids of his own and was devoted to being a good stepdad, even when we didn't want his help. As such, he almost always answered my calls. And with everything going on now, I knew he was probably watching his phone, just waiting for an SOS.

"Izzy, darlin'," he said in his big voice. "Are you all right?"

"Not exactly. The cops are here searching my place."

"What the— Why didn't George give me a heads-up on that?" George was his friend at the police department.

"Considering the detective on the case, it could have happened fast and without many people knowing." I explained about the warrant, how they wanted "standards" from my place. "Maggie is here with me, and we're trying to figure out specifically why they want my DNA. Can you call—"

"Immediately," he said before I could finish, and he hung up.

Maggie and I stood in the hallway, waiting.

"Let me read the rest of this stuff," Maggie said. She continued scanning the warrant. Two vertical lines appeared between her eyes. "It says that Vaughn interviewed Zac Ellis, Jane's husband, and as of yesterday Zac informed him that Jane's Emmy Award is missing from the living room of their home."

"What does that have to do with me?"

Maggie pursed her mouth as she flicked through the pages of the other affidavit. "They think that due to the nature of the trauma, blah, blah, blah…Wow."

"Wow, what?" I was so anxious my skin twitched.

"They think whoever killed Jane beat her with an Emmy Award before they strangled her."

"You're kidding."

"I'm not kidding." Maggie glanced up at me, eyes scared. "And they think it was you."

77

I was still standing there, staring at Maggie, when my phone rang. It was my mother.

"Hi, Boo," she said. "Are you…are you somewhere you can talk?"

"I'm standing outside my front door with Maggie. The cops are inside." I looked around. The landing outside my condo was nondescript, decorated with mustard-colored walls and wood moldings. The stairs, which had never bothered me before, seemed too close to my front door now, giving me the feeling that one wrong move would send me tumbling into a dark chasm.

"Spence asked me to call," my mother said.

"Oh, no, is it that bad?"

"Well, it's… Listen, Izzy, you know I'm not judgmental, right? Whatever you want to experiment with in your life and your lifestyle, especially now that you and Sam have hit a rough patch, I'm fine with that. You know that, right?"

I pointed at the phone and made a *She's crazy* face at Maggie. "Thanks, Mom. I appreciate that. And if you're referring to the cops saying they thought I kissed Jane or whatever, it's not true. Jane and I were just friends. If I do decide to come out of the closet, I'll let you take me shopping for my first rainbow T-shirt. In the meantime, please tell me if Spence learned anything."

"Yes, well, that's what I'm referring to." She said nothing.

"Mom, c'mon!" I said exasperated.

"I don't know how to say it."

"Just *say* it!"

"Well, Spence told his friend he wouldn't say anything, and this is rather distasteful." She exhaled loudly. "Okay, George told Spence that they found a small amount of fluid on Jane's bed on the day she died. They shined some kind of light on it. I don't know what the light was… Spence!" she yelled away from the phone. "What kind of light was it?"

"Doesn't matter, Mom. Keep going."

"Of course. So the fluid didn't appear to be male or whatever. It wasn't…" A pause. "Sperm."

It was the first time I'd heard my mom say that word. She wasn't the one who had told me about sex. It was Bunny Loveland.

Now, my mother kept rolling along, though. "They tested the fluid in the lab just to be sure, and they were right. It wasn't sperm. In fact, DNA analysis showed that the fluid was actually from two different people, both female." My mother sighed here, as if in pain from what she was relating, but she soldiered on. "Because of this finding, your detective apparently believes it was vaginal fluid from two women." She said this quickly, as if she was desperate to get the conversation over with. "He wants DNA samples to try and show that one of the fluid samples belonged to you."

"What?" I said, but inside my brain, things were adding up. That's why Vaughn suspected me. He believed the killer was a woman, someone who'd been with Jane, in her bed, that day.

Maggie mouthed, *What? What?*

I heard Spence yelling in the background.

"Yes, yes," my mother said. "Spence is telling me that the fluids could be mucus, saliva, what have you. They can only say it was from two different people, both women. But this apparently was enough for the search warrant for DNA materials from you."

Vaughn opened my front door, the two uniformed cops behind him like statues, both holding black plastic bags.

"I have to go, Mom. Tell Spence thanks."

Vaughn handed Maggie a handwritten list. "Here's a re-covered item inventory." I saw a few things on the list— *computer, laptop…* "We'll get you an official inventory later." He took a step forward. "See you, ladies."

"Hold up." I put my hands on my hips and blocked Vaughn, not caring that my back was to the stairs now, to that dark well. "You found fluids in Jane's bed from two women, and you think she and I were in bed together on the day she died? You really think I killed her?"

"Yeah," Vaughn said. "That's what I think."

He tried to move around me but I held firm, fists digging further into my hips. "Why? Why *me?*"

"There were secretions in her bed. They were fresh. And DNA shows the fluids were from two different women." He cocked his head and gave me a pleased smile. "And who was Jane supposed to get together with? Who took over her job? Who took over her boyfriend? Who was obsessed with Jane?" He leaned forward at the waist. "You."

"It wasn't me!" My yell ricocheted off the walls of the small stairwell. One of the cops actually flinched.

"Iz," Maggie said in a stern voice, a hand on my arm. "Quiet. Don't say anything else."

I shook off her hand. I leaned forward so that Vaughn's face and mine were about two inches apart. "I'm telling you. It. Wasn't. Me."

He didn't flinch like the other cop. He didn't even blink. "So if it wasn't you, who was it?"

"Maybe Zoey. Zac's ex, who he's dating again. He said that Jane knew Zoey, that they were sort of friends. He said Jane was fine with Zoey being around their lives. Maybe that's because she and Zoey had something going on?"

I didn't like throwing out accusations when they might not be true, but I was scrambling to think of what woman Jane might have been involved with. And then, I wasn't scrambling. My fury drained away, the swirling questions and suspicions disappeared. And they left in their wake only the image of one face.

78

Maggie and I sprinted toward her car, leading a trail of shouting, scrambling reporters.

"Go!" I yelled when we were in the car.

A minute ago in the stairwell, I'd asked Vaughn if he was going to arrest me. When he'd said, "Not yet," I grabbed Maggie and propelled her down the stairs with me.

Now she peeled away from the curb in her little Honda.

I turned around and saw Vaughn coming out of my building. He stood on the front step watching us, while most of the media ran back to him, holding up microphones and pointing cameras.

I had the fear, familiar now, that Vaughn would make a statement, that he would say something horrible about me. But the damage had been done, I realized. There was no reason to struggle against that damage. Just a reason—my life—to fight it.

"So where are we going?" Maggie looked in the rearview mirror. "I think I lost the press."

"Trial TV."

She sped up Sedgwick, then glanced at me. Maybe she could see me thinking, maybe she could tell that there was nothing, as a lawyer or a best friend, that she could do now. Except drive.

I ran through it all in my head. "What do I need to do to establish chain of custody in a criminal case?" I asked.

"What do you mean?"

"If we find something incriminating, how do we make sure it's admissible later in court?"

Maggie thought about it. "Make sure other people see you find the evidence. Be careful that it doesn't look like it's planted."

"How do I do that?"

She turned onto Clybourn and floored the Honda. "Well, the best way would be to let the cops find it."

"So they'd need a warrant."

"Right."

"And Trial TV is already listed on the search warrant," I said, excited.

"That's true."

I stared at Maggie. "So basically, you're saying that I should make Vaughn work for me?"

She shrugged. "If you can."

I pulled out my cell phone, called the Belmont police station and got his damned message again. I called back and spoke to the dispatcher, telling her I was sure Vaughn would want to call me back if she could reach him.

A minute later, my phone rang with a 773 area code.

"It's Izzy," I answered.

"I got that much," Vaughn said dryly.

"Meet me at Trial TV. And bring that search warrant."

I hung up. He called back. I let it go to voice mail. Ten minutes later, we pulled into the Trial TV parking lot. I knew Vaughn would be heading there. He wouldn't be able to resist.

Maggie barreled up to the curb and put her hazards on. She scampered behind me as I went into the building and sweet-talked the security guard so he would give Maggie a visitor's pass.

It was Sunday and a quiet news day, so the hallway was deserted. I'd been told that a skeleton crew manned the network on the weekends, showing mostly pretaped shows.

It dawned on me that the executive offices were probably going to be locked, especially the one I wanted to get in.

But when I reached the door, it was open, the lights on inside.

I stood in the hallway, Maggie behind me. I looked at my watch. Vaughn probably wouldn't be here for at least five minutes.

"Izzy?"

I turned. It was Faith Lowe, the producer who'd come into the Fig Leaf with her bridesmaids.

"Faith, hi," I said. "What are you doing here on a Sunday?"

"I'm working overtime so I can take time off for my honeymoon. But, uh…what are you doing here?"

Faith had nearly blown my cover when I was at the Fig Leaf, but maybe like Vaughn, she could help me now.

"Faith," I said, "did you just see me walk in here?"

"Yeah."

"Okay, I have a favor to ask you. Could you wait here with us for a few minutes? The cops are coming. It has to do with Jane's death. I just don't want to do anything without them here."

"I guess," she said slowly, as if she was thinking. "We're running tape. Won't be done for twenty minutes or so." She glanced around the hallway and seemed to realize we were alone, that *she* was alone with a "person of interest" and her friend.

"Faith," I said. "I didn't do anything to Jane."

"Right. Sure. It's just that…" She looked around the hall again. Muted sounds trickled in from the set, but otherwise all was quiet. There seemed to be no one around. "This is kind of weird."

"Who else is here today?" I asked. Maybe we should get whoever was at the station out here with us. I didn't want this woman to be frightened.

"Uh…let's see. Well, C.J. is in an editing suite."

"C.J. is here?" I couldn't help the alarm from creeping into my voice.

"Yeah, she's working with an editor on a tribute to Jane. They're going to run it this week. Anyway, I should probably tell her you're here."

"No, let me tell her. Which suite is she in?"

"Number eight, but…" Faith's eyes narrowed, as if she was unsure what to do. She looked around again.

"Faith, let me ask you something," I said. "How long have you been in the news business?"

She looked at the ceiling for a minute. "I left the law three years ago."

"Do you remember when Jane won an Emmy Award for some story about a vice cop?"

Ever since Vaughn had looked at me in the stairwell and said, *So if it wasn't you, who was it?* I hadn't been able to get C.J. from my mind. I glanced in the office now—C.J.'s office. The moving boxes were still there, still unpacked— full of office crap and personal mementos. And awards. I could see that box, the one with the plaques and trophies sitting right there by C.J.'s desk. I itched to look inside.

I kept thinking of C.J. telling me that the story about Jackson Prince was one that could win an Emmy. I thought about how, during that same conversation, I'd mentioned that Jane had won an Emmy. C.J. told me then that she had worked on the story with Jane. There had been a moment when she had sighed and looked over my shoulder, and her face had been awash with grief. It hadn't been a surprise. After all, C.J. and Jane had been a team for years. Everyone knew how close they were—C.J. often wrote Jane's stories, while Jane did the interviewing and the research. Working with them, I'd once thought their professional relationship was almost symbiotic. But now I wondered if their relationship had been more than that outside the business world. I wondered if that grief of C.J.'s was because she had loved Jane. And she had killed Jane.

"Oh, yeah," Faith was saying, "everyone remembers the Emmy Awards from that year. It was right after I started at Chicagoland TV."

"C.J. was the producer on that story, right?"

Faith laughed, then she looked around as if feeling guilty.

"What?" I asked. "Did C.J. get an Emmy, too? Isn't that what usually happens?"

"That's what *usually* happens." She paused. "You really don't know the story?"

I shook my head no. Maggie did, too, fast, her gold hair ruffling

Faith dropped her voice low. "C.J. worked on that story. In fact, the word on the street was that she wrote most of it, like she used to do for Jane. But when the station submitted the story, they accidentally left C.J.'s name off."

"You're kidding."

Faith shrugged. "I guess this has happened more than once. It's a clerical error more than anything else, but C.J. didn't take it that way. She was pissed off. I mean, really pissed off."

"At Jane?"

Another shrug. "At everybody." She looked at her watch. "Listen, I should go." Another glance around the hallway. "And I'm thinking that you should probably go, too."

"I will. I am. I just have to ask C.J. something." *And keep her away from her office until Vaughn can search it.* I started walking away, still talking. "Maggie, stay here with Faith, all right? And have Vaughn use that search warrant in there—" I pointed at C.J.'s office "—when he gets here."

The hallway that contained the editing bays was quiet, the carpeted floor sucking up any sound. My legs felt awkward as I walked. My eyes kept swiveling around, nervous.

There were ten editing suites. Every few steps or so, lights flickered from one, but no noise emanated from their soundproof interiors. I quickly walked past them, slowing at the end, stopping outside number eight.

Through the small rectangular window, I could see the backs of C.J. and an editor, a guy with long black hair. Their shoulders were hunched over a desk filled with grids and consoles. Every so often, they looked up at monitors at eye level and rolled tape.

As I stood outside, I could see Jane's face gracing the monitors. Different shots showed different sides of her—Jane's competent anchor personality, her kind smile during a tough interview, her sad eyes when covering a verdict, her mouth laughing and wide, the shot obviously taken when she had flubbed a line.

I took a step closer to the editing bay, careful not to let my shadow fall over the room. I could see C.J.'s face now, lit by the flickering images of Jane. C.J.'s eyes were wide, almost as if she were in shock.

The door of the editing bay opened, nearly knocking into me, startling me. "Oh, hey," I heard a voice say. It was the editor with black hair. He must have gotten up while I was watching C.J.

C.J. turned to look. Her brows furrowed a bit when she saw me.

The editor looked at me, then over his shoulder at C.J., as if for a clue on what to do.

"I'm here to ask C.J. about a story we're working on," I said.

"Yeah, about Jackson Prince," C.J. said. She nodded at the editor. "It's okay."

The editor threw a curious glance at me, then left.

"C'mon," C.J. said, standing, "let's go talk in my office."

"No!" I said fast. I had to keep her away from her office. Just for a few minutes. At least until Vaughn could get there and Maggie could convince him to search the place. C.J. might not have won her own Emmy but she might have Jane's.

I stepped into the dark of the bay, right in front of her.

C.J. paused, looked at me. Did she wonder for a second

if something was off? I remembered her talking to me yesterday; I heard her say to go ahead with the Jackson Prince piece for Jane, *Do it for her legacy.*

The air in the editing bay smelled stale, closed-up, overly personal—the smells of different people in a room together for hours.

Despite the open door, darkness hung like a veil, making the lights on the console shimmer eerily. On the monitors an image was frozen—Jane watching a news conference, her legs crossed, her face pensive.

I looked at C.J. and searched her face for an answer to my question—*Did you kill her?*

She said nothing, but she stared right back. Then she pulled me inside and pushed the door closed.

79

"What's going on, Izzy?" she said quietly.

"Um, nothing. Why would you ask?"

"Because you just barged into my editing suite and said you needed to talk to me about a story." Her words sounded like the usual surly C.J., but again, she was calm. Overly calm.

"The story. Right. Well, the story is going well," I said, trying not to let my imagination go wild. I gave her a quick retelling of the doctors Mayburn had spoken to, the ones we hoped to get interviews with.

When I stopped talking, she stood there gazing at me. The electricity from the editing equipment hummed. The atmosphere in the room felt constricted, as if the fresh air was slowly being cut off.

"So, I guess I wanted to ask you," I said, stalling for time, "about anonymous interviews with some of the doctors. You know, where their faces can't be seen. Is that okay?"

She stepped back and sat in her chair, then nudged the editor's chair with her foot. It bumped me in the knee. "Sit," she said.

I hesitated, staring at the chair. The room was lit only by the square of light from the hallway and the lights on the console. Was Vaughn here by now? Had I given him enough time to see if there was anything in those boxes in C.J.'s office? There was that one in particular, filled with broadcast awards and plaques. But Vaughn might not even be here yet. It was only minutes since I'd left Maggie and Faith in the hallway.

I pulled the chair back, sat in it. But now, my back was to the door, the chair blocking it, and it became even more apparent to me that it was just C.J. and me. Alone in a mostly dark room.

I tried to lighten the mood. "How's the tribute going?" I nodded at a frozen image on the monitors—in the frame, Jane's body language and face were relaxed. There was no artifice, no camera-ready poise. Instead, in her thoughtful gaze, you could see the person behind that beautiful face, a person who was fascinated by life, who had her own demons, her own questions.

"The network wanted to do five or ten minutes, can you believe that?" C.J. said. "Like Jane wasn't worth an hour or two." She shook her head slowly, staring at Jane on the monitor.

"With everything that's been going on," I said, "I keep forgetting to check in with how you're doing. I mean, you and Jane were tight."

She turned her gaze to me. "We were."

"You were best friends professionally."

"Yeah." Her voice was rough for a second. She cleared her throat.

We sat in the silence of the editing bay for a few seconds. "You were more than that, weren't you?" I asked. I paused. Then I decided to go for it. "You and Jane were lovers."

C.J. took off her glasses. For a moment, in the square of light, I saw her eyes—smaller than they seemed when she had glasses on, but more clear, more intense. She moved her head away, so that the light of the door fell only on her shoulder. I couldn't see her eyes any longer.

She reached forward onto the console and clicked a button. The monitors went blank. Jane disappeared. I heard the sound of C.J. touching another button, and the colored lights of the console went dark, too, dying out with a fading hiss.

80

Detective Vaughn strode into the headquarters of Trial TV, trailed by his officers. Two more squad cars on their way.

He shook his head at the thought of Trial TV. It would be better for him, and all of law enforcement, if people weren't so goddamned interested in the police and the law. He blamed the detective shows. Not that he'd ever seen one. He got enough of that shit at work.

The truth was, he loved his work. And he was good at it. His instincts were almost never wrong. He'd known in this case a woman was involved. So many things pointed to it, especially the DNA evidence from the bed, and then there was Isabel McNeil with her obvious crush on Jane, and all things Jane.

In order to figure out if his instincts were right, the law gave a certain amount of latitude to detectives like him. He could, for example, lie his face off to a witness during interrogation and hey, if that witness was being processed at one station and then suddenly taken somewhere else for booking and shuttled to a whole other place for holding, that was fine. And hey, if that witness's attorney and family members couldn't find them for a while, that was fine, too. The law, he figured, treated him well and let him pretty much do what he wanted. What he didn't like right now was that he was being told what to do. By his own suspect.

He stopped a guy with long hair turning the corner, a coffee mug in his hand.

"Excuse me," Vaughn said. He didn't need to show his badge. The officers behind him gave him more than enough credibility. "Do you know where Isabel McNeil is?"

"Yeah," the guy said, his eyes a little jittery. And it wasn't from the coffee. You could tell he was excited by the presence of the police. He was in the news business, after all. He probably loved to get the scoop on everything, whether for work or not.

"She here now?" Vaughn asked.

"She's in an editing suite." He pointed. "Down that way. Past the offices. Or I can take you the short way, through the kitchen." The guy gestured behind him.

"Let's do it."

Vaughn followed the guy to the left, through an empty staff kitchen and into a hallway beyond that. He would find out what was going on here at Trial TV, because he had a new instinct, one that told him that Isabel McNeil was about to go up in flames, right here in front of him.

81

I felt C.J.'s hand snake around my wrist, warm and yet hard. It squeezed me, cutting off the blood flow.

"C.J., please don't." My words were as calm as hers, but my body was at once vividly alert.

"Don't tell me what to do," she said. "Ever. Ever. Ever."

She kept repeating the word like a creepy mantra—*Ever, ever, ever.* She squeezed my wrist tighter. I could hear her breathing; could smell a trace of something coming off her, something like sweat, something like fear. I wondered if she could smell mine.

"You hated that Jane got the glory." My voice was low, but it wouldn't matter if I raised it. With the booths being soundproof, no one would hear us.

"Shut up." Her words snapped into the air with such force, such crisp enunciation that I flinched. She tightened her grip around my wrist. "Do you know how much of an idiot you are?"

I said nothing, which just made her squeeze harder, lean closer.

"Do you know how little you know about life?" she asked. "How little you know about the news, about the law, about *anything?*"

"Yes." If there was one thing I'd learned over the last year, it was how little I actually knew, compared with how much there was to know about the world. The thing was—I had thought there was a lot more time left to figure it out.

C.J. yanked my wrist, pulled me close to her. I felt alarm swoop in, felt my mind careening wildly.

"Do you know how little you know about love?" C.J. hissed.

"Yes," I said again. Another easy answer. "C.J., did you love Jane?"

"Shut up." A pause. "Who did you tell?"

"Tell what?"

"That you think Jane and I were lovers."

"It's true, isn't it?" The bones of her fingers pressed tighter into my flesh. I ignored the pain, the fuzzy feeling in my fingers. "Did Jane end your relationship?" I asked. "Or did she try to?"

Fingers tighter. "Why do you ask?" Her voice was calm again. So calm.

"On the day she died, Jane told me she was going to see a friend. She also said she had to tell the friend that she wouldn't be around much because she needed to focus on her marriage."

C.J. laughed, although it sounded more like a choke. "She was always talking like that."

"But was it more real this time?" I thought of everything I knew about C.J. and Jane from working with them, from what Jane had said. "Because Jane had already left you professionally, right? First by winning the Emmy a few years ago and leaving you out, and then by going to Trial TV without you?"

"I understood that Jane needed to grow up. I understood she needed to experiment." C.J. sounded slightly wistful, almost like a mother, one who has to watch her kid make mistakes.

"You looked after her."

"When she let me."

"And you loved her because you knew everything about her. You were one of the few people."

"I *told* her she had to stop sleeping around with random guys." Her grip got tighter. "I *told* her it would get her into trouble."

"What do you mean, trouble?" I said the question quietly.

"You can't *do* that," C.J. said. "You can't cheat on your husband and fool around with different people and not have it come back to haunt you. I was always trying to warn her about that."

"How did you warn her?" Then it occurred to me. "Were you the one who left the flowers? And the noose?"

I heard a sound in the dark, something coming from C.J.'s throat, a combination of a groan and a grimace, a sound of someone in pain.

"How do you know about that?" she asked.

"Jane called me when she found them."

She tugged on my wrist, her hand tightening even more. "I can't believe she called you," C.J. said. *"You."*

"We were friends."

"No, *we* were friends. She was supposed to call *me*, the person she always called, the person she always relied on."

"She was always turning to other people," I said. "She was always leaving you behind."

She yanked my wrist then.

Instinctively, I yanked back hard, and she fell partially on me. I tried to shove her, but she was so much bigger than me that she wouldn't budge. "Who did you tell?" she said, and her voice sounded like a growl.

"I…"

Suddenly, her hands slipped around my neck.

I struggled against her, but she was as strong as a man and pressing down hard with the weight of her body, the grip of her hands.

"How do you like it," she said, her hands constricting my neck even more. "Does this make you feel good? It was good enough for Jane."

I heard myself choking, tried to swallow against the pressure, but my throat was blocked.

"Who did you tell?" Her voice was now tinged with tranquility. Still, she squeezed my neck.

"I didn't tell anyone," I managed to choke out, pushing hard with my arms. It was true. I hadn't even told Maggie my suspicion that C.J. had been the one who was having a relationship with Jane. C.J. was the one who worked closely with Jane on a professional basis. Jane won an Emmy one year, and C.J. should have won one, too. She did most of the work on that story, but the station screwed up. Jane got all the glory. Then Jane left C.J. behind to come to Trial TV. Jane said she wanted only staff with legal backgrounds, but she was also trying to step out into her own as a reporter and an anchor. But C.J. didn't like that. And my guess was that C.J. really didn't like it when Jane told her their personal relationship was over, too. Probably Jane had told her this before. Probably this was why C.J. had tried to scare Jane by leaving a noose in her house and the flowers. She thought Jane would turn to her. But she didn't. Jane still wanted to end things. She was trying to tell C.J. that on the day she died.

Most of these thoughts were suppositions, guesses, but they seemed more and more like conclusions the longer C.J. held me around the neck. I began to pant with the short breaths I could barely get in. I felt my face heat. My head felt dizzy, as if the dark editing suite was swirling around me.

Don't give up, I told myself. With a guttural groan, I pried C.J.'s fingers half an inch away from my neck. I squirmed, but I couldn't move her grasp any farther. We struggled against each other.

"You killed her," I gasped.

C.J. yelled. No, she roared. She leapt off me at the same time. Stunned by the absence of her weight, I froze for a second. In the low light from the door's window I saw her reaching the desk, grabbing something square and black— a small console of some kind. She held it over her head. She yelled again, and I saw the thing coming at me, felt my mouth open, felt myself scream. I kicked at her. I clamored to move away, but the suite was so small.

Then the room was bathed with light. And I was falling backward.

82

There was a clamor, a scuffle above my head. I was, I realized, lying on my back in the hallway. The door had been opened, and I'd been yanked out. By Vaughn.

"Hold up, hold up!" he yelled, apparently at C.J.

I saw one of the uniformed officers draw his gun. Another pulled me to my feet. Vaughn was facing C.J. in the dark editing suite, his own gun drawn. Her glasses had fallen somewhere and her eyes darted from one officer to another.

"What's going on?" Vaughn barked.

"Did you search her office?" I asked.

He shot a glance at me but stayed with his body toward C.J., who was still holding the piece of equipment. "Put that down," he demanded, gesturing at her.

She complied, and Vaughn looked at me. "Now, what are you talking about?"

I poured out the whole story. "I know you're looking for a woman, someone who was with Jane that day in her bed, someone who killed her with an Emmy, but you shouldn't be looking at me. You should be looking at *her*. Vaughn, this is C. J. Lyons."

"I know who she is. I've interviewed nearly everyone at this network."

"Well, you should interview her again! And you should search her office for Jane's Emmy. She's got boxes of stuff in there. One is full of awards and trophies. I saw it in her office one day, and the same day she told me about the Emmy that Jane had won. She talked about winning an Emmy for a story we were working on."

"And?" said Vaughn dismissively.

"And *she* was the one in a relationship with Jane, not me." I told him my theory, my words spilling over one another. "They were together Monday afternoon, but Jane told her it was the last time. I think for the first time, C.J. knew Jane was serious."

Vaughn gestured at C.J.. "Did you have a relationship with Jane?"

"Professionally, yes." C.J.'s eyes looked lost without her glasses, but otherwise she was composed again. "As I've told you, Jane and I worked together for years."

"Nothing more than that?"

She shook her head, a short, dismissive movement. It wasn't exactly the firmest denial. Vaughn's eyes flicked from her to me and back again.

"You see her on Monday?" he asked her.

She said nothing.

"Were you in her bed?"

We both looked at C.J. Although her face was composed, her black hair appeared thin, her pale skin overly delicate. It seemed as if tough, strong C.J. was aging before our eyes.

"C.J. loved Jane," I said.

C.J. took a step back then, her body fading into the shadows of the editing suite. And then her knees went out from under her, and she began to fall backward as if she'd been shot.

"Hey!" one of the officers said, trying to grab her. But C.J. landed on the floor of the editing bay with a thud.

"Get up!" Vaughn barked at her.

She just sat there as if she hadn't heard him.

"Get her up," Vaughn yelled at his officer.

The cop bent toward her.

"No!" C.J. bellowed. "Don't touch me!" The raw agony of her voice froze us all.

C.J. curled her knees up to her chest and wrapped her arms around them. She began to shake her head back and forth, back and forth, as if saying *no, no, no* to some internal words that no one could hear.

Vaughn stared at her, his gun still pointed. He looked at me. "Where's her office?"

I pointed down the hallway. "Maggie is there, along with another Trial TV person."

Vaughn nodded at one of his officers. "Stay here." He took the other officer and left.

And then in the dark of the editing bay, like a child who finally gives in to anguish they feel deep inside, C.J. put her head on her knees and cried.

83

I hear a knock on the bedroom door.

I try to call out, "Come in," but my voice is hoarse from lack of use.

Another knock.

I clear my throat and sit up, swinging my feet over the side of the bed.

I look around the room. It bears a helter-skelter appearance—scattered clothes, plates of half-eaten food, mugs of half-drunk tea. A couple of prescription bottles are lined up on the nightstand. *Diazepam. Halcion.*

Another knock on the door and this time it opens.

My brother's mop of curly hair enters the room first, then I see his face and an expression he doesn't normally wear—worry.

"You awake?" he asks.

I clear my throat. "Yeah," I croak out. "What day is it?"

"Tuesday."

Two days since the cops searched my place, two days since I confronted C.J. at Trial TV.

It all happened so fast.

Jane's Emmy was found in C.J.'s office, in that box. C.J. had tried to wipe the trophy clean, to make it truly hers, but one tiny speck of blood was left from the vibrant force that had been Jane Augustine. And the half fingerprint that was left matched C.J.'s. So did the DNA from Jane's bed. That was enough to get the crime lab and the cops to agree—C.J. had killed Jane.

I was interrogated again. But the interrogation was different. Vaughn asked questions and actually listened. When I left, he stopped Maggie and me at the door.

"Got something to say?" Maggie asked, sarcastic, triumphant.

Vaughn only shook his head. But for an instant, our eyes met, and he gave me the briefest of nods. It was the closest thing to an apology I would ever get from him.

I have been sleeping for most of the last two days at my mom's house. The prescription bottles are hers.

Just in case, she had said. *You might have a hard time sleeping.*

But I hadn't needed them. Sleep had been easy. The difficult part was the moments I was awake, usually at odd hours, scrounging the kitchen for food to bring back to the guest room and trying not to be angry. I have been telling myself that Vaughn, although misguided in his suspicions of me, was just doing his job, a job he had a passion for. Such reminders haven't worked. I didn't kill Jane, and I live with my own passion now—a passion to see Detective Vaughn get the shit kicked out of him by me or someone close to me.

I get up, tie a robe around my waist and pick up my cell phone from the nightstand. I look at the calls that came in while I was sleeping. Theo, three times. Grady, twice. No Sam.

"He's outside," Charlie says.

"What?"

"Sam. He's sitting outside in his car. He says you need to get out of the house." Charlie gives me a once-over. I haven't showered in days.

I stand and peek through the wooden blinds onto State Street. Sam's car is parked half a block down. I smile and turn to Charlie. "I'll call him."

"Mom and Spence are at the store," my brother continues, "and I'm taking off for a job interview."

My eyes open fast. "Are you kidding? A job interview?"

"Yeah, who knows? I might be a working stiff soon." He shrugs and grins, then leaves.

My cell phone rings. Mayburn.

"You all right?" he asks.

I hear that worry in his voice, but the answer comes quick. "I am."

"Good. Got some news you'll like. You know your buddy, Mick, that writer you told me about? Well, I did a little digging. Found out that a couple of years ago on Christmas Eve, he got hammered, and tried to hammer his own dad."

"What do you mean?"

"They got in a fistfight. Apparently, Mick won and beat the hell out of his father. Both were arrested, both were loaded. They were about to get charged with disorderly conduct and assault, but at the last minute, the dad's agent did some sweet-talking—and some sweet bribing—and no charges were brought. The whole thing was hushed up, and both Mick and his famous father really, *really* want to keep this thing quiet."

"If that's true then maybe I—"

"Already took care of it. Had a talk with Mick. We're not going to mention this again, and he's going to scrap the book about the news personalities."

"He's not publishing it?"

"Nope."

I close my eyes and feel a wave of relief for Jane. I open them again. "You're the best."

"I know," he says, and hangs up.

I dial Sam's number. "Why aren't you at work?"

"Look, I know you're supposed to be saving yourself," he says, "but I want to make sure someone's watching over you."

"Sam."

"Come downstairs."

"I need a shower."

"I'll be waiting."

84

Sam drives, and we're silent.

I have the sense that we're waiting, holding everything back until we're sitting somewhere and can look each other in the eye. The waiting makes the car feel like a ticking clock, as if we both know that this moment, which seems so mundane, so *Sam-and-me-just-driving-in-the-car,* is so much more than that.

I look out the window. I tell myself not to be scared of the weight of the moment, not to jump ahead of it.

Sam turns from Clark, then onto Lincoln Avenue. The day is vivid, full of light. The more I stare out the window, the more I feel that I'm waking up and the more I realize that the fear about what's going to happen to Sam and me is nothing compared to the fear I felt when I found Jane and then the terror of being wrongfully accused. Now that it's over, I can see that terror from afar—like a sharp, blue light that cuts through and crystallizes everything else, leaving only the dust of memories and the force of the fear itself.

I study Sam. He's been in the sun lately with rugby practice, and his skin looks warm and golden.

"Did you get a haircut?" I ask. "It's shorter than when we went to North Pond."

"Yeah. She did something different." He points at his forehead. His hair is pushed up at a different angle than normal. "Like it?"

I keep looking at his hair. It is so miniscule, that change, but it is a change. "I like it," I tell him.

I turn and stare out the window. Then I roll it down, letting the sounds of the city seep in, letting the breeze—balmy and invigorating—twirl its way through my hair, through me.

Chicago seems to have sprung to life since I last paid attention. Music bleeds from second-floor windows. The smokers, usually huddled outside bars bearing haunted looks, stand tall in the spring sun, talking and gesturing with their cigarettes, laughing loud. There is color everywhere—orange and red tulips dotting otherwise feeble front lawns; cherry-blossom trees sprouting pink and white; bushes bursting with yellow bulbs. The urban landscape looks as if it's been painted by an artist, one unafraid of vivid splashes of color.

"Where are we going?" I ask Sam.

"A dive bar. Just for you."

"Which one?"

"You'll see."

He keeps going on Lincoln Avenue. He passes Fullerton, then Wrightwood, then pulls over and parks at a meter. Town houses run along one side of the street, and a Mobil station sits on the other.

"Rose's," Sam says, and he points.

Next to the gas station is an old, brick three-flat apartment. The bottom floor has a wooden front, painted a bleak ivory color, with two high octagonal windows that are dark, revealing nothing about what's inside. Only the *Old Style On Tap* sign that hangs above the door indicates it's a bar.

"I haven't been here in years," Sam says. "But I thought if the press was still following you, they'd never be able to see inside."

We get out of the car and look up and down the street. No press. They had been crawling all over my lawn, making my neighbors crazy, and so I'd escaped to my mom's house, hoping to lose them. And now, apparently I have. Or maybe it's more simple—maybe my part of Jane's story is over.

We wait for a few stray cars to pass, and we cross the street.

Stepping inside Rose's is like stepping into a bar somewhere in Wisconsin in the 1970s. The dark wood furniture is mismatched, scarred. Many of the seats of the bar stools are duct-taped. A sagging pool table is wedged next to an ancient jukebox croaking a Sinatra tune. I love it.

Two guys sit at the end of the bar. They look a bit tougher, less styled, than the usual Lincoln Park crowd. Cops, I guess. The thought sends a reactionary frisson of fear through me, but I see it and I let it loose. I have nothing to fear. At least not right now.

Sam and I sit at the bar, and a woman with gray hair, stooped with age, asks what we'd like to drink.

"Do you have Blue Moon?" Sam asks.

"No." She shakes her head at the notion. "I have Polish beers. They're the best."

"I'll try one."

"Make it two," I say.

She gives us beers in the bottle and dumps a few pretzels onto a white paper plate. Then she leaves us alone.

We talk about everything we haven't talked about in months, everything except us. It feels good, in a dark bar with no indication of time or even of season, to spend these moments with Sam.

He stops, though. He's in the middle of a story about his landlord—*He's trying to raise the rent, and I said, you can't do this, I've got a two-year lease, and then he said…* And Sam just stops. Just like that.

Sam looks at me. "We have to decide."

"Decide what?"

"Us."

"There's a word I haven't heard you use in a long time."

"I know." Sam turns on his stool to face me. "Because

we've been so back and forth. We're not engaged, but we haven't broken up. We're sort of dating, but we're sort of not. We're kind of together, but we're kind of not. Let's pick one. I need something certain, Izzy. You do, too."

I think about what he's said. "Actually, I'm okay with not nailing it down."

Something about Jane's death, and her life, has made me rethink the way I want to live. Jane had a million accomplishments, but C.J. voided them in one instant. And yet what still lives on from Jane, what she'll be remembered for, is her passion. There's that word again. The story of Jane and C.J.'s passion for each other and the end result of it—*Lesbian Lover Scorned*—has been splashed all over the papers and the news. So far nothing has come out about the scarfing. Nothing about the other affairs. I assume many will scorn Jane's passion and the way she acted it out. But her fervor for life, for the news, for love was undeniable, and it still remains.

And what I have been thinking in my waking hours is that I want to be known for my passion, too. I don't want to act it out like Jane. I don't want to emulate her in any way, except that I want to get in touch with my passions, wherever they lie, and I want to feel them, to wrap my arms around them, to taste them. The thing is, I'm not sure where my passions lie—not romantically or professionally,

I've decided that in the interim, an uncertain life, an uncertain relationship don't necessarily point to a bleak future or even a bleak today. And so I don't have to put labels on Sam and me. We can ride it and see whether that passion we had is alive, whether it wants to keep living.

But Sam, apparently, doesn't agree with me. He shakes his head, pushes away his half-empty beer. "I don't want this anymore, Iz. Not like this. It's too hard."

"Relationships are always hard."

He gives me a long, indecipherable look. "Says who?"

"Says everyone."

"It doesn't mean that it's right." He takes one of my hands. He has the smoothest skin, so familiar that it almost feels like my own. "Can you promise me it will be easier someday?"

Reflexively, I start to say yes, but then I close my mouth. I want to say the truth—to me, to him, to *us*. "No," I say. "But that doesn't mean it will be bad. In fact, we might find a lot of joy that way."

The song on the jukebox dies. The cops leave the bar. The bartender shambles over to us, holding her back with one hand. "You want something else?"

"Yes," Sam says, but he's looking in my eyes. "I'm sorry, Iz, but I want something else."

85

When I walk out of the bar, the city feels razor-fresh. My senses are heightened. Sam is still inside, and for now I'm on my own. And I am fine. More than fine.

The brick of the buildings, which so recently looked dusty red, is vividly bright now, each brick like a poppy in a bouquet. The El train's rumble is melodic. The smell of food cooking, of car exhaust, of spring earth—it all mixes in the air and wafts down the street. The sirens, so frequent in the city, are no longer in the background. Now, even though distant, they cut through my mind like bands, each one clear, bright, distinguishable. I will never hear a siren and not think of Jane. And after a while, that won't be a bad thing.

After a while, Sam and I might get back together, or we won't. We will be friends, people forever bonded, or we won't. I will investigate the story of Jackson Prince and get back into the news business, or I won't. I will find myself in the law again, or I won't. Maggie will forgive Wyatt again or she won't. Q will find a new profession he loves, or he won't. My brother Charlie will get the job and not rely so much on my mother, or he won't.

I will be okay with starting over again, or…or I will.

* * * * *

*Overleaf is a preview of
RED, WHITE & DEAD,
the next book in the
Izzy McNeil trilogy
by
Laura Caldwell*

Dez Romano told me it had been a wonderful night, that he'd like to see me again. "I guess I should have asked before," he said with a sigh that surprised me. "You're single, right?"

I answered honestly. "I am."

A few short months before, I'd juggled three men, and then suddenly there were none. Today, one was staging a comeback, and I wasn't sure what to do about that. In the meantime, although I was occasionally tortured about those who had left my life, I was free to date whomever I wanted. Even a ranking member of the mafia, if only as a part-time job for John Mayburn.

If I hadn't known who he was and what he did for a living, I wouldn't have blinked before agreeing to go out with Dez. I was about to turn thirty, and with my birthday fast approaching, it seemed the dating gods had flipped a switch in my head. I had never dated anyone much older than myself, never really been interested, but now Dez's forty-some years compared to my twenty-nine seemed just fine.

Dez leaned his elbows on the green-and-white tablecloth and shot me a sexy kind of smile over his shoulder. "Would you go out with me sometime? Officially?"

Officially, I was about to say *Sure*. This was what Mayburn had hoped would happen—I would listen for anything having to do with Michael DeSanto, and if nothing came up, I'd establish a contact with Dez so I could see him again, so I might learn something about Michael in the future.

I looked out the window once more, thought about how to phrase my answer. And then I saw him.

He was standing across the street at a stop sign, wearing a blue blazer and a scowl. He glanced at his watch, then up again, and as the cars slowed, he began to cross the street, right toward us.

I opened my mouth. I must have looked shocked, because Dez followed my gaze.

"Hey, it's DeSanto," he said fondly. He looked back at me.

I clamped my mouth shut and met his eyes, trying to cover my panic with a bland expression.

His eyes narrowed. "You know DeSanto?"

"Um…" What to say here? *Actually, we met when I was pretending to be friends with his wife, Lucy, in order to sneak into his office and download files to incriminate him. It was another job I had for Mayburn. Isn't that ironic?*

Mayburn and I had decided that if I was successful tonight and got to Dez Romano, and if I could somehow steer the conversation toward Michael DeSanto's name, I would ask about Michael, maybe volunteer that I'd once met his wife, Lucy—the woman Mayburn was now in love with—at the gym, or someplace similarly benign. But that plan had assumed I wouldn't actually *see* Michael; it assumed that Michael wouldn't pull open the door to Gibsons, and walk right in, and find me with his buddy Dez.

I stood up. I leaned forward, hoping to distract Dez with a little cleavage. It worked. His narrowed stare relaxed. He glanced up at me and, to his credit, kept his eyes there.

Meanwhile, my eyes shot toward the door. And there was Michael DeSanto, stopping to say hello to the maître d'.

Frig, I thought, attempting to stick with my stop-swearing campaign despite the circumstances. *Fuck,* I thought. *What is he doing here?*

According to Lucy, her wayward husband, Michael DeSanto, was out of jail on bond, and although he was friendly with his compatriots of old, like Dez (all of whom had managed to avoid prosecution through one loophole or another) he wasn't doing business with them anymore. Rarely saw them much at all.

Yet now Michael was *here,* just out of jail, clearly stopping in to see Dez Romano. And about to come face-to-face with the person who was instrumental in putting him in jail. Me.

I took a step away from Dez, muttering, "Be right back."

I moved in the direction of the bathrooms, but when I realized it would put me on a collision course with DeSanto, I shifted, started to go the other way. I froze when I realized the exit and bathrooms were all just beyond where Michael was standing.

He stopped then—completely still—looking at me with his eerily light brown eyes. He froze in exactly the same way an animal does when assessing a dire situation—with the knowledge that this might be the end, this might be the time to meet the maker, but with a sure clarity that there was going to be a fight before the end came.

I froze, too. I wished at that moment that I was better at this stuff, but no matter how much I'd learned from Mayburn, the whole undercover thing was simply not in my blood.

And so, lacking anything better to do, I gave Michael DeSanto the same smile I gave lawyers at the Chicago Bar Association events when I didn't recognize them—a sort of *Hi, how are you? Good to see you* kind of smile.

Physically, DeSanto looked a little like Dez Romano, but he wasn't even looking at his friend right now. His intent stare stayed focused exactly on me. He cocked his head ever so minutely. His face jutted slightly forward then, as if strain-

ing to understand. And I knew in that minute that it was one
of those situations—he'd recognized me, sort of, but he
couldn't place me. Yet. I was sure he'd figure it out any
second.

I didn't wait for the wheels to start clicking in his mind.
Instead, I averted my gaze and hightailed it right, then
veered back behind him. I glanced across the room at the
front door. It was clotted with a huge group of people saying
goodbyes, giving each other boozy pats on the back. I could
sense Michael turning around to stare at me, and so I darted
up the staircase, and bolted for the bathroom.

I panted inside the stall, trying to work it out. *Should I
somehow try to say goodbye to Dez? Should I give up on
the infiltration job and just take off for the calm confines
of my condo?*

It wasn't much of an infiltration job anyway, just a job
that required chatting up someone at a bar, a task I used to
be rather good at, if I say so myself.

Eight months ago I'd been on top of the world—the highest paid associate at a big, glitzy law firm, en route to part-
nership not only with the firm but with my fiancé. And then
poof, all gone, rendering me tired and stunned and jobless.
What I'd been doing for the past few months consisted of
nothing more than feeling guilty about doing nothing.

And so this request from Mayburn, who believed
Michael DeSanto wasn't as squeaky clean as he was telling
his wife, had led me to Dez Romano. But enough was
enough.

I left the bathroom, went down the first flight of stairs,
peeked down the rest of the way, my hands on the silver
banister. I saw no one. The large group appeared to have left.
I trotted down as fast as my high heels would allow.

My breath was managing only shallow forays into my
lungs, so I stopped once to suck in air. A few more steps and
I was at the bottom, the front door only a few feet away.

The maître d' gave me a bored nod as if to say a mild

good-night. But then he glanced to the right, and a questioning expression took over his face. I peeked to see what he was looking at. Michael. Across the room, Michael was talking to Dez, his arms waving, gesturing.

Right then, Dez looked over Michael's shoulder and saw me. "Hey!" he said, his eyes narrowed in anger.

There were only a handful of diners in the restaurant, but Dez's voice was loud enough to get everyone's attention. They looked at Dez, then at me. Suddenly Dez and Michael were coming toward me, the furious looks on their faces enough to catapult me into action.

I reached down, pulled off my high heels and dashed out the door onto Rush Street.

It's going to be a

RED HOT SUMMER

LAURA CALDWELL

MIRA®

It's going to be a RED HOT SUMMER with a new trilogy from LAURA CALDWELL

SAVE $1.00

June 2009 July 2009 August 2009

- -

SAVE $1.00 on the purchase price of one book in Laura Caldwell's red-hot trilogy.

Offer valid from May 26, 2009, to August 31, 2009. Redeemable at participating retail outlets. Limit one coupon per purchase. Valid in the U.S. and Canada only.

52608692

5 65373 00076 2 (8100)0 11606

MLCTRI09CPN

® and TM are trademarks owned and used by the trademark owner and/or its licensee.
© 2009 Harlequin Enterprises Limited

REQUEST YOUR FREE BOOKS!

2 FREE NOVELS
FROM THE ROMANCE/SUSPENSE
COLLECTION PLUS 2 FREE GIFTS!

YES! Please send me 2 FREE novels from the Romance/Suspense Collection and my 2 FREE gifts (gifts are worth about $10). After receiving them, if I don't wish to receive any more books, I can return the shipping statement marked "cancel." If I don't cancel, I will receive 4 brand-new novels every month and be billed just $5.74 per book in the U.S. or $6.24 per book in Canada. That's a savings of at least 28% off the cover price. It's quite a bargain! Shipping and handling is just 50¢ per book.* I understand that accepting the 2 free books and gifts places me under no obligation to buy anything. I can always return a shipment and cancel at any time. Even if I never buy another book from the Reader Service, the two free books and gifts are mine to keep forever.

185 MDN EYNQ 385 MDN EYN2

Name _____ (PLEASE PRINT)

Address _____ Apt. #

City _____ State/Prov. _____ Zip/Postal Code

Signature (if under 18, a parent or guardian must sign)

Mail to **The Reader Service:**
IN U.S.A.: P.O. Box 1867, Buffalo, NY 14240-1867
IN CANADA: P.O. Box 609, Fort Erie, Ontario L2A 5X3

Not valid to current subscribers of the Romance Collection,
the Suspense Collection or the Romance/Suspense Collection.

Want to try two free books from another line?
Call 1-800-873-8635 or visit www.morefreebooks.com.

* Terms and prices subject to change without notice. Prices do not include applicable taxes. Sales tax applicable in N.Y. Canadian residents will be charged applicable provincial taxes and GST. Offer not valid in Quebec. This offer is limited to one order per household. All orders subject to approval. Credit or debit balances in a customer's account(s) may be offset by any other outstanding balance owed by or to the customer. Please allow 4 to 6 weeks for delivery. Offer available while quantities last.

Your Privacy: Harlequin is committed to protecting your privacy. Our Privacy Policy is available online at www.eHarlequin.com or upon request from the Reader Service. From time to time we make our lists of customers available to reputable third parties who may have a product or service of interest to you. If you would prefer we not share your name and address, please check here. ☐

BOB09

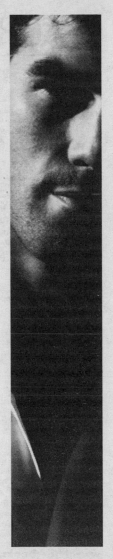

LAURA CALDWELL

32183 LOOK CLOSELY	___ $6.99 U.S.	___ $8.50 CAN.
32309 THE ROME AFFAIR	___ $6.99 U.S.	___ $8.50 CAN.

(limited quantities available)

TOTAL AMOUNT	$ _____
POSTAGE & HANDLING	$ _____
($1.00 for 1 book, 50¢ for each additional)	
APPLICABLE TAXES*	$ _____
TOTAL PAYABLE	$ _____

(check or money order—please do not send cash)

To order, complete this form and send it, along with a check or money order for the total above, payable to MIRA Books, to: **In the U.S.:** 3010 Walden Avenue, P.O. Box 9077, Buffalo, NY 14269-9077; **In Canada:** P.O. Box 636, Fort Erie, Ontario, L2A 5X3.

Name: _____
Address: _____ City: _____
State/Prov.: _____ Zip/Postal Code: _____
Account Number (if applicable): _____

075 CSAS

*New York residents remit applicable sales taxes.
*Canadian residents remit applicable GST and provincial taxes.

MIRA®

www.MIRABooks.com

MLC0609BL